DO NOT FORGET ME QUITE

D0268428

RICHARD PIKE

Matador
9 Priory Business Park
Kibworth Beauchamp
Leicestershire LE8 0RX, UK
Tel: (+44) 116 279 2299
Fax: (+44) 116 279 2277
Email: books@troubador.co.uk
Web: www.troubador.co.uk/matador

ISBN 978 1783064 526

British Library Cataloguing in Publication Data.
A catalogue record for this book is available from the British Library.

Front cover photograph © Hulton-Deutsch Collection/CORBIS

Typeset in 11pt Aldine401 BT Roman by Troubador Publishing Ltd, Leicester, UK
Printed and bound in the UK by TJ International, Padstow, Cornwall

Matador is an imprint of Troubador Publishing Ltd

For Ann

ACKNOWLEDGEMENTS

The quotations from Ivor Gurney's songs/poems *Severn Meadows* and *The Songs I Had* are reproduced with kind permission of the Ivor Gurney Estate. The words of the Gurney song *In Flanders* are by F.W. Harvey and are reproduced by kind permission of Eileen Griffiths. The poem itself can be found in F.W. Harvey, *Collected Poems 1912 – 1957* (McLean, 2009). Details of both the Ivor Gurney Society and Trust, and the F.W. Harvey Society can readily be found online.

Many of Gurney's and Harvey's poems can be found online. Recordings of many of Gurney's songs and other music mentioned in this book can be found online or on disc.

Many people have encouraged and helped me in the writing of this book, most particularly my fellow writers at Leicester, Ancaster and Peterborough. I am very grateful to them. I also want to thank Tim Wilson for his unfailing encouragement and support through different drafts.

ONE

There are no photographs of my father. Someone destroyed them all years ago, tore them up to be rid of him, as if he had disgraced us all. Poor Daddy – black sheep of the family. I was the only one of us children who really knew him, and I adored him. I remember that last night in France. I must have just turned six. Most memories of him now are of last times, or saying goodbye.

He always seemed to be going away.

Mother appeared, a candle in her hand. She had a white apron over her dark dress.

"Dorothy, close your scrapbook now. Gather up your things. It's time for bed."

"Oh, Mama, must I?" We were in a hotel parlour somewhere in France, and I was enjoying listening to Daddy playing a duet on his violin with a French girl from the town. She was on the piano.

"Yes, you must." Mother was always strict. "Tomorrow's a long day for all of us. You won't want to feel tired."

I stood up. I knew we had to go home but I didn't know why. They must have kept all the panic and whispering away from me. "Daddy, will you play my tune for me?" I hoped to stay up a little longer.

"I will, my sweet. Not now. When I know you're in bed, Mamselle and I will play it specially for you, and you'll hear it drifting up through the floorboards like fairy music."

"What nonsense is this?" Mother asked.

Daddy rested his violin and bow on top of the piano. "Oh, you know: Edward Elgar's little piece, *Salut D'Amour*. Dorothy's taken quite a fancy to it."

"You'll spoil that girl, John, if you indulge her." She turned to me. "Now say good night to your father."

He crouched down, I kissed him on his cheek and giggled. His big moustache always tickled.

"Night, night, *mon petit chou*."

"I'm not your little cabbage!" I said. Daddy spoke fluent French and had taught me a few snippets, even then: counting, names of things and so on.

Mother unlatched the door into the passageway and I saw the candle flame bend and struggle against the sudden inrush of air. It was all candles or oil lamps in those days. Out in the country, anyway.

"Mama, how *are* we to get back to England?"

She sighed. "Don't worry about that now. You'll see."

I remember it all so clearly. It was the end of everything.

Or you could say the beginning.

★ ★ ★

What were we doing in France? Daddy was a schoolteacher then – I think it was a public school in Kent – and he always had long holidays. He loved France and I know he prided himself on keeping up his French. But you'd think September 1914 was a silly time to be out there, especially after Mons. The war had already started. But France is huge, and we were away from it all, deep in the rural part. Perhaps Daddy thought the war would all blow over. He was always the optimist. Mother was the one with her feet on the ground.

Normally you could never hurry him, but next day he clumped up and down the stairs to their room.

"Come on, my dear," I heard him say, "why does it take the whole morning to pack our belongings into the trunk? When can we get off?" I knew something was the matter then.

"All right, all right," Mother said. I hated seeing her flustered. So unlike her – all red-faced and puffing. Having to pack in a hurry must have unsettled her. She liked life to be steady and ordered. Everything in its place.

And there must have been other factors which I didn't understand then. She had to see to my brother, Rowley, of course. He was only a baby and would have needed a sleep. It was after noon before we set off.

★ ★ ★

I don't remember much about the journey back. It wasn't quick, not like nowadays when you can take an aeroplane or even a train. It must have taken weeks because we had to come back a roundabout route via Marseilles. Too dangerous to make for the Channel ports, I should imagine. We'd no idea how far south the Germans had advanced. Somebody must have decided it was safer to take the long way home. Daddy, probably.

The journey seemed to take for ever. Motor vehicles were still a rarity in those days; you pointed it out when you saw one. We relied on horses then, so we certainly travelled some of the way by horse and cart. You know, I can recall seeing horse buses, even in London, before the war. Daddy could certainly ride and I suppose Mother could drive a pony and trap if she had to.

If I close my eyes now, I can still feel that terrific afternoon heat.

"Is it far now, Daddy?"

"Just be patient, my sweet. *Eh! Vas-y, Vas-y!*" He slapped the reins on the horse's back.

But the horse, used to pulling heavy loads of melons or other produce, still ambled across the open countryside. I was fascinated how, when flies danced around its head, it flicked its ears and whisked its tail. It ignored us, refusing to move any faster in spite of Daddy's urging.

For long hours, the sun pinned us down to the sandy road – small figures in the wide French landscape; only in the distance, a few clouds tumbled over the tops of the hills. It's like an old snapshot or when you pause a video.

It was as if time stood still for the last time.

"We're never going to get home at this rate!" Mother, red-faced in her sun bonnet, tried to shade the baby with an old lace parasol.

★ ★ ★

I've never forgotten one place we stayed overnight. After a late meal, we returned to our *pension* and headed upstairs to our room. Mother checked Rowley for the last time, planted a kiss on my forehead and turned the lamp down.

"Sleep tight everyone," she said.

Darkness flooded over the room, and there was silence. A bedspring clunked as Daddy turned over and began to settle.

The sound of a distant clock chiming ten filtered through the shutters.

"Mama, something's tickling me."

"Go to sleep, Dorothy. It's your imagination. You've had a long day. We all have."

"Daddy, will you look? I'm not telling lies, and it's not my imagination."

Mother turned over and gave an exasperated sigh.

"I will check she's all right," Daddy said.

"You give in to her too easily. She's got to learn. I've never heard such a to-do."

He eased off the bed, fumbled for the matches and lit the candle. "Now, what's the matter, my sweet? Oh, good God!"

"What is it?" Mother turned violently and sat up.

All over the walls, tiny black dots, the size of apple pips, scurried away from the light, seeking the safety of cracks in the wallpaper, the window frame, the tassels of the carpet. Within seconds, the walls were clear.

I sat up, blinking. "What are they, Daddy?"

"It's all right, Dorothy, they've gone now." He turned towards Mother. "Bed bugs."

She pointed a frantic finger across the room. "Rowley's crib.

Move it quickly! Away from the wall! They'll love to hide in the wicker. And pass me the matches."

She scrambled out of bed, flinging the covers back. She lit the oil lamp. "Dorothy, get up! Let Daddy move your bed away from the wall and check your sheets."

I sat on the edge of my bed and said nothing.

Holding the oil lamp in one hand, Mother checked the sheets of the double bed. "That's clear." She moved across the room to rummage in the bedding of the crib. "And so is Rowley's, thank goodness."

The baby began whimpering. Mother picked him up and held him close. Making soothing noises, she nursed him until he drifted back to sleep.

"Look, we can't leave now." Daddy was adamant. "Not at this hour. But I don't trust the beds. The blighters could be hiding in the frame or the woodwork. We'll have to sleep on the floor – the bedding's not infested – and leave the lamp on. They don't like the light." He hurried to his violin case, opened it up and moved it closer to the lamp.

With pillows and blankets on the floor and the beds pushed well clear, we settled down again. They left the lamp burning, but Daddy shaded us with Mother's parasol to avoid the glare. A trail of black smoke meandered towards the ceiling; a smell of paraffin hung in the air.

"Mama," I called quietly from the other side of their bundle of bodies, "my arm itches."

She huffed and turned her back on us all. "Shall we ever get out of this God-forsaken country?"

TWO

John watched Emma sidle off the bank and into the river. She held Dorothy's hand and, once sure of her footing, encouraged the girl to join her.

"Oh, Mama, it's cold." Her squeal echoed round the meadow.

"Don't fuss, Dorothy." Her tone always quick, clipped. Even her rare endearments to him sounded impatient.

He'd never seen his wife naked and knew he shouldn't watch now as she freed her hair, bobbed down into the water and removed her remaining undergarments. Dorothy did the same. He turned away. Emma had insisted on leaving the *pension* as soon as the children woke up, saying they needed to bathe to be sure they were all free of those wretched creatures.

They were lucky to find this oasis. The Saône swirled and slipped past; here it formed a tranquil pool where willows arched and concealed bathers from any eye on river or land.

His turn next.

He turned towards the trunk of the huge overhanging tree where Rowland kicked and struggled in his crib. At fifteen months, the boy seemed slow to take to his feet, but what did John know about such things? He left child-rearing to Emma. Given half a chance, the baby crabbed around on his bottom, quickly covering any room where he had freedom.

He began to undress the boy. At least there'd be no soiled napkin to worry about. Emma had begun training him on the pot very early. John left the suitcase open for her to find a change of clothes for herself and Dorothy, and moved a few yards away. Cradling his son in his arms, he stood, back turned, until he heard the sloosh of Emma and Dorothy leaving the river. He made his way down to the bank and stepped into the water, naked apart from his white shirt.

He moved in deeper, felt the chill reach his midriff; his shirt tails floated like flippers at his side. He began to scoop up water with his right hand and trickle it over his son. The boy gasped, tensed, gurgled. John was reminded of a baptism. Total immersion.

Slowly he ducked down, still cradling Rowland before his chest, until the water lapped his shoulders and the boy almost floated in front of his face.

"You're a small, little fellow, aren't you?" he murmured. "You must take after your mother."

With a cupped right hand, he ladled water over his own head and let it trickle down his face and off the ends of his moustache.

He began to wade towards the bank. In the green shade-cocoon of the tree, Emma and Dorothy had covered up. How tiny his wife seemed – little bigger than a girl, though she was already thirty. Sloping shoulders, oval face. She'd hate this forced indignity; something she couldn't prepare for.

His wet shirt clung to him as he scrambled out of the water.

"Here you are, my dear, one baptised son!"

Already a ripple of shivers had started to tense the baby's body. Emma quickly surrounded him with a towel.

"Be quick now," she said, "we need these clothes out in the sun to dry. And for heaven's sake, let us be on our way."

★ ★ ★

They found the station at about two o'clock. Everywhere quiet. The houses had closed shutters against the heat, as if turning their backs on the stranded family.

"Must be siesta time," he said.

The square stood deserted apart from one carriage in the shade of the station building. The old nag hung his head and occasionally scraped a hoof on the cobbles. The hollow clop echoed. The driver himself sprawled in the back, arms folded, cap tipped forward over his eyes.

Even the trees in front of the station seemed to drowse.

"Isn't that our trunk?" Emma pointed at a long one-wheeled barrow, abandoned at the entrance.

"You're right, my dear, I must make arrangements for that. At least they've brought it this far. And I'll get our tickets." He encouraged her to take the children to the platform for Lyon. "Do mind how you cross the lines. And Dorothy, stay close to Mama, and be sure no train is coming either way."

"John!" Emma said, when he rejoined them, "it's no good. We'll have to leave the crib here. I can't keep carrying Rowland around. It's extra weight and very tiring. My shoulders and arms ache so." She picked the baby up and jockeyed him onto her hip. "Put all that bedding and stuff in the suitcase, will you? If it'll go."

John eased his violin case off his back, opened the suitcase and crammed in the extra items.

"Just have to learn to walk now, won't you, old son?" He touched Rowland lightly on the nose. "We'll take turns carrying him."

"What have you done about shipping the trunk home?" Emma said. Two furrows appeared at the bridge of her nose – a sure sign she was worried.

"We have to trust them. They said to leave it on the barrow. They'll put it on the next available train."

"Not our train, of course. I do hate this *laissez-faire* attitude. You've paid for it, I suppose."

"Well, not exactly. I've arranged for it to be despatched to Percy. Cash on delivery."

"Is that really best?"

"Well, it could arrive before us," he said. "We don't know yet how we'll travel back. The trunk would be shipped as freight."

"I don't mean that. Percy's the stingiest man I know."

"Oh, I say, Em, steady on. He is my brother, after all."

"Well, that's as may be, but he has no friends that we've seen, no wife, and thinks only of saving every penny. Is he likely to pay out to receive our trunk?"

"Oh, come on, Em. I think you're being unduly harsh."

"Am I? Well, we shall see. He's not one to give to charity, and he's always envied you. Why should he help us?"

★ ★ ★

The train slipped into the station, hissing steam. John inhaled deeply; he loved the smell of hot oil, the constant roar from the firebox. A squeal of brakes, a jolt, and the tall-funnelled monster stood panting, ready to receive them.

He pulled on the brass handle of the door to allow Em to board. He passed up the baby to her. "Now you, Dorothy."

"Daddy, Daddy, hurry, the train will go without you!"

"It's all right. Plenty of time."

Towards the back of the train, a whistle shrilled.

"Daddy!"

He hooked his violin over his back and picked up the suitcase. At that moment, the leather strap of the handle snapped, and its full weight dangled lopsidedly from his hand.

"Damnation take it!" He stumbled aboard, fell to his knees and shovelled the case before him. He managed to scramble up and close the door behind him.

The engine whistle blew, the brakes jolted free, and the train began sliding from the station. Something made him glance back towards Rowley's crib, forlorn and abandoned in the shade of a plane tree.

"Is it far?" Emma asked, as he joined his family on the slatted wooden bench. "This isn't very comfortable."

At Lyon station, she pointed to a large poster on the wall. "Have you seen this? They're everywhere."

He looked at the imposing lettering printed below two French flags.

ORDRE
DE MOBILISATION GÉNÉRALE

"Now will you believe me when I say there's a war on?" She seemed determined to make a point. "Even I can understand that."

He smiled, put his arm around her shoulder and pulled her to him. "Yes, my dear, I know!"

Now was not the time to tell her what he had already decided.

★ ★ ★

Daddy walked very fast through Lyon. He'd mended our suitcase with rope from somewhere. I almost needed to run to keep up with him.

"Where are we going now?" I asked.

He glanced down at me and strode on. He wasn't smiley now. I remember looking up and noticing the dark patches under the armpits of his shirt and a glisten of moisture on the tangle of hair on his chest. Unusually for him, he wore his shirt open and his body smelled like one of those soft cheeses he loved to eat.

Mother walked behind, also hurrying; she wore her sun bonnet which hid all her hair and made her face look like a red figure **0**. I was glad I didn't have to wear long dresses. Rowland rode on her hip, shaded by a towel draped over his head and shoulders. His dress was rucked up so people could see his frilly pants. I hated that.

In a large square near the centre, a line of men edged towards a tall building, queuing into the darkness inside. Some wore suits; others looked as though they'd come straight from the fields. A few carried sticks or hay forks.

Somewhere in the distance I heard singing.

Two women in dark dresses held a banner above their heads and paraded up and down alongside the line of men. I tried to read it: *A bas les Boches.* A group of small boys marched behind, chanting: "*Boches, Boches, à bas les Boches.*"

I didn't know many French words then, only ones I'd heard

people say often. *Boches.* I remember thinking did that mean *mouth,* or was it *pocket?*

"What are those men waiting for, Daddy?"

He turned to look at me. "It's a *Bureau Militaire*, darling. Nothing to do with us. Keep going."

I shook my head. "Where are we going, Daddy?" My sandals were beginning to rub and make my feet sore.

"Down to the river. We must hurry. It's our only hope now."

★ ★ ★

"Will they take us?" Mother sat on the low wall overlooking the river. I nestled beside her, my doll on my lap.

Daddy leaned against the drinking fountain at the edge of the quay and drank from the brass cup. He dipped his handkerchief under the tap and mopped his brow.

"Our luck seems to have changed again, Em. It won't be easy but better than waiting for a train which might never come. It'll mean roughing it, I'm afraid. Two of us will have to sleep on deck under the stars, and I shall have to do some crewing since the captain says he's now two men short. Gone to sign up, he thinks. That queue we saw, probably. But the trip won't cost anything, thank goodness. I shall be working our passage. It suits us, and it suits them."

"Will the journey take long? I hate feeling like a bunch of wandering gypsies."

"As far as I can gather, two days. Maybe longer. It's all downstream and the Rhône is pretty fast-flowing, even now. We'll have a couple of hours sailing before dusk; the captain won't go through locks in the dark. Not with three barges in tow. Tomorrow's an early start. He hopes to reach Avignon mid-afternoon. Another night, and we should see Arles sometime on Thursday. That's as far as he can take us. I'm sorry, it's the best we can do."

"Well, if we must, we must. As long as we're getting on."

"It's all in the right direction. Arles is excellent. You can almost smell the sea there. After that, Marseilles, then home."

Mother snorted and sat up straight. "You make it sound so easy."

The river tug that would be our home for the next few days seemed very wide and flat, and thick ropes snaked across the deck. I could hear a hiss of steam; a trail of smoke wandered from the tall, thin funnel.

"Be very careful on this boat, Dorothy," Mother said. "It's not a pleasure steamer and there's no rail to stop you falling over the side. Definitely no running."

I nodded.

"And don't go bothering Daddy when he's working. We don't want any accidents."

I nodded again.

★ ★ ★

Through my feet I felt the pulse of the engine increase, heard the peep of the little steam whistle. The boat shuddered and strained as it headed for the centre of the river. A sound of creaking and tightening; water dripped off the ropes as they lifted out of the river. Behind, three rusty barges eased into the stream, grinding and jostling against each other – a hollow screech and boom.

I covered my ears with my hands.

Daddy was far away on the last barge, hauling in the huge rope which had tied the craft up.

"What jobs will you have to do?" Mother asked, when he returned.

"Oh, I'm deckhand, lowest of the low. I'll have to tie up and untie the barges once we get to a mooring. But the other thing I've got to learn is to handle a quant pole. The river's shallow in places and there are tricky mud flats to negotiate. Going round a wide bend, the barges can slew right out. My job's to keep them from running aground. Push them off, in other words. At least, I think that's what he said. It taxed even my French – this Provençal accent."

"You ought to wear gloves," she said. "Protect your hands. You're not cut out for rough work."

★ ★ ★

Mother perched on a low bollard, preparing food. I sat cross-legged on the deck; Daddy spread himself on a nearby hatch cover. Rowland, tired by the heat, sat and blinked at the passing trees.

"At last, moving again," Daddy said.

Another picnic. Mother had bought bread and cheese, some strange slices of sausage with white lumps inside, and a bright red vegetable mixture with bits in it which Daddy said was a speciality of the area.

"You say it, Dorothy, rat-tat-oo-ee."

I giggled. "Sounds like someone knocking on the door and calling." I was very suspicious of it, but Mother said it contained tomatoes and other good-for-you vegetables. Eat it, or go without. I was hungry, so I ate some.

Rowley was lucky. He had bread and warm milk in a bowl and bit the spoon as if he really enjoyed it. Daddy ate everything and drank red wine out of a cup kept in the suitcase. He loved his drink as he loved France; our upbringing was different. Moderation only, ever since…

Mother made herself some weak lemon tea with hot water from the galley. She didn't seem hungry.

Daddy was soon laughing and wiping his moustache with the back of his hand.

"Haven't you got big teeth, Daddy?"

"Dorothy, mind your manners! It's rude to make personal remarks, even if it is only Daddy." She made me jump.

"Oh, I don't mind," Daddy said. "I'm used to it. The boys at school often think I'm smiling when I'm not. It's the teeth. Whenever I'm talking, whatever I'm saying, they think I'm smiling. In fact, one particularly clever boy, Lambert his name is, came up with a nickname which has stuck."

13

"I didn't know that," Mother said.

"What do they call you, Daddy?"

"*Souris*. It's French, my sweet, and that's why I think the boy who made it up is so clever. It can mean a little smile, but it can also mean a tiny little mouse." He leaned across and tickled my tummy. I giggled. "And all because of my big front teeth."

"They sound very rude young men to me," Mother said. "Don't they teach respect in your school? It sounds like they're asking if you're a man or a mouse."

"Oh, don't take it like that. They mean no harm. I think it suggests they quite like me."

I laughed. "Why are you always so happy, Daddy?" He was smiley again now.

"Oh, that's easy. Because I'm with the people I love."

★ ★ ★

Later that evening, I found Mother sitting on a bench tucked against the cabin of the boat. She'd settled Rowland down and sat, elbows on knees, head in hands. A cool breeze blew down river, and long shadows crept across the water from the tree-lined bank. The sun had almost gone.

Daddy was on the furthest barge, hauling on a huge rope which looked as thick as my arm. I waved to him but he was too far away, busy putting the boat to bed and making it safe. *Monsieur le capitaine* had him working hard again.

I shivered, put my head on one side. She seemed to be crying. I stood awkwardly beside her. "Mama, are you all right?"

She looked up and sniffed. Her cheeks were wet, her eyes red. "It's nothing. I'm quite all right," she said.

"What is it?" I wondered if I'd done anything wrong.

"You wouldn't understand."

I rested my arm around her. "I don't like to see you cry."

"I'm all right, Dorothy. It's a grown-up thing. Nothing to worry little girls about. I'm better now." She sniffed again and tried a weak smile. "Ten minutes, and then you must think about bedding down. When Daddy comes back, say good night to him. And promise me one thing: on no account tell him you've seen me like this. I mean it. I'll tell him myself when I'm good and ready."

"Oh, I won't, Mama." Strange! Grown-ups didn't cry.

THREE

John stood on the stern of the rearmost barge and raised his violin to the hushing world. But what to play?

He felt isolated, at peace after the day's haste and confusion, a spiritual closeness to God and his creation. Such times often fed a melancholy in him which he welcomed but the practical Emma had no time for. He accepted that. She was very different from him; he often praised her steadiness. "You keep me anchored," he once told her. "Without you, I'm adrift."

"Get away with such stuff. I'm your wife, it's my job to make life easier for you, and bring up our children."

For sleeping on the boat, they agreed he and Dorothy would lie on deck, partly sheltered by an awning, and Emma and the baby would move into the cramped below-deck cabin. She took the bunk there, complained of the heat and the smell from the galley, and made a cot-nest for Rowland in the suitcase on the floor.

He began playing a Beethoven *Romance* while darkness spread over the water. He imagined the orchestra joining in, as the thin sound wafted away. He had played the piece as a piano duet with Mamselle only last weekend. How distant that life seemed already.

Somewhere a moorhen squawked, its call echoing round. A flash of light as a fish jumped, leaving the river's tranquillity circling and rocking.

Everywhere so dark! His violin sang on, soothing, lamenting. He finished the first section, letting the sound drift into the darkness, lowered his bow. A hint of mist rising like a wraith from the river.

"To think – all those miles away young men are dying, fighting for their country," he murmured. "You'd never know it here, not in this heaven." The air smelt sweet, warm – a hint of freshness with the mist.

He seized a bucket on a rope and lobbed it into the river. He hauled it up, leaning out to avoid cannoning the metal hull of the barge. Proper seaman stuff! He set it on the stern, peeled back his braces, stripped off his shirt and sluiced his body thoroughly. Twice in one day he'd bathed in river water. But needs must...

He smiled, remembering Emma's Victorian precept: "Horses sweat, gentleman perspire, and ladies merely glow." She often recited it to Dorothy.

"Must be a horse, then." He rinsed liberally round the back of his neck, tipped the pail of water over the side, heard it cascade into the darkness. He dabbed at his face and neck with a drying cloth.

Emma liked a good tune but didn't respond to music in the way Dorothy did. Even at six, she had already taken to that Elgar piece, had made it her own. He was so glad their first child was a girl; he saw reflections of himself in his daughter.

Standing bare-chested, he patted his stomach. Nearly thirty-five and already signs of a belly. What did they call it? Getting a paunch?

He straightened up. Something of a stoop, too.

Have to take exercise.

"God, I love this country." His fervour startled him. "All the more reason I must... Surely I must... I cannot stand by and see it overrun. But my family..."

He hated dilemmas. He knelt down on the metal deck, cleared his mind and let words drift into his head:

Keep me as the apple of an eye,
Hide me under the shadow of thy wings.

He often went to Compline in the school chapel during term time. A peaceful end to the day, before going home: only a few boys there, the chaplain leading the brief service. An intimate solitude, the light through the stained glass windows slowly fading. But now, what was The Lord calling him to do?

★ ★ ★

The deck still felt warm under his bare feet, the wood slow to give up the heat of the day. Beneath, he heard the slap and trickle as the river caressed the boat. He saw Dorothy lift her head from the makeshift pillow and look around.

"Can't you sleep, darling?" He knelt at her side.

She sat up. "I heard you playing. It was lovely. It felt sad, though. Will you play my tune, Daddy?"

"Not now, darling, others are trying to sleep. We have the world to ourselves. Look up there." He whispered now, his voice a rustle on the air. "All those stars."

"They look like pinpricks in the sky," she said.

The vast speckled silence overawed him. He put one hand on her shoulder and pointed up to the dark. "They're such a long way away. We're a tiny dot, too, to anyone up there who can see our world. If it wasn't for God looking after us, we might think the things we do on earth aren't the slightest bit important."

"How many stars are there, Daddy?"

"Oh, you'd never count them all, my sweet. There are millions of them, and they're millions of miles away, too."

"What does millions mean, Daddy?"

★ ★ ★

The next afternoon, the boats going fast downstream with the flow, he saw another low bridge coming up. Better take up my post; big bend, too. Can't be that far from Avignon.

Sure-footed now, he leapt onto the bow of the following barge and hurried down the narrow outside deck. He set foot on the third vessel, stooped and picked up a huge pole, almost the length of the craft, and manhandled it upright.

As he expected, the flow of the stream flung the rear barge out towards the waiting shallows. With two hands, he strained and thrust the long pole against the mud and gravel to keep the vessel from running aground. Now, sure of deeper water, he strained it against his thigh to act as a primitive rudder.

Panting, standing tall, he took pride in keeping the craft in line with the tug. "I am the captain of my ship," he said to the world, with a grin. He could feel sweat dripping off his face, a cool run of moisture down his back.

But he also knew he should have listened to Emma.

★ ★ ★

To someone as young as I was, the journey seemed to take for ever. I've often tried tracing our route on the map. Without much success, I must say. The only thing I knew: I must look out for the sea. Getting to the coast as quickly as possible was our first objective. But I do remember something of Avignon – not the history or the buildings, though I think Daddy stood me on the bridge and sang the old song to me, you know, *Sur le pont d'Avignon...*

Easing onto a berth kept him busy with the pole and hawsers. His back must have ached after all that labouring. When the convoy was lashed firm to the bank, the tug engine shut down, leaving a putter of smoke trailing across river. Then we knew Daddy's work was done, the family free to go ashore.

"I shall stay a while," Mother said, "and get my land legs back. I feel quite giddy at the moment." She sat on a bench on the bank and placed Rowland beside her. "When I'm rested, I shall make up a sling to carry Rowley and search out some food. Don't wait for me. You and Dorothy go and explore while there's time."

Daddy was concerned and asked if she was all right. I expect she glanced at me suspiciously as if I'd blabbed but gave her usual answer, *Yes, perfectly, thank you* in that clipped way of hers. He shook his head and smiled, knowing how she hated any fuss.

The heat struck up from the cobbles of the huge square. In the distance, several booths in faded canvas revealed a scatter of market stalls. I held out my hand but Daddy didn't take it, which puzzled me, and we hurried into the dusty heat of the town. That was unusual. I used to like holding Daddy's hands. They were huge and soft, and whenever I was upset, I only had to put my hands in his to feel secure again.

I trotted beside him. "Ooh, pretty pictures." I remember pointing to some crude prints hanging from the canvas of one of the stalls.

"Oh, yes. That's a field of lavender, my sweet, they grow a lot round here and harvest it for ladies' perfume. Very nice smell. Grandma Hemingby likes lavender."

"I wish I could have them for my scrapbook, Dad." I was a terrible wheedler in those days and he often spoiled me.

"What, the picture? How much are they?" he asked the stallholder; he turned back. "I don't see why not. They're only a few sous." He eased his hand into his pocket for the money.

"And will you buy me that red one as well, please? I like them. I want to give them a whole page in my book. What's the red one, Daddy?"

"That's a field of poppies. They only grow where the soil has been ploughed up or disturbed."

"Is every little red dot a flower?"

"Yes, that's right."

"All those flowers. There must be millions."

I kept that picture for years; but now, even that Monet picture with the poppies upsets me when I think about the significance of those flowers.

★ ★ ★

We took a trophy back to the boat. Gingerly, Daddy pushed it up the gangplank and onto the deck. "It isn't new, I'm afraid, Em, but it folds easily, so if we have to, we can carry it. In comparison with a perambulator, though, it's very insubstantial. No hood to protect the little chap and only a canvas seat."

She looked at the spoked wheels of the pushchair, the solid white tyres, the thin tubular framework.

"Very thoughtful, dear. Thank you. Anything to avoid carrying Rowley all the time. And there'll be space on the foot rest for a parcel or two. Stand it over there, will you? Oh, by the by, I've finally managed to master the range." She looked pleased. "You wait until the coal is glowing and the smoke has died down, and then you can cook. Tonight we shall be eating like the French. It's a one-pot supper – *coq au vin*. Unfortunately, search where I might, I couldn't find potatoes."

"Never mind, Em, it's well done. You always cook good meals."

"I'm feeding everybody tonight. There's enough for the captain and the mate, even Rowley will have some bread soaked in the chicken gravy, and I've mashed him up a few vegetables."

After our meal, I said to Daddy: "Will you play *sloodamore* on your fiddle for me?"

"We say *Salut D'Amour*, my sweet." He looked at me. "I'm sorry, I'd rather not. Not tonight."

"Oh! Why?" Perhaps he would give in.

"I'm afraid my hands hurt rather." He looked away towards the far-off bridge.

"Show me!" Mother caught at his hand and turned it over. "Oh, John, for heaven's sake!" She sighed. "What did I say? I thought something was wrong, the way you held your spoon."

I only caught a glimpse. At the bottom of each finger, the skin had wrinkled and looked red and raw. Elsewhere, yellow cushions had puffed up on his hand and looked ready to burst. I looked away and bit my lip. His hands must hurt.

"Wait there!" Mother hurried off into the cabin.

21

"Where's she going?"

He did not reply.

She returned and squatted on the bench. She held a white petticoat between her hands, strained at it and began tearing the cloth into wide strips.

"You silly, silly man, what did I say about gloves? You should know you're not suited to manual work."

I looked down. I didn't like seeing Daddy told off.

FOUR

Daddy, his hands bandaged with dirty strips of cloth, could just about manage the pushchair with the base of his palms. He refused to show me his blisters, and Mother did all the handshaking as we said farewell to M'sieur le Capitaine and the mate.

At last we were on land again and hurrying across this new town. Someone said we might get transport to Marseilles. All around, the walls seemed very high, the streets narrow, shady and crowding. Would that have been Arles?

No one told me where we were. Daddy strode on, his face screwed up, cross. Perhaps he was worrying. You couldn't always tell what he was thinking.

I know I wasn't allowed to linger, though the market was fascinating with all its noise, smells and colours. At the head of a flight of steps, my parents stood waiting.

"Pick your feet up, Dorothy, and stay close now," my mother said.

"Mama," I said, "what is Kaiser?" I'd seen notices everywhere. I pronounced the word Kayser, I remember that.

"Ssh, Dorothy, not now!"

A crowd of people had gathered around a vehicle about the size of a lorry. I stared at the solid white tyres and spoked wheels and the strange engine which looked like a huge barrel in front of the cab.

"Is this a bus, Daddy?"

"It is – not like London, just a little French country bus, but it'll do. It's going where we want to go."

"No doubt it goes all round the villages and will take for ever to get to Marseilles." Mother's lips looked very tight. "This journey is taking an eternity."

A man standing on the roof of the bus shouted and whistled at

Daddy when he tried to take our suitcase and pushchair inside. Someone picked up a short ladder and leaned it against the bus. All luggage, even some of the men, had to travel on the roof.

All very primitive, I think now. I remember the bus had no windows. Just air. I could wave my arm out into the street. When we were about to leave, a well-built woman came billowing down the steps towards the bus. She carried a large basket and an old sack with something struggling inside it.

I had to make room and sit on Daddy's lap. That lady – she must have been a real French peasant – smelt of flour, and yeast, and garlic, and looked very hot. She passed the writhing sack through the window space to the man with the ladder. He drew out a brown chicken which began to flap and squawk.

Holding the bird by its legs, he passed it to the man above who lashed its feet to the low barrier rail on the roof.

I heard the thump of footsteps overhead and hated the way the bird hung flapping and squawking at the side of the bus. Its eye glared at me and its beak gaped. And then another hen came out of the bag and joined it upside down at the window. I watched a feather float to the ground.

I'll never forget that – typical rural France for you.

"At last," Daddy said, as we set off, "perhaps it'll be cooler now. You know, my dear," he said to Mother, "we're very lucky. We just managed to pay for this ride. Apart from a few sous, this has cleaned us out. I shall need to cash one of those Travellers' Cheques when we get to Marseilles."

Mother probably said nothing – she was good at the grim silences – and closed her eyes. I always knew when she wasn't pleased about something.

Even though we all fell asleep, except Daddy, the journey must have taken hours.

The bus felt very hot and I remember my bare leg stuck to the leather seat. I woke up when we stopped at some thatched houses way out in the country, and the fat lady struggled out.

"*Au revoir, ma petite, au revoir, m'sieur, madame,*" she said and waddled away from the bus, her basket over one arm and the two chickens dangling and flapping in her left hand. I was glad they'd gone.

Mother now stirred and sat up. "Oh, heavens," she said, "how much longer?" Rowland woke then, screwed up his face, looked around, and wailed. A nightmare journey. Eventually the bus stopped outside the railway station in Marseilles. The sun was already setting, and I shivered with the cold. "Mama, I've seen the sea." I thought it would please her.

"Have you now?"

"Yes, and lots of ships in the harbour. Will one of them take us back to England?"

"We'll see. Probably tomorrow. Now we must eat and find somewhere to sleep."

"What about money?" Daddy said.

"Just as well I have some put by, isn't it? You'll find no banks open now." And she gave him a look as if he was a careless child.

★ ★ ★

In a tree-lined road, leading away from the port, we discovered a restaurant about to open for the evening, gas lights flaring into the dusk.

"Wait here." Daddy went in and spoke to someone in the depths of the kitchens. A fishy food smell wafted out.

"Oh, Mama, I'm hungry, and thirsty."

"We all are, Dorothy. Just be patient."

Daddy returned, smiling broadly. "This is a family place. They were suspicious at first, but I explained our predicament and reassured them we were English not German. Madame said there's a room upstairs we can have. No bed, but they'll let us have blankets and pillows. We can sleep on the floor. There *is* floor covering."

"No bugs this time, I hope," Mother said.

"I shouldn't think so. And do you know, they've just made a new batch of *bouillabaisse*. I'm bucked about that. I've never tasted it. Read about it, of course, but now we can try a speciality of Marseilles."

She tutted and sighed. On her brow, the two frown lines appeared.

We found the entrance passageway at the side of the restaurant, pushed the chair deep inside and all clumped up a dark staircase covered in fraying linoleum. On the second floor, we found the room. Huge curtain-less windows looked out over the street. I was surprised to see the tops of trees below me.

"Well, we shall have to make do," Mother said. "The linoleum's rather dusty but at least the children will get their sleep."

Downstairs in the restaurant, we found a table in a corner, at the back.

"What is it we're having, Daddy?" It was the first time I'd ever heard the word. Whenever I come across it now, it takes me right back.

"Bouillabaisse? It's a delicious fish stew – lots of different types of seafood and vegetables, and bread, of course. Lovely! I think we deserve a carafe of wine tonight."

"John! I cannot believe what I'm hearing. You tell me you've managed to blue all Grandad's money on this supposed trip of a lifetime. And now it's run out, you're still behaving as if you're an English lord. Have you forgotten?"

"Oh, hush, Em, don't spoil our last night."

"My word, you are confident we'll get away."

"Please, *pas devant*. Let's not argue in front of the children."

I looked down, shrank on my chair and began stroking the tablecloth.

"Very well, I'll just say this." Mother seemed to hiss her words. "I may not have your education, but I'm not a fool. And I certainly know how to manage money properly after years of keeping Father's books."

I sneaked a look at them. What had Daddy done wrong now?

★ ★ ★

26

I liked that special morning time. There weren't many occasions when I had my mother close and all to myself, and we talked quietly while she worked my hair into plaits for the day. I daren't turn round, though, for fear of a scolding; sometimes she tugged my hair, and that hurt. I asked where Daddy had gone.

"He went out early, we shall see him later. He needs money from the bank, and he'll ask around to see if there's a ship that'll take us to England."

"What sort of ship?"

"Who can say? Probably not a passenger boat. Maybe no one will want to do the journey. Not now. But any ship which has room for all of us. Beggars can't be choosers."

Another expression I'd never heard, and I wondered if our wanderings had somehow literally turned us into beggars. I thought of grubby men in ragged coats who stood on street corners selling matches or holding their cap out to passers-by.

"Finish this bit yourself, if you can, Dorothy. I shan't be a minute." Mother pushed the half-finished plait over my shoulder, dropped a ribbon in my lap and hurried from the room. "Keep an eye on Rowley, will you? But don't try picking him up."

I heard her hurrying down the stairs and went to the window to see if she came out onto the street. No sign. So, paying a visit, I assumed.

When Mother returned, she was dabbing her mouth with a large piece of cloth. I asked if she was all right.

"Perfectly, thank you. Only a little upset. These things happen. Nothing to worry about. I expect some of the fish didn't agree with me."

I didn't know what all this meant – we didn't in those days – and asked her if she'd have any breakfast.

"Perhaps not," she said. "I'll see. Oh, and by the by, miss, a reminder: I don't want you tittle-tattling to your father about me being poorly. He'll know about it soon enough."

FIVE

John suspected the bank had never seen someone with a Travellers' Cheque before. The clerks stared at his bandaged hands and made a great fuss of checking his passport and signature. They huddled together, whispering as if confronted by a German spy. Eventually, after a hushed telephone conversation, they gave him the money.

Stupid! He thought afterwards, how much longer will we need francs anyway?

He headed towards the port, feeling trapped. Marseilles seemed busier than London: horse-drawn vehicles – carriages, carts, buses – clopped across his path. Amongst them, motor cars and lorries wove in and out, even the odd motorcycle. He smiled. The French had scant respect for any rule of the road.

He dodged between the traffic and hurried down to the harbour. A bell clanged behind him, and he jumped back as a horse-drawn tram rumbled past on tracks set into the cobbles. Goods littered the quayside: boxes, heaps of coal, loads of timber. And huge piles of barrels. He picked his way through, waiting while two men rumbled a cask into the stack. A ship alongside flared steam across his path from a vent below the deck-line. Different smells assaulted him: fish, coal, horse droppings and, again, hot oil and steam.

Everywhere, the salt odour of the sea.

He gazed around, surprised to see so many sailing boats, tall-masted schooners, even small fishing boats like Egyptian feluccas.

We need a steam ship, surely, if we're ever to reach home. But which?

He looked up at the city's cathedral, dominant and incongruous above all this confusion. O Lord – almost a prayer – what on earth do I do? There must be a harbour-master, somebody to help somewhere.

Ahead, a knot of people on the quayside, stationary amongst all the noise and bustle, blocked his path.

"*Pardonnez-moi*," he said.

No one looked up.

He shuffled his feet, swallowed. Had they heard him? They had to be French.

Two of the women continued to bend forward and slash and slosh amongst the fish in the barrels before them. Every few seconds, a hand darted out and tossed a fish, newly gutted, into a wicker basket. The silver creature flashed and slid across the pile.

When the basket was full, a girl, little more than thirteen, bent down and swung the basket onto her head.

He cleared his throat. "*Excusez-moi…*"

As one, the whole group stared at him as at a camera. The girl with the basket stamped her clog and planted a fist on her hip. Five of the women glared and gripped their gutting knives more tightly. Big-bosomed, with thick muscular arms and blood-spattered aprons tied just below the breast. A group of men stepped forward as if to protect them. One adjusted his cap, picked up a bucket and held it at a menacing angle, ready to souse its oily contents at John's feet. Another – a huge fellow in a tan bowler hat and brown corduroy trousers – puffed a pipe and breathed out smoke like a threatening dragon.

The third appeared to be a gendarme. He wore a kepi and white trousers, and an ancient belt across his grubby blue tunic held his sagging bulk together. He looked away and continued drinking from a glass. Flecks of beer-foam clung to his whiskers.

They all stared.

"*Allemand?*" The bowler-hatted man spat on the cobbles and then onto his palms.

Lord, do I really look German? He considered turning back. Try a smile. "*Mais, non! Je suis anglais.*"

"*Anglais?*" The other man lowered the bucket. "*Anglais, là-bas!*" He flung out an arm, stabbed his finger towards a distant part of the harbour and turned away.

"Merci, beaucoup." John stepped forward: no one moved. Nothing for it but to edge between them all and the drop into the oily water. They ignored him and turned back to their work as if he was a mere fly bothering them.

★ ★ ★

The restaurant appeared different now: darker and less welcoming without its gas lights, cooler because the glass doors had been folded back to let in breezes from the sea.

"Daddy!" Dorothy jumped down from her chair and rushed to greet him.

He stopped in the middle of the restaurant. "We sail at six tonight!" He felt his grin broaden, and he gave an affectionate tug to one of her plaits. "Good morning, Dollycoddle."

"You haven't found something? Already?" Emma said.

"You'll never believe it: a British boat in port, sailing for England tonight. Somebody up there must be looking after us."

"Thank goodness! You might make the beginning of term after all." Her brow furrowed. "What kind of boat?"

"Trawler, I think. The SS Ben Lawers."

"What on earth is a British trawler doing in Marseilles?"

"I didn't ask. Fishing, I suppose, maybe trading, and now refuelling and re-provisioning for the home run. I met the captain – Mr McCann – a very pleasant man, and he said they also had official business in port. Apparently they lost a crew member recently. Drowned. Perhaps it's to do with that. Anyway, I explained our situation and they're happy to make space for us if -"

"You haven't volunteered to crew again, have you?" Emma's eyes sharpened.

"No, no, of course not." He shushed her with his bandaged hands. "I've learned my lesson. No, I was going to say, if we don't mind cramped quarters, they'll make a tiny cabin available so we can be together as a family."

Emma jumped up. "Nurse Rowley for me, will you?" She thrust the boy at John as he sat down. "I'm just going…"

She hurried out of the restaurant.

"What's the matter?" he said to Dorothy as he bounced the boy on his knee. "Is Mama all right?"

"Perfectly." She spoke in a confidential whisper. "But I think it's something she ate."

★ ★ ★

"She's moored over there," he said. "Rather a walk. Hard going on cobbles. Are you up to pushing the chair, Em?"

The suitcase nestled in the pushchair; John carried Rowland in the crook of his arm and pointed out ships and bright flags to the boy. Dorothy trotted alongside.

"I shall manage, thank you!" That crisp reply. "Now, which one? I've never seen so many boats."

"You see that far quay jutting into the harbour? She's the last one moored there."

"I hope the ship's bigger than it looks." Emma's lips tightened.

"Oh, cheer up, Em. It's not a liner, just a trawler, but it's British, thank The Lord. It says *Aberdeen* on the stern. And they'll take us all the way home. The crew are Scots, I gather."

"Dadad!" Rowland swivelled round on his father's arm and began tugging at the dark ends of his moustache.

"You're lively today, young fellow. Anyone would think you like the smell of the sea."

★ ★ ★

He watched her turn her critical eye around the cabin. "You and I can have a bunk each, Em. It's where we put the children, that's the question."

"Rowland will sleep with me," she said. "Neither of us takes up much room. You have the other bunk. You need the space. The area under mine will make a bed of sorts for Dorothy."

"Good old, Em. Always practical. So what do you think of our home for the next few days?"

She stood with her hands on her hips. "I don't mind the wooden walls, could be worse, could be cold metal. Not much daylight, though. Tiny porthole, can't be more than six inches. But what do we do about that? It's so hot in here." She pointed at a small lamp above the porthole which roared bright light into the cabin.

"Nothing. It's acetylene, I think. Stays on all the time."

A knock at the cabin door. A young man in crisp white shirt and dark uniform craned his head in.

"Good afternoon, sir; Mrs Hemingby, welcome aboard."

"It's good of you to give us all a passage," Emma said. "A great relief, I assure you, and you've no idea what a pleasure it is to hear English spoken again."

The man smiled, tipped his cap and disappeared.

"There you are, Em," John said. "We shall manage perfectly."

SIX

He walked back from the galley, slopping a bucket of hot water. Already the sun shone. He relished the swoop and lilt beneath his feet as the Mediterranean caressed the ship. Perfect weather. At the stern, white furrows glittered.

He knocked on their cabin door and entered.

"Morning, my dear, hot water for washing."

"See to the children for me!" Emma, hand to her mouth, rushed past and disappeared.

"Oh, dear," he said to Dorothy, "I always thought Mama was a good sailor. Perhaps it's the smell of fish."

Later she emerged and, outside the bridge house, shared a deckchair with Dorothy. She looked huddled, diminished, wearing a ruched bonnet against the light wind.

"What was it, my dear – the smell of fish, the coal? The smoke, perhaps?"

"Something like that, I expect," she said. "Now, don't fuss. I'm better now." The captain emerged from the wheelhouse. She turned towards him and asked how long the voyage would take.

"Hard to tell, Mrs Hemingby. Depends on weather, especially the winds. If Biscay is kind, a week, ten days. Maybe more. We'll need to put in at Gibraltar and Lisbon for coaling and re-provisioning. Maybe also Corunna."

"I shall never forget this kindness," she said. "I don't know what we'd have done otherwise. But what brings a Scottish trawler so far South?"

"The silver darlings, Ma'am. They go mad for 'em down here."

She looked puzzled.

"It's what we call the herring. Barrel loads we brought 'em, gutted and packed."

"And now, with this war, will you keep up the trade?"

The captain rubbed his chin and scratched his growth of beard.

"Ach, well. That depends on the U-boats. We shall see, ma'am, we shall see."

"Yes, I understand. A great concern." She seemed conscious of Dorothy looking at her and stopped.

"Mama, where's my drawing book?"

"Are you tired of all this sea, my sweet?" John said. "It is a long journey, isn't it?"

"Oh, don't pander to her. The child must learn patience." Emma turned to Dorothy. "Go into our cabin. Pull out the suitcase under your father's bunk. Open it, lift up the clothes carefully, and look at the back on the left-hand side. You'll find your book there. Will you want your crayons?"

"Yes, please."

"Also at the back, but on the right-hand side."

Everything in its place, John thought, and tidied away. Wonder where she'd keep me if..? He turned and gazed far out to sea, deep in thought. How could he pray for guidance without any privacy?

★ ★ ★

He could not sleep. Emma and Dorothy, buried beneath their blankets, hid from the force of the storm. He looked over the edge of his bunk. A bucket on the floor swayed and slopped.

He covered his mouth with a handkerchief, held on to the metal frame of his bunk and slipped his feet down. He manoeuvred to stand astride and gain balance, feeling the trawler roll and rear, then drop helpless into a trough. The ship's propellers roared, sounding as if they churned only in air.

He hardly felt sick at all.

His watch swung by its chain from the light on the bulkhead.

Five-thirty. Nearly dawn. A chance to experience a storm at sea.

He struggled up the companionway and battled the short distance along the deck. A salt wind skimmed the breakers and stung his face. He wrestled with the door to the wheelhouse, heaved it open, let it bang behind him.

"Good morning, may I join you?"

"Brave man, sir." The mate stood close to the wheel, gripping it tight.

They had to shout above the howl of the wind. It chattered and rattled at the door, tugging to prise it open. Around them, the bridge house creaked and cracked.

"Were you expecting this, Mr McKillop?" he said.

"Aye. Did you no see the storm cones hoisted at Corunna?"

"Don't know about them."

"Well, skipper knew what we were in for. Decided to run with it, only just gone below. Aye, she's doing her worst." McKillop struggled to hold the wheel steady. "Wind wants to blow us in all the time." A cascade of water buffeted the bows; the ship lurched. "You have to decide – put into shore and risk the rocks, or stay out and run the waves. We're pressing on."

"Makes your arms ache, no doubt."

"Aye." McKillop stared straight ahead.

John peered through the fog of spray and watched huge quiffs of water curl up from the bows and sluice and sweep along the main decks. "Everything lashed down which needs to be, I suppose."

"Aye. All hatches battened."

"Aren't you afraid the ship will turn over?"

"Steer into the wave. He wants to buck and toss us. It's like riding a horse over a jump."

"Oh, I know about horses. So that's it, is it?"

A blue-green wall of water reared ahead. It towered above the ship – green, dense. John took a deep breath and held it. The bows rose in a slow heave, until the angle seemed close to toppling point – seventy-five degrees, at least. Spray skimmed and leaped over the bridge house.

The wave hit the ship like an explosion and burst out sideways, flinging spray; the sea boiled and whipped, soused and settled over the deck.

John put his head back and laughed in exhilaration.

"No afraid, then, sir?" McKillop wrestled to change course.

"Oh, no, I love this. I've faith The Lord will protect us." He took a deep breath and began singing:

> *Jesu, lover of my soul,*
> *Let me to Thy bosom fly,*
> *While the nearer waters roll,*
> *While the tempest still is high:*

A huge wave smashed and scattered against the bridge; he gasped and staggered, hurled towards the door.

Another breath.

> *Hide me, O my Saviour, hide,*
> *Till the storm of life is past:*
> *Safe into the haven guide,*
> *O receive my soul at last.*

Water siled down the windows. The wind screamed and howled over the ship; the bridge house shuddered.

The mate turned to look at him, shook his head and grinned.

"You see," John shouted, "valiant 'gainst all disaster. The Lord's testing me."

SEVEN

I do remember one moment on that terrible journey across The Bay of Biscay. In the mess room below deck, little Rowley – he can only have been about fifteen months – sat on the floor and laughed at every buck and toss of the ship. He didn't seem to mind the bad weather. He clapped his hands as the ship rose, and chuckled at the sudden lurch and drop. Daddy smiled at him.

Mother and I huddled on the bench seat, our backs to the portholes and the storm outside. I'd tucked myself into the shelter of her body, my hands limp in my lap; I glanced up and caught Daddy's eye but I couldn't smile. Two off-duty crew played cribbage on the corner of the table, pausing now and then to catch a tin mug which skidded across the table; another man sat forward, head bowed, hands clasped as if in prayer. I knew how he felt.

The air hung heavy with the smell of sweat, vomit and the lingering odour of fish and cigarette smoke. Horrible! The carbide light flared bright heat into the room.

Daddy tried to keep Rowley at his feet, but my brother edged across the floor on his bottom, reached for the vertical brass rod which supported the table, seized it in a small, fat fist and hauled himself to his feet. Arms held aloft as if in surrender, he let go and took his first step.

In that cramped mess, we all watched: Rowley steadied himself against the pitch and roll of the ship and achieved two more jerky steps.

"Mama," he said, "Mama!" and set off towards us.

Everyone cheered and clapped, and Rowley's face split into a grin. He applauded himself, too, and promptly thumped to the floor on his bottom.

"Well, if the wee laddie isn't born to the sea…" The man caught the tin mug as it was about to fall. A slop of tea trickled to the floor.

"Well done, Rowley," Daddy shouted. "That's my boy! At least you've found your sea legs."

"I've never seen a wee bairn so surefooted, and in this sea, too. He's a natural." Prophetic really, in view of Rowley's later career. He might have made an admiral, if…

EIGHT

John woke before dawn, feeling the ship free of the rear and drop of the night. He lay and listened to the thud of the pistons, the drilling of the propellers through the water.

Across the cabin, Emma and Dorothy, fast asleep, their breathing still regular. But Rowland sucked his thumb and stared at the ceiling.

John got out of bed and eased the boy from the opposite bunk over Emma's body; he edged the enamel chamber pot out and sat the boy on it, then tugged a blanket from his bunk to wrap himself and Rowland in.

Outside, the sea was slate-blue and calm, the ship ploughing a steady furrow through the water. Black smoke spiralled behind them, hanging and spreading like a pall.

He took a deep breath. "Look, old chap, all the storm gone! Can you see the seagulls?" He hoicked the child up on his arm and pointed at the squabbling flock. "There must be fish there."

"Birds," the boy said.

A figure in a dark mackintosh motionless up in the bows.

"Good heavens – McKillop!"

"Morning, sir, all's well after yesterday's blow, I'm glad to say."

"Yes, indeed. Where are we now, do you know?"

"See that – way over to starboard?" He pointed to a smudge of land rising like a monster out of the mist and sea. They watched it slipping past. "The Isle of Ushant. Start of the English Channel."

"Thank God! Nearing home, then."

"Aye. But the skipper wants an extra watch just now. He's a wee bit leery. They say German U-boats patrol hereabouts."

The sun flung up above the horizon ahead of them, casting a scarlet track across the water. John placed a hand across Rowland's eyes. Within a minute, the sea had turned blood-red in the morning light.

"Will the ship keep working if the war gets tough?" he said. "After all, the country will still need fish."

"There's talk, sir, that the navy is commissioning trawlers and arming them. Protection vessels for convoys, minesweepers and such like. Anyway, the lads are all game for whate'er they give us."

"So what would Captain McCann do now, if a German submarine surfaced in front of us?"

McKillop straightened his tie and grinned. "Och, well, we'd ram her, sir. No doubt about it. Slice the wee bugger in two. Show the braggart Hun what a good bit o' Scottish steel can do."

"My godfathers! Just like that. You'd have no worries about killing, then?"

"Would you, sir?"

John did not reply. He shut his eyes, desperate to block out the image of men struggling and writhing in black, oily water.

★ ★ ★

They leaned over the port rail, looking towards the English coast. John took a deep breath. "Last night at sea, Em, last meal on board."

She pulled her shawl around her. "I hope I do it justice. I'm not over hungry. And we're hardly dressed for ceremonial, are we?"

"Don't worry. The crew are friends now. It's just an agreeable way of saying farewell. Who'd have thought this voyage would take so long?"

"It's a lovely September evening," she said. "I hope this weather lasts until your birthday. How calm it seems after those rough seas. Sometimes I wanted to die."

He bent low over her, put his arm round her and hugged her to him. "Look, the Isle of Wight. Soon be home." He broke away and rubbed his hands together. "Oh, Em, I can't wait to share a bed with you again. It's been so long."

"Yes, I know, John, but there's something you need to be aware of. We shall have to be careful. I'm expecting again. At least two months gone, by my reckoning."

"Are you sure?"

"I recognise the signs. Not sea-sickness at all. But we'll see what the doctor says."

He stood back and turned her towards him and gazed into her eyes. The breeze played with the loose hair over her ears. "That's wonderful news, wonderful. So when's it due?"

"Around the end of April, I think."

"You know, I hadn't any idea." He glanced around the deck, checked no one could see them, and kissed her. "So is it my turn to think of names? I chose Dorothy; you named Rowley."

"I wonder where he is now, he must be nearly twenty-one." She stared out across the water. "New Zealand's such a long way away. I wonder if I'll ever see him again."

"What, your brother? Oh, he'll come back. When he's made his fortune."

"We'll see," she said. "Father took it badly, his going. He's not been well since Row emigrated, and with Mother dying -"

"Oh, cheer up, old thing! Don't go on. Now what do you say to calling our new little one Benedict, if it's a boy. And how about Beatrice for a girl? Both names sort of mean *blessed*." Again he leaned over, put an arm around her slight shoulder and kissed her.

She stiffened. "Let's not be hasty, John. April's a long way off, and so many things could happen."

"We are blessed, getting home safely. All these adventures. This child can be a symbol of how The Lord looked after us."

"I'm sorry, you know I don't feel the same about all this God business."

He bit his lip and said nothing.

"Don't you fear for the world we're bringing our children into?" she said. "All this talk of war so near to home. We'll manage and see it through, of course we will, make them as secure as we can. But I hate the thought of war. Thank goodness you've got a safe job. There'll always be need for schoolmasters. You won't have to go. Anyway, you're probably too old to be a soldier."

"What, at thirty-five? For heaven's sake, Em! Anyway, look on the bright side, this war won't last. Probably all over by Christmas."

"You say so. You're always the optimist. But we'll see."

He turned away. A distant lighthouse winked its welcome to their homecoming.

Damnation, he thought, damnation! How do I tell her now?

★ ★ ★

On the wooden table in the cottage kitchen, under the domed mesh of a meat safe, someone had left a joint of ham, butter, a bowl of eggs and some bread. A pint jug of milk stood with a beaded doily covering it.

"How kind," Emma said, "I wondered how we should manage tonight."

"Someone in the refectory is very thoughtful. They must have got my telegram." His eye fell on a letter propped up against the meat safe. "Mr J F Hemingby," he said, reading the envelope. "That's me, unless someone wants my father."

"John! Don't be silly!" She tutted.

He took a kitchen knife from the table drawer and slit the letter open.

"FROM THE HEADMASTER, it says." He walked away towards the window and scanned the handwritten note.

Dear Hemingby

I trust you have had a safe return from the continent, and that your family is all well. I should be obliged if you would call in to see me at your earliest convenience – this evening before dinner, if at all possible. I have a matter of some importance that I should like to discuss with you.

Yours etc.

"Curiouser and curiouser," he said, "I wonder what the old man wants." He showed it to Emma.

"You definitely must be first in the bath," she said. "I'll start carrying water up. You can't go as you are, that's for certain. And have a shave! You look very dark along the chin."

★ ★ ★

"Feels very strange getting back into these togs after two months. I really struggled with my collar and tie, and I never realised how rough this tweed suit was. How do I look?" John stood at the foot of the cottage stairs.

"You need a barber. Still, can't be helped now. Let me brush your hair down, make it look tidy." She fetched a brush and comb from a drawer, made him sit on a kitchen chair, and flattened his damp hair against his head.

"Oh, heavens, I suppose I shall need my gown," he said. "Now, where on earth did I leave it?"

"Go to the closet on the landing, and you'll find it hanging on the back of the door. I put it there myself."

"Oh, Em, what would I do without you?"

He reappeared, easing the gown over his right shoulder. "Looking a bit green, isn't it? Still, can't be helped."

"Now, be off with you. Don't be late. You know he likes dinner prompt at seven-thirty."

He hurried across the college lawn, a short cut to the wing where the headmaster's rooms were. His gown billowed behind him; a glance at his watch: six-fifty. The day eased into dusk; above him, in nearby trees, a lone thrush whistled peace to the world.

A solitary gaslight flared above the stairs to the headmaster's study. John stood in the gloom before the heavy oak door and knocked.

He swallowed.

"Come!" said a voice.

43

He turned the brass knob and went in. An oil lamp on the desk, a trickle of smoke rising from its chimney. The headmaster stood by the window and began drawing down the blinds.

"Hemingby? Ah, good man. Thank you for coming so promptly. Back today, I hear. How was France, polished up your accent and topped up the patois?" He waved John into a Windsor chair before the desk. "Sherry?"

"Thank you, Headmaster." John tucked his gown around him and sat. He longed to turn the wick of the oil lamp down, but watched the man busying with the decanter and the glasses. The old boy had decided on making it formal, was even wearing his hood as well as his gown. Strange character: greying hair, centrally parted, and beard trimmed to a point like a naval officer, or the King. When he needed them – pince-nez.

One of the old school.

"Wife well, I trust? And the family? Good, good."

Didn't he ever wait for a reply? Had the man no inkling of the family's difficulties abroad?

The head placed a glass of sherry in front of him. "Now, look here, I'll be straight with you. A lot of the younger men have caught war fever and are convinced they must go and do their bit for the country. Quite a few have volunteered already and say they won't be returning this term. Probably be away for the duration. I'm all in favour of patriotism, but it's dashed inconvenient, I must say, when we've a school to run. It means we shall be short-staffed. Of course, we shall have to do some doubling up – I may even have to teach myself – and I've managed to call one or two stalwarts out of retirement to see us through. But –"

"Perhaps it'll all be over by Christmas, sir."

"That's as may be. The boys' numbers are down, too. Quite a few of the Upper Sixth have also volunteered to join up, as they call it. Particularly those prominent in the cadet force. Several even turned down decent offers of places at Oxbridge. World's gone mad, I say."

44

John sipped his sherry. "So, why have you sent for me, Headmaster?"

"Well, I know I can rely on you as one of our older members of staff. You've made a good fist of getting French off the ground for Higher Matric, even poaching a few away from Classics. Now that *is* some achievement. I like the way you've mixed in and helped boost the school orchestra with your teaching and your playing –"

"Well, thank you very much, sir."

"Now, not to put too fine a point on it: term begins next Wednesday and I need a core of staff I can rely on to hold the school together in these difficult times. I'm asking you to take on School House – your wife would make an excellent matron, I'm sure – and run that while Carswell is away. I'll make it worth your while, of course, but the fact is, Hemingby, it's very good experience for future promotion elsewhere. Your own language faculty, good extra-curricular work, and head of a house. What more can any school want? This war will be the making of you, you mark my words."

"Well, thank you, sir…" John drained his glass.

"What are you laughing at, man?"

"Sorry, sir, I'm not. Far from it. It's natural, my teeth, I'm afraid. I shall need to think this over. This puts a whole new complexion –"

"Very well. Let me have your decision by ten o'clock Monday morning. Three days should be enough."

Outside the door, he stopped and took a deep breath. "Oh, Lord, help me. What do I do now?"

NINE

The family set off in the school's pony and trap. John drove, letting the reins lie slack on his knees. The horse clopped on, seeming to know the way.

"Where are we going now?" Dorothy asked. "I don't want any more journeys. I want to stay at home."

"Don't whine," Emma said. "We're going to Canterbury for some shopping, and your father is going up to London for a couple of days."

John glanced at his daughter who sat squashed between them. "I'm going to see Aunty Helen first and then Uncle Percy in Stoke Newington when he's finished work."

"I wish you the best of luck," Emma said.

"And I might go and see Grandpa and Grandma Hemingby, if there's time."

Dorothy gazed up at him. "Can I come? I like seeing Aunty Helen."

"Not this time, sweet. I want to see what's happened to our trunk, if it has arrived from France. I'll be back late tomorrow." He turned to Emma. "Now, are you sure you'll be all right driving back on your own?"

"I shall be all right," she said, "as long as there aren't too many motor cars, and Canterbury isn't as crowded as Dover was the other day. All those trains arriving, full of soldiers. And the troop ships, I didn't like that. I'm glad we were travelling away from the port."

"What about Rowley? If you're driving, how will you –"

"Don't fuss! I shall manage." Her eyes flashed.

He raised his hands to pacify her.

★ ★ ★

"Fordie!" Helen flung the door open, and moved to embrace him, even though she had a baby in her arms. "My, how lean and brown you look, not your usual scholarly self at all. Positively bohemian." She ruffled his long hair and laughed. "France must have suited you."

He kissed her and wiped his feet carefully, conscious of the Turkish carpet in the hall. "I've not seen you for ages and ages, Sis," he said. "How I've missed your smile."

The baby watched him with an intent gaze, jerked his head away and buried his face in his mother's neck.

She laughed. "Come through to the back parlour. Tell me everything."

"Yes, let me wash my hands. They're all sooty from the train door handles."

She led the way down the hall to a room which overlooked the back of the house. He caught a glimpse of a rose bush tossing pink heads in the breeze.

"Are you ready now for lunch?" she said. "Mrs Banks has left a steak and kidney pie in the oven."

She took her children upstairs for a nap, and over the meal he recounted some of the family's adventures getting home from France.

"You won't see Ma and Pops this visit," she said. "No, they decided on an autumn trip North and set out for Leeds two days ago."

He felt relieved. That discussion could now wait. Talking to his father was never easy.

"Pops wanted to see Uncle Will before winter set in," she said. "You know what he's like."

Eventually he managed to broach the issue that had troubled him ever since the meeting with the headmaster.

"Helen," he concluded, "I really don't know what to do. Of course it's attractive – security, promotion and so forth. But even while we were still in France and I knew that war had broken out,

I've had this deep calling – yes, that strong – that I should do something to help, to support my country. You know me, I've been worrying about it quietly and praying. I feel I cannot stand by and let France – a country I love – suffer a foreign invasion. I suppose I should have expected it but I was shocked when I saw all the young men here in London, and in Dover two days ago, flocking to join up and do their bit. I'm beginning to believe The Lord wants me to get involved."

She paused and dabbed at her mouth, let her napkin rest in her lap. "Fordie, dear, you know you don't have to fight. You're married, and they say married men are exempt. And sorry to say it, you're probably too old. Anyway, it'd be hard physical stuff. Hardly you, is it? Howard says soldiering is a young man's game. He's glad he won't have to enlist, though a lot of younger men have already left the bank to join up. Besides, what does Emma say?"

"I haven't really discussed it with her yet. I wanted to be sure; I need to be clear in my own mind what I feel I'm called to do. That's the confounded trouble: what I feel I must do goes against all that would seem prudent. I know I'm getting on a bit. Besides – I shouldn't tell you this – Em's expecting again. Next spring, we shall have *three* children. And that's a further turn of the screw. Whatever I decide won't be fair on her."

"Oh, that's lovely news. At least you're keeping the London Hemingby name alive. I know Pops would be pleased. He's very keen to keep his branch of the family going. And there's not much sign of Perce settling down, is there?" She laughed. "Anyway, can you really see yourself as a soldier? I can't. You're much too gentle."

"Do you know, it seems silly, but I even think the headmaster's offer is some kind of temptation which I must resist. Strange to think of him as the devil. But what he wants me to do seems all too easy. I don't think I should have a comfortable life when others are suffering. I feel that isn't what God wants for me and yet…"

"You poor dear, you're a good man, you know, but you always manage to find guilt somewhere, don't you?" She stood up, listening to sounds from upstairs. "That's Philip crying. He's woken up, so PJ will want to get up, too. Just remember this: you felt guilty when you became a schoolmaster, all because Ma once said she always thought you'd become a doctor. Do what you have to do, John. You'll come to the right conclusion, I'm sure." She hurried away towards the stairs.

"Yes, but Helen, the head wants my decision by Monday."

"As I say, you'll know. Remember the still, small voice in the bible." She paused three steps up. "Don't forget you're a family man. I know Howard would say you can serve God and mankind just as well in the form room as you can on any battlefield."

★ ★ ★

He recognised his brother from some distance away. Percy's light-footed bustle and the bob of his bowler hat showed a man confident of his position and authority within the borough. He carried an attaché case chained and padlocked to his left wrist.

John thought of a convict and smiled. "Heavens, Perce, half-past six. They work you late, don't they?"

Percy stopped, his small feet neatly side by side, and drew out his watch on its leather strap.

"It's a case of needs must, my dear fellow. We can't all have easy-going, regular hours and long holidays like you. The Borough Treasurer made it obvious at my appointment that some evenings, especially Friday and the weekend, I'd need to be out collecting after office hours. I accept the pay, I have to accept the conditions. It's wise to collect rate money before some of them go out and spend it."

"Well, it's good to see you, anyway." John reached out his right hand.

His brother offered small, cold fingers, pudgy, moist. "What brings you North of the river?" he said. "I thought you preferred the South these days."

"I've come to see you, say hello," John said. He searched his brother's suspicious blue eyes. "I thought I'd treat you to supper tonight."

"Well, I hadn't planned for that," Percy said. "I'm expecting to find a mutton stew waiting for me. I just have to heat it up and boil a few potatoes. Mrs Rogers said she'd leave me something which would last two days."

"She doesn't live in, then?"

"Good Lord, no. I couldn't be doing with that."

"Well, now, why not change your routine! Let's go out, for once. It's not often I come calling."

They walked up the black and red quarry tile path to the front door. Percy reached into the right-hand pocket of his trousers and pulled out a set of keys on a chain. He undid two locks on the front door. "Come in, then," he said. "I need to finish off first. You'll have to bear with me."

On a small square table, he placed the attaché case, opened it and took out a cash box and a huge leather wallet. He freed himself from the padlock, slipped off his dark suit jacket and eased his thumb under his braces. He stretched.

John looked at the sharp creases of Percy's white shirt, the high vertical collar: starched, of course. The sober tie. The highly polished black shoes. His brother took out a well-thumbed ledger from the suitcase. He reached for a pencil from the breast pocket of his jacket, licked it and began totting up the day's takings.

"I need to get this right," he said, "make sure everything tallies. They rely on me at the town hall."

He slipped on a fingerstall and riffled through the pound and ten shilling notes and picked out the occasional fiver; he counted the sovereigns into piles of ten and stacked the smaller denomination coins. With his pencil stub, he jotted down the totals for everything and scribbled them on a square of paper.

"Good, everything adds up." He selected another key from the chained bunch and opened a safe, set into the floorboards near the fireplace. "Now, you can all go away until Monday morning," he said. He hid the money and ledger from sight and locked the safe.

"Did our trunk arrive, Perce?"

Silence.

"Perce?"

"I sent it back."

"What? Why did you do that?"

"I couldn't see why you had it delivered to me. What's the point of them bringing it here? It's only by chance I was in when they called. It was all rather inconvenient. Why didn't you pay in advance?"

John looked down. "I wanted someone trustworthy to take it in. I knew the school would be closed for six weeks, and there'd be no porter or anybody to receive it. Besides, I was short of cash, quite frankly."

"So you thought of me?"

"Yes, of course. Everyone knows they can rely on you."

"John, did you really think I'd fork out for a delivery of your dirty laundry, or whatever it was, all the way from France? I can't afford that sort of thing. Not without careful planning. Besides, where would I store it until you bothered to collect it? No one knew where you were."

"I see." Em was right – as usual. "So, where is it now?"

"Back at Carter Paterson's. Wapping or somewhere. I couldn't have it here, cluttering the place up. Never put upon family, that's my motto."

"Oh, I say, Perce, that's a bit thick. Now I shall have to trail over there tomorrow." Blasted man, he thought, always wants things his own way.

TEN

The crash of the kettle onto the range, Emma's determined sawing at the bread, the thud of the slices being buttered told him all he needed to know. He had not slept well, and his face felt sore where he had cut himself shaving. The last stair creaked as he came into the kitchen. Dorothy sat at one end of the table drawing and colouring. She looked up.

"Happy Birthday, Daddy. I'm doing a picture for you."

"That's nice, dear. Thank you." He bent down and kissed her forehead. "Morning, young sir," he said to Rowley who sucked on a rusk in his high chair. John tickled him under the chin.

"Bikwit," the boy said and held it out.

"What's happened to your hair, Daddy? You look like you're a soldier," Dorothy said.

His stomach lurched, then he laughed. "No, darling, but would you believe Uncle Percy wouldn't go out for supper until I'd been to the barber's?"

"How typical," Emma said. "What a fusspot!"

"And he was very reluctant to put me up for the night. I had to sleep downstairs on the couch. Perce said, 'There's only the big bed upstairs, and I'm certainly not sharing that with you.'"

Emma snorted and turned back to the range. "Ten minutes, Dorothy, then we must set off. It's a fine morning, only a slight dew. We can walk across the fields to school. And make sure you've been."

Dorothy put her pencil down and stood up. "I know what your birthday present is," she said in the voice of a conspirator.

"Do you now?" he said, and smiled. "Well, don't tell me. Let it be a secret."

Emma brought him a soft-boiled egg and bread and butter. She glanced down at Dorothy's picture.

"Heavens, child, what have you drawn? The Red Sea?"

"No! It's a poppy field, silly. Like we saw in France."

"Dorothy! I will not be spoken to like that. Now, you will say sorry this instant."

Dorothy's face crumpled; the room fell silent. "Sorry, Mama." She ran off outside to the water closet.

"Don't be harsh on the girl, she didn't mean anything," he said. "She knows I liked those fields in Provence. It shows she has a good memory."

"Oh, you would take her side. That young lady is becoming rather too impertinent for my liking. We shall have to slap her down more before it gets out of hand. In any case, how was I to know? It looked like a sea of blood to me. Not what you want at all."

★ ★ ★

He knelt alone in a front pew of the chapel. Decision time and no clearer what he should do. After a night of constant turning, exhaustion sat on him. At one point Emma had woken, complained in the darkness and clamped an arm around him as if to pin him down. He dared not move and slept fitfully.

A strong smell of beeswax, and the odour of the yellow and gold chrysanthemums on the altar hung on the air. A wasp batted and buzzed against a window somewhere.

He liked the intimacy of the place; it could never hold the whole school – a year group of boys at a squeeze. But empty, it exuded stillness and peace.

The morning sun filtered through the surrounding trees and cast a glow onto the woodwork. Behind him, a pew cracked and settled. Dust motes danced in a shaft of ruby light from a stained glass window.

He closed his eyes and clenched his hands.

"Oh, Lord, help me, please. What will You have me do?" His knuckles hurt.

Nothing.

His right leg itched.

He looked up at the stained glass windows, two either side: the Four Evangelists. Above his head, Matthew and Mark gazed into the chapel with benign indifference. On the opposite side, Luke and John stared down. A shaft of purple sunlight from St Luke's garment shone on a brass plaque to commemorate the school's fallen in the Boer War. The plate flashed in a starburst of colour.

Saint Luke – patron saint of doctors.

And then at last he knew. An answer to his prayers.

★ ★ ★

Outside the headmaster's door, he hitched his gown onto his shoulder and swallowed at the command "Enter!" His throat constricted, his stomach jittered. Quickly, he wiped his hands on his gown.

The headmaster put aside his book of Horace *Odes* and peered at him over his pince-nez. He smiled.

"Ah, Hemingby, good man, come in. On time, too. Now, what do you have to tell me?" He waved John towards the chair.

"I've come to say, Headmaster…" He remained standing. "I regret to tell you…" He swallowed again. "I'm afraid… that I cannot take up your kind offer of Head of School House."

"What are you saying, man – don't you want it?"

"No, I'm not saying that, sir, I'd like the position very much –"

"Well, then –"

"But, after much thought, I've decided that my duty has to lie in serving my country while we are at war. I intend to volunteer for the Medical Corps. There are likely to be many casualties as the fighting goes on, and I feel I must do my bit to help the injured and wounded however I can. I don't feel I should take part in the

54

fighting, I don't want to be associated with killing anyone, but…"

"It's a pretty speech, Hemingby, but very foolish and short-sighted." The headmaster glared at him. "Are you not a family man with responsibilities?"

"Yes, sir, a young family, too, but I think Mrs Hemingby would struggle to fulfil a matron's duties in the way that both you and she would wish, especially as next spring we shall have two children under the age of three."

"I am at a loss. Have you discussed it with her?"

"No, sir, I still have to do that, but I wanted to be clear in my own head where my path lay. I have to follow my conscience. It is something I've wrestled with, I assure you."

The head's colour had risen to a deep flush and he gripped the edge of the desk.

"Words fail me," he said. "How can you be so foolish as to turn down an opportunity of advancement such as I have offered you? We need good, sound men at home." He drummed the desk with his fingertips. "I assume you realise your decision has consequences. Have you thought them through?"

"How do you mean, sir?"

"Well, think about it, man, think about it now. Or do you need time to reconsider? You're in the employ of the school and currently live in a grace-and-favour house as a valued member of staff. Now, if you leave us to go to war, as you say you propose to do, we cannot hold your position or your accommodation open indefinitely."

"Of course, sir, I understand." Fresh lodgings shouldn't be a problem.

"I can have a word with the governors, of course, and I shall do, but the facts are likely to be these: we shall pay you two months' salary as a good-will gesture, but I'm afraid that you and your family would have to leave that house by the end of the month, so that we can offer it as an inducement to others to take up a post here. Unfortunately, that is sooner than both of us would like."

John swallowed and looked at the floor. Hadn't thought of that.

"After that, your remuneration would be in the hands of His Majesty. Do I make the position clear?"

He could hear the head breathing heavily. "Yes, sir, admirably."

"Well, what then, man?"

He held the silence for a moment; his shoulders dropped. "My mind is made up, sir."

Now he had to tell Em.

ELEVEN

Emma took off her shawl, refilled the kettle and stood it on the range. Her skirt was damp from the dew. "I'll make some tea by and by," she said. "I thought we might have tears from Dorothy, or some nonsense like that, she's been away so long. But not a bit of it. She ran straight through the school door. Scarcely a backward glance."

"Good." His reply an abstracted murmur. How was he going to tell her? He swallowed.

She eased Rowland out of the baby sling and set him in the corner under the clock. "Now, here's your bear and some toys. Be a good boy and play quietly." She turned to John. "Now we've a moment, I'll fetch your birthday present."

The boards creaked overhead as she moved about in Rowland's room. She returned holding a bulky parcel wrapped in brown paper and tied with string.

"You know what I'm like," she said, "I decided to get something practical, it seemed apt for this time of year. Many happy returns, dear, I hope you think it suitable." She rested a hand on his shoulder, gave him a kiss on his temple, and placed the parcel on the table.

"Thank you very much, Em. Very kind." He bit his lip. When, oh Lord, when?

The parcel gave to his touch. He began unpicking the knots.

"Give me the string, when you've undone it," she said. "I'll save it. And the paper."

He lifted a black academic gown.

"They assured me it's good quality." She began folding the paper into a square. "I thought it time you replaced that old one that's going green. I'm sure you weren't aware how smelly it was, either. You men must live in a tobacco fog in that common room."

"Oh dear," he said. "I..." He cleared his throat, aware of her steady gaze up at him. He started rolling up the string. "Em, it's very kind and would have been ideal –"

"Would have? What do you mean 'would have'?" A sharpness in her tone. The lid of the kettle began to chatter. She swept across the kitchen and banged it to the side of the hot plate. "What do you mean?"

A deep breath, he hung his head. "I don't know how to tell you this. I've had a real struggle, been praying a great deal."

She huffed. "Tell me what?"

Say it quickly, all at once. You owe her that. "I've resigned my position here."

"You've done what? Why?"

As he explained what he had told the headmaster, her eyes widened, her hand went up to her mouth. He felt for her. She couldn't have expected any of this. "I'm sorry. I must follow my conscience, Em – my calling, if you like."

"What calling? I thought we'd agreed you're too old to fight."

"No, I shan't enlist as a fighting soldier – far from it – but I must do something; I'm aware of this terrible sense of responsibility. I want to be of service, and so I've decided to volunteer for the Medical Corps."

The lid began chattering again. "Blast the thing," she said. She strode across and, with a cloth around the handle, lifted the kettle down. "And what did the head have to say about all this?"

"He wasn't best pleased, I'm afraid."

"I'm sure he wasn't. Neither am I –"

"Especially as he'd offered me Head of School House."

"And you've turned that down? What *are* you thinking of?" She wiped a tear quickly from her cheek.

"I'm sorry, Em, but I cannot stand by and have a comfortable life here when others… Do you know that many boys from the sixth form have already signed up and gone off to war? Some of the younger men, too. They volunteered during the summer vac. While we were still in France. And that clever boy, Lambert – the one I told you about, do you remember? He's deferred his place at Oxford and left. If he feels that strongly about fighting for his country… I must support my boys. It's the least I can do."

"Your boys! What about us, your wife and family? Don't you have any responsibility towards us? What's to become of us? Shall we be able to stay here?"

He stood up and began pacing.

"This house isn't ideal," he said. "We'll find something more convenient. More modern."

"I'm not happy. Come on! Are you telling me we must leave here?"

"There's sure to be a house in the village we can rent. It'll be better for Dorothy going to school."

"Oh, no! I don't want some poky place in the village. Not if I'm to manage things on my own." She sounded breathless, her voice tight. "I'm here because you're here. If you go away, I want to be amongst people I know. Especially in my condition and with Mother gone. I don't want to be stuck out here on my own. I want somewhere civilised. I want to be near my family, especially Dora and Father."

"Back to Anerley, then."

"Somewhere like that. Nearby, anyway. I hope you haven't made the wrong decision. I accept – I will try to understand your reasons for wanting to do this, but I don't share them. I'm only going along because I made that promise to obey you – what is it, eight, nine years ago?" She began twisting the handkerchief from her skirt pocket and would not look at him.

"It's nine, now."

"I don't agree with what you're doing at all, I think you're being very foolish, but I don't break a promise I made in public." She paused, breathing heavily. "I thought you loved your family." Another tear trickled down. She dabbed at it quickly.

"Oh, heavens, Em, I do. This isn't going to be easy for me."

"Well, quite. And how are you with the sight of blood? You're not a practical man."

"I shan't be comfortable, but I shall have to get used to it. I can't be squeamish."

"And are you up to all that physical labour, all that lugging about or whatever you'll have to do? Remember what happened on the river. You got yourself in an awful state."

He felt himself growing hotter; his pacing quickened.

She went on. "And what shall we all do if you get killed? I dread the thought. Or injured? I couldn't bear it. What, then? Don't you care what happens to your family?"

He stopped, turned and glared at her, panting.

"Emma! I cannot help it! It's what I have to do! I feel that strongly about it."

Rowland, playing with his wooden bricks, looked up, startled. The tower of bricks wavered, bent, and clattered to the floor. He searched his mother's face, turned to stare at his father. His face broke, and he wailed.

★ ★ ★

John wandered away into the surrounding woods and paused to look back at the house. A curl of smoke went up from the range chimney, a wisp of grey silhouetted against the dark trees.

Like something out of a fairy story.

He stopped and saw through the uncurtained window Emma rolling pastry on the kitchen table, unaware of his gaze; the oil lamp beside her cast a yellow glow over the scene. Homely. Warm. What he'd leave behind.

It felt like exile.

He walked on into the woods, scuffing the new-fallen leaves, heard a twig crack under his feet. He was glad he'd remembered his violin. Apart from playing a hornpipe for Dorothy on board ship, he'd scarcely touched it. Now he needed it to soothe the melancholy catch in his throat. Had he done the right thing, had he followed the promptings of the True God? Why hadn't he realised it would mean his family being displaced? Again… Was that really the sacrifice God demanded?

He reached a clearing where the moon shone onto the thin grass, grey in the pale light.

Far enough away now.

With his back to a soaring beech tree, conscious of leaves fluttering down around him, he placed the instrument to his chin and began playing Bach's First Sonata for solo violin. He knew it by heart. Head back, he closed his eyes. Playing pandered to his melancholy but he continued nonetheless. No one as witness; a oneness with nature, the peace of the darkness. Closer to God.

The violin spoke for him, soothed his soul.

He made decisions in that moment of stillness: he would see Em and the children settled before he volunteered. They must be secure. He'd send them money. And, if possible, this old fiddle would go with him. He needed its companionship, its familiarity, its calm.

What would his world be without music?

He gave a rueful smile: a German composer, giving him peace. He'd once thought them the most sensitive and cultured of nations. And now…

He played the Adagio to the end, not caring who heard or thought him odd.

He was most truly himself.

He lowered the fiddle, feeling purged now of his sorrow, and listened to the sounds of the wood. A barn owl skimmed past like a silent spirit on a soundless hunt; it turned wide cat-eyes upon him and swivelled its head away; a rabbit raced across the clearing, its white scut an exclamation mark of fear.

And in the distance, a late bird began singing, the sound echoing and dominating the silence of the wood. It fluted, chuckled, then paused, as if waiting for a response. He held his breath. At times, the birdsong burbled like water welling up from an underground spring; at other times, the keening whistle was unbearable, as if his world would never be the same again.

TWELVE

"You're doing the right thing, lad. It's The Lord's work."

At sixty-three, John's father looked like an Old Testament prophet – a tangle of curly white hair and full beard. They did not always see eye to eye: talking to Father was often like listening to a set of pronouncements. The lingering Yorkshire accent made him sound dogmatic, and he reserved the right to give his approval – or otherwise – whether you wanted it or not. Very little discussion; you disagreed with him at your peril. John wished sometimes he could share the Old Man's certainty about everything.

"Now, what does Emma say about it all?" His mother wiped her hands on her apron. "She's supporting you, of course."

"You know Em," John said, "she's a good, loyal wife but she never says much about her feelings. Keeps them hidden. Let's say she's going along with it, but I'm sure she wasn't happy about having to move, especially as our third child is on the way."

"Oh, I'm so pleased! I wonder which she'll have this time."

"Ordinarily a child would be a blessing," his father said. "But war isn't normal. How will she manage?"

"The school has granted me two months' pay which I shall make over to her. That should see her through until Christmas, I hope. She's a good manager."

"And what about you, son?" His mother wouldn't look at him, but he saw the wrinkled brow, heard the Suffolk burr become more pronounced, signalling anxiety and uncertainty. She slipped off her apron and began pouring tea. He was honoured – the best tea service...

"Oh, I shall be all right. I've taken the King's Shilling already." He brought out the shiny coin from his pocket and spun it in the air. "Everything's all found in the army. I shall be all right."

"And where's she going to live?" His father stroked his beard.

"She insisted on being South of the river, she wants to be near her father – he's not well, you know – and Dora."

"Tell her she wants to come back to Stoke Newington where she knows the folk she was brought up with." His father took out a handkerchief and blew his nose like a trumpet.

"So we're renting a small house in Catford," John said. "Em seemed to take to it. Her choice really."

"Catford! Well, it'll be difficult to get over to visit, it's rather a journey." His mother shook her head.

"Tell her she's always welcome here," his father said. "Say JF said so. We'll help with the babies –"

"It'd be nice to hear children in this house again." His mother smiled. "We see Helen's, of course, but they never stay."

"It's quiet and safe here. She won't know there's a war on," his father said.

"I'll tell her." John thought of Emma's likely reaction.

"Now, lad, tell us what happened when you volunteered."

"Well, it was straightforward, really." He told them about joining a Territorial Unit for the Medical Corps and recounted the tedious attestation process: several examinations – including a medical – and a lot of form-filling.

"Then I raised my right hand – there were several of us – and swore loyalty to His Majesty. I felt rather foolish, we all looked like Baden Powell's Boy Scouts."

"Never mock service to God or the Crown, lad."

John tightened his lips.

"So where are they sending you?" Ma's wrinkled brow again.

"I don't know yet. They asked me which regiment I wanted to join and I couldn't say, I hadn't given it thought. Well, the fellow in front said he wanted to join the Wessex regiment, because he came from Hampshire originally, so I said that would do for me also."

"You didn't! Whatever for? You could have mentioned the Suffolks or the Yorkshires. You'll be miles away."

"As long as I'm serving, Mother, it doesn't matter. Anyway, they sent me home and said I'd receive my joining instructions and travel warrant in a day or two."

"The important thing is that you won't be fighting," his father said. "You'll keep that Sixth Commandment."

"What about Percy? Has he shown any signs of wanting to volunteer?" he said.

"They're not having my Perce." His mother folded her arms across her breast. "'Sides, his job is too important. They'd never let him go."

"Not tall enough," his father said.

"He'd never pass the medical, not with his asthma. Poor old Perce." His mother began clearing away.

"He seemed fit enough when I last saw him," John said. "But it must feel good to be indispensable." He smiled. "So I'm the only Hemingby going to war, then? Wish me luck, won't you?"

THIRTEEN

The first I knew about our life changing was when they told me I had to leave the village school. That meant saying goodbye to my friends, and I assumed it was because I'd done something wrong, something dreadful. But I couldn't think what it was. You know what young children are like. But I hated the thought that I'd never see Vera and Bessie again.

Mother was very cross about the move – I remember that – but she said little beyond, 'Do as you're told, child, and make yourself useful.' So I packed up my books and crayons, my paints and my dolls. But her face looked blank and sad, like a stone, as she bustled and packed and scrubbed the floors and beat the carpets on the clothes line. I loved that nice little cottage in the woods near the school, but no one told me why we were leaving, except that we needed to move near Grandad and Aunt Dora.

I sat up in bed in that new house, wishing I could change things back. No doubt I shed a lot of tears, but already I'd learned how to stop myself quickly. I decided the reason they gave for the move must have been a fib – because we hadn't seen Grandad, or Aunt Dora, since we arrived.

Except grown-ups didn't tell fibs. That was a puzzle.

I'd no idea where we now lived. Some place near London, I thought. I knew it was noisy and difficult to get to sleep at night because of the trains puffing and whistling past at the bottom of the garden. And I worried about what would happen if I got lost coming home from my new school. I wouldn't be able to tell anybody where I lived.

And what was worse – I learned Daddy was going away but he couldn't say where, and I didn't know why.

I heard his footsteps on the stairs. He was coming to say goodnight as he promised, but I knew it was the last time I would see him. He wouldn't be there in the morning.

He came into the room with his shirt sleeves rolled up and his white braces showing. He carried his fiddle which he put on the bedroom chair near the dressing table.

"I don't want you to go, Daddy." I bit my lip so I wouldn't cry again. "Please don't leave me. I won't be naughty again, I promise."

"Honestly, my sweet, you've done nothing wrong. You haven't been naughty. I'm sorry, I have to go. Sometimes when you're grown up, you have to do things because it's your duty."

He looked strange now. The tickly tails of his moustache had been cut short above his top lip so he looked different and even more smiley.

I hardly dared ask. "Will you be coming back?"

"If God goes with me, wherever they send me, I shall be kept safe and come home to you all by and by."

That was a relief.

He went on. "I want you to be a good, brave girl. Work hard in your new school, make some new friends –"

"But I want to see my old friends again. I liked them."

"You may not see them for the present, but think of them and remember them in your heart, and in your prayers. Just as they remember you. Do you understand?"

I nodded.

"And next year, when you're a big girl of almost seven, when the time comes, be sure to support Mama. She'll be very busy. Help her by looking after Rowley. Hold his hand when you're out in the street. Get him ready for bed, and help out with him at meal times."

"Yes, Daddy. But how will I know when the time comes?"

He laughed. "You'll know, my sweet. Just be a good girl and do as Mama says."

I promised him I'd behave better and work hard at school, learning my tables and my spellings. And then I said: "Please will you play my tune now? I like it so." I eased down in the bed and lay back on the pillow.

He tucked the violin under his chin, briefly checked its tuning and began to play.

That night, his fiddle sang me a lullaby. I closed my eyes and let the music surround me. Daddy's playing took away all the tears. I looked at him once and saw him swaying to the music, eyes closed, his bow stroking the fiddle to bring out the lovely, singing tune. I relaxed: I knew everything would be all right. The music said so. But nowadays I can't listen for long to someone playing a violin, it always brings tears.

When I opened my eyes again and looked towards the window, the sky had darkened to a yellow green, and a golden moon peeped huge above the roof of the house opposite. I listened as the last notes faded away.

"Thank you, Daddy, that was lovely. I like my tune."

He laid the fiddle and bow gently on the bedroom chair again. Then he drew the curtains and came to sit on the bed.

"Have I ever told you what *Salut d'Amour* means?" he said.

I shook my head.

"It means *Love's Greeting*. And whenever you hear that tune in the future, in the bandstand, as you pass some tea rooms, perhaps even on a gramophone, I want you to know that wherever I am, I'm thinking of you and remembering you with love." He bent forward and kissed me on the brow. "Night, night, my Dolly Daydream. *Sois sage,* and may God bless you and keep you."

I smiled. "Night, night. Thank you for playing my tune. Come back to me, won't you?"

"I will." He picked up his violin and bow, stood for a moment in the doorway, blew me a kiss, and left.

FOURTEEN

Soon after, I asked my mother where War was. She met me from school and seemed in a dreadful hurry to get back. She walked very fast with that old pushchair. I know I struggled to keep up.

"What are you saying, child?" She looked down at me.

"Where *is* War? I don't understand. Today, Teacher said that now we've gone to War, we must do all we can to help our brave boys. What did she mean? Where is War?"

"War isn't a place, Dorothy. It's a saying – something that's happening to this country. England, Great Britain has gone to war."

"So what does it mean?"

She thought for a moment. "I expect you've seen boys in your form fall out with each other, they quarrel –"

"Yes, two boys were fighting in the school yard today – Tommy Trent and Alfie Morton." And I prattled on, no doubt about all the ins and outs of my school life.

"Well, can you imagine two countries falling out and starting a fight with each other? This war started when the Germans did something wrong. Their army crossed the border and took the fight to Belgium."

I struggled. "So, why are *we* at war?"

"Lots of countries are. Belgium, France, England all think that the Germans are wrong and should be stopped and taught a lesson. Everybody has taken sides – it's as if the whole world has been spoiling for a fight."

At a corner near the parade of shops on the main road, Rowley sat up in the chair, flung an arm out and pointed at a huge poster on the side of the corner house.

"Wook!" he said. He was very slow pronouncing his 'Ls'. He used to talk about his 'swippers' or said he 'wiked' things.

That must have been the first time I saw that poster. Very effective, that big bushy moustache, the way Kitchener stared and pointed at you. I struggled to read it then but eventually worked it out. I thought it meant he wanted me.

Mother laughed for once. "No, don't worry. He doesn't want little girls or boys. Though heaven knows some of them are young enough."

That must have been the first time I realised where Daddy had gone.

"That's right. Your father has gone to join up."

More jargon, more confusion. I had a childish picture of him standing in a circle holding hands, like we did in the school yard.

"Come on, Dorothy, don't dawdle." Mother had had enough; she was never very patient with me. We went into a grocer's shop where she ordered half a pound of broken biscuits from a shiny tin box on the floor, a dozen eggs, two pounds of flour and half a pound of green back bacon. I realise now she must already have been thinking of economising.

I used to love watching the man turning the wheel of the bacon slicer. It would glide backwards and forwards, and rashers dropped off and were laid on the paper at the side.

We hurried on towards home. "Mama, is my daddy fighting in the war?"

"Not fighting, no. He's joined up so he can help men who've been hurt in the fighting."

"Like a doctor?"

"Something like that."

"So will he be safe?"

"Oh, all these questions!" She sounded cross, but I persisted. "Yes, I expect so." She paused, sniffed, and dabbed at her nose with a handkerchief. "I hope so." She rarely let us see when she was worried or upset. True Victorian in many ways.

★ ★ ★

My dear Em,

October has sped away. Catford feels so distant since I came down here, and you and the children in another world. I do hope you are settling into the house, that the children are no trouble and that Dorothy is liking her new school. I miss you all so. If you can, my dear, do take time to rest during the day. You'll be so busy next year when April comes.

We are undergoing – I might almost say enduring – what they call basic training. I find it a trial since it seems so pointless. We are drilled in marching and standing to attention for what seems like hours on end. They haven't issued us with a rifle as such, thank goodness, but we still drill up and down the parade ground with a broomstick sloped over the shoulder. I find the quick march particularly difficult. It's as if my legs aren't made to step that fast. I am frequently singled out and shouted at.

Sergeant Plum – yes, that is his real name – seems to despise us medics, as he calls us, and often berates us in a sing-song Welsh accent for what he calls our 'posh ideas' and 'la-di-dah ways'. "You may not be going to *fight* for King and Country," he says, "but we still have to turn you into proper soldiers with smartness and discipline about you."

It's such a different world. I do realise I'm the lowest of the low, which suits me well enough – a private – though there's precious little that's private about life here.

The food is adequate and plenty of it, we had pork and beans the other day. But nothing matches the quality of your beautiful meat pies. How I long to taste them again. I have had to learn sock darning also – not half so neat or comfortable as yours, unfortunately.

I've teamed up with a pleasant fellow from near Exeter. His name is Walter Poundsbury, and he has a very strong

Devon accent. It's all nicknames here. I have quickly become Smiler for all the obvious reasons, but you too would smile, I should imagine, to hear Poundsbury come out with, "I don't loike standing in loin, Smoiler." Try saying it aloud and you'll get the effect. Nevertheless, he's a capital fellow and cheerful company. I gave him a nickname which has quickly caught on. Poundsbury is Sov, short for sovereign, again for obvious reasons. I dare not say what some of the men call Sergeant Plum. Too coarse for your sensibilities, my dear.

We've had one or two lectures on the way the Medical Corps works in the field, but I struggle to remember the difference between a Regimental Aid Post, a Casualty Clearing Station and a Field Hospital. There's no sign yet of how we'll be required to serve. From what shocking rumours I hear coming into Portsmouth, I cannot imagine it'll be long before they need us in France or Belgium. We hear terrible things of our lads suffering over there. All of that, I realise now, they keep quiet back home.

So far, though, our experience is restricted to practising being stretcher-bearers. Imagine two long poles which support a canvas bed or hammock slung in between. This folds or rolls up when not in use. Each stretcher has short metal feet and stands some four to six inches off the ground. We have to practise lifting two or three sandbags on the stretcher without injuring ourselves. Many fellows have strained their backs by too hasty a lift and had to report sick. There's no point in being there to assist casualties if we end up crocks ourselves.

My dear, we're close to lights out, so I must finish. I send all of you my love and fond thoughts. I miss home life terribly. Homesickness, they call it. It makes some men weep. Give the children a kiss from their father, especially little Rowley who's walking ever more confidently each day,

I imagine. Tell Dorothy I love her very much. And to you I send particular and special love, and my thanks for your support and devotion.

Until the next time, your loving husband,
JFH

★ ★ ★

It must have been long after school time. Dark outside. I liked to sit in a wicker chair close to the window overlooking the backyard. Practising drawing flowers in a book on my lap, I expect. No idea where Rowley would have been.

Only the hiss of the central gas lamp disturbed the room. Mother had lit just two of the mantles, and she had a rule we couldn't light the fire until six o'clock. I asked if I could have the day blanket over my knees. That was allowed. I loved its bright patchwork of knitted squares. I'm not sure who had it afterwards.

Mother worked in the scullery preparing a fidget pie for tea with bacon, and apples from the garden. I liked the crisp sound of fruit being peeled and sliced.

"You're very quiet, Dorothy. Are you all right?"

"Yes, thank you, Mama."

"You're usually full of chatter when you come back from school. Has anyone upset you?"

"No, Mama." You could hear the clatter of a train going past the bottom of the garden. Bright squares of light chasing across the lawn. I had something on my mind but I never knew with Mother how she would react. Would she be cross? I didn't know whether to say something or hope the dread would go away before bedtime.

I remember putting my drawing book down and leaning against the scullery doorway, that blanket wrapped around my shoulders like a shawl. And then I came out with it: "Mama, will Daddy come home?"

She looked up from her chopping and put the knife down on

the board. "Is that what's troubling you, child? Why should you worry about that all of a sudden? What's happened?"

I told her about the teacher cuddling one of the girls at school who couldn't stop crying: "Frances's mama told her that her daddy wouldn't be coming home. 'Ever again', she said."

"Heavens! Whatever was her mother thinking of, sending the poor mite to school with news like that?"

Mother was very good, I'll give her that. She slipped off her pinafore and came out of the scullery. She sat in the big chair where she usually read me bedtime stories. "Come on now, here by me."

I remember wriggling into the seat and putting my face down into her lap. It felt easier that way.

"Mama, what does 'killed' mean?" Her dark dress smelt faintly of bacon and coal, perhaps onions. I'll always remember that.

"It means that Frances's daddy has lost his life. In the war, is it?"

I just sniffed and nodded.

"What does 'being dead' mean?" My voice came out all muffled.

"Oh, child, it's when your life ends. You're dead when your heart stops and you don't breathe anymore. It happens to everybody."

"Will I be dead one day, Mama?"

She paused and took a deep breath.

"Yes, my dear, one day. But it'll be a long, long time before that happens. Try not to think about all that now. Put it out of your mind. There's nothing anyone can do about it."

"And do dead people go to heaven? Is Frances's daddy with Jesus now?"

Again, she paused. "That's what people say."

"Could my Daddy be killed in the war?"

And she didn't reply.

When I lifted my head again, I saw the glisten of tears in her eyes.

I think she loved him in her way.

FIFTEEN

"Hemingby, you grinning, stumbling oaf! On your feet!"

That Welsh shout – he knew it distinctly. He swung his legs off the bunk and stood to attention as his tormentor swaggered into the hut. "Sergeant!" he said. His voice sounded husky.

"You must be doing something right with your stuck-up, la-di-dah ways, you ponce-arsed toff. Captain wants to see you at oh-nine-thirty hours. And get smartened up, boy – we don't want you looking like a rag bag – take that grin off your face, and have a proper shave."

John cleared his throat. "Yes, thank you, sergeant."

"Oi hope you're not in trouble, Smoiler." Sov looked up from writing home and gave him a grin.

"So do I." John began to strop his razor with extra care. "Not even my wife orders me around as much as this."

★ ★ ★

He first noticed the blue eyes of the man behind the desk. The gaze was direct and challenging, the lips thin, the jaw determined.

"Ah, Hemingby, good. Come in, man." The captain's voice was crisp, educated. Reedy like an oboe.

"Thank you, sir." John stood to attention.

"No, no, at ease. Nothing formal. Take a seat." The captain motioned him towards an office chair at the side of the desk.

John sat down and wondered whether it was proper to cross his legs.

Everything about the captain suggested formality. His hair had a straight centre parting and was brilliantined firmly to his head. His uniform was tightly buttoned, the leather Sam Browne belt glowed, and the insignia of the Medical Corps gleamed at his lapels. Maybe two or three years younger. Doctor, probably.

"Would you say you're a fish out of water, Hemingby?"

"Sir?"

"I mean, you're not ordinary rank and file, are you?"

"Well, I –"

"Look at your background, man. Master at a public school, educated, good family. Speak fluent French, don't you? And aren't you musical, did I hear?"

John tried to speak.

"Not to put too fine a point on it, we could use you. Have you thought of a commission?"

"Well, no, I actually –"

"Oh, come on, man, you're one of us. That's plain enough. You don't have to slum it. Surely you don't want to remain in the ranks? You're officer material. I ought to be calling *you* sir, with your background. A lot of young fellows from public schools have become officers. You'd have a good rapport with them."

"I just want to serve my country; I don't feel it appropriate to be exalted above my fellow men, sir."

"Exalted? What sort of biblical tosh is that? We're talking about promotion here." The captain put his elbow on the arm of his chair, his forefinger at his lips. "Hang on..." He pointed at John. "... You're not one of those CO types, are you?"

"CO, sir?"

"One of those wallahs who object to the war on conscientious grounds."

"I have a religious conscience about fighting which is why I joined the Medical Corps. I don't want to bear arms, certainly not be responsible for killing another human being, but I do believe I should serve my country."

"Test question, then: what would you do if you saw a group of Huns threatening your wife and children, or about to rape your sister?"

John winced. "I'd fight to protect my family, tooth and nail, sir."

"Good, good. But you're adamant you won't let me recommend you for a commission?"

"I'd rather not, sir."

"This damn war is turning dirty, you know, Hemingby. We need men like you."

"Not over by Christmas, then, sir?"

"I fear not. I think we shall soon be kept very busy. They say the Boche used gas shells on the French only the other day at Neuve Chapelle. Caused violent sneezing fits."

John smiled.

"You may laugh, Hemingby, but the consequences can be serious; it could all get out of hand. I hear talk of things our chaps are preparing. Nasty stuff. I hope you don't regret your decision to remain in the ranks."

★ ★ ★

My dear, dear Fordie,

Christmas will be so strange this year without all the family. Ma still insists on having us all over, but for once she has forgone roasting a goose and has opted for a large capon. She says we must all make economies as if the war is some great thing that dominates our lives. But apart from seeing recruiting posters everywhere and men in uniform, our little routines continue much as before. Howard is subscribing to a serial magazine called *The War of the Nations* in the hope of understanding the complexities of it all. Beyond me, I'm afraid.

Emma isn't coming until after Christmas Eve. She says she would prefer to arrive after the excitement of the children opening their stockings. So we shall be a somewhat diminished family at church on Christmas Day. It's not certain we shall see Perce until after dinner. He says he has to attend to other things before he can come. Such a close, private chap. Ma, of course, is very disappointed that she'll be without both her sons on Christmas morning. But at least she'll have all four grandchildren on Christmas night. I can't imagine they'll get much sleep, all together in the attic.

It'll be very jolly to see Emma and your two. Finding Dorothy's present was easy. I've bought her a lovely little paintbox – at least I hope she finds it so – her first step towards watercolours. What a great little artist! I'm so looking forward to seeing Rowley now he's walking. We hear that he's very steady on his feet and quite the little adventurer. He has no fear of stairs, so we shall have to watch him.

John looked up from the letter and smiled, remembering the boy's confident first steps against the lurches of the ship in Biscay.

I thought of buying him a clockwork train, but Howard advised against it, saying he was too young yet awhile, his fingers not strong enough to wind the key. He would be forever pestering Em to make it run for him. So I've settled on a smart wooden train and carriages which caught my eye in Hamley's the other day. He'll just have to shunt that around. Our two boys look forward to seeing their cousins and playing games with them. I expect Mother will organise Hunt the Thimble in the afternoon. That should go down well.

The hut door banged. "Hemingby, Poundsbury! On your feet."

The two men jumped up as if guilty. John laid his letter and parcel to one side on his bed and stood to attention. "Sergeant!" they said in unison.

"You may think it's a holiday, boys, but I'm not yer ruddy Father Christmas. The log fires in the officers' mess need recharging. The scuttles are already low. We can't have the officers feeling the cold now, can we? To the wood store, you two, at the double, and thirty minutes sawing and chopping pine logs."

Plum laughed like a pantomime villain and turned on his heels out of the hut. As the door banged behind him, they heard the sound of his boots scuffing the ground, and a strong Welsh voice singing:

> "Bring me flesh and bring me wine,
> Bring me pine logs hither;
> Thou and I will see him dine,
> When we bear them thither."

"Blimey," Sov said, "old Plum Pudding, he got a sense of humour after all."

"It's the drink," John said, "didn't you see his cheeks?"

Later, his hands red and aching from wielding the axe, John flopped down on his bed and resumed reading his sister's letter:

I hope you'll welcome this little parcel. It's so difficult to know what to get you soldiers. Anyway, I thought small bars of Fry's chocolate to share would go down well but knowing your sweet tooth, you'll probably keep them all to yourself! I don't know how much time you get for reading, but here's the latest Edgar Wallace. Pretty light stuff, I know, but you can always pass it on. The newspapers urge us constantly to remember our brave lads, and so I hope you'll enjoy *The Kitchener Army Song Book* which they say you can use in camp or in the field. I expect you'll have a cheery time entertaining your fellows with a tune on the old fiddle, and having a good sing-song. I shall miss our duet at Christmas teatime but no doubt shall strum a few tunes on the piano for us to sing to.

I'm sorry you chafe at delays and frustrations. However, I thank God you're not in harm's way. Two of my unmarried friends volunteered as Red Cross Nurses and have gone straight to the Front. We all hope and pray they fare well.

The Medical Corps must be training you for skilled work with all that bandaging. Quite the little doctor, aren't you? Ma must be so proud! I never knew so many ways of trussing up men's arms and legs. I wonder you can keep still long enough while others practise on you, though. How I laughed at the idea of you and your great legs on a stretcher being carried up and down dunes and hollows in the heath. How many men does it take to lift you, I wonder?

Is your arm less sore now? Does the inoculation mean you're about to be sent overseas? I know your few days with Em and the family will be precious, but do come and see us when you get embarkation leave. I miss you so, when you are away.

In the meantime, don't let the squad drill, and the stretcher practice and all those lectures get you down. Think of all the useful stuff you're learning! And isn't it nice that they're giving you riding time? I imagine you galloping through the New Forest. They'll be transferring you to the cavalry next!

John grimaced. The smallpox vaccination scab on his arm came off early while he was riding, and now his backside was distinctly saddle-sore. Is this what he joined up for?

I loved the photograph of you in uniform. Don't you look dashing? But why has the RAMC got a snake on its badge? Horrid! Keep well and fit, and enjoy a Christmas with absolutely nothing to do but kick your heels. When the weather's cold, it's a jolly good time for loafing about, I dare say.

We are all thinking of you and send you our love, but I do especially. Keep smiling, Smiler!

Your loving sister, Helen.'

"Hemingby!"

The Welsh shout startled him out of the letter. The sergeant glared from the doorway.

"On your feet, man! It's time you and Poundsbury got coke shovelling. All the stoves need riddling and refilling. Do you want us all to die of cold this Christmas?"

"No, sergeant. Coming! Right away." He looked down at his hands. Already blisters were beginning to form. He could still hear Emma's chiding on the boat; only her face had begun to fade.

SIXTEEN

"Now, you men are all Territorials, and for that reason, we've gone easy so far with your induction into the Corps – which is why you experienced – I won't say 'enjoyed' – a pretty trouble-free Christmas." The major paused and smiled, showing very even teeth; he stroked one side of his moustache with the back of a forefinger.

John gazed round the gloomy drill hall, caught Sov's eye and grimaced. He ran his thumb over the blisters at the base of his fingers. Not a quiet Christmas for some, anyway.

"And on the subject of the festive season, let me say two things. First, it will now have dawned on you that this conflict was far from over by Christmas, as many of you expected when you enlisted. We realised that would be the case soon after Marne. The Boche are going to take some beating, I tell you now."

That's ambiguous. Which does he mean? John looked at the flickers of snow outside the windows. Were his own lessons this boring?

"You may have also heard of the despicable fraternisation that occurred in a few places at the Front on Christmas Day itself. I certainly don't wish to dwell on such unmanly behaviour on the part of a very small minority of our troops, except to say this. Any such cowardice in future in the face of the enemy will be subject to court martial and the severest of penalties."

Sov looked down at his knees and whispered. "What happened?"

"They sang carols and played football with the Germans on Christmas Day," John said.

"Oh, blimey."

"Silence in the ranks!" A bark from the sergeant, somewhere at the back. John put his finger to his lips.

The major continued: "Now it's time to give you men an introduction to some of the issues you're likely to face in the Medical Corps. I'm sure many of you enlisted out of idealism or a wish to help the national effort. Possibly even your fellow man. But very few of you will be alive to the realities you're likely to face when dealing with wounded men after battle. Many of you will also be unaware of your likely response when faced with the sight of blood. A great deal of it sometimes, I assure you. That aspect – that test – will be rectified soon enough and may well determine the role you'll play within the Corps. So, today, I want to talk about wounds. The first rule in assisting the injured is to remember *Every Wound is Infected*."

The major wrote the words on the blackboard, and faced the men. Again he stroked his moustache with his finger.

"There's no such thing as a clean cut. Infection can get into a wound not only from an encounter with a weapon, but also via the man's clothing and especially the ground itself. You need to be aware at all times of –"

He wrote in capital letters: GOOD HYGIENE AND USE OF DISINFECTANT.

"And after that, the first line of defence against complications due to infection is the anti-tetanus injection. Unfortunately, there will be occasions where it's not possible for a qualified medic to administer that. Some of you will have to learn the technique of doing so, maybe under difficult circumstances. Fact of war, I'm afraid. That is another hurdle you will all have to go through."

"Over." John covered his mouth to avoid being seen.

"Those of you that don't like needles may struggle with giving injections. And we shall need to find that out. Now, there are two basic types of wound."

On the blackboard he wrote WOUNDS and underlined it firmly. Then he wrote:

1. Penetration Wound
2. Laceration Wound.

"A penetration wound is exactly what it suggests. Something has penetrated the soldier's body. A bullet is most likely, either from a machine gun or a rifle, or it could be a thrust from a bayonet –"

Sov drew his breath in with a hiss.

" – but it might also involve metal fragments from shells or grenades. You will be amazed at what finds its way into the human body in warfare. But, in my view, the worst kind of wound is that caused by shrapnel."

He wrote the word in capital letters on the blackboard.

"Sounds like a Boche word but it isn't. What is it? Well, it's metal balls or fragments that are scattered when a shell, bomb, or bullet explodes. There are even some shells that are designed to do exactly that. Nasty things. They explode in the air and send stuff flying everywhere. At their worst, they can rip large chunks out of a man's body or tear off limbs, and many wounds you will see subsequently lead to amputations because of shrapnel damage. Any questions?"

John bowed his head and tried to block the images out.

A soldier some distance away put up his hand.

"Yes, you, soldier." The major pointed over the heads of the men.

"Sir, which parts of the body are likely to be injured?"

"Generally, or by shrapnel?"

"Either, sir."

"We're finding injuries to spinal columns, the abdomen –"

Another intake of breath. Sov looked down and gripped the edge of his chair.

"– the chest, head and, of course, arms and legs. Everywhere, in fact. You would be amazed what weapons men seize if it comes to hand-to-hand fighting: rifle butts, boots, shovels, knives – all of them can make serious wounds in the hands of a desperate man."

John raised his hand and waited for the officer to acknowledge him. "Sir, what protection will we have at the Front, particularly as we shall be unarmed?"

"Good question. But no clear answer, I'm afraid. Your uniform, of course, possibly your greatcoat. We have to hope that the enemy respects the Red Cross arm band. Usually, of course, you'll go in after the fighting when things have quietened down, so you'll be less in the line of fire."

"Thank you, sir." He bit his lip.

"One tip I will say at this point: think carefully what you put in your pockets when you're out in the field. You don't want to be anywhere near a shell-burst. Many casualties have been injured by their own possessions. We've seen the contents of men's pockets driven deep into their wounds by a blast. Penknives, coins, pencils – and from outside, pebbles and bits of masonry. I have even known bones and soft tissue from a nearby victim lodge in a soldier hard by."

John turned as a chair scraped somewhere at the back of the hall. A red-headed young soldier, his hand stuffed to his mouth, hurried from the hall.

"Eyes, front!" The sergeant's bellow made several men jump. "Pay attention to the officer."

"Yes, thank you, sergeant. I will finish where I started, by saying…" He tapped the blackboard with his fingernail "… every wound is infected. Grease, dirt, bits of clothing are all likely to be driven into the wounds. Out in the field, you will not have time to achieve perfection. Your job, gentlemen, will be to patch up and move on. That must be your constant watchword."

John pursed his lips. Words of the popular poem, easily modified, slipped into his mind. 'What is this life, if, *en pleine guerre*, we have no time to give due care?'

What had he let himself in for?

★ ★ ★

My dear Dolly Daydream

I hope you are well and being good and all that sort of thing, and I do hope, my sweet, you think a lot about your Daddy

84

who loves you even if he has to go away from you when he doesn't want to.

In our camp here, we start our day very early (before you wake up, I expect) and they march us out for two miles in all weathers before breakfast. It always seems to be raining and I get soaked through. They keep us hard at work all day and we sleep sixteen in a room, not a bit of furniture apart from our lockers. Not like home at all. And someone snores!

Soon I shall be going to work at a nearby hospital so I can help poorly soldiers.

Be very good to Mama and tell her I love her, and give her a big hug for me, and please, please send one of your pictures to me. I miss you all so much and send you big kisses.

Your loving Daddy

★ ★ ★

He had never seen an amputee before and did not know how the wound would look or what his reaction would be.

But that was the point.

The soldier seemed so ordinary, so young. Only the screw of pain on his face showed that he had experienced anything unusual. He looked about eighteen.

"Good morning, Private," the hospital doctor said, "this is Private Hemingby of the Wessex Field Ambulance. We'd both like to look how your leg is progressing after the operation. Now, show us the wound, will you?"

The young man wriggled and eased up his left trouser leg. The doctor leaned forward and gestured to John to unwind the bandage.

No brown bloodstains, thank God. John found he could look at the leg without feeling queasy. The wound still glowed a hot pink as if angry at being disturbed.

Not a stump at all. More like the end of a worm, he thought, smooth, rounded, tapered. He'd expected a straight cut across like a log, but no bone glistened. Stitches, like coarse black hairs, sprouted from the folded surplus skin. Would it hurt when they had to be removed?

"Any pain at all, Harry?" John said.

"Don't yet know it's gone, sir. The itches from foot rot still playing me up. Very odd, sir."

"So, what happened?"

"I slipped, sir, just as the field gun kicked back, and me leg went underneath the wheel. Me own fault really, I shouldn't have been hurrying with that next shell. But we was under orders for rapid firing and –"

"Where are you from, Harry?"

"Deptford, sir. Me and a group of pals all joined up at the same time. Wanted to be together. Only two of the five still going strong."

"Right, Private Hemingby, paint iodine on this man's wound and re-bandage it. Firmly, but not so tightly as to constrict it." The captain straightened up, casually felt the young man's pulse and folded away the stethoscope. "When you've done that, join me further up the line. There's a very unusual shrapnel case I'd like to show you."

"Yes, sir." John knelt down and fumbled in the dressing box the matron had issued to him. "This might sting somewhat," he said, "but I've got to clean it." He soaked a swab in surgical spirit and began dabbing at the pink stub.

"No, sir, I can take it. Feels nice and cool, actually."

"How old are you, Harry?"

"Well, I can tell the truth now, I s'pose. Leastways, I don't mind you knowing. I lied about me age, didn't I, so's I wouldn't be left out. I was jest seventeen when we joined up, eighteen come this August, I am."

John sat back on his heels and closed his eyes. "So young! I'm twice your age."

He dressed the wound. When he had finished winding the bandage around, he cut down the centre to create two long tapes. With these, he tied off round the leg just below Harry's knee.

"Well, at least the war's over for you now, soldier."

"I hope me life ain't an'all, sir. I mean, what am I going to do now I can't stand properly, and what use am I going to be on a football field of a Saturday? I used to live for that."

"You'll find something, Harry, another door will open, I'm sure. We have to believe it." He straightened up and began repacking the dressing box as he had been taught.

A smell of disinfectant hung in the air. Somewhere, a man groaned. John stood up, lifted the box and gave a grin of encouragement to Harry.

★ ★ ★

In the gloomiest part of the ward, away from the light of the windows, a young soldier crouched, huddled into the very corner of the room. John had not noticed him before but the man wore the blue uniform of a patient.

His face was hidden, buried deep on his knees. If his eyes were open, they looked only at his feet. And his hands, fingers spread, rested on his head as if to protect it, or tear his thick blond hair out, or exclude the world. He seemed like a man in the extremities of grief, shut out from all life. John turned away, shocked.

At the far end of the ward, the doctor waved to him: "Over here, Hemingby."

★ ★ ★

The next patient, a man in his early twenties, John guessed, sat on a deal chair at the end of his bed. His uniform was neat, the red tie done up tightly. An epitome of smartness. Yet he stared into space with a milky gaze.

The doctor touched him lightly on the shoulder. The young man started but did not speak. Still he stared ahead.

"It's all right, Private, I'm the doctor." He turned to John. "I don't know whether he can hear me or not. I have to assume he can." He faced the patient again and in a raised voice said, "This is Private Hemingby, he's helping me on the ward today."

No reaction. A nurse went past, carrying a syringe in a bowl, her skirts a brisk rustle.

The doctor shepherded John a short distance away. They talked in whispers.

"Now, what would you make of this, Hemingby?"

"It's amazing, isn't it, sir? Not a mark on him except –"

"Yes, quite. We think it's probably a shrapnel wound, but it may have been caused by a thrust to the face with a bayonet or even a trenching tool."

A V-shaped crevice, starting above the man's eyebrows, plunged into his head and ended at the bridge of his nose. John struggled with the idea that the cavity created another opening into the head. He tried to block out the notion of it filling with water.

"He's had some reconstructive work, of course. There's not much more we can do, not when something has stove in the brow like that."

"So what damage has it done, would you say, sir?"

"He's blind, of course, and never speaks. But we don't know whether it's shock and he'll recover speech in due course. My guess is the frontal lobes have been damaged which isn't a good prognosis. But we're not going to trepan him just so we can take a look. Poor devil's been through enough."

John looked at the young man again. The hair was neatly parted, his uniform impeccable – some nurse had lovingly tended and dressed him – and his skin smooth and boy-like. He stared into an alien world he'd never escape, his lips full and sensual, parted in an expression of fear and surprise.

"He looks haunted," John said.

"Unspeakably monstrous, isn't it? Someone said he was a solicitor's clerk before he joined up, you know – able, ambitious, trusted. The sort of fellow you want on your side. In line for promotion, too. But keep up your heart, Hemingby. Sadly, he's one of many. We have to move on."

★ ★ ★

"The next one may turn your stomach, so be prepared, Hemingby. Bed number twenty-six on the other side."

John checked the numbering on the beds. Twenty-five patients each side of the long room. The bed in question stood in the opposite corner of the ward, protected by thin curtains which lifted and rustled in the draught from the window.

Even on a cold day, let God's fresh air in. It's good for you. He could hear his father's pronouncement even now.

Certainly practised here. But what would the old man make of all this?

A cry of pain from the far end of the ward distracted him for a moment.

"Now this fellow has had a lucky escape." The doctor again spoke in a whisper. "If you can call it lucky. He won't talk to you for obvious reasons, but he's *compos*. Just. He's due for reconstruction work shortly but we have to build him up first. He's lost a lot of blood. At the moment, we have to help him along with rest, beef tea, glucose and regular injections of morphine." He spoke more loudly now. "Good afternoon, Lieutenant. May I introduce Private Hemingby? He's ward orderly today." John admired the doctor's cheerful manner.

The man's eyelids opened to an apathetic droop and he raised an index finger off the sheets. He made a vague gargling sound.

The injury had damaged his mouth and cheek. What remained of his mouth was fixed now in a permanent gape. A tangled mess of purple flesh, congealed blood and skin showed that something had hit, cut or smashed his right cheek and bottom jaw.

But as he became used to the gloom, John realised the man's bottom teeth and part of the jaw hung through the shattered lip and rested on a padded dressing placed below his neck.

"Oh, dear God!" John closed his eyes and turned away, his back to the patient. He clasped his hands in an attitude of prayer, tensed himself to look again towards the bed.

The doctor tugged the curtains back, hurried over and hissed at him: "For God's sake, man, I did warn you. Now, get a grip. Do you realise what you could have done to that soldier's morale? Never, ever, show that you find a patient's wounds disturbing or disgusting. Fortunately, this time, he's so hazy he probably won't remember. That man hasn't seen himself in the mirror. But he's got to live with himself for the rest of his days. Your reaction now will show him how people see him, and what he can expect from the rest of society."

John sniffed, blew his nose and cleared his throat. "I'm sorry, Captain, I couldn't help myself."

"And I'm sorry to chew you up like that, but it's a valuable lesson to learn. Medics are the front line to a man's recovery. If the patient gets this far, someone decided they'd got a chance. We leave behind the ones we don't think will make it. So we don't want to be responsible for setbacks at this stage."

Dear God, John thought.

"But I don't mind telling you that many an evening after a day on the wards, I've returned to the mess and reached for a dram or two to see me through. You'll get hardened to it, so that eventually you'll come to hate yourself for your callousness. Took me about four months. Now go and look at the men in beds –" he consulted a check sheet – "thirty-seven, thirty-eight and forty-four. All need dressings changed. Clean 'em up, chat a bit and move on. There shouldn't be anything too stomach-churning. When you've finished, ask for me at the nursing station or Matron's cubby hole. Any questions, I'll go over 'em then."

★ ★ ★

"You will find Captain Henshaw in his snug." The matron seemed to tower over him; her crisp uniform, her formal manner intimidating. He hesitated.

"Go through the ward, down the passage, turn right into the corridor, on into Isolation. We've set aside a room there, at the far end."

She sniffed and turned away.

The smell of pipe tobacco accosted him. He knocked on the door and walked into the atmosphere of a gentlemen's club. A billow of smoke swirled around his head.

"Ah, Hemingby, come in, man." The doctor had his feet up on the mantelpiece. "Put your baggage down and come and take a seat." He indicated an armchair in shiny brown leather. Brass studs traced the curl of the arms.

"Oh, thank you, sir." John eased himself into the chair and instinctively spread his hands towards the fire.

"Now, in here, army rules don't apply." The doctor put his feet down. "I can't be doing with all that Captain – Private nonsense. Keep it for the wards. Both of us are volunteers; here we meet as equals. In the world we come from, we're professional men and could easily meet socially. So, how do you do? I'm Hubert Henshaw." He put down his pipe and proffered his hand.

John leaned across and received a firm handshake.

"John Hemingby." He rested back against the cushion and observed the doctor, now with his uniform unbuttoned: bald head, round face and grey hair full and thick over his ears and at the back of his head. Not a typical military man, and about twenty years older.

"Care for a fill of Sobranie, John?"

"No, thanks, sir – er, Hubert, I don't smoke. Used to take snuff, but my wife complained I was always sniffing. She didn't like the state my handkerchiefs got into. So I thought I'd better stop. Found it easy to give up, thank goodness."

"Ah, the ladies. Always a civilising influence. Now, any questions?"

"No, not really. Changing those dressings was straightforward. But tell me about –" John looked at his checklist. "– that young private, number thirty-seven, the one with the foot wound. He tells me he was about to clean his rifle, wasn't aware there was still a round in the chamber. Do you believe that? Sounds rather careless."

"I wondered what you'd make of that." A long pause while Henshaw lit his pipe with a spill and puffed to get it going again. "We had a communiqué about this sort of thing. SIW they call it."

"SIW?"

"Self-Inflicted Wound. Wouldn't credit it, would you? But it seems they're on the increase."

"You mean that fellow shot himself deliberately?"

"No one can prove it, of course. But it does seem fortuitous that a man should receive a flesh wound bad enough to take him out of the front line, but hardly life-threatening. Thank God *we* don't have to decide whether the man's a coward or not."

John shifted in his chair and stroked his chin. Late afternoon: getting stubbly. "That's a court martial offence, isn't it?"

"If he presented with a wound like that in my surgery at home, I'd talk to him, find out what was in his mind. Can't do it here, of course. The military wouldn't allow it. But a chap doesn't shoot himself in the foot for no reason, I say."

"You believe in all this new psychological stuff, then?"

"Well, you can't dismiss it completely. It interests me. But here we don't worry about niceties. Our orders are clear enough: patch 'em up and send 'em back."

"I don't suppose that young Tommy will be too happy about that." John glanced up at the clock. "Before I go, though, Hubert, tell me about the young man crouching in the corner. He didn't move all the time I was on the ward."

"Ah, number fifty. Now, that's my difficult case. I don't know what to do about him. Is he faking? Are we dealing with a cunning coward? Or is it something else – something we've never seen before? A new illness produced by this damned war?"

"Very disturbing, I must say," John said. "I can't imagine how it must feel to be locked in on yourself as he seems to be."

SEVENTEEN

My dear John,

All well here, I'm glad to say, Dorothy seems settled at school now. They say she's very imaginative. She likes artwork, especially painting, as you know, but her teacher says she responds to poetry and can recite quite long pieces very prettily. Her reading is above average also.

At home, we have general teething troubles. Rowley is developing his milk teeth just as Dorothy is beginning to lose hers. She's come home with some nonsense about The Tooth Fairy rewarding children by leaving threepence for each young tooth lost, and against my better judgement I've gone along with it. I'd rather it were a penny, of course. One time, though, I left the money under the pillow but quite forgot to take the old tooth away. Needless to say, Dorothy foolishly began to wonder whether she might be rewarded twice. I had to say you cannot fool The Tooth Fairy!

My confinement, now little more than a month away, concerns me greatly. I've decided the children will be better staying with your parents when my time comes. Although Dora and Father live nearer, neither of them has much inkling about how to relate to young children. It's better that Dorothy and Rowley don't go to them. I've arranged to visit Stoke Newington for Easter and stay there with the children so, whilst I'm with them, they get to know their grandparents better. That should mean they won't find the week or so of my confinement so strange or unsettling. I hope also they'll see something of Helen and their cousins. That could make for a very jolly time.

Well, I'd better close and prepare for bed. I do hope you're keeping well and getting enough food. Are your working boots cosier now?

My best love to you. Until the next time,

Your loving wife, Em.

★ ★ ★

"I been thinking," Sov said. "I mean, who says if a man's a coward or not?"

"That's a solemn subject for this late hour," John said.

The pair lingered on the railway platform, part of a group waiting for the 'special' bringing the wounded back to England. Other men from the section stood idly, smoking, chatting.

"No, I'm serious, Smiler, who gets to say whether a man's a coward or not?"

"In the field, I suppose it'd be your senior officer first, but eventually a court martial would decide."

"You see, I been thinking about that young Tommy Atkins with the foot wound, the SIW you was telling me about. Who'd decide if he was a coward or not?"

John took a deep breath, remembering his horror as a schoolboy when he first learned of the Roman practice of decimation. Random slaughter of the ranks to improve morale. He sighed. "Here in Blighty, the doctor would get involved," he said. "He might have to have the last say, or at least submit a report. I suppose that's humane, though I'm not sure Captain Henshaw would relish that. Doctors are meant to preserve life, not assist in taking it."

"Yes, I've heard they've started shooting 'en now. Keep others on the straight and narrow."

"I can't bear the thought." John turned to look down the track.

Execution by firing squad; not a hero's death. And would the family feel the disgrace or mourn the loss?

A forlorn train whistle sounded in the distance. He straightened up. "Right, here she comes. Ready, Sov?"

The whole company stirred, even before Sergeant Plum gave the order. Many tidied and tugged at their uniforms; others discarded their cigarettes and ground them under foot. Routine now.

A gibbous moon peered round the edge of a cloud, tingeing the surrounding fields a soft yellow. Grey smoke and white steam from the engine rolled and tumbled away over the hedges. The train chuffed round the bend and eased alongside the platform. Minimal clanking and jerking as it came to a stop, gentle as a nurse.

Then, silence; only the chiff-chaff of steam from the stationary locomotive. All along the train, double doors opened outwards from the special carriages and lamp light flooded onto the platform.

"Company! Stand by!" Sergeant Plum's orders echoed round the station.

"As if we don't know the drill by now."

"Oh, Sov, you do enjoy your grumbles!" John said.

Along the platform, the thirty-six stretcher-bearers gathered in groups of four or six. Somewhere behind them in the cobbled yard, a horse at the head of one of the ambulance wagons flubbered its lips and stamped its foot.

"I do hope this lot ain't too bad," Sov said, "I hate it when they cry out while you're shiftin' 'em."

"It should be OK. They'll have had some treatment in France, or an op on the train. The worst'll be sedated." John picked up the stretcher from the platform.

The Red Cross nurse on the train towered above them. "Now, you men, go gently with these lads. And make sure you look after them." She wore a cape as protection against the chill of the March night. "Come aboard, please, we're ready for you now."

In pairs, the men tramped up boxed wooden steps which

seemed to have appeared from nowhere. John and Sov climbed into the coach and unfurled their stretcher.

Hot, fetid air and body odour. John turned away and gagged. Strong disinfectant caught at his throat. By the light of the overhead lamps, he saw the bunks ranged in threes along the sides of the whole carriage.

Those nearest the doors first, he thought. Us two to hold the stretcher and two to ease the patient off the bunk.

The other orderlies squeezed past and took up position at the patient's head and feet. A middle-aged nurse watched anxiously.

"Middle bunk first, lads. That's easiest," John said.

The two men jockeyed round John and Sov to lift the man onto the stretcher. The soldier on the top bunk peered over the edge to watch.

"God, lad, you weigh a bloody ton," one of the orderlies said.

The patient lifted his head and grinned, then winced.

"Steady, boys, don't jolt him," John said, "and lift his greatcoat up."

He and Sov gripped the handles of the stretcher, took the strain and moved towards the exit. Two more bearers, ready to pick up the next man, shrank back to let them pass.

"We've left you top or bottom, boys. Take your pick." John grinned. For the higher berth, you needed the stretcher up on your shoulders; working to clear the bottom bunk always strained your back.

"Oh, thank *you*, Smiler, for nothing." The bearers moved further along the lines of bunks.

Behind them, from the depths of the carriage, John heard a groan: "Oh, God, are we home yet?"

"They're coming, soldier, be patient, wait your turn." The sister's voice firm but kind.

John always brought up the rear; Sov, the big Devonian, coming off the train, had the difficult task of keeping the stretcher level. He straightened his arms above his head as they laboured down the steps.

"Oh, Jesus, for fuck's sake watch it, will you!" the patient said.

"Steady, soldier, take it easy, soon have you off," John said.

"Now then, Smiler, where's us goin' to put 'en to?"

"Over there, Sov, back of the platform. Leave plenty of room for the rest."

They eased the man down, putting him close to the paling fence. Again they set off to pick up a new stretcher.

In the darkness, all along the platform, the patients lay close to the ground, awaiting bearers to the ambulances. An officer with a checklist, head bowed, peered at each tally card with a lamp and ticked each patient off on a list. Behind him, a nurse went along the ranks, bending to tidy blankets, saying a few words.

In the light of a station gas lamp, John could just see at the rear of the train the 'walking wounded' – men in greatcoats, with bandaged heads and strapped-up arms, filing off onto the platform. A group of women surged towards them, their long dresses swishing, their fox furs pinned tight around their necks against the night air.

"Now, would any of you men like a cup of tea?"

Another flashed a small silver case. "Care for a cigarette, soldier?"

The men stood around in a huddle, some of them glad of a smoke. Most would travel in the motor ambulances. The section had only two but, in spite of the regulation slow pace, these men would reach hospital first.

Because of their experience with horses, he and Sov took it in turns to drive the ambulance wagon. They usually transported two or three stretcher cases, occasionally a few walking wounded.

"Right, that's our lot." Sov helped a nurse into the back of the wagon and clambered up front himself. "Lovely job. We can make a start now. OK, let 'em go now, Harry, we'll see you later."

The orderly patted the muzzle of the leading horse and stepped back.

"Lights all checked and working, lads."

"Come on, then, boys!" John clicked his tongue and slapped the back of the right-hand horse with the reins. He loved feeling the cold leather straps in his hands. The two great Suffolk Punch horses lumbered into motion. "Steady now, Samson, slow and steady." Not too quickly, especially over the cobbles. Even so, a cry of pain from the back of the wagon as one of the patients was jolted.

The two horses set off for the three-mile journey to the hospital. The slow clop and swivel of those splayed, shaggy hooves, the jingling harness. He smiled, remembering a walk with Grandad Ford in the Suffolk countryside, near Lavenham. Twenty years ago, at least. They stopped to watch a team strain to plough a great belly of a hill for next year's wheat. Up at the top, silhouette against the sky. Fascinating, the rhythm, the time-steady motion, the oneness between man and beasts. *Remember this, John boy. This is your glimpse into the past. Time standing still. We'll lose it soon enough.*

Suffolk Punches.

"Why do we have to do this late at night when everybody else is asleep?" Sov yawned. "I been ready to bunk down for at least two hours now."

"Government policy, I heard, so the public don't know how bad things are in France. They bring the wounded back when everyone else is in bed. Keep up morale."

"They want to think about having hospitals in France, 'stead of here, save the poor devils this long journey."

"My guess is it'll come to that," John said.

The lights of the town faded and the wagon trundled on into the dark lanes. The wheels ground and crackled on the grit of the road. Above them, moonlight flickered through the branches of the tall trees, turning the way ahead silver. John looked up startled, and strained to hear. From the back of the wagon, a sound of someone snoring, growling defiance into the night.

"I hope I don't show funk if it ever comes to it, I don't want to be shot."

"Oh, Sov, are we back there again?"

"Isn't it something everybody's afraid of, Smiler, being a coward? You don't know how you'll be when it comes to it."

"I know the army harps on about being manly," John said, "as if manliness and courage go hand-in-hand. But they say courage is when people face danger without giving way to fear."

"So, if I do my duty, if I do what's expected at all times, no one will accuse me of bein' a coward?"

"Yes, that's right. But I don't think it's as easy as that. Courage, bravery, call it what you will, is going ahead and acting even when you're frightened, I should imagine."

"Oh, that's all right. I'm not so afraid now of being thought a coward. It's all right to be frightened as long as you carry on."

John smiled. "That's about the measure of it. But, for me, cowardice would be not acting for the best when you can and you should. I just pray I'm never in a situation where that happens."

★ ★ ★

After Church Parade on Easter Sunday, he slipped back into chapel, his mind a whirl. Em's letter had reminded him: the birth of their third child was only three weeks away. He half hoped for a girl again – a little companion for Dorothy. Whatever The Lord gave, though, the family would be blessed. But would Em remember his suggestions for names when it came to registering the birth? He smiled to himself: how life had changed in the seven months since the journey back from Marseilles. No prospect of leave at present; when would he see the new arrival? He thought of them, now with his parents. Father was never easy. Would Em manage to guard her tongue?

He knelt down, hands clasped tightly. Sounds of laughter outside drifted through the chapel windows, unsettled him. So many things to pray for: safe delivery for Em; his children's wellbeing and security in time of war; his parents, his sister and brother. He paused, thinking of Percy. How could two brothers be so different? Why..?

He hauled his mind back, prayed for the recovery of patients in the hospital. He found himself staring at the altar. Two young soldiers lost during the last week; both from shock after tricky double amputations. Could he cope?

He had to pray for himself. "Please, Lord, you know this work has not been easy. May your strength go with me, help me to continue this work with diligence and compassion. And in the future, may I do nothing mean-spirited or cowardly, but only Thy will. Amen." It helped hearing the words aloud.

He opened his eyes again and looked at his fervent, clenched fingers, the knuckles showing white. All this pain, this struggle – it had to be the right decision. So what was it he feared?

EIGHTEEN

"I'm a father for the third time." He could not control himself any longer. "Look!"

He pulled the telegram from the back pocket of his trousers. He'd kept it there while they worked on the ward. Now, on a break in the hospital snug, he'd a chance to share his news. He passed the telegram over to Hubert Henshaw, who stood, back towards the fire, enjoying a quick pipe.

"Congratulations, old man," Henshaw said, "and this is your –"

"Second girl. Beatrice Ford Hemingby," he said. "I'm jolly bucked about that. My wife named her, I wasn't sure she'd remember. Beatrice was my suggestion, if it was a girl. Months ago, actually. And she's even given her my middle name."

"What, Ford?"

"Yes, my mother's maiden name. An old Suffolk family, the Fords."

"I once did a locum in Suffolk," Henshaw said, "Bury St Edmunds. I remember a big funeral back in '02, I think it was. Or maybe the year the old Queen died. In the papers, big procession. Now he was a Ford, I think. Master of the local workhouse at one time. No relation, I suppose."

"Well, I'm dashed," John said. "That was my grandfather. And I travelled up for his funeral, naturally."

"So our paths have crossed before, so to speak, though we just didn't know it. Charming place, Bury."

"Small world, eh? And I'll tell you something else," John said. He started pacing up and down. "I was *in* that workhouse. Only for a short time. So they told me later. I was very small, so I don't remember. Not an inmate, we were visiting Grandad."

"Of course," Henshaw said. "You're hardly a *work'us brat*. Dreadful places. It's time they abolished them and found a better system. Just pray you never see the inside of one again." He laughed. "Not very likely, I must say. Anyway..." He laid his pipe in an ashtray. "Come on, old chap, duty calls."

★ ★ ★

My dear, dear Fordie,

I do hope you're keeping well and that you're bearing up under all the work. We're all so thankful they're holding you back in England on home duty. From what we hear and read, things are horrid in France, so many of our brave lads being wounded etc., etc. You're well out of it, I'd say. Howard and I were shocked to learn that the wretched Huns are now using poison gas as a weapon. How barbaric! The papers don't dwell on details, but I gather the effects are extremely unpleasant. To think that little Bea came into the world just as they started using that dreadful stuff.

She's a beautiful little thing, quite small. Let's hope she also has your hazel eyes, like Dorothy. Now you're not to worry, John dear, it's reasonably routine in these days of modern medicine. But little Bea has developed slight jaundice since her birth. That should pass of its own accord in a few days. But Emma has experienced one or two complications since the birth. You know what she's like, makes light of her troubles and keeps on going. But the fact is, she is very tired, poor dear, and somewhat anaemic. There are one or two other ladies' things which you don't need to know about, but the result is that Doctor says she needs rest, building up and some treatment, and they are soon to admit her to St Thomas's for about a week. Little Bea will go with her and at least be cared for in the same hospital, but your other two are coming over to SN again to stay with Ma and Pops towards the end of the month. Things worked out nicely at Easter. They have the space, the children know their grandparents and should be quite happy. I shall look in as often as I can with the boys.

Now, you're not to worry! I volunteered to write and tell you since I'm sure I owe you a letter. Emma is well enough in herself considering, apart from the dreadful fatigue and the complications, and the baby will pick up soon enough.

So, no cause for alarm, but do write if you want to know anything further.

With fondest love from your little sister,
Helen.

He put the letter down on his bed and stared across the hut. *Complications.* Did that mean things were serious?

★ ★ ★

Strange sounds outside the window of the snug: coughing, shuffling, the scuff and crunch of boots on gravel. John stowed a rolled bandage in his medical kit and looked out. An army of beggars struggled past. Each soldier rested his hand on the shoulder of the man in front, or tagged onto the tail of his jacket. Men in groups of three or four, all in muddy uniform, some without hats, shambled along, several Red Cross nurses beside them as guides. From time to time, the women put out a hand to steer one of the soldiers.

Every man's head drooped: some had lint pads across their eyes; others shaded their faces with a hand as if it hurt to look at daylight. In the rear, a sergeant thrust out his chest and marched at a funereal pace.

"Dear God, it *is* the blind leading the blind," John said, his voice little more than a murmur. "Hubert, look at this."

The doctor wandered over. "Poor devils! The first of many, I fear. Look at them – walking wounded, but not a mark on them. Bloody barbarism. Doing this to men isn't civilised." He explained these were the first poison gas victims brought back from Ypres. "The medics don't know what to do with them out there. I don't know that we're much better placed."

"So what's caused this?"

"We had a wire about this, and indications are that it's chlorine. Those that weren't too badly affected talked of a greeny yellow cloud of gas and a smell like a mixture of pepper and pineapple. Medical wisdom has it that –"

"Chlorine? Is that all? Isn't it a water disinfectant? Don't they use it in public swimming pools?"

"Yes, it's soluble in water. But get it in greater concentrations, or as a gas, and it's bloody corrosive. Spray it over these poor chaps, make them breath it in, and it mixes with the water in the eyes and throat, and in the lungs, and creates hydrochloric acid."

John flinched and closed his eyes. "Oh my Lord, what is civilisation coming to?"

"I'm at a loss to know what we or anyone can do to help these men," Henshaw said. "I really am. The damage is done." He stood up and began buttoning his jacket.

"Oh, Hubert," John said. "There is one thing, something worrying me. About my wife. Could I just ask –"

"I'm sorry. Will it keep, old man? I ought to check on that tricky chest wound. The poor chap will be coming round about now."

"No, of course, I understand. Later, then." He sighed.

Later could be too late.

★ ★ ★

"I must get home, sergeant, I'm worried," John said. "My wife has to go into hospital, and our new baby isn't well. My family needs me. What are my chances of getting forty-eight hours' leave?" He needed to stoop; Plum scarcely reached John's shoulder.

"Well, you could try 'compassionate'," Plum said. "But from what I've heard, boy, you'll be bloody lucky. They need all the medics here. So many casualties coming through from Portsmouth, we'll be running round like blue-arsed flies. We're a Clearing Station now for anyone with a Blighty. But try your luck, go through the adjutant. You might get a word with the captain. But, bit of advice: get a proper shine on those boots – look at them, they're a disgrace, you know what a stickler the captain is – and make sure you wipe that bloody smile off your face."

John sighed. "It's natural, Sarge, I can't help it. It's the way The Lord made me. Big teeth. This is no laughing matter, I promise. I'm very anxious."

★ ★ ★

He huddled into the shelter of the station doorway. Sunday – they locked the waiting room now to save lighting the fire. Economy because of the war. Not even a man behind the ticket window. Pay on the train, he supposed, or at the other end.

A cold wind, flecks of rain in it. He shivered and turned the collar of his greatcoat up. Not good this, for early May. Where was spring?

Would little Bea look yellow? That was all he knew, you turned yellow with jaundice. Where was it, in the liver? What rotten luck, being born with a diseased liver! Did this mean she'd always be sickly? Would she even live?

He shut his eyes to block out the thought.

And what about Em? Helen's letter seemed so discreet. But what complications did women have after birth? Problems internally or externally? Had she lost a lot of blood? Perhaps she'd need stitches, even a full operation? Or was it something else? They said some women went funny in the head after giving birth, got a bit down. Not Em, surely, she was too practical, feet on the ground. She wasn't given to funny turns. And nothing strange happened before.

Feeding the baby? That could be the trouble. He remembered

Ma talking once of someone down the road. The woman couldn't feed her baby herself, and a neighbour who'd also recently given birth had to express some milk in order to help out. Mysterious thing, childbirth.

If only he could get under way. If all went smoothly, he'd be home by midnight. "Come on, train!"

He glanced up at the station clock. Ten minutes late already. Touch and go whether he caught the late tram from Waterloo. He strained for the sound of distant puffing. Nothing, but...

The sound of segs on boots scuffing the cobbles of the station yard. Someone coming. Military perhaps. But not marching; only one man by the sound of it.

He shrank back into the doorway.

Not coming already, surely.

The footsteps sounded closer. Whoever it was headed straight for the station entrance. Another soldier to catch the train? Bit late. He wondered whether to move away, hide in the urinals.

He held his breath.

"I thought I might find you here, you daft old bugger." The Devon accent was unmistakable. "Come on now, Smiler, this ain't the answer. You know that."

"Sov! How did you know where to find me?"

"I can read you like a book, my old son. I guessed what you'd go trying on, so I thought I'd better come and find you afore they closed the gates and you really got yourself into trouble."

"I've got to get away, Sov. I need to see my family."

"Well, this ain't the way to do it, mind. Not after they said no leave. You'll find yourself on a charge, and God knows where that'd lead. Good job no one's missed you yet awhile. Now, come on back wi' me and we'll march in the gates together." He put an arm round John's shoulder and began shepherding him out of the station.

John cast a despairing glance down the line in the hope of seeing the train. He sighed, bowed his head and began walking back.

In one of the shortcut side streets, the doors of a Presbyterian chapel opened and light flooded out. The congregation began spilling out and surrounded the two men with the chatter of real life.

"I been thinkin'," Sov said, "why not talk to Doc Henshaw about it? You know him. He'll put you right about what's going on with your wife and the little one. I'd do that, set your mind at rest."

★ ★ ★

"Try not to worry, old chap," Henshaw said when they had a quiet moment. "Many babies are born with jaundice. It soon passes when the body itself rights the balance. I'll spare you the technical details. Let Nature take its course. Baby will be fine."

"That's a relief," John said. "But what about Emma?"

"Harder to say about your wife. It can't be too serious or the doctor himself would have made contact. And then you'd have had something to show the captain to support your case. Your sister's tone here hardly sounds as if matters are urgent." Henshaw tapped Helen's letter which lay on the mantelpiece.

"I've heard something about childbed fever," John said, "and I've been worrying myself into a frenzy about it."

"Rest assured, old chap, if this was urgent, your wife would be in hospital already. I think we can safely conclude it's not puerperal fever. It's most probable that the doctor has decided Emma needs rest, and time away from the children, particularly with the anaemia. There may also be one or two patch-up jobs, as we call them, that need doing after the birth. They're common enough."

Tears began pricking John's eyes. "I've been so worried, my imagination runs away with me."

"I'll tell you one thing, old chap, you're getting overwrought."

"The work here, the suffering all around us, it's unrelenting. And then this worry. I feel so helpless not being with my family when they need me."

Henshaw put his hand on John's shoulder. "Everything will

work out, John, trust me; your family will soon be back to full health. You need to look after yourself now, stop yourself cracking up with the pressure. Find something that relaxes you, something that restores and brings back the old John, the civilised John."

★ ★ ★

"I couldn't give tuppence for military etiquette. A lot of stuff and nonsense." Henshaw ruffled up the long tufts of hair at the back of his head and smoothed them down again. "It's an excellent idea, so let's go ahead."

"Shall we make a start this weekend?" John said.

"Why not? The music may not be everybody's cupper tea, but at least it'll be different. Better for the men than staring at the walls of the ward all day. They can stare at us. It'll be entertainment of a sort and will break up the monotony of hospital routine." He took a sip of whisky.

"All right," John said, "I'm keen if you are."

"I'll sort out any objections. We're not on the Base, and over here I'm King, or Prince Regent, at least. With Matron's permission, of course. So, to Hades with all this no-fraternisation nonsense. What we do with our spare time is entirely up to us."

John looked forward to playing duets again. He had hardly touched the violin since joining up and he longed to nestle the instrument beneath his chin again and coax out some music. "There's plenty of Mozart and Haydn available, I expect," he said. "But getting our fingers round some of Beethoven could pose more of a problem."

"Look, old lad, why don't we include some modern stuff? Educate ourselves as well as the men. They can watch us enjoying ourselves."

John grinned. "What, some of Elgar's pieces?"

"No! Well, yes, but let's be adventurous. Something a little less *thé dansant*. How's your sight-reading? Ever come across the César

Franck Violin Sonata? And do you know Vaughan Williams at all?"

"Can't say I do."

"Now he's one to watch, they say. Keen on using folk tunes. Good stuff – some of it. He's one of us, you know."

"How do you mean?"

"Joined the Medical Corps, so I heard on the grapevine. Didn't need to, of course – and he's even older than you, my boy." Henshaw playfully punched John on the shoulder.

"How do you know all this?"

"Letty, my elder daughter, plays with the Marion Scott all-women orchestra. Miss Scott's big in the RCM, you know. Anyway, Letty comes back with all the music gossip. I pick it up. It seems ages since she and I used to play duets." Henshaw looked wistful.

"Well, I hope my playing's up to snuff."

"You'll be fine. Look, I'll wire my wife and get her to send all my music down, post haste, and I'll also contact Boosey's and see what they can come up with. I'll tell 'em it's part of the war effort to entertain the troops, and they might let us have it *gratis*."

Henshaw grinned, drained his glass, came over to the mantelpiece and poured himself another scotch. He waved the bottle over the other glass, but John held up his hand in gentle refusal.

"Here's to you, then," Henshaw said. "You know, I'm very lucky. I've got a lovely, supportive wife and two intelligent modern-thinking daughters. They all spoil me. But sometimes, just sometimes, I wish we'd had a son. Someone I could relate to man to man. Share a few thoughts with. Like yourself perhaps. Someone with a bit of nous. There! That's embarrassed you." He grinned and patted John on the back.

★ ★ ★

When they had finished playing, a man with a crushed shoulder, his left arm missing, beckoned John over.

"Excuse me." John laid his violin and bow on top of the piano.

Henshaw continued shuffling and tidying the music, putting it into a battered leather music case.

The soldier, a stocky fellow, with a lined, round face and bulbous blue eyes, seemed an unlikely supporter of classical music.

"Smiler," he said, "what's that music you just played?"

"That last piece? That was from Max Bruch's violin concerto." John took care to anglicise the name: Max Brook's. Mention of anything German-sounding could easily offend some soldiers. You had to think of these things, however pleasing the music was.

"That sweet, singing tune was beautiful, really lovely," the man said. "And I've decided. That's the music I want played at my funeral."

"Oh, come on, soldier, buck up! Let's not have talk like that," John said. "The worst is over, you're safe now and getting better. You're back in Blighty, remember, no danger from the war here. Not this far from the front line."

NINETEEN

May 1915

Their bedroom door stood ajar. I hesitated as if facing forbidden territory, then pushed it open. After the low lights left burning on the landing for me, the room seemed very dark, but I managed to locate the bed from the sound of Grandpa snoring.

"Grandma," I said in a loud whisper. "Are you awake?"

I heard a grunt and a sigh. "What is it, child, what's the matter?" A scrape of a match and Grandma lit a candle. She had a white frilly cap on her head.

"Come here, Dorothy, let me see. Are you very wet?"

"No, Grandma, it's not that." I felt indignant.

"What's going on, woman? Put that light out and go back to sleep."

I began sucking my thumb and shrank into the shadows. I was afraid of Grandpa when he was gruff.

"It's Dorothy, John, she's come down, she's worried about something. What is it, dear?"

"There's a bumblebee in the sky and it woke me up," I said. I laugh about it now.

"Bumblebee? I don't think so, not at night. They only fly in the day. It must have been a dream. Shall we take you back up? I'll sit with you for a bit."

"It's not a dream. I can still hear it. Honestly."

"What, in here?" Grandma cocked her head. "I can't hear anything." She addressed the bed. "It couldn't be that hornets' nest in the roof space that she's heard, could it, John?"

"Don't be so foolish, woman. They're quiet at night, too. Now settle down the pair of you and let's get some sleep."

"Even if there is a bumblebee outside, Dorothy, it won't hurt you," Grandma said.

"Will you look out of the window with me? It's up there now."

She sighed and swung her feet out from the bed. "Let's have a look, then. It's a moonlit night. If it's there, we'll see it. Then you must go back to bed."

The brass rings rattled overhead as she flung back one of the heavy curtains. She heaved up the bottom sash window and we both leaned out. The slate roofs of the houses at the back glistened bright, as if wet from rain.

I could hear the sound clearly now, a puttering, a whirring, high in the sky. No, not a bee. I looked up and saw a funny, silvery shape very high up. It seemed to be moving away.

But there was no wind.

I asked Grandma if she could hear it.

"No, sorry, dear, not a thing. There's nothing there."

"What's that thing up –"

From somewhere nearby, a shattering roar and the sound of slates breaking.

"Oh, dear God, what was that?" Grandma pulled back quickly and hit her head on the bottom sash. Her cap was thrust forward over her face. She snatched it off and sat on the edge of the bed, rubbing her head.

I looked out again and saw a fountain of orange sparks shoot upwards from a house about two streets away.

"Come away from the window, child. We don't know what's out there. John, you take a look, see what's happening!"

Grandpa groaned and eased out of bed. He stood up and scratched his beard. His nightshirt fell and settled over his feet. He shuffled to the window.

"It's a fire," he said. "Somewhere towards the station. One of the houses. A great red glow of smoke. Over Alkham Road way, possibly. I'd better get dressed. See if I can help."

"What is it, then, John?"

"Gas explosion, most likely. Blown a hole in t'roof. Let's hope no one's hurt."

From further away, another explosion; the whole house shook and the bottom sash slammed down. The glass ornaments on Grandma's dressing table jingled and her hairbrush bounced to the floor.

I screamed and rushed to the bed and buried my face in her nightdress. I know I said I wanted to go home, as children do.

"Oh, my Lord, what's going on? It's like the end of the world." Grandma pulled me close and put her hands over my ears. "What about Rowley? He's upstairs still. Come with me, child, we'd better see he's safe." She picked up the candle.

"You know what I think it is," Grandpa said, "it's not houses blowing up, it's something dropping from sky. That noise the child heard. It wasn't a bee. I reckon it's one of them zeppelins. We're having a raid."

"A zeppelin over London? I'll get Rowley. Dorothy, stay with Grandpa! Oh, dear God, the Germans are coming. The Germans are coming." Grandma hurried from the room, shielding the candle flame with her hand as it bent towards her.

The room went dark. I asked Grandpa what a zeppelin was. I hadn't even heard of them then. I sniffed and wiped my eyes with the back of my hand.

He did his best to explain: "... And it has motors. That must have been what you heard. But why it's flying over London, I've no idea. We're not a military target."

"What is the zepp... What's it doing?"

"Dropping bombs on innocent civilians, wrecking houses. That's what it's doing." Grandpa was gruff again. "Keep back, child, in case the glass shatters."

I shrank back towards the bed. Moonlight glanced in through the window.

Grandma came back into the room, carrying Rowley, his head lolling, his arms and legs splayed in sleep. "You'd never credit it," she said. "This poor mite has slept through it all." She laid Rowley in the bed and covered him up. "Do you know how I found him? Little bits of plaster from the attic ceiling all over his chest. How he slept through it, I don't know." She stroked the boy's cheek as if brushing dust off.

I sat on their bed, uncertain what to do.

She turned to Grandpa who stood back from the window, but still stared outside. "So are these Hun barbarians attacking defenceless people now?"

"Seems so." Grandpa stroked his beard.

"Dropping bombs on people's houses. We could all have been murdered in our beds. And what's Mr Asquith going to do about it?" she said.

"I reckon we're safe now. The thing's moved on. They can't turn round that easy. It won't be back tonight, any road."

"Are you saying it could happen again? Will it come back tomorrow night?" Grandma said.

Grandpa sighed and looked at her. "Happen it might," he said.

I glanced down at Rowley asleep under the eiderdown, his fist at the side of his face. I began swinging my legs over the side of the bed. It was then I missed my father; I knew all this was something to do with the war and I felt sure he would know how to stop the zepp coming back.

TWENTY

Next morning, I padded down from the attic, still in my nightdress. I hate the feel of cold lino on my feet; for once, Mother forgot to pack my slippers. Downstairs, sunshine streamed through the kitchen window. Grandma sat in her chair, helping Rowley build a castle with his bricks. He glanced up and smiled at me.

"I am glad you went back off," Grandma said. "It's late now. Can you tell what the time is?"

I looked up at the wall clock with its busy pendulum, stared at the little hand and worked out the time. "Is it about nine o'clock, Grandma?"

"Good girl!"

I hesitated and asked whether I'd had a bad dream or not.

"No, my little one, I'm afraid it wasn't."

I looked down and bit my lip.

A rapid knock at the scullery door made us jump. "Now, who'd that be?" Grandma said. She began untying her apron.

A small man in a dark suit and carrying a briefcase bustled in. "I can't stop," he said, "I came to make sure you were unhurt. Where's Father?"

"He's gone to get a paper, find out about last night."

Rowley stared at the stranger and withdrew to the safety of the table leg and the maroon chenille cloth. I went and stood close to Grandma, pressing against her.

"Oh, come, child, don't be shy. You know your Uncle Perce, don't you?"

I said nothing. Something about him made me feel uneasy.

"Good morning, young Dorothy. My, haven't you grown!" He chucked me under the chin. "Were you woken up last night by all the noise?"

I nodded and clung to Grandma's skirt.

"She's not long awake," Grandma said. "You know, that blessed thing went right over here. Scared us half to death. The child woke us, or we'd have all been blown out of our beds."

"They say the zeppelin was dropping high explosive and incendiary bombs. That's what did for the house in Alkham Road."

"What's incendiary?" Grandma said.

"It causes fires, Mother – deliberately," Uncle Percy said.

"Oh, that's shocking. Barbarians!"

"A bobby said he saw it following Newington High Street. Eventually it turned back east."

"Terrible," Grandma said. "First the *Lusitania*, now this."

I studied Uncle Percy. He looked so different from my father. How could he be his brother? Daddy was big, warm and cuddly, and smiled a lot, but Uncle Perce seemed small, neat, with jerky movements like a bird fussing about after breadcrumbs. And I remember he smelt sweet, not like Grandpa and Daddy, and it tickled my nose, I thought I would sneeze. But Grandma didn't seem to notice. I spotted a touch of blood on his high, stiff collar where he'd cut himself shaving. Rude to say anything, though.

"Well, I'm glad there's no harm, no damage here after last night's misadventure," Percy said. "Now, I'd better be on my way and get started. It's always a big round on Tuesday. Goodbye, Ma." Percy put an arm round and kissed her on the cheek. "Oh, look at that!" Still holding on to his briefcase, he bent down and rubbed a mark off his highly polished shoe.

"Goodbye, Perce, I expect Helen will be down later, see how we are. Now, don't you take any risks, mind."

"I won't, but council business calls. Rates must be collected even though we're at war. Goodbye, young Dorothy." He pressed a moist hand to my brow and patted my head.

"Say goodbye now, child," Grandma said.

I managed to squeeze out the necessary word, but Rowley,

seeing his turn coming, spun away, gripped the table leg and buried his face in the cloth.

★ ★ ★

Grandpa and I stood in Alkham Road, looking up at the bombed house. I clung to his hand. You could still smell burning wood, though I couldn't see any smoke. The roof timbers, charred and scaly like crocodile skin, pointed towards the sky. Black marks streaked the walls at the front of the house where the water from the hoses had run down. I listened, fascinated, to people in the crowd.

"The fire brigade got here quick enough," said a young woman with a baby in her arms, "and they soon had the fire out, but imagine havin' to tumble out of bed and come down here in your night clothes. They didn't know what was goin' on. They say it smashed through the roof and set fire to the bedroom and the back room on the top floor."

"How many was in there?"

"Well, Mr Lovell, his wife and two children, that's four, and two others. Lodgers, maybe."

"Where are they now? Not *in* there, surely to God."

"Gone down his mother's, I heard."

But something else puzzled me. I was aware of a strange smell. I asked Grandpa what it was.

He stroked his beard and began sniffing. "By, you've got a good nose, lass! I reckon that's tar, is that. The Germans *are* wicked."

"What's the tar for, Grandpa?"

"Never you mind, Dorothy. You don't need to know. It's part of the bomb. Come on, let's go."

We moved among the crowd, always looking up at the skeleton of the roof.

"Are these big bombs what they're droppin'?" someone said.

"Nah! Someone said they'd seen one what didn't go off and it was like a big black pear, 'bout a foot long."

117

"I heard," another said, "a bomb dropped beside a house and made a hole so bleedin' big you could've stood fifty blokes in there, easy."

"Cor, blimey!"

"And the explosion went up'ards and out'ards and wrecked the bottom part of the 'ouse – not the roof, like 'ere – and all the windows was smashed in, right along the street. You could even see into the basements, specially where the inside walls was blown down."

"Come on, Dorothy, let's get off home to Grandma, see if our Helen's come."

But I lingered.

A stout woman, legs astride, hands on hips, stared up at the flaking rafters. She whirled round and addressed the group. "Did you hear about that couple they found? I don't know where, not this place. Charred bodies they was, kneeling by their bed and saying their prayers. Probally thought the end of the world had come. All his hair was burnt off and he had his arm round his wife. She had a large piece of her own hair in her hand. I reckon she musta pulled at it in pain, and it all come away."

"Come on now, little lass," Grandpa put his arm round me. "This is no place for thee and me. We've seen what's what, and it's not a pretty sight. I reckon things could get ugly, the way these folk are talking."

A rasping, scraping sound from the roof of the shattered house. Slates began slipping down the lower roof; several lodged in the cast-iron guttering. I remember watching two accelerate and slide over the edge to shatter into black needles on the ground.

"Let's go, Grandpa, I don't like it here."

But that wasn't the end of it. "Get behind me, child." Grandpa crowded me against the brick wall of a corner house. He gripped his walking stick as if he might hit someone.

I pressed close to his leg. "What's happening?"

I heard a babble of voices, mostly female, and saw a group of women and old men half-running down the road towards the high street. They carried broomsticks, spades; one woman held a brick in each hand.

"Bloody Huns," somebody shouted. "Creepin' over in the dead of night. Them buggers are spies. Told 'em where to come. Get 'em, show 'em what for!"

Grandpa clapped his hand over my ear and pulled me close. I could feel the roughness of his tweed jacket against my cheek, sounds became muffled.

"We shall have to bide a while, lass," his voice seemed to boom now, "till they're done. We don't want to tangle with the likes of them."

I peered up at his face, his eyes staring, his beard jutting. Good to feel the closeness of his arm against my shoulder, I must say.

★ ★ ★

We stood against that brick wall on the street corner as if sheltering from a storm. Grandpa scooped me up and held me close. Now his face, his tangled grey hair and his beard came level with my eyes. I'd never been that close to him before. He seemed breathless and kept looking round. Not half so frightening.

"Best stay here till things have settled down. Now, look at that." His voice went quieter, calmer and he tried to distract me by pointing out a blackbird flying to its nest, or something. He hugged me close. "We'll be all right, little lass."

But from round the corner, out of sight, came babbled cries, the breaking of glass, the splintering of wood. I heard people shouting, "Bread, bread! Go on, son, now's your chance, nip in and get it." And I swivelled my head towards the noise.

A woman with a hatchet in one hand and two children at her side ran across the junction. She held the tails of her apron and cradled loaves of bread in it. The two children, not much older than me, had more tucked under their arms.

119

I asked Grandpa what was happening.

"That's wicked thieving, is that. They've done folk no harm."

I began fretting and urged him to take me home.

"Aye, I will. In a minute. When coast's clear." He looked up and down the road as if he had forgotten the way.

Coming from the alleyway that ran at the back of all the shops, the sound of scurrying footsteps, someone crying. A big woman, her face screwed with terror, tripped and stumbled towards us. Her blouse was ripped and dangled loose from her shoulder; a trickle of blood ran down her arm as if she'd been clawed by a wild cat; her fair hair tumbled in a straggle beside her face. She gasped when she saw us.

"Oh, Mr Heming, Mr Heming, they are breaking now our shop. What must we do? Help us, please."

"Don't stay here, Mrs Englemann, get off away while you can. I'll see if I can find a policeman."

The woman stared at him in horror. "But my man, he is there still."

"Go, madam, go. It's not safe here for you. Not now. Not today."

"There she is!" A big man with a red face and staring eyes came running down the passageway, his boots crunching on the ash path.

Grandpa turned to Mrs Englemann. "Go, woman, in God's name, go!"

I held onto Grandpa, both arms tight around his neck. The woman gasped; the rapid clatter of her boots on the pavement faded into the distance.

The drunken man reached the pavement where Grandpa stood.

"And you, sir, leave that woman be," Grandpa said. "She's done you no harm."

"What's it to you, old man? Hun lover, are you?" The man swayed on his feet and drew back his fist, ready to strike.

I screamed and seized Grandpa.

"Oh no you don't, me lad."

In a swinging sweep with his stick, Grandpa lurched sideways and hit the drunk behind the legs. The man fell onto his knees and tumbled to the ground. Grandpa tucked the stick under his arm, gripped me and began to run, back the way we'd come.

"Let go now, lass, you're hurting, that's my beard you've got." His voice drained, now little more than a whispered gulp.

He jerked and bumped me away. He managed only a gasping lope and had to stop after about twenty yards. He hesitated, looked back and dodged into a garden with a tall privet hedge. There he set me down and bent double, panting wildly. "By gum, child, I'm not built for all this, not at my age."

I said nothing. Through a gap in the hedge, I looked up the road and saw a group of people running towards us. In the middle of the knot of bodies, men dragged a stout man who struggled and stumbled, trying to get free. His clothes were covered in flour, his mouth dripping blood. They hurried him along in wrenches and jerks, hauling him by his collar. Someone kicked him from behind, causing him to stagger; another thumped him hard in the back. And then he went down, and I couldn't see any more. The crowd gathered round, shouting and jeering: "Filthy Germans! Lock 'em up. Intern 'em all."

A woman screamed: "Go on, kick him!"

I buried my face in Grandpa's waistcoat. I could feel his hand on the back of my head and the cold hard metal of his watch chain against my cheek.

"It's all right, Dorothy, the police are coming."

Very cautiously I pulled away, kept hold of his hand and peered round the gatepost to look down the road. Two men wearing plain clothes pedalled at a sedate pace towards the crowd.

"Bobbies!" The yell caused them all to look up. One of the policemen blew his whistle. His bicycle wobbled beneath him.

"Quick, lads, scram! Scarper!"

The knot of people untangled, many running back towards the shops.

In the road, the man lay face down, his hands still protecting his balding head. A strand of dark hair, lank and damp with sweat, drooped over his face.

The policemen glanced at him and cycled past.

"Hey, aren't you going to do anything about this man?" Grandpa ventured out onto the pavement, his voice returning to a shout.

"Not us. It's a military matter," one policeman said without looking across. They pedalled on slowly, as if sweeping the streets of trouble.

"Dorothy, stay there!" Grandpa walked out into the road. "It's all right, Mr Englemann, they've gone now. Let's get you up."

The man's apron had swivelled round to the back of his body, and his arms, bare because of rolled-up sleeves, were covered in dirt and grazes from lying in the road; on one shoulder of his waistcoat, traces of horse manure clung.

Grandpa helped him to a sitting position and eased him onto his feet. "Can you stand all right? It's terrible, is that. I've never seen owt like it."

"I have my shop since ten years," the man said. "I am no enemy to England. I was born here. My parents live here fifty years almost."

"I know, old lad, I know. It isn't right. But this is war, and people think and do silly things, especially after last night. Now, mind how you go." Grandpa patted the man on the shoulder and returned to the gateway. "Come on, then, lass."

I didn't look up, just slipped my hand into the safety of his fist and we set off in silence. Grandpa said we'd take a roundabout route in order to avoid the shops. He no longer carried me but I kept tight hold of his hand. From time to time, I glanced up, worried. Apart from the tap of his stick on the pavement, he puffed a lot through his whiskers, as if still out of breath. He was old: I didn't know what I'd do if he fell down. And I'd no idea how to find Grandma and the house where we were staying.

After about twenty minutes, I began to recognise trees and some of the front doors in the street.

"Nearly there, lass."

I said nothing.

Inside, I waited in the hallway while Grandpa put his stick away and rattled the bolts across the front door. He moved very slowly. Coming from the parlour, the sounds of small boys laughing and singing. Dancing, too. Over it all, the clear, happy voice of Aunty Helen:

> *"Do you know the muffin man,*
> *The muffin man, the muffin man,*
> *Do you know the muffin man*
> *That lives in Drury Lane?"*

Grandpa opened the door. Rowley, our two cousins and Aunty Helen, hands linked, were dancing round in a circle, the two youngest doing little more than jumping round in excitement. Grandma, in her chair, clapped her hands.

> *"We all know the muffin man,*
> *The muffin man –"*

The song stopped. "Here she is! Here's Dorothy!" The dancing ended and there was silence.

"Dorfy," Rowland said and pointed. A smile lit his features. He was a lovely little boy then.

I looked at all those happy faces, the panting circle of three small boys, the laughing, smiling Aunty Helen.

Silence.

Nobody moved.

Then I broke. My hands went to my eyes and I burst into tears. I rushed to a corner of the room, my back to the others and howled.

"Oh, my darling, whatever's happened?" Aunty Helen hurried to my side, crouched down, holding me close. I felt a kiss on my hair and an arm round my body. A comforting perfume surrounded her. I leaned in close. I'd never been cuddled like that before. But I still cried, louder and louder.

"We ran into trouble," Grandpa said. "Nasty stuff. Couldn't avoid it. People protesting and rioting. I couldn't do owt about it. Caught in the middle."

Again, I burst out at the memory and filled the room with my cries. Rowley and my cousins sat on the floor wide-eyed and watching.

"Oh, poor mite, what a thing to happen," Grandma said. "But leave her be, Helen, let her cry herself out. It's better that way."

"I can't leave the poor child in distress," Aunty Helen said. She squatted down and pulled me onto her lap. "It's all right, darling, you're safe now. You've been a very brave girl, I'm sure, but no one can hurt you here, I promise."

"She *has* been brave," Grandpa said. "Now, excuse me, I'm away upstairs to change. I'm wringing wet after all the excitement and running."

"And I'll put the kettle on," said Grandma. "We could all do with a drink, I'm sure."

Aunty Helen held me and stroked my hair. The tears subsided, the silence in the room broken only by my juddering sniffs. "You're all right, darling, it's all over now. Are you beginning to feel a little better?"

I just nodded dumbly, knowing all I wanted to do was go home.

★ ★ ★

I don't think I ever saw my grandparents again. Rowley did. Mother had no time for them really, and this episode was the last straw. I think she always blamed them, though it wasn't really their fault. I suspect she thought Grandma was a bit simple and under the thumb of a bombastic old fool who shouldn't have exposed me to danger like that. Mother was never very forgiving.

But I wish we'd kept in touch with Helen. She might have helped us all when trouble really came.

TWENTY-ONE

My dear John,

I'm so glad to be home. My stay was mostly convalescent since Nurse Cooke and the doctor thought I should have minor surgery and rest after Bea's sudden arrival. For once, I did as I was told and ate all the liver they gave me without too much protest. You know how I hate it. Now I feel almost normal.

As you can imagine, I'm very annoyed that the children were both exposed to danger from the zeppelins. But no help for it, I suppose. Nowhere in London is truly safe from aerial bombardment any longer. I assume the enemy had the nearby railway as their target.

You'll want to defend your father's actions, no doubt, but for me it seems utter foolishness to go out sightseeing the day after the raid. Of course there'd be anger on the streets! The silly man should have considered that possibility. Certainly Dorothy has been very subdued since. I think it'll be some long time before I contemplate sending the children there again. Anyway, enough on that matter.

John tightened his lips and sighed. No closer to his parents, then. Why were families so difficult?

★ ★ ★

The door of the company hut banged. He looked up.

"Right, boys, on your feet! Gas Drill, parade ground, five minutes!" Sergeant Plum paced around, slapping his legs with a rolled-up newspaper. "Hurry, hurry, hurry, your life depends on this. Hemingby, get a move on, boy. Put that bloody letter away."

"Sarge!" John crammed Emma's letter into its envelope and tucked it inside his tunic.

On the parade ground, the men stood at ease while Plum prowled.

"Today, you learn about protecting yourselves from gas," he said. "First thing: how will you know it's gas?"

"See it coming, Sarge?" someone said.

"Yes, but don't be like the stupid Frogs and think it's a bloody smoke screen. Yes, you'll see it coming, and if the cloud is yellowish green and smells godawful, that's your first clue. It's chlorine gas. Then what? You can't depend on hearing the look-out with the warning rattle. So, when you see the cloud, what do you do? You don't duck down in the trench or lie on the ground, hoping it'll blow over. What don't you do, soldier?" He pointed at someone in the third row.

"Don't duck down, Sarge."

"You don't duck down. Why not? Because the bloody stuff's heavier than air and will hang about in the trench or at ground level. That's where it'll get you. And you don't panic, and you don't run away."

He strutted up and down in front of the company, bent down and picked up a small khaki bag.

"Now, inside here is a smoke helmet."

He pulled out a fabric hood and tucked it under his chin, letting it dangle for a second.

"It's a grain bag off our farm," Sov said, in a whisper.

"What's that, Poundsbury?"

"Nothing Sarge, sorry Sarge."

"Well, pay attention, boy. This'll keep you alive. Now, look at it. This fabric is soaked in a chemical to protect you. What are the signs of gas?

"Eyes hurting, Sarge, and throat smarting," Sov said.

"At first, yes. Now, you'll all be issued with a helmet in a canvas bag which you keep on your left-hand side. Any cack-handed buggers here?"

Two soldiers at the back raised their hands.

"You ponce-arsed types sling it on the right, then. Where you can get at it easy. Now, you will give your smoke helmets regular inspections. First the seams, are they tight?" He took the hood and tugged at the joins in the fabric. "No tears, no pulls? Now the eyepiece – no cracks in the mica. Is it fixed in tight? Now, these hoods come in five sizes. Poundsbury! Hemingby!"

"Yes, Sarge!" they both said together.

"Great gawks like you will take size five. More normal men – that's the rest of us – have a size four or three. Any questions?"

"Sarge, what do we do if we get caught without any protection?"

"You'd better not, but in your case, Hemingby, you whip out what you lah-di-dah folk call your hanky, or you take a swab, and you u-rin-ate on it. You hold that in front of your nose and mouth."

"You're serious? That'll give us protection?" John said.

"They say that'll do the job, but in *your* case, Poundsbury, be safe and stick your whole head in a bucket of piss, just to be sure."

"I know you're having me on, Sarge, but does all this gas training mean we're going to France soon?"

"Who can tell, boy, this is the army. You don't know nothing, you do as you're bloody told."

"Sarge!"

Plum spun back: "And one other thing: someone may tell you gas makes your todger drop off, I'll leave you to find out how to avoid that."

John grinned. "Better not drop our trousers, then, Sov."

★ ★ ★

During a break, he picked up Emma's letter again:

And now for my news. I've decided to move house again.

We shall stay here until the end of June. The landlord seemed happy enough with my say-so rather than yours. How quickly times change! But being close to the railway here worries me now.

John paused and stared across the parade ground. Another move. Now it'd be even more difficult to imagine life at home. But if it meant that the children... He turned back to the letter.

In hospital, I met a nice woman whose husband is also away. He's in the navy. Mrs Daphne Struther has asked me to share a large house in Streatham. This will suit us both. The children and I will have the first floor and the attics, and her family will use the ground floor and basements. We'll share other facilities, even the cooking, and I won't be skipping meals in order to see the children fed. The doctors scolded me for that. It'll certainly be easier financially to join forces, and I shall feel safer – the railway line is at least a mile away. Of course, I'm still near enough to visit Father and Dora if needs be. Uprooting will be tiresome, but all in all it's for the best. I only wish they'd give you leave so you could be involved in family life again. You haven't even seen Bea yet! She's a dear little thing, quite small, but a good baby. If she was our first, I'd worry about how placid she is, but as things are I welcome her quietness. Rowley is becoming quite a handful with his boisterous behaviour.

I asked Dorothy what she'd like for her birthday and she won't shift from the notion that she wants to see you. I'd thought of books or paints, something like that, but she insists that seeing her daddy is all she wants. Foolishly, I've said I'll see what can be done, and now she talks of nothing else. I assume you'll manage some free time if we do come, perhaps you could arrange lodgings for a night or two. A respectable woman who doesn't mind children would suit very well. But I certainly don't want people thinking I'm a camp follower. Write back soon and tell me what you think.

With my love, as always,

Emma.

John put the letter down and stroked his moustache. Wonderful! All the family together again. Some treat for Dorothy's seventh birthday. He smiled to himself and folded the letter away.

★ ★ ★

"I don't think I can do this, Smiler."

The big Devonian swallowed, gave a nervous smile and cast about as if looking for an escape.

"We'll be quite safe, Sov. It's only an exercise. We put our helmets on, go inside the hut, find the bench, you sit down and pull up one trouser leg and I put a bandage on you, below the knee. Then we get out. That's all."

"But, Smiler, that's real gas in there. God knows what it could do. What if these bloody helmets don't work? I don't want to die that way. Not through gas. I seen the agony folks go through."

The two looked towards the opening of the hut which stood about twenty yards away.

"It's as black as hell in there," Sov said, "look at them bits o' gas driftin' out. And I'd wager old Plum'll top it up specially for us."

"Looks like a pea-souper, doesn't it? But we'll manage. We won't be long in there." John straightened up. "Right, standby, here's The Taff now."

Plum marched up the line towards them. He pushed his cap back to look up at them.

"Right, then, let's see how you big fellas do. Knowing your luck, you'll be head and shoulders above the gas."

"Not when we sit down, Sarge."

"Haven't got the wind up, have we, Poundsbury?"

"No, Sarge."

"Better not. I don't want no cowards on my watch. Right, boys, your own time, hats off."

The two men laid their caps on the ground and each fumbled to undo the bag containing the hood. John took his out, shook it and held it against his chest for a moment. Sov did the same.

"Here we go, then." John crammed on the coarse hood and pulled it down till he could feel it on the top of his head. Is this how it feels for a man about to be hanged? he thought. The eyepiece came below his view and he tugged the hood down at the back until he could see out through the dim yellow pane. He watched Sov wrestling with the fabric and strode over to help.

"Now, tuck it in the top of your jacket." His voice appeared as a muffled shout. He unbuttoned Sov's uniform and began cramming the hood inside and did the same himself. Both men buttoned up the tunics tightly. His stomach jittered. "Come on, then, old boy." He swallowed. "Let's do it."

Wisps of green vapour curled round the edges of the entrance. John paused; as a reflex, he took a deep breath, held it and plunged into the swirling semi-darkness. He could feel Sov's hand on his arm and wondered if he'd got his eyes shut. Two canvas baffles had been fitted inside so that the bench they had to find was not obvious in the gloom.

Foolish not to breathe normally. Have to trust the helmet. He paused, took a quick gasp, and another, inhaling the smell of cotton and bicarbonate. No sharp smell, or taste of gas. It worked!

Through the blurred pane, he saw the trestle bench in the far corner. He pointed and began to fetch out a bandage from the medical kit.

"I can't, Smiler, I can't." The whites of Sov's eyes flashed behind the pane of the hood. "I can't breathe in this. I got to get out."

"Easy, old lad, we'll only have to do it again, if we don't do it right."

"Smiler, for God's sake, don't make me do it. Please! I'm

choking." Sov clutched at his hood and began ripping it off his head.

"Stop! Don't be a fool! Don't take it off!" He could already see the white of Sov's neck. He dropped the medical bag, dimly aware of the bandage unravelling across the floor. Have to do something! He looked around, took a swing and punched Sov. His hand grazed against the coarse fabric of the hood and his knuckles hurt.

His friend crumpled and toppled forward; John caught him and took the weight upon his shoulder. In a swooping lift, he picked him up and staggered towards the exit with Sov's body draped over his back.

He covered the twenty yards with his knees buckling and laid Sov down on the parade ground.

"All right, all right!" Sergeant Plum came running towards them. "What's happened here? Which man is that?"

"I'll get the medic bag, Sarge, I think he fainted." John turned back to the hut, hoping Sov would forgive him.

TWENTY-TWO

"I'm sorry, Smiler, I don't know what come over me. Don't usually panic like that. But thanks for coverin' up. Old Plum didn't twig, did he?"

"Let's hope not, old lad. Wasn't a proper test, anyway. In reality, we'd put our hoods on when we're already surrounded by gas. No, Plum wanted his tea, otherwise he'd have had us doing it again and again till we got it right. Pass the dubbin, will you?" The two men sat on their bunks working their boots, ready for the next day. A comfortable time winding down to lights out.

"You don't half pack a punch, though, Smiler." Sov rubbed his chin. "Proper job, that was. I ent felt like that since I downed three pints one harvest supper. That floored me, an'all." He paused. "That's going back a while. Before I walked out wi' my old gel, I reckon."

"Yes. I've never had scrumpy."

Sov stared. "You all right, boy? You're quiet tonight. Not with us, like."

"No, I'm OK. A lot of things on my mind since I got Em's letter. Family worries, if you like."

After lights out, John was slow to capture sleep. Several worrying hints in the letter: Emma seemed to suggest that she struggled financially. Not like her at all: she prided herself on getting by. Had she been neglecting herself, missing meals in order to see the children fed? That wouldn't do. And house-sharing. It might save money, but were they equal partners, or had Em become live-in housekeeper? She was so proud; she wouldn't say.

He stroked his moustache.

But he sent as much as he could, kept back very little. Would things be different if he'd taken the commission? More money, at least. Had he been selfish? Should he have accepted?

He tried praying. Wrong, not being on his knees. But to avoid comment, even ridicule, from the others, he'd decided long since to wait till darkness surrounded him before praying. But it didn't feel right, flat on your back.

One thing clamoured: was it The Lord's will that his family struggled because he'd volunteered for the army? It seemed the whole world had to suffer with this war.

He prayed, feeling the comfort of tightly clenched hands. Would he receive an answer?

Nothing.

He lay there, mind a blank, the only sound the drilling snore of a man near the hut entrance.

The flutter of shadow leaves on the ceiling: the trees outside filtered light from the lamp on the parade ground.

He moved his lips in silent prayer: "Oh, Lord, please keep my children safe, from all bombs and unrest in London, and all the confusion war brings, protect them from hunger and want so they grow up strong and healthy citizens in a new world of Thy making. Please keep my parents out of harm's way: give them wisdom and safety in old age, and protect them from all dangers, and bring us all through this war and into Thy peace. Amen."

He turned over and covered his eyes to block out the flickering. He sighed. Hadn't prayed for Em, or Perce, for that matter. Or Hubert. He began the drift towards sleep, random thoughts still pestering.

He tried again to get comfortable. What did Em mean about Bea's sudden arrival?

He shifted; a bedspring clanked. Would it matter if Dorothy missed school so she could visit? Was seeing him so important?

The hours plodded by before he slept.

★ ★ ★

133

Beneath the brick arches of the station, the little group waited, Emma in the centre with the baby and Rowland at her side. Dorothy, separated by the suitcase from her mother, stood on the other, taller now in a long dress in dark green velvet.

Her hair's grown, I'm sure. Quite the young lady!

He gave a broad smile and waved.

"Daddy!" All decorum gone, Dorothy ran towards him. In one movement, he knelt down and gathered her into his arms.

"Hullo, my darling. Oh, it's so lovely to see you. Belated Happy Birthday!"

"Daddy, my daddy!" she said, her arms tight around his neck. "You're a soldier for The King now."

"That's right, I am." He kissed her cheek and set her free. "Now, take my hand. I want to say hullo to Mama and the others. How are you? Feeling stronger, my dear?" he called.

"Quite well, thank you." He'd forgotten how crisp, almost abrupt, her voice could be.

He put his arm around her shoulder, bent to kiss her, drawing her towards him, only to find Rowland had squirmed between them.

"Rowley, dear, don't be silly," Emma said. "This is your daddy. Say hello to him."

"No!" The boy clung to her and buried his face in her skirts.

"He doesn't remember you. He'll come round," she said.

"And this is little Beatrice," John said. The tiny form, now two months old, writhed and stirred in her mother's arms. "Hullo, my little one, I'm your daddy." He tickled the baby's tummy and grinned. "You're a beautiful girl." A gentle kiss on her forehead. "So, who does she look like, Em?"

"She's definitely inherited your eyes, but I see a lot of Baxter there, especially around the mouth."

The baby yawned.

"Come on, then, let's get to your lodgings." He picked up the suitcase, offered Dorothy a hand and began to walk from the station.

"Haven't you got noisy feet now, Daddy?" Dorothy said. She looked up at him and smiled. "Do you still play your fiddle?"

"I do, my sweet, when I can. Some of the poorly soldiers like to hear it."

★ ★ ★

The landlady agreed to mind the children. John returned at eight o'clock, and he and Emma strolled through a nearby park in the July warmth.

"Walking out again, just you and me," he said. "It was as warm as this when we married, all that time ago. Do you remember?"

She slipped her arm through his. "I'm surprised you do. I didn't think men were sentimental. Now here we are, ten years later, with three children and the world at war. I never thought to see my husband in khaki." She stopped, stepped back to look at him. "Quite handsome, really." She patted his chest. "But we're managing, both of us, to get through, in our different ways. I'm glad, though, the generals are keeping you older Territorials back in England. It makes good sense."

"Yes, but, I er –" He tightened his lips. "*Are* you managing, my dear? You would tell me if things were a struggle, I hope. This Mrs Struther, this house you've moved into –"

"We're coping perfectly well, thank you." Her tone and the sudden set of her lips said there'd be no more of the matter that evening.

"May I know why Bea's arrival was so sudden? Will you tell me?"

"There's no great mystery. I was doing the washing."

"What happened?"

"It can be heavy work, you know, and I'd just finished stirring the week's sheets in the tub and was heaving them out, ready for rinsing and mangling, when I got signs that something was imminent. I expect all the lugging and hauling had brought everything on. I rushed the laundry through and just had time to peg things out – I didn't want to leave them indoors. I had to hurry inside. I just made it. And that's how Bea arrived – on the kitchen floor, amongst the washing."

"You were alone? You delivered her yourself? Couldn't you call anybody?"

"Oh, don't fuss about it, it's not as if she was my first. I managed. It wasn't ideal, but I managed."

"You are extraordinary, you know that, Em?" He kissed her forehead and slipped an arm round her shoulder. "And very brave."

"Oh, fiddlesticks! You do what you have to."

They walked along in silence for a while, admiring the red, white and blue of the bedding in the park's flower borders.

He took a deep breath. "I've something to tell you, Em. I don't know for certain, so many rumours fly round the camp, but they all seem to be saying we're about to be sent to France."

"Oh, dear. How definite is it?"

"No one can be sure until orders come through. But it's a good time and a bad time for you all to be here. We're on exercises tomorrow and you'll be able to watch from a distance and get an idea of what we do. But everyone is saying these manoeuvres are final preparation for going overseas. I'm not looking forward to it. It's sure to be strenuous and very tiring."

"So where will you be tomorrow?"

"Near Brockenhurst, perhaps. But I'll get word to you."

"This could be goodbye, then, John." Her eyes searched his face.

"Not quite, my dear. That's one thing I do know. Before embarkation, everyone gets a few days' leave. I shall come home and get to see the new house and meet Mrs Struther, after all."

TWENTY-THREE

I'd heard the word but didn't know what it meant. Certainly couldn't spell it. It puzzled me: man oovers – what the soldiers were going to do. Daddy had arranged for us to ride out to the heathland in the New Forest, where they'd be. Mother would drive, we'd packed a picnic, and I looked forward to seeing him as a real soldier.

We reached an area of scrub and trees where the ground was bumpy and hollowed, and all the soldiers, horses, wagons and guns were gathered. Mother stopped the trap close to a boundary rope. "This'll do," she said. "You can get down now, Dorothy, and see if you can spot Daddy. He'll be somewhere there."

Scattered along the edge of the heath, close to the road, small groups of people, mostly women, also lingered to watch.

I went up to the barrier and began looking for a tall man with a moustache, but, of course, there were so many of them. But by chance the sun flashed on one man's teeth, and I could relax. He was among a group gathering about fifty yards away.

Someone I couldn't see gave a long, loud shout and all the men stiffened to attention. The man oovers were starting.

Daddy stood straight as a wooden soldier beside a huge draft horse. I used to love their fluffy, cloppy feet. Still do, but you don't often see them nowadays. I could only see his profile. He wore his cap pulled down so I struggled to make out his face.

He wasn't smiling.

I remember being very proud and thinking how smart and brave he looked. All his badges, buckles and boots shone, and his puttees were tight and neatly wound round his legs. I wanted to call out, but some instinct told me that'd be wrong: he wouldn't look at me.

I hated the fact he didn't know I was there. I asked Mother for the box camera to record the moment.

She passed it down: "Remember what I told you. And only two pictures, mind."

In those days, you had to squint into a glass rectangle on the top of the camera.

"Don't forget, hold it steady, Dorothy."

I concentrated hard, saw I'd captured him in the viewfinder, pressed down the shutter with my thumb, and waited for the click.

"Give it to me. I'll wind it on."

Rowley wasn't the least bit interested in what was going on. He squatted on the floor of the trap at Mother's feet, busy spinning the wheels of a toy cart as fast as he could. I tutted and looked back.

Besides my father, another man stood close to the horse, patting its cheek. He was whispering to the animal, as if it needed calming.

From across the heath, a puff of white smoke, followed by the echoing slog of the gun. I jumped and clapped my hands over my ears; the pony behind skittered and tugged at the trap. The big horse reared. And then Daddy put his foot in a stirrup and swung up to sit astride.

I had to have another snap. All over the heath, men took up different positions. Something was about to happen, I was sure.

"Now, easy," Mother said, "take your time."

Daddy sat very straight and tall on his horse; I pointed the camera and clicked the shutter.

That was special. I'd never seen Daddy ride a horse before. And it was a perfect snap, though I say it myself. I loved that picture, kept it for ages, often took it out while he was away to remind myself what he looked like.

Haven't got it now, of course.

The gun boomed again and the whole company lurched into action. Daddy rode the leading horse of three which pulled an ambulance – just a big closed cart with a red cross painted on the side. All the men cantered away, hooves thudding, the ambulance rocking and ricketing from side to side over the rough ground.

In the distance, Daddy jumped down; another huge fellow joined him, and they stooped and picked up someone on the ground. They eased him onto a stretcher and carried him, in and out of trees, up and down the hollows, over stiles and fallen logs.

I remember asking why they didn't put the man in the cart and take him straight to hospital.

"It's only pretend," Mother said. "Just practising."

So many people rushing around in different directions! I remember wondering how it would seem to God, looking down from above. I was religious in those days. Daddy's influence, I suppose.

Once, in the Catford house, I turned up some crazy paving in the garden to see what was underneath and disturbed an ants' nest. All those creatures scurrying down little pathways, going down holes in the ground, trying to hide. I remember being fascinated by those ants which struggled with huge weights, often bigger than they were. Moving their eggs to safety. They all seemed to know what to do, everything tidy and organised. It didn't seem long before they'd all disappeared, except for a few stragglers wandering blindly.

I never told Mother about the ants. She'd have poured boiling water over everything.

Two soldiers began running across the open space; they lit cardboard tubes which they dropped on the ground and white smoke poured out; the men went on running.

I remember a whistle blew; someone far away shouted, "Gas, Gas, Gas!"

Across the open space where Daddy and the other men worked, a cloud of white smoke drifted. It seemed to float and gather until it became a fog swirling round them.

Everything changed. They all stopped running. In the distance, Daddy and his friend put their stretcher down and each began rummaging in a case hanging from their shoulders. They struggled to put yellow-brown bags over their heads; Daddy knelt down and lifted up the man on the stretcher and tried fitting one over his head; two other soldiers seized the horse and held it firm, though it struggled and panicked, eyes rolling; one man had an arm around its neck while another forced a bag over its nose and eyes. It reared and whinnied. There were muffled shouts, swirling smoke everywhere. I hated it.

A whistle blew and the gun thundered again. For a second, everyone froze; I watched in horror as some men dropped to the ground, their heads still uncovered. They lay still. The others put on caps over their hoods and began to return to their starting place. I tried to see which was Daddy's ambulance, but now every wagon looked the same and I couldn't make him out.

But they weren't humans now; an army of man-frogs clustered, like goblins, bulge-eyed and staring, and they marched at a steady tramp towards me.

I screamed.

"That's it," Mother said. She urged me to climb back in the trap. "We've seen quite enough."

I clambered up, barking my shin on the step, and tumbled into the trap.

Rowland probably just stared at me. He stayed on the floor as Mother clicked her tongue and slapped the back of the pony with the reins. We set off at a trot away from the heathland.

"Come up beside me, Dorothy, and dry your eyes," she said. "No need for all that fuss. Quite enough excitement for one day. I knew we shouldn't have come, this isn't for little girls to see, but you did want it. Now, stop crying. It was only a practice. Nobody got hurt. You'll see Daddy again before we go home." She thrust a hanky at me, and I sat there, sniffing and dabbing at my tears. "Now, have a look in the back and see if all the noise has woken Bea."

Those goblin men stayed with me over the years. I was frightened to go to sleep in case they appeared again in some nightmare.

I've always hated gas masks.

TWENTY-FOUR

January 1917

Darkness crowded the Streatham church where John knelt, hands cupped to receive Holy Communion. A single gas chandelier hissed earnestly; candles on the altar, like sentries on guard, did not waver. Six-thirty a.m.; he should have waited until the family service at half-past nine.

Still be here on my own, though.

The vicar, a relic from Victorian times, all grey, dundreary whiskers and fluting voice, intoned *"The Body of Christ"* and placed the white bread into John's hands. He moved on.

John lifted the morsel to his mouth, his mind reaching out for sincere spiritual union. He stood up, took a step back, bowed his head. The vicar, back at the altar, drained the chalice and fussed with a cloth to cover it. Only three other communicants, all elderly women in black with dark, beaded lace covering their heads.

Was this really how the world worshipped The Lord God Almighty?

* * *

"Why not take Rowley with you to see your parents?" Emma said. "The girls will be happy enough at home, there's plenty to occupy Dorothy here. For once, she'll have to do without you, but I want Rowley to get to know you. Boys need their father to look up to. I'm concerned he sees you as a stranger who's suddenly appeared in this house."

John worried about coping with his son, now nearly four.

Carrying him seemed inappropriate; Emma had dressed the boy in a new sailor suit and short trousers, so he was quite capable of walking, even though their pace seemed leisurely. John knew about boys aged thirteen onwards, but this trusting manikin, whose little legs busied along beside him, seemed a wonder.

"Hold my hand, old chap, on this busy road. We have to cross to catch the tram to Grandpa's." He marvelled how the little hand crept into his at moments of uncertainty. Perhaps Rowley would accept him after all.

He arrived at Stoke Newington at midday – giving his parents time to return from Morning Prayer.

His father opened the door. "Come in, lad. It's good to see you." They shook hands. "By, the army's put some muscles on you! You're bigger than ever. And who's this come with you?"

"Rowley." The boy reached for his father's hand.

"How do you do, young sir?" The old man stooped forward. "You don't remember me, do you?" Rowland accepted his grandfather's handshake with solemnity; he let John take his little cape off. John senior stowed the coats in the understairs cupboard.

"Are we in the front room today?" John said with surprise.

"Aye, parlour and dining room today. None of your eating in the kitchen. Your mother's gone all formal in your honour." His father stood back to let John and Rowley enter the room.

Augusta Hemingby sat upright in a high-backed Windsor chair to the left of the fireplace. Her clasped hands rested in her lap but a busy thumb worried at the backs of her fingers. Her carefully gathered hair had turned white. Dear God, what's done that to her?

He knelt at her feet. "How are you, Ma? It's so good to see you again." He kissed her cheek.

"I'm better for seeing you," she said. "I've been worried how you've been doing, but, my, you do look well. Don't you think our John cuts a fine figure in his uniform, Father?"

"Aye, he does, Gussie, proper soldier now."

John got to his feet again, aware of the creak of leather shoes behind him. Percy left the window seat and appeared at his side.

"Isn't it good to have him home, Perce?" his mother said.

"Yes, indeed." Percy gave his usual moist handshake. "Welcome home, albeit briefly." He straightened his tie, cleared his throat and stood back.

John's mother looked at Rowland who clung to his father's trousers. "My word, look at you, Rowley. Quite the little man in your sailor suit. And that lovely blond hair. How long will it stay like that, I wonder? Now, see, there's a tumpty over there." She indicated a pouffe near the fireplace. "You may sit on that and talk to Sam, but be gentle when you stroke him. He's quite old now."

Rowland did as he was told and sat watching the grown-ups while he stroked the long-haired cat.

"Hasn't Emma breeched him rather early?" she said in a quiet voice. "I hope he can manage buttons."

"I suspect she did it for this leave – her way of showing me she's managing well to bring the children up. I daren't ask where she found the money, though."

"So, how is the family?" Augusta said.

"Well enough, I hope. Little Bea will be two in April, and Dorothy is eight and a half as she boasted when I got back."

"Aye, it's a great pity we've not seen the lass, not seen any of 'em since that cursed air raid. Has Emma got something against us?" his father said.

"Shouldn't think so for a minute. I'm sure she's very busy. Bringing three children up in war time can't be easy."

"So what have they had you doing since you joined up?" his mother said.

"Well, we spent the best part of a year in a Casualty Clearing hospital in Hampshire – general medical work really. And a lot of training, too. Even though we've stayed in England, they like to prepare us for battle conditions, so we're always ready to go. They've had us out in the New Forest more than once. We even camped there for a week. In the fog, if you please. And we've spent a couple of years in Maidstone, general nursing in convalescent homes, and working with shellshock cases. And that is a challenge."

"Now then, what exactly is this shellshock? I read a lot about it in the papers. It seems to be a new thing," his father said. "But nobody can tell me what it is."

"Nobody knows is one answer," John replied.

Percy cleared his throat. "Go on with you. It's something faked by cowards and shirkers who've had enough of fighting and want to get out of doing their duty. Not a mark on some, so I've heard."

"It's not that at all!" John struggled to keep his voice down. "It's a genuine medical condition but nobody quite knows the cause, or how to cure it. I've seen lots of different methods. All I do know is that some of the bravest suffer from it – many of them officers." He glanced towards Rowland, now engrossed in a large book of animal pictures. "There are several theories but the main one is that noise and heavy vibration from the guns have made subtle shifts in the brain and nervous system. A bit technical. Some say that a bursting shell creates a vacuum and the air rushing in disturbs the working of the brain."

"Rank nonsense, if you ask me," Percy said. "These fellows are scrimshanking – malingerers who've found a clever way of working their passage home. They should be tried for cowardice."

"Some of them are, believe me," John said, "with all the consequences that entails if found guilty. Or they get sent back to France, many of them right to the Front, where often the inevitable happens."

"Good," his father said. "You don't want to go soft on types like that."

John glanced briefly at his mother who sat clutching a handkerchief close to her mouth. "The worst part is the stare. So many gaze past you into the distance, as if looking at something hundreds of yards away," he said. "I've seen it so many times, and I've come across others who've lost the power to speak, even though there's nothing wrong with their vocal cords. One man I remember had terrible facial twitches which he couldn't control. It emerged later that he'd been involved in bayonet attacks and –"

Augusta stood up and spoke sharply: "Rowley, will you come with me? I want to show you our kitchen, see if you remember it, and we can look at how the brisket's getting along. Then it'll be nearly lunch."

Rowland closed the book with a thud, laid it on the pouffe and followed his grandmother.

A look passed between Percy and his father.

"Aye, well, I'd better go and mend the fires." His father shuffled out.

Percy waited until the door closed. "I say, I do think all these details are a bit much. You might have guarded your tongue in front of Mother. Particularly with your impending departure. She's easily upset, you know. And neither she nor Father is getting any younger. They'll both be sixty-six this year."

"Well, that's the trouble; folks at home aren't really interested in what's going on. Pa asked me specifically about shellshock but when I start to tell you all, they want me to shut up. I'm surprised he didn't tell me to hold my tongue, like in the old days. It feels just the same with Emma, too. People in England haven't any conception of what war's like. They only know silly things like not hearing Big Ben anymore –"

"They see the casualty lists in the papers. That's terrible enough, and everybody knows someone who –"

"Yes, but they can't imagine the strain of sitting in a trench in all weathers, waiting for a shell or something to land on one's head. I can't. But I've seen the results of all that and it won't be long before I have to experience it myself." He struggled for breath, his hands clenched, his voice raised.

"So this time it's not a false alarm?" Percy stood, his back to the fire, hands thrust into his pockets. He rocked forward onto his toes. "You're definitely going overseas?"

A downdraught from the chimney wafted smoke into the room. Percy coughed and stepped out of the way.

145

"I have to go," John said. "This time it's not rumour. Heaven knows we've had enough of those. We've been lucky to be spared for so long. This time, my group really is mobilised. But what about you? Hasn't anyone challenged you about still being at home?"

"Oh, one or two silly women tried to white feather me, but I soon put them right. One came up to me only the other day, produced a feather and said: 'Here's a gift for a brave soldier.' I looked at her and said: 'My dear lady, you should know I am engaged in vital local government work.' Once they hear that, they leave me alone. I'm no coward, I assure you, but my health isn't a hundred per cent with my asthma and so forth. Anyway, somebody has to keep life going at home."

Fair enough, but I wish you weren't quite so smug about it. John chewed his bottom lip.

★ ★ ★

Percy vanished after lunch, but John and Rowley lingered over tea. Eventually, John checked the clock on the mantelpiece. "Best get the little fellow home. The sun's already low. I'll get our coats."

His parents both came to the front door. He shook his father's hand. "Goodbye, Father. Goodbye, Ma. Wish me luck."

His mother gave a choking sound and put her handkerchief to her mouth.

He put his arms around her. "Now, don't cry, Mother, it's all right. The Lord will care for me."

She gulped and dabbed at her eyes. "I thought they'd keep you in this country. You're doing good work here. I didn't think they'd send you to all that – slaughter. What'll I do if you don't come back..?"

"Oh, hush! With God's grace, I shall. This wretched war can't last much longer. A day of reckoning will come. I don't think any of the combatants have much stomach for fighting now. They'll make peace soon."

His father patted her shoulder. "Now, now, Gussie. It's right is that. No question of it. He's got to do his bit. We may not like it, but now they've brought conscription in, like as not he'd be going anyway."

"But it doesn't make it any easier." She dabbed at her eyes, turned away, and blew her nose.

A pony and trap clopped past, the busy trundle of its wheels breaking the silence.

John gulped and broke away, scooped Rowley into his arms and strode down the steps.

He did not look back.

TWENTY-FIVE

"I can't imagine life over there, Em," he said. "It won't be the same, I'm sure. We've had things easy so far."

They sat side by side in the bar: he wore his uniform which she'd sponged and brushed; she had dressed in her smartest clothes. Tomorrow – entrain for France. "But I can't shake it off, I wish I could, this fear I have about going."

She said nothing but linked her arm through his and squeezed the back of his hand.

Perhaps she understood.

He continued to spear his remaining chips and stared straight ahead, taking comfort from contact with her body. They rarely sat close in public, but he insisted on a last evening together: "... as if we're still sweethearts walking out. I've seen so little of you these last two years."

He needed more beer. He raised his finger and caught the eye of the barman. The man brought the jug to their table and refilled his glass. John took a large swallow, sighed and gazed around. "I want to remember this, Em: you, this very English meal, this beer, even your cup of tea. They're memories I'll take with me. It's what life's all about. I'm afraid something's going to happen. I don't know what. I have this strange feeling which won't leave me. I still believe God will sustain me and be with me, but He seems distant tonight, no more than a whisper. I can't hear His voice."

She leaned her head on his shoulder, careful not to dislodge her hat. "I don't know what to say, I wish I did. Try not to think so much. I'm sure you make it worse for yourself. It must be difficult not knowing where you're going, what you'll be doing."

"That doesn't help, certainly. All they've said is we'll have mission-specific training when we get there, but what that is... Do you realise I've not even seen a dead body yet? I don't know how I'll be about that. I think I'm all right with the sight of blood now, but a corpse... I've only dealt with the living." He took a drink of beer.

"Hush, dear," she said. "Don't upset yourself. When it comes to it, you'll cope, I know you will. Now, look here, I've got something for you."

From her handbag, she brought out an envelope which contained a selection of photographs. "I had these done just before Christmas. Two of me with the children, and one of each of them on their own."

"That's lovely, Em, thank you. I'll cherish these and tuck them away, close to my heart." He patted the breast pocket of his uniform. "So I shall have my family with me out there." He smiled. "Dorothy looks quite the young lady here."

"Yes, it's that hat. Helen bought it for her, and she's very taken with it. She'd wear it all the time if I let her. Oh, by the by, be sure to read her little message on the back. She insisted I pointed it out."

He turned the picture over. In neat script, she had written: *To the Best Daddy in the World, with much love from Dorothy. Come home safe to me.*

"That's lovely," he said, "it's more than I..." He shook his head and looked away.

Emma squeezed his hand again. Silence gathered. She said: "What about your old fiddle? Will you take that to France with you? Will they let you?"

"I do hope so. I'd be lost without that. I can't be without music. Amidst all that lugging and heaving and chaos, I must have something... Something to connect me to my old self."

★ ★ ★

"Ssh," she said, as they climbed the stairs. "Don't clomp so much. You'll wake the whole house."

149

"Let them hear me," he said. "It's my last night." He couldn't quite control his mouth; it kept wanting to grin. "This time tomorrow I shall be far away – in France."

"Come on! Shush!" she said. "Let's get into our room."

He paused at the top of the stairs. "Goodnight, Blighty," he said to the landing. "England expects that every man this day will do his duty." He rested his forehead on the door jamb, then lurched upright and saluted.

"John!" An urgent whisper.

"She is the very model of a modern major general!" He banged the door behind him and staggered towards the bed. "Em, where's the po?"

"Where it always is." She turned away, took her hat off and began undressing. "Hurry into bed. There's a nip in the air tonight."

"Pass the candle, old dear, a chap needs to see what he's doing when he's hunting a jerry." He knelt on the floor at the foot of the bed.

"Don't be coarse, John. It's not you. You can see perfectly well." She slipped into bed. "Oh, lovely! Hurry up! Daphne's put a hot water bottle in."

"I like your Mrs Struther. She seems nice. Do you think she can hear us now?" He sat on the bed and began undressing. He unlaced his left boot and let it fall to the floor.

"Oh shush, John, quietly! She'll certainly have heard that."

"I'll keep her guessing, then." He took off his other boot and laid it with care on the floor. He stripped off quickly, placing his trousers over the end of the bed. "She'll think you've brought home a one-legged man tonight." His night shirt settled around him and he bundled into bed. He shivered and snuggled close. "Warm me up, Em." Her slender body quickly roused him, and he began gathering up their nightclothes above the waist. She raised herself off the bed to help him.

His love-making was urgent, needy. She took him, though he could sense she was scarcely ready. "Gently, my dear, gently," she said, as if her murmur in his ear could check him. He rode on without her, dimly aware in the light of the candle that she bit her lip and that her hands merely rested on his back.

He finished quickly, pulled away and lay on his back gasping.

"Thank you, thank you," he said. He moved and thrashed his feet around, making the bed squeak. "Now I'm hot!" He giggled as the eiderdown slid off the bed. "And we don't need this either." With a hook of his foot, he ejected the hot water bottle. It landed with a thud.

"Did you hear that, too, Daphne?" he said.

"John! Be careful! I hope you haven't cracked it."

He turned on his side to look at her. The candle flame on the bedside table danced in the air currents. He stroked her cheek, his fingers tangling in the nest of her hair. "Shall I ever see you again? My rock, my Em. Without you, I'm nothing, you know."

"Ssh, ssh, you mustn't talk like that."

He gathered her to him and began kissing her, stroking her legs, her belly. "Oh, my darling one, I need you so much. I can't get enough of you tonight. I wish you could surround me." He thrust deep into her again as if he could draw strength and comfort from her body.

"Oh, my dear, ssh, ssh, don't rush," she said. "You've never needed me this much before. Be gentle, please. Let's just stay like this and hold each other for a moment." He felt her arms wrap around him and her cheek against his.

But the imperative to move inside her overcame him and, seeking oblivion, he again began thrusting at an increasing pace. She put her hands up in surrender and gripped the pillow at her head.

At last he arched away from her and shuddered. His body twitched as if he was possessed. She pulled him down to the hollow of her neck, cradling the back of his head as she would a baby. She turned and gently kissed the side of his brow.

His body shook in a final spasm and he buried his face in the pillow.

And then the tears came.

TWENTY-SIX

He stuffed his hands into his greatcoat pockets, shivered and stared at the dark smudge of the French coastline. The sun had already gone, leaving a flare of yellow sky merging into purple above the grey water. He had never seen the sea so still – oil-smooth with dark dapples like treacle clogging the surface. No wind, the evening settling into a hard frost. No sound, except the relentless throb of the engines.

He swallowed, his future slipping inexorably towards him.

Around him, men talked in murmurs now, their breath drifting onto the air like departing ghosts, their laughter, the hilarity and singing that enlivened embarkation, now evaporated. A few lights from the shore blinked at them.

"So is this Boulogne, then, Smiler?" Sov pronounced the name to rhyme with Cologne.

He nodded. He had been through the town many times, understood the people. But now... So many things different.

"And you speak the lingo?"

Again, he nodded.

"Us'll be all right here, then. I'll stick with you."

The ship slowed and began gliding into the harbour. The port seemed so busy, he wondered where they would moor. Three ships to starboard, crammed side by side against the quay, pointed seaward. One, an old paddle steamer, now a strange grey outline with bat-shaped black camouflage, was under steam, its dark smoke dawdling skyward. Hospital ship, perhaps, making ready to return to Folkestone.

"Look at all they motor ambilances," Sov said. "I never seen so many. Not all together, like." He began counting. "Five. Kitted out with red cross and all. Reckon they'm for us?"

"More likely casualties for Blighty," he said. A struggle to get the

152

words out; he cleared his throat. Clusters of men loitered on the quay near the ambulances, smoking, talking. Waiting.

"I wish they'd told us where we was sleeping tonight," Sov said. "I need to know where I'm to get my head down. I'm not hungry, like, not after the bully and biscuits, I shall be all right till morning, but I'm ready for my kip. Must be the sea air."

"Yes."

The ship shuddered as the engines went into reverse. The glide slowed.

"Could do with a drink, though."

"Use your water bottle."

A sailor flung a slender rope ashore; someone hauled it in. The huge bow hawser attached to it snaked over the side of the ship and plashed into the water below.

Soon be tied to France.

"Hey, look yonder." Sov wiped his mouth and pointed to the main harbour basin. A tiny sea-plane, like a frantic moorhen, scooted into safety from the open sea where it had landed, its nose-wave sending surges of oily water up the side of the dock. Engine and propeller chattering, it headed for the concrete ramp out of the water. Somewhere astern, a tug fussed and blew its whistle.

On shore, a clock chimed five; the gas lights around the harbour brightened; darkness settled.

The rattle of chains at the stern of the boat and a crash as the gangway hit the cobbles of the quay. Soon be on land. A slight off-shore breeze wafted smells of coffee and frying garlic towards them.

Back again, then. If only there was something welcoming, familiar...

"Good Lord, look at all them." Sov said, as they tramped down the gangway.

At the back of the quay, a line of eight double-decked vehicles – unmistakably London buses, but no longer scarlet. Painted brown, they looked drab: spattered with mud, war-weary. The army had covered the downstairs windows with rough planking to offer some cover against the glass shattering; little protection from a direct hit.

"Troop transport," the sergeant said as he checked them ashore. "Not for the likes of you. You stay here tonight. Up country in the morning." He motioned them to a holding area near the harbour wall where the company gathered, restless, uncertain. Waiting.

The fighting men, carrying rifles and packs, bundled down the gangway and onto the buses. A lot of joshing as if going on an outing. Several men swung up the outside staircase to the open top deck, their boots clattering on the metal treads.

"Pukka soldiers?" someone said. "They're just like kids. Always want to ride on top. How many'll the bus carry?"

"Supposed to be twenty-five, but coming back from the Front, they cram on as many as they can." A newcomer to their section, Gosforth, seemed to know everything.

"Wouldn't like to be downstairs," John said. "Dark in there. Where do they get the drivers, anyway?"

"Even LGOC drivers join up, you know." Gosforth again.

"Busman's holiday, then." John gave a tight-lipped grin.

A grinding of gears; the vehicles lurched away, and a cheer went up from the men on board.

"Oh, come on, Sarge, let's be off, too," Sov's voice a mumble. "My toes is freezin'."

As if in response, a whistle shrilled, the men fell silent and the new sergeant shouted to the company.

"Right, let's get you Wessex lads kipping down. No, we're not billeted in town. It's a village about five miles away. Nice and quiet out there. Make the most of it. Won't always be a cosy night. Ranks of four – fall IN!"

The men jostled into position, hefting their packs and bags onto their backs. John eased his violin case over his shoulders.

"That's all we want, boy," Sov said, "a bloody route march at the end of the day."

★ ★ ★

"Right, B section, this 'ere schoolroom's your billet. Forty in here."

The men began shuffling in.

"No bunks, Sarge?" Atherstone was another newcomer. Little more than a boy, he wore spectacles and sniffed a lot.

"No, and no mother to tuck you up, neither. You're at war now, lad. Get used to it. Now, hold this."

The sergeant thrust a hurricane lamp into the young man's hands, and took out a piece of chalk from his breast pocket. He bent down and, walking backwards, began drawing approximate straight lines across the floor. He completed the grid with other lines at right angles.

"Looks as though we'll have about six foot by two foot each. Cor, lummy, you'd have more room in a grave," someone said.

John looked at the accommodation: a bare wooden floor which stank of carbolic. Beneath their feet a crackle; someone had swept the room hastily, using disinfected sand to pick up dust and debris. He remembered the school janitor doing such work.

Ages ago, another world.

He unwound his puttees and eased his boots off. Now, do I want Gosforth's head or feet near my nose? The best arrangement would be feet to feet and head to head.

"Corp, is it just one blanket?" someone asked.

"That's the issue, lad."

"But it's ruddy freezing, much colder than London –"

"Use your bloody greatcoat, man. That'll keep the draughts out. You don't get undressed here. Reveillé at oh-five thirty, parade at six."

"What time's it now?

"I heard a church clock chime eight."

"That'll do me. S'been a long day. I'm for me kip."

"Sarge, where do we wash in the morning?"

"There's a brook across the road –"

"Oh, blimey."

155

"For anything else, there's a bucket in the corridor, or a five-holer at the far end of the kiddies' playground. Right, last man by the door, put that light out."

John chose a space near the wall. Worried about his violin which he had nursed over The Channel, he decided it wouldn't get kicked if he leant it between him and the wall. He arranged his pack to form a rough pillow, stood his boots at his feet and jockeyed the blanket and greatcoat over himself. Couldn't be helped: have to be shoulders out, feet under cover. Never could sleep with cold feet. He settled: I can touch five other men without moving. He looked up at the beams of the school room. In the corner, near an air vent, a cluster of bats, like a growth of black fungus against the ceiling.

He turned on his side towards the wall and tucked his knees up under his greatcoat.

The yellow glare of the lamp vanished and the room took on sudden darkness. Someone coughed; another man turned over and the floor rustled. Within a minute, someone at the far end began snoring.

Out of the black, a sigh of exasperation. "Oh, Jesus, is this it?"

★ ★ ★

He awoke to a thunderous rap. "All right, you 'orrible bloody lot, on your feet." The sergeant strode in, banging his stick against the walls. He marched round the perimeter, stepping over men's heads, giving feet a hefty kick. "Time for ablutions, all of you. Buck your bloody ideas up. Smells like a fucking pigs' party in here."

All around, sounds of men yawning, groaning, stretching, farting. "Oh, yes," someone said, "better out than in!"

"Did you sleep?" John asked Gosforth.

"Only snatches. Too cold."

"Cold? See this?" Sov's mess tin had traces of ice in it. "Frozen! That was hanging by my head last night."

The brook lay behind a low flood wall on the other side of the

156

road. Still dark. John could hear the trickle of water but not see it. Reluctantly, he pulled his shirt out of his trousers at the front and let it hang down at the back. In a line of about twenty, he knelt down at the water's edge. The cold of frozen earth immediately struck up through his uniform.

At the edge of the water, a wafer-glaze of ice gave under the weight of his hand. Nearer the middle, the brook busied past, an urgent chatter over the stones.

He gasped. Perishing!

He found a small pool, dipped his flannel in and rubbed some Wright's soap onto the cloth. Touching his chest made him tense up. He scrubbed at his neck, under his arms, gave his sides and stomach a perfunctory wash and reached for his towel: cold and hard – partly frozen in the night, and someone, searching for washing space, had trodden it into the mud. He dried himself as best he could, pulled on his shirt again and tucked the collar inside. Have to shave by touch. Didn't want to be on a charge. He soaped his brush and circled it over his chin. He began drawing his razor over his face, hearing the rasp of the bristles yielding. From time to time, he swirled the blade in the brook and prepared to shave below his chin where the darkest growth occurred.

A man, who had already washed, pushed past. John paused, not wanting to get his elbow jogged while he worked close to his Adam's apple.

"Come on, you idle bastards, let's have you, parade five minutes." No mistaking that bellow.

"And two whole hours afore breakfast," Sov said. "I could kill for a bacon sandwich."

★ ★ ★

After an hour and a quarter's march, the company milled around at the railhead.

"It's no good, Poundsbury, you'll never cut it."

Sov put down his knife and glared at Gosforth. "Bloody Frog bread. Why can't they make a proper loaf? I'm starvin', I am." He picked up the French stick and began smashing it against a stone. "I'll break the bugger, then. Get it that way."

"Give up, Sov," John said. "It's frozen solid, probably stale, too."

"And I've had the bugger down my shirt, trying to thaw en, all five miles of this soddin' route." Sov threw it down in disgust.

The field kitchen had arrived first, and the morning air was filled with steam, smoke, the smells of the primus stove, and cooking bacon.

"Oh, sniff that, boys," Sov inhaled deeply. "You can't beat it. A man could live on beer, bacon and cheese – and proper bread, o' course."

"Hot water up, lads!" The catering orderly leaned down and set steaming enamel pitchers on the table at the back of the field kitchen.

"Bread up!" Another man tumbled warmed loaves onto the table.

"I'll get them." Atherstone sniffed. The other members of the section rummaged in their packs for mess tins and their rations of sugar and tea.

"No tea for me, boys, till I've had my bit o' bacon. Hey, Corp," Sov called to the men at the kitchen, "give us some of that. I'm starvin' over 'ere."

"Sorry, chum, bacon's officers only this morning. One of the wagons come off the road. Didn't you see? This is all we got."

"Well, bugger me," Sov said, "we done the march, they just sat there on they horses, all nose-in-air, like." He glanced over to where the officers gathered round a table and sat on folding chairs.

"'Ere you are, chum, you can 'ave a drop o' this." An orderly ladled into Sov's mess tin some of the fat they had fried the bacon in.

"Oh, lovely job, thanks, soldier. I'm famished." Sov dipped chunks of his bread into the fat before it cooled and hardened in the cold. He looked around. "You want to try this. Going down a treat."

"No thanks, old lad, I'll stick to bread and jam," John said.

"Don't you worry. I'll have that for afters." Sov mopped the inside of his mess tin with a wedge of bread, tipped two spoons of sugar and some tea leaves into the tin and poured on the hot water. "No milk, I s'pose." He glanced at the others. "Thought not. Our luck's right out this morning."

★ ★ ★

The train lurched and set off. Inside, the men staggered and grabbed for something to steady themselves. The clink of the couplings tightening, the wheels squealing in torture on a tight curve sounded up through the floor of the wagon. They could hear the determined huffing of the engine. Gosforth found a hook on the wagon's wall and hung up the unlit hurricane lamp. Before long, the rhythm of the wheels settled them all down.

"How long are we all going to be in here? Anyone know where we're going?" Atherstone said.

"Why, son? Thinking of jumping train?"

"No, it's... I don't like enclosed spaces. It makes me feel... Can we have a bit of air?" He sniffed and inched a door open. A cold gust swept in.

"Steady, lad, not too much, or it'll blow all this stuff around."

"What's the straw for anyway?"

"I hope I'm wrong," John said. "But I reckon it's for sleeping on. Plenty of it."

"Shall we be in here that long?" Atherstone looked anxious.

"Could be," Gosforth said. "Why else would they issue iron rations and order us to eat them at sunset?"

"So that's why we've got a bucket." The man pointed into the corner. "What do we do when it's full?"

"Open the door and cosh it out, of course."

"I can't credit it," Sov said. "We're the British Army, not flaming cattle. Is this the best they can do? We only put our beasts in these when we're sending them to slaughter."

"Yes, well..." John said. "Could be a long day." He lifted his violin from its case and tucked it under his chin. He plucked the strings to test the tuning, picked up his bow and began to play. "Now then, chaps, do you know this one?" The jogtrot rhythm of the train on the rails suggested the tune *Narcissus* and, in time with the wheel taps, he began to play. "Join in, whistle along, if you know it," he said.

One by one, the men relaxed; they sprawled on the floor, made little nests in the straw, settled down. John stood with his back to the doors of the wagon, looked round and saw men smiling. Several whistled the jaunty tune in time with his playing.

Someone made up words: "Oh, we're OK, on top of a load of hay. Hard at work, with nothing to do all day."

Soon all joined in, bellowing the words out. Even Atherstone managed a sickly smile, sat cross-legged at the door and began to whistle.

"Well done, Smiler," Sov said. "This'll 'elp pass the time."

John swayed to the music and looked around. He saw smiling faces, the tension fading, the group's bonhomie.

He relaxed. Things'll be OK, after all. We belong together; we can work things out.

Someone lit a cigarette and blew smoke into the air.

"Careful," Gosforth said. "It's a tinder box in here. All this stuff."

"What do you think I am? An idiot? Course I'll take care." The man glared and Gosforth lifted his hands to pacify him.

"Do you know this one?" John said. He started a piece from *Carmen*; again, the men joined in. They did not know the words but managed various sounds to accompany the tune. For the next half hour, he played several well-known melodies from operas.

"I wonder, can they hear us next door?" Sov gestured with his head. "They don't know what they're missing."

★ ★ ★

The train dawdled on. It stopped often, jolted into motion again. Once, after a long pause, it reversed direction. The wagon became their world; some slept; others smoked; someone lit the lamp and a few read in the dim light; two of the section became engrossed in pocket draughts. John took out the photographs of his children and studied them. He closed his eyes and prayed silently.

Again the brakes squealed, the train jerked to a stop, and silence swept over the wagon. Up ahead, the engine panted rhythmically.

"Wonder where we are," someone said. "Open the door, Athers, take a look."

Atherstone slid the heavy door back. A swirl of snow gusted inside; several men shouted and swore; outside, the wind drove the flakes horizontally across wide, empty fields.

The engine blew its whistle and let off steam.

Silence.

"Listen now," someone said, "see if you can hear the guns."

Silence.

"Where the hell are we?"

"Let me look," Gosforth said. "Hang onto me, Hemingby, while I take a peek."

John stood legs apart at the entrance and strained backwards, holding onto Gosforth's arm while he leaned out into the driving snow.

"You'll never believe it," he called. "I can see the sun. It's struggling to get through in all this snow. Now, that's very interesting." He swung back into the wagon.

"Shut that bloody door!" someone said. "Stop mucking about. It's bollock-freezing in here."

"I'll tell you one thing," Gosforth said. "Judging by where the sun is, we're not getting near the Front, we're going away from it."

★ ★ ★

"Welcome to Rouen, gentlemen," the commanding officer

addressed the morning parade. "I trust your journey was adequate. Now, we're keeping you Territorials in reserve, but that doesn't mean you'll be idle. This is the Base Hospital of the Fifty-Fifth Infantry Division, and all the skills you acquired in Blighty will be necessary here. You'll also have to manage many ailments peculiar to men under combat conditions. What we do expect is that every soldier you treat will be able to return to the Front as soon as possible. Duties begin tomorrow at 08.45. Make sure you study the roster in your billet."

He handed over to the sergeant major to dismiss the men; a junior officer hurried forward, carrying a piece of paper. He approached the sergeant major and whispered.

The sergeant major straightened up. "Hemingby! Identify yourself! One pace forward, move!"

John swallowed and stamped out of the line. Lord, what have I done?

The officer hurried up. "At ease, Hemingby. Letter for you."

So soon. That's quick.

The adjutant thrust the letter towards him and looked away. "I'm sorry," he said.

John took it. He saw the tell-tale black border around the envelope, shut his eyes momentarily and began opening the letter.

TWENTY-SEVEN

He chafed at having to wait for a chance to reply:

My dear Em,

I'm so sorry. I wish I could be with you at this difficult time. How rotten that your father should go on the day we landed in France. (Unfortunately, I can't tell you where I am. All outgoing letters have to be checked now.)

I do hope the funeral arrangements haven't fallen on you alone, and that Dora is bearing up well. It'll be a great blow to her, I'm sure, after all the care she's given the old man, all the more so for the apparent suddenness of it all, but we've both known for a long time it was coming. I trust she hasn't gone all a-flutter as we both know she can. You can do without that.

I can picture you gritting your teeth through the long service and hating all the pomp and prayers of the day. I pray the weather is kind: a burial in rain or biting wind can be the cruellest thing. Certainly we've had little let-up in the cold here.

I shall pray for you all, especially now. I wonder who'll be present as mourners. You and Dora, of course, but anybody else? Your brothers? I don't suppose our children understand what's happened. Will Daphne mind them while you're away?

You say you feel very alone. Talk like that, my rock, upsets me. But there's no help for it. I'm so sorry not to be able to support you on the day.

With all my love and sympathy, John.

He sighed, put the letter in the envelope and left it unsealed. She ought to get it in two days – before the funeral anyway.

Now he needed to rush for the evening round. Have to be on his mettle. Didn't do to be late on the Officers' Ward, certainly not with the major. Old School stickler. He picked up his ward kit from the dispensary and hurried off. His partner, Underwood, had gone on ahead.

He hoped to be inconspicuous as he scurried through the ward; he dodged past two Red Cross nurses with a smile and a greeting, but without warning, one patient accosted him: "Good heavens, sir, what are you doing here?"

"I beg your pardon, sir," John said. "Should I... Can I help at all?"

"You don't recognise me, do you?" The man smiled.

"Sorry, sir, I'm afraid I..." He stared hard at the young lieutenant who sat in an armchair beside his bed. A walking stick, ready to hand, lay propped against the chair. Something familiar about him. The tilt of the head, perhaps the boyish grin.

"Would it help if I called you 'Souris'?" He seemed to be enjoying the joke.

A long pause.

"Good Lord, I don't believe it. Lambert! Of all places... What a coincidence! How are you?" They both laughed. "Sorry, stupid question. Anyway, back at school, your hair wasn't that short and you certainly didn't have a moustache. You're in disguise now. So I can be forgiven. But I'm sorry, I ought definitely to be calling *you* sir."

"Oh, don't worry about that. Sickness is a great leveller. To me, you'll always have *sir* status."

John looked over his shoulder. "Look, I'd love to stay for a chinwag but I'm on duty at the moment. They tell me the major's a stickler, and I'm already late. Can we make it tomorrow when I'm off? Late afternoon perhaps."

"Certainly, I'm not going anywhere. But don't worry about Old

Huff and Puff. Heart of gold, really. Blame me, say I detained you. That should square it. When he saw me here, he refused to treat me, said there was nothing he could do, let nature take its course."

"Did that worry you?" Have to be careful, mustn't criticise the boss. But it did sound rather cavalier.

"Good Lord, no. I knew he didn't mean it. He's my godfather, you know."

★ ★ ★

Lambert shivered under a pile of scarlet blankets. "Rats as big as cats," he murmured. His words sounded slurred, his eyes rolled unfocussed. The metal bed frame chattered with his shaking.

John fetched out his thermometer, lifted up the young man's head and put the instrument into his mouth. "Under the tongue, old chap." Lambert's hair was lank, his head and neck greasy with sweat.

John looked around: only one other officer in bed on the ward. "How's this happened?" he said to the Red Cross nurse sitting at the table in the centre. "He seemed in good spirits last night."

"It comes on without warning," she said. They spoke in whispers. "About every five, maybe six, days. They get to dread it."

He hurried back to Lambert and removed the thermometer. The curtains at the window were drawn and he squinted to read the temperature in the gloom. "Good Lord, hundred and five," he said. He looked down again. "That's high, old chap."

The young man opened bleared eyes. "Blasted duckboards."

John spoke to the nurse again. "Is he infectious? I thought I saw a rash. Not scarlet fever, is it?"

"No, don't worry. But wait until you get on the general ward. It's an epidemic there. Nothing we can do, just make them comfortable. Trench fever, you know."

★ ★ ★

"The men christened it shin-bone fever," Lambert said. "I'd go along with that. It makes my legs ache like billy-ho, and it crocks me up frightfully." He stood now; John had helped dress him but the young man leant heavily on his walking stick. "I think I'd rather have a nice clean bullet wound. At least you know what you're dealing with, and you can see progress. With this..."

"How many times has the fever laid you low?"

"I think this last was my fifth. Lost count. I hope I've seen the back of it now. I don't mind telling you it gets me down. I feel as weak as a kitten but I can't do anything. One has to accept it. The trouble is I feel I'm letting the men down, I look a fraud, not a mark on me. I want to get back to my outfit, not sit around feeling sorry for myself."

"They'll return you soon enough," John said. "Sit in your chair, tell me how it all came on."

With several groans and sighs, Lambert eased himself down. "As I remember it, we were about to make an attack on Beaumont Hamel and I wanted to patrol the trench to encourage the men. Then my sergeant appeared and said he'd 'found' a barrel of rum."

"A barrel? Good Lord."

"Well, these things happen. You don't ask questions. I didn't need to know where he'd got it from. He suggested I distribute it, on top of the men's usual ration. 'It might give the lads more courage, sir.' I remember him saying that. Many of the men were shaking with fear. I hated that. Wasn't from the cold. God only knew how many would survive going over the top. But they realised. I thought the rum would at least give a morale-boost and steady their nerves. I learnt early that it's quite usual for officers to increase rum ration before an attack."

"Really? How extraordinary."

"Not that you'll find it written down anywhere. So I OK'd an extra tot all round. Didn't have any myself, mind you. Needed a clear head, since I'd be leading them. It's a close call. You have to decide, do you want drunken troops or men with guts?"

"Dutch courage, eh?"

166

"So I checked I had my whistle, inspected my pistol, and up I came out of the dugout. At first I felt rather giddy, and I remember thinking, 'Must get these duckboards fixed, they're not stable.' It was most extraordinary; I couldn't stand up or walk in a straight line. It was like being drunk. Only worse."

"I suppose you were afraid the men would think you'd –"

"For a moment, I clung on to the planking in the trench wall, hoping the world would stop spinning. I felt sick and had a blinding headache. 'Devil of a time to catch the 'flu,' I thought. And I said to myself, 'Must stagger on, the men expect it.' I managed another two steps and dropped. Like a stone. I think some of the men thought a sniper had got me."

"That sudden?"

"Yes, honestly. Down I went. I just about remember lying face down, my nose in muddy water, and I was aware of my revolver digging into my hip. It hurt damnably and it felt as though I'd wrecked my back. Don't remember the stretcher-bearers at all. I was vaguely aware of the Regimental Aid Post and shivering like mad, my eyeballs hurting. Couldn't get warm. But I knew it wasn't a sniper."

"So what happened about the attack?"

"I'm afraid I've no idea. I feel terrible about letting them down. My guess is the sergeant took over and led the men, but I don't know. I keep asking, but they either don't know here, or they won't tell me."

John struggled to know what to say. He didn't believe in false comfort. But the chances of war meant that Lieutenant Lambert was likely to be posted to a completely new unit when he returned. "Don't dwell on that now, old chap. Concentrate on getting well again." He looked up at the wall clock. "Better press on, or I shall be late for duty."

To elaborate further would be like getting Lambert out of his chair and onto his feet, then deliberately kicking away the walking stick.

★ ★ ★

"I feel guilty, you know," John said. "So far, I've had it easy. For me, it's not The Great War at all. We've not been near the front line; I've not encountered danger; I don't feel I've been tested at all. I haven't even come across lice yet."

"Be careful what you wish for, Monsieur, isn't that the old adage?"

"Oh, that old *Monkey's Paw* stuff," he said.

He and Lambert had discovered a discreet café off the old market square in Rouen. They talked and relaxed together, drank café au lait and, as the young lieutenant grew stronger, enjoyed a carafe of red wine. Here, out of uniform, they set aside military etiquette and called each other *Monsieur* as a compromise.

"I mean, have I been fair to my family?" John went on. "They've been uprooted, are probably short of money – though Emma never complains – are deprived of a proper life together, and all because of my religious calling to serve in The Medical Corps. I can't get out of it now. Two and a half years on, and I'm wondering if what I've done is selfish or vainglorious. What's my purpose in all this?"

"Remember the old saying, Monsieur," Lambert said. "How does it go? 'They also serve who only stand and wait'."

* * *

"Do you miss your violin?" Lambert said, as they wandered back. He leaned much less on the walking stick now.

"Wouldn't be without it," John said. "I managed to bring it, you know. More or less kept it in one piece."

"That's marvellous." He hesitated. "Monsieur, would you play for me tonight? I'd love to hear proper music – something with soul. In the trenches, you hear harmonicas or the accordion, or singing, or men whistling while they march. Occasionally, you even hear someone playing the bagpipes. But I'd love to listen to something classical to remind me of the old days – The Queen's

Hall, concerts at St Edward's, you know, the life we've left behind."

"I'll do that with pleasure. If you can think of somewhere we won't disturb others, I'll get my fiddle."

In a quiet corner of the day room, now in semi-gloom, Lambert slumped into a leather armchair in the shadows.

"I wonder if you'll know this," John said. "French composer – Massenet. The fellow certainly knew how to write a good tune." He began to play the *Méditation* from *Thaïs* and for the next four minutes lost himself in the music.

When he finished, he looked towards the young lieutenant and smiled.

Silence. Lambert hung his head, looked away, blew his nose furiously.

John hurried over and knelt at his side. "Oh, my dear boy, I didn't want to upset you. Too melancholy by far. I'm sorry."

"No, it's exactly what I needed. It helped. Something that lasts even though I may not." Lambert tightened his lips. His eyes stared into the distance. "Something of the old days that puts me into perspective."

"Oh, my dear chap, you mustn't think like that. Remember that university place waiting for you."

"I don't think I'm meant to see Oxford. Out here, people get these feelings. You know what's waiting for you but you carry on." Lambert blew his nose again and wiped tears from his eyes. "I don't mind dying if I have to. I'm not sure I believe all this stuff the newspapers trumpet about a hero's death. I've seen enough out here to know that war can be pretty ugly." He smiled ruefully. "But if I were to have a prayer about my own death, it would be that I meet it bravely, while doing my duty, that I don't let anybody down – and, if I'm lucky, that it comes quickly. I shan't mind losing my life if a better, saner world comes out of all this horror."

John bowed his head. "You put me to shame. But Amen to that."

TWENTY-EIGHT

April 1917

"Someone's arrived on the wards who might interest you," Lambert said. They sat in a quiet corner of their café, drinking red wine and "setting the sun with talk", as John called it. A candle guttered on the table.

John raised his eyebrows.

"Nothing medical at all, don't worry. The poor fellow *has* been wounded, stopped a bullet in the shoulder. But his interests are very much in your line. Musical. It seems we've a composer in our midst."

"Composer?" John said. "We haven't picked up a German, have we?"

Lambert smiled. "No, he's no Fritz, far from it. Very English, I should say: Cotswolds, West Country, that sort of area. And not only that, word is he's a poet as well."

"Poet and composer. That's unusual. Will I have heard of him?"

"Chap called Gurney. Private Gurney. Strange fellow, rather down at the moment, I gather. Never says much. You get the impression of great intensity, of a lot going on up here." Lambert tapped the side of his head. "When you have the time, you might find him interesting to chat to. If he *will* talk..."

"Gurney – name's not familiar. How will I know him? I can't exactly hunt through patients' cards, can I?"

"Oh, it'll be easy enough. He's the one that looks like Schubert."

* * *

The ragbag of a man sat reading in a dark corner of the patients' lounge. His wavy, brown hair had not been combed and below the jacket slung over his shoulders, he wore striped blue pyjama trousers, as if he had become bored with dressing. He lobbed a small leather-bound book onto the table in front of him, took off his spectacles and rubbed the dark circles of his eyes. He stared straight ahead, mouth set halfway between sadness and determination. He looked at nothing as if aware only of an intense inner life.

John strolled into the lounge. "What are you reading, soldier? May I?" He leaned forward and picked up the volume which would tuck easily into the breast pocket of a tunic.

He began turning the pages.

The man made no move.

"Housman, eh? *Loveliest of trees* – oh, I know this poem. You must be Gurney, am I right?"

"I B Gurney, Private, sir!"

John smiled, the name sounded distinctly rustic in this West Country accent. Not broad like Sov, though.

"Relax, soldier, I'm not an officer. Like you, just a private... Hemingby, John Hemingby. Wessex Field Ambulance. I'd like to take a look at your wound. Will you follow me to the side ward where I can check it and dress it for you?" Thank God, he thought, as Gurney followed him, someone cultured. He missed the times with Henshaw.

He untied the sling, eased off the shirt and with great care unwrapped the bandages on the man's arm. "You're a lucky chap. The bullet seems to have missed any bones completely. Very clean." A neat, red-ringed circle in the upper forearm and a splayed exit wound at the back, high on the man's shoulder. John checked the medical notes. "Two days ago? They brought you down here fast enough, my word. Whoever picked you up did a good job, anyway."

"Stretcher-bearers bound it. Machine gun fire, constant spray,"

Gurney said. No eye contact. "Lucky. Someone saw me go down and called them. In the way, of course. No use in the trench once you're wounded. They put a pad on very quickly. Still bled, though."

"Now, this may sting a bit. I'll be as quick and gentle as I can." John fetched out the surgical spirit, poured some on a lint pad and began dabbing the area round the bullet hole. Gurney clenched his left hand into a fist and stood up, ram-rod straight, teeth gritted. "Hold on," John said, "soon be finished." Ask him questions, see if he relaxes. "Where are you from, soldier? Have you got a sweetheart?"

Gurney stared straight ahead. John finished the dabbing. "Arm up, please." He began the slow winding of the bandage round the shoulder again. "There, that's you done," he said. "Did it hurt much when you were hit?" Get him talking. Buck him up a bit.

The answer a growl. "Like being on fire. Blazing."

"You knew what had happened, then? I've heard some people aren't even aware –"

"Couldn't use the arm, couldn't reach for my field dressing. Couldn't nothing."

"Looks a clean wound, though. Should close up and heal all right. Probably take a month, six weeks. How do you feel?"

"Weak as a rabbit."

"What did you think when you knew you'd been hit?"

No reply.

"Gurney?"

"It's the end of music for me."

"Yes, I've heard something about that, but maybe it's not the end, soldier. The wound'll heal. It says in your notes you're suffering from battle fatigue."

"Don't know; you lose track. Three weeks, was it, in line, constant fire? Food running out. And always my bloody, bloody guts."

John started to edge Gurney's shirt on. "You're well out of it here. You'll get some rest. I can see you're tired."

"I have a brain that won't move," he said as John eased the jacket over Gurney's shoulders. He pursed his lips and his dull eyes blazed for a second. "I'm going weaker and frizzier in the head. Constipated in the brains, that's me."

John shook his head. How to help, that was the challenge.

* * *

"I wouldn't have said Schubert," John said, "but I see what you mean." He and Lambert in the café again, a carafe of wine on the table. "The spectacles, perhaps. Maybe the wayward hair. But I'm sure Schubert had a rounder face. Certainly more cheerful than this fellow, I'd guess. He's very doleful. I'm wondering if he's shellshocked. Hubert would know."

"Hubert?"

"Hubert Henshaw, my old MO. He stayed on in Maidstone. He wasn't posted with us. I miss him. We got on well. He took a keen interest in shellshock, reckons half the chaps who get court-martialled and shot for cowardice need medical support." He took a drink of wine. "They don't always get it. But I gather he's still out on a limb. Not many support that idea."

"I had to make that decision," Lambert said, his voice a murmur. "Shortly before an attack. I was resting in my dugout when the sergeant appeared and asked me as a matter of urgency to go up with him. I found one of my young soldiers lying in the trench, nursing his hand, bullet wound through the palm. Scarcely eighteen, I'd say. Not much younger than me."

"What did you do?"

"What I had to. Sent for a medical orderly and had the man arrested."

"What? Oh, my Lord, no."

"I had to assume he shot himself to avoid taking part in the attack. You can't allow such behaviour to go unpunished. It could encourage others to do the same."

173

"SIW – guilty until proved innocent, is that it?"

"'Fraid so," Lambert said. He looked down at the table and toyed with his glass. He took a deep breath. "They're sending me back, you know. My new posting's through. The fever's not recurred, and the MO says I'm fit for duty." He stood up. "So this evening has to be farewell, I'm afraid."

John stood up. "My dear chap, you should have said." They shook hands.

"Au revoir, Monsieur Souris," Lambert said. "Thank you for your friendship, your encouragement, your kindness to me here and at school, and your music. Best of luck with Gurney. You've speeded my recovery. Perhaps we can... I hope the war is kind to you."

John swallowed. "When all this wretched business is over, and things are settled again, come and look me up at school and we'll arrange to hear a concert together. My treat. We'll go and listen to some modern English music. Perhaps this chap Gurney, if he's had anything published."

"Thank you. I'll look forward to that." Lambert looked down at his feet.

"I raise my glass to you," John said. "May God bless you and keep you and cause his face to shine upon you."

Still standing, they drained their glasses. Their eyes met, they smiled, and John saluted.

"Thank you, Private, thank you very much," Lambert said. He pursed his lips.

"Before you go, sir," John said. "May I ask: what happened with the young SIW?"

Lambert breathed in deeply, his voice little more than a whisper. "Shot at dawn, I'm afraid."

John held his breath and closed his eyes.

TWENTY-NINE

Dear Daddy,
    I hope you are very well. I am. Here are some flowers I painted for you. Mama says you've had very cold weather in France, so I'm sending some crocuses and snowdrops to remind you of spring. I hope you like my pictures.

He stopped reading, put the letter aside and looked at the carefully folded pictures. Her artwork showed progress, increased skill. She'd painted the snowdrops on coarse blue paper so the white paint stood out, and green leaves speared up. He smiled at the yellow and purple ovals of the crocuses.

He gazed across the hut and sighed. "Oh, to be in England, now that April's there..."

"Sorry, what say, Smiler?" Sov looked up from polishing his boots.

"Nothing, old lad, only thinking aloud." He picked up her letter again. Spring? Everything here an autumnal palette: red, white, brown.

Mama takes us swimming on Saturday mornings. I can nearly do a width of the baths now, but Rowley splashes about doing the doggy-paddle. Mama doesn't come in the water. She sits with Bea and watches. She hasn't been very well in the mornings lately but she tells me not to worry. I don't think it's anything she ate. She says you'll know what she means and to tell you it's the usual trouble. She says don't fret about it but expect news in the autumn.
    Lots of love from Dorothy

He tucked the letter and pictures back into the envelope, shook his head. They all seemed so far away. Another life. Now they were growing up without him, doing things, learning skills he'd never see. What kind of father didn't rear his children, didn't watch them develop or give them love or guidance? He couldn't even say he was truly fighting *for* them. And now that hint. Did it really mean a fourth child on the way – a result of those few days' leave in January? Was it responsible to have another child and leave Em to bring the family up? He should have shown restraint. How on earth would she manage? He resolved to pray about it later.

★ ★ ★

"I haven't even heard the guns, yet," John said. "Not been anywhere near the trenches. I feel a fraud. What's it like under bombardment? I can only imagine..."

"Nothing but noise and apprehension," Gurney said. "Or long blanks of tedium. The trenches are the cause of three things: cold feet, lice and fear. And stink. Four things. Soldiers piss and shit themselves out there."

"I've heard it said. People really do, then?"

"Oh, yes, when they're scared. He detests it, but you get used to the stench of death and uniforms stinking. Many lads have stopped wearing underclothes. Too difficult to keep clean. Can't wash them or yourself properly. Hate it, but it makes sense. One less place for lice to hide. Long gaps between baths." Gurney sighed. "I feel ill-used. And always my naughty, naughty insides playing up. If the shelling gets bad, some men weep for exhaustion and misery. And the guns – his ears sing some nights. It gets so that you long for a Blighty. Although he hates it in this damn place, it's a good stroke of business being in hospital, away from the Front for a while."

"You do need the rest, old chap."

"I hate getting the Blues. He needs something to steady him down, get him over this dry-up of thought. Nothing in his brain seems to be moving. The old lethargy. If only they'd let him walk some miles. Walking always helps."

"Who's he, old fellow? You keep mentioning 'he'."

"Out here in this damned country for ten months now. Nearly a year."

"Who, old chap, who?"

"Gurney, of course, Ivor Gurney." Impatient now. "Always with me."

★ ★ ★

"Good heavens, man, what on earth are you doing?" John ran forward.

Gurney leaned over a table, the sling hanging loose under his jacket. He had freed his wounded arm and now propped it up with his left hand as he attempted to write a postcard.

"I'll do that," John said. "Let me write it." He reached out for the pencil.

"No, it's a good thing if I do it, you get frightfully slack, doing nothing." He protected the card. "'Sides, I must let Miss Scott know where I am, what's happened."

"Who's she – your sweetheart?"

"Heavens, no, nothing like that. She's a lifeline, looks after him, organises him. He depends on her totally. He's expecting a letter from her about the preface he sent. She's next of kin."

"Do you not have family, then?"

Gurney sighed. "I could do with a pipeful. I haven't had a smoke since I've been here. Do you use tobacco?"

"Not me, I'm afraid, old chap. But I think I know where I could scrounge some." He thought of Gosforth puffing on his pipe before releasing a further nugget of his wisdom on the world. "Would some John Cotton's do for you?"

"Anything sweet and soothing. That sounds excellent. Keep me calm, my spirits up." Suddenly, Gurney burst out: "Oh God, don't

177

you just hate the flatness of this country? It's not so bad round here, few hills, I suppose, but bloody, bloody Belgium... Makes you brood. Much of it's below sea level, you know. Or feels it. I'd give anything now to watch the sun set behind the Malverns. Or see some warm, Cotswold stone. Give me some proper hills!" Gurney's foot jiggled with suppressed energy.

"You're overwrought, old chap." Gurney did not react. "Anyway, where's home for you?" Can't get through, John thought. How can I help him?

"Home is... Outdoors preferably, under the stars. I live anywhere. Last week, the trenches. Now it's here, where are we? – Rouen. I *come* from Gloucester but I live where I find myself. High Wycombe, Fulham, wherever I am. I'd live in the Royal College if they'd give me a room. But home..."

"That's the Royal College of Music, I take it?"

"All those has-been oompah men, making up rules he doesn't want to follow. It's not easy. He's searching for something new. Real English music. Move away from the Germans, what do they know? Miss Scott sends me ruled composition paper, but what can you do out here in exile? I've jotted down a few pieces..." He stared into space.

"So, if this had been a Blighty – and thank The Lord it isn't – where would you go, Ivor?"

"That's why I write poetry out here. Easier. But words are sullen, often won't come... Had to push her to find a publisher, though. Nearly every letter he sends her, there's a poem. She types them out. At least twenty now."

"Is that what your preface was for?"

"*Severn and Somme*. That's what he called the book. They're going to publish it. I don't know why it's taking so long."

"But which would you rather be, Ivor? May I call you Ivor? Poet or composer?"

"Composer first, poet second."

* * *

178

"Strange cove," Gosforth said. He paused, the only sound the pupping of his lips as he drew on the pipe. He tapped out the spill on the side of the fireplace and blew out a billow of smoke. "I changed his dressing the other morning. Chap never said a word. Sat there as if he was dumb. I even had to go and look for him. When I found him, he was on his own in the day room, rubbing his chin and staring at the ceiling. Odd fellow." Gosforth reached into his pack. "But yes, he can have this tin. It's spare, not even opened. My mother sends them. I think she thinks I need tobacco like a steamer needs coal."

"Thank you very much, Gosforth," John said. "I'll give it to him. I'm sure he'll appreciate the kindness."

"Palled up with him, have you? If you ask me, that fellow thinks too much."

John slipped the tin into his pocket and walked away. Gurney might be a troubled soul but he was interesting, a challenge. Might even learn something.

★ ★ ★

He found a pretty embroidered postcard with the words *A Present for a Good Girl* and prepared it to send home.

'My dearest Dorothy

Thank you so much for your pictures. I love the yellow and purple crocuses. They really do remind me of spring. I showed them to some of my friends, and I keep them by my bed where I can see them every morning. Please tell Mama that I love to have letters from home. I want to know all her news. Letters mean so much to us out here.

I miss you. Write again soon.

All my love, Daddy.'

★ ★ ★

"Ivor, your pack's finally followed you here, and my friend Poundsbury is pack storekeeper this week. He's taken an inventory of your personal effects and has sent quite a lot of stuff for washing. He's found these papers at the bottom of the pack and asks me to say, 'Do you want them or can he burn them?'"

"Tell him to leave them be. They're my stuff, not any old rubbish!" Gurney stood up, fists clenched at his side, eyes staring with anger.

"All right, all right, old chap. I understand. If they're important –" John handed over a tangle of folded, dirty papers which had obviously been crammed at the bottom of the pack.

"'Course they're important, that's my music, and poems I'm working on!" Still a flare of anger. Gurney sat down again and hung his head. "I feel so low. I've run dry. I need to get my head moving again."

"Bit of a muddle, though, old chap, would you like me to look through them for you?"

Gurney, eyes lowered, passed the bundle across the table.

John began to separate the papers. "This one's rather messy, Ivor. What's this staining?"

"Mud, probably. I wrote that lying on a damp sandbag, trying to get the damned tune down before it evaporated."

"I see. Now, what about this? This music's printed. *In Flanders*. You've had it published already."

"Miss Scott saw to that. I wrote that Christmas Day at Thiepval as a setting for Willy's poem. Do you know Will?"

"Will who, Ivor?"

"Will Harvey, F W Harvey. We write when we can."

"An extraordinary first line: *I'm homesick for my hills again –*" The words sang in his mind. "Goodness..."

"He's imprisoned, you know."

"Oh, I'm sorry."

"Last August. I thought we'd lost him. Believed he was dead. Didn't know what to do with myself. Such days we had before the war – walking our hills. Then, October, I heard he'd been captured."

"Oh, prisoner of war!" John smiled, relieved.

"Isn't that obvious!" Gurney glared.

"All right, all right." He held his hands up in surrender. "Ivor, may I beg a favour? I have a violin here. May I fetch it and play some of these over? I'd love to hear how these sound."

Gurney gave a gesture of resignation. "If you wish. I've never heard it. Only up here." He tapped his head.

John sighed. A little trust, at last.

★ ★ ★

The music was for piano and voice. John decided to play the vocal line, and soon the violin sang out all the pain of nostalgia. Gurney sat head bowed, stroking his chin.

When he had finished, John put down his violin and bow and applauded Gurney. "That's amazing, and it's been performed already – the world must surely like it," he said. "It's extraordinarily beautiful. Never heard anything like it. Such yearning there. It really describes being in the trenches and longing to be back home again. How do you manage to capture such feeling? I couldn't show my feelings like that. It's new. In a way, not English."

"It's *very* English." Gurney's correction almost a reprimand. "That says everything for me. And fortunately you play it as if you understand, too, I'll say that. To hear strings again, strings that can tear the heart out of any mystery." He lowered his head and whispered. "Thank you."

"Before I go to bed, I must try it another way," John said. "Will you come through to the day room? I want to play it through on the piano." They walked together into the darkened lounge. John carried an oil lamp and stood it on top of the piano. "I'll give us some privacy," he said. He pushed the double doors to and walked back to the keyboard. Gurney shrank into the shadows.

John played the accompaniment now, the slow, soft notes of the opening to the song. He began to sing:

> *I'm homesick for my hills again –*
> *My hills again!*
> *To see above the Severn plain,*
> *Unscabbarded against the sky,*
> *The blue high blade of Cotswold lie;*
> *The giant clouds go royally*
> *By jagged Malvern with a train*
> *Of shadows. Where the land is low*
> *Like a huge imprisoning O*
> *I hear a heart that's sound and high,*
> *I hear the heart within me cry:*

> *"I'm homesick for my hills again –*
> *My hills again!*
> *Cotswold or Malvern, sun or rain!*
> *My hills again!"*

"Oh, heavens! That comes from the heart. I couldn't... I daren't let myself feel like that. You've really captured it – being homesick," John said. "Extraordinary. Unnerving."

"First time I've heard it sung. Not so bad. What do you think? Work of a genius, wouldn't you say?" Gurney smiled mockingly.

"Genius, and something totally different. Wonderful, delicate, emotional music."

THIRTY

He awoke, convinced he'd been crying. Had anyone heard? He lifted his head off the pillow. Still dark, sounds of sleeping all around. A distant owl screeched.

Had he really whimpered or cried out, or only in his dreams? And what was he dreaming? What would make him cry? He screwed his eyes up, trying to reach back into the dark.

He didn't cry. Wasn't allowed to. Well, yes, that one time he did, but that was the drink. He felt ashamed afterwards but Em accepted it, told him not to be so silly when he apologised.

But Father – he could hear him still: "Stop crying this instant, lad, or I'll give you something to cry about. Only girls cry." Those fierce eyebrows, that twitching beard. Like God.

He didn't cry.

So why the sob, the tears in the dark?

He thought of singing Gurney's song just before bed. Hardly a lullaby, more a song of loss and pain. Did that spark off something? Desperation there, longing – but what exactly was homesickness?

Gurney's longing seemed to be for the place, the geography, the hills. The man wouldn't talk about his people. Not his family. Gurney was rooted in the soil, the landscape of Gloucestershire. That was what he missed.

For himself, it wasn't absence from place. What was there to nourish roots in Stoke Newington or Catford, or now Streatham? He smiled in the darkness. Living and working in Kent was pleasant enough, but no roots, no pull there.

Homesickness meant people: Dorothy, Helen, Em, of course, his parents. If he knew there were people to go back to, people who accepted him... He could wander anywhere if he knew someone waited for him. Keeping the home fires burning, as the song went.

But Gurney didn't have that. Something askew there, couldn't put his finger on it. An inner wound, perhaps, as well as the arm. Some deep-seated soul-pain. What would cure that?

Was Gurney crying inside?

Around him, men began to stir.

"Oh, God!" A distant yawn. "Another bloody day."

★ ★ ★

"What do you make of our Private Gurney, sir?"

The Medical Officer finished scrawling on the notes and looked at John. "Gurney? Coming along nicely, I'd say. Wound closing up. No sign of infection. Had his tetanus?" He glanced down and checked. "Yes, good. About another month I'd guess, perhaps less if we're lucky."

Try another tack: "He keeps complaining of stomach trouble. It seems to be chronic with him."

The doctor glared. "Can't expect much else after such a poor diet. I thought rations were getting through to the trenches now. Anyway, I've asked the Red Cross to make sure he eats properly while he's here. Build him up again. Odd fish. Fellow seems absent–minded to the point of distraction. Needs to concentrate on getting himself fit again."

"You don't think it's something else? Nerves, perhaps, sir?"

"Nerves?" He tapped the notes. "Battle fatigue, it says here. That's common enough. Rest and good food, that's what he needs."

"Certainly looks fit only for the knackers' yard as he is. Are you worried about his irregular heartbeat?"

"Oh, don't fuss, Hemingby, it'll all settle down as he gets back on his feet. He's a young man." He looked again at the notes. "We don't know what he's like when he's normal. It's not what we're here for. Anyway, why this special pleading? Why are you hinting shellshock to me? It's pretty unlikely. When he stands up straight, he looks manly enough to me."

Oh, dear God, straight out of the ark. He tried again: "I'm concerned about him, sir. I feel there's something not quite right. He's a very talented young man, in my view. Rather special. Needs looking after."

"What's the matter with you, Hemingby? He doesn't need a mother hen. He's a twenty-six-year-old soldier with a wound. Nothing special about that. I can't concern myself about a man's talents or otherwise. This is war. We have to deal with the job in hand: patch him up, get him back on his feet and pack him off again."

Yes, but something's not right. Why does Gurney block the world out?

* * *

My dear Helen,

It was so good to have your letter. It does help to know life back home continues just as I imagine it.

I believe Em is pregnant again, though she hasn't yet said so herself. I've written to her after the merest hint through Dorothy. I cannot imagine being father to four children. As it is, I hardly know two of them already because of this confounded war. Rowley viewed me with great suspicion last time I went home and little Bea doesn't remember me from one leave to the next. I hate being a stranger to them all.

You ask if I've made many friends out here. We all know each other well in our section. We live and work together and are often assigned tasks as a unit, but we're very different people: Gosforth, our self-appointed mentor, was a bank clerk and can be pompous, Atherstone a baker's assistant. Underwood's a fine fellow, he used to be a printer. And so on, and so on. We all rely on each other, but I think you know I feel closest to Sov Poundsbury, one-time farmworker and my first friend in the army. He may not be the brightest star in the firmament but is certainly warm and dependable. I should be extremely sad if a transfer or some worse misfortune separated us. I feel safe with him.

Currently, I count myself lucky to have encountered one patient – a young Gloucester man who, despite his eccentricities, is a talented and thought-provoking companion musically. I'm quite thick with him. He gives me intellectual stimulation, rare out here. But I must enjoy his company while I can. His circumstances and the nature of our work are essentially transient. But he's an interesting fellow, and I should certainly like, God willing, to renew his acquaintance when this war is over.

With all my love to you and yours
Fordie

★ ★ ★

Gurney slumped forward in his chair in a dark corner of the day-room, his head in his hands. A curl of smoke from his abandoned pipe; a plug of dottle in the ashtray.

"Ivor, is everything all right?" He rested a hand on the man's shoulder. Certainly looked like shellshock.

Gurney flinched.

"Sorry, it's only me. Are you in pain, old chap?"

"It's like living, only half-awake." The voice a mumble. "I need to push myself physically. I'm not doing anything here."

"It's only a fortnight since –"

"I've nothing to read. Nothing I want, anyway. No money for books either."

"What about the Housman poems? Have you exhausted them?"

No reply. This was hard work.

"I could lend you my bible, old chap. For a while. That always helps, I find."

Gurney turned to look up at him, his eyes heavy-lidded and lifeless, his face gaunt. "Thank you, no. I'm polite to God, but..."

"What about chess? Someone'll give you a game."

Gurney stroked his chin and blew heavily through his lips.

"I see." Come on, Smiler, think of something. "Now, music I know will buck you up. Why not play the piano in the recreation room? Your arm will take gentle movement now."

Gurney shook his head. "Don't feel like it. Can't remember the tunes of the songs the others enjoy, and they won't like my stuff. Nobody does. Best left."

John sighed. What's best left, you or this issue? He took a deep breath. "We've got to find something to take you out of yourself. Let's see if we can sort out some leave – perhaps a couple of hours to start with away from the ward, and when I'm free, I'll join you and we'll go into the town, find something that's more your cupper tea."

★ ★ ★

The heavy door sighed shut behind them and the latch clinked, enclosing them in a world of stillness and silence. Their bootsteps chittered and echoed off the cold stone. Amid the must of ages, the odour of stale incense oppressed the air. John feared he would sneeze. Ever since they had wandered away from the hospital, Rouen itself had dwarfed them: narrow, curving streets, lofty buildings, some with timber frames, and now the cathedral itself. It dominated them: tall soaring columns and arches either side of the long narrow nave. They felt compelled to whisper.

"I don't fear cathedrals," Gurney said, "not since my days at Gloucester. But this place..."

"Yes?" John said. It was the first time Ivor had started any conversation.

"You get used to them, come to feel like home. I made friends there."

"Excuse me," John said, "I must..." He moved away. He knew what he had to do – what he always did: he knelt down a few chairs in from the central aisle and readied himself to talk to God. "Dear Lord Jesus, I pray for..."

But nothing would come.

He knew he should pray for his family, particularly for Em with her fourth pregnancy. He wanted to pray for Ivor but could think of nothing to say. He needed to pray for himself, but all his thoughts seemed clichéd, stale, as if God had turned his face away and would not listen. Was it because he'd walked into a Catholic cathedral? The only words that came into his head were Hamlet's: *How weary, stale, flat, and unprofitable Seem to me all the uses of this world!*

What on earth's the matter with me? He scrambled to his feet and rejoined Gurney who had wandered ahead, neck craning in admiration at the procession of fluted pillars and arches. "There's peace here," Gurney said. He held his right arm as if it hurt. "But also gloom today. Light liked to flood in at home. I don't like the gloom of God."

"Are you in pain? Does your arm hurt? Shall we rest awhile, old chap?" John gestured towards a row of chairs. They sat down side by side, subdued by cold silence. He stared woodenly ahead. Why couldn't he pray? In all this, where was God? He watched a nun up near the altar, moving like an earnest bat to tend the red glow of the sanctuary light. Her garments rustled; she bowed to the altar and her sandals flapped against the stone floor as she busied away into the shadows.

Somewhere behind them, out of the heavy stillness and darkening silence, organ music burst onto the air, shook and tumbled through the cathedral. John guessed immediately it was Bach.

"I know this," Gurney said, "I like playing it. Not as fast as that, though, this fool thinks you have to hurry."

John composed his face for listening but could only hear climbing notes which sounded very much like the tune to Humpty Dumpty. Like he used to sing to Rowley.

Humpty Dumpty sat on a wall. The rhythm fitted. Once thought, the idea wouldn't leave, though the tune wandered quickly away from the nursery rhyme.

What's the matter with me? What's going on?

Gurney leaned over to whisper. "I was on sentry duty last time I heard this."

"Really?"

"Misty night, but stars overhead. Last October, I think. Dog-tired, No Man's Land completely black. A struggle to keep alert. But it lifted me."

"Where was the music coming from?"

"Up here." Gurney tapped his head. "I listened to it all up here. Bach's an old friend, you know. Kept me awake. Often comes to me like that. I was a dreamer ever."

"You're lucky being able to recreate music in your head."

"Listen to it now! Don't you just envy the old man his felicity? It all flows out of him. If only I could... Everything I do is born out of sorrow and pain."

"My dear chap, don't..."

"You're lucky. Your feet are on the ground, yet you still know how to coax the soul out of a piece. Great gift." A long silence as if Gurney had lost his train of thought. "Will you do something for me, John?"

The first time Gurney had used his name.

"If I can help, of course."

"I need to know, whether I live or die, I need to know... I have a piece..." He patted his breast pocket. "It captures the heart of me. I know it does. When I wrote the words, I heard it as a song. Now I've given it the music it needs, but I want to know just once that Schubert didn't always do it better. When we get back, will you play it for me? Sing it, too, perhaps?"

"Of course, old chap. Gladly. You know I rate your music. Any excuse to play the old fiddle." At last, he's let me in. Now what will I learn of the real Ivor Gurney?

★ ★ ★

189

No, not shellshock. He was more certain now. He remembered how Hubert Henshaw quickly distanced himself from thinking the cases were physical victims of the guns who needed electric shocks or plunge baths to jolt their nervous system back to normality. Henshaw had begun to suspect some form of mental illness afflicted the men – something which needed sympathetic diagnosis and treatment, perhaps even the talking cure. Shellshock victims seemed withdrawn, locked in, or afflicted by fear. Hard to reach, certainly.

And that wasn't Gurney.

John believed he was now witnessing in the soldier a slow emergence from debilitating melancholy, like a cloud passing or a fog lifting. The catalyst, the healing agent, seemed to be music and literature. Certainly, the man wasn't the outcast who'd isolated himself when he first arrived.

★ ★ ★

"Had my picture taken three days ago," Gurney said. "Want to see it? I found an old photographer in one of the side streets. He did it for me. Only charged a few sous. Just for the paper and the plate." He passed over the sepia print.

John recoiled at the image. "What was your reason for having this done?"

"Miss Scott wants one of me as a soldier. Go with *Severn and Somme*, I suppose."

John looked at the picture: the greatcoat sagging open and hanging half off the wounded arm; the tunic rumpled, and Gurney's breast pocket unbuttoned, a slip of folded paper just visible.

And the face – a sullen stare straight to camera, the eyes heavy-lidded and lifeless. He looked tired out.

"Rather doleful, wouldn't you say?" Gurney gave a wry smile.

"Not you at your best, old chap. You should have worn your glasses. And let's say you wouldn't pass a CO's inspection."

Gurney opened the palms of his hands in a gesture of

resignation, his shoulder too painful for a Gallic shrug.

"Get another one taken, why don't you? This doesn't show a dashing soldier-poet."

"Don't much feel the type," Gurney said. "I'm dumb now."

"The words'll come back, old chap, I'm sure of it. Now, what about that poem you mentioned? Still want me to see it?"

Gurney fiddled in his tunic and produced a large folded paper. He passed it over.

John opened it up and looked at the neat handwriting. "Now, what's this mean, Ivor? It says 'Caulaincourt' at the top." John showed him the draft.

"That's the place I wrote it."

"Very challenging first couple of lines. *Only the wanderer knows England's graces.* Makes you think."

"We were sheltering in a mausoleum. Some big estate. January. Had to get out of the intense cold, and that wind. Colincourt, the lads called it. Danger of Boche booby traps there. But we needed time under cover. The fields everywhere froze shortly after New Year and just... For ever, it seemed. Unrelenting. Temperatures well below. I can remember my fingers being frozen; tips went yellow; I could scarcely hold a pencil; ink would have turned to ice. Had to get this down, though. Wouldn't leave me alone. Trenches aren't the best place to write a work of genius." He grinned. "Can't be idle, but it's easier writing poetry, you don't have to worry about the right paper."

"But you knew you wanted to set it to music?"

"That came a couple of months later. Don't do it often, rarely use my own stuff."

John puzzled at the music manuscript with the words and notes dashed in. "Is all your music as disorganised as this? It's difficult to read."

"Make allowances, won't you? I work at speed. Have to get it down before it skitters away."

"Well, let me give the melody a try. I've brought the fiddle." John went across to a nearby armchair where his violin nestled in its case.

He picked the instrument up, checked the tuning and began to play the voice line. A plaintive tune, sweet, poignant. He began to sway to the music.

Gurney's shout startled him. "C sharp, it's C sharp. For God's sake, don't jigger it!"

John lowered his violin, took a deep breath and puffed his lips out. The temperament of a genius! "I'm sorry, Ivor, doing my best; I *am* sight-reading, it's incredibly difficult to tell what key you want it in."

"Two sharps – F sharp and C sharp. Isn't it obvious?"

John said nothing, waited a few seconds before resuming the tune. He let the final notes fade away and lowered his violin. "Yes, lovely," he said.

"Not such a jolly wanderer as Schubert's, but I've tried to capture the best of homesickness in the world."

"You'll see Gloucestershire again, Ivor. We must never despair."

"Not quite vanished, then."

"Sorry, what?"

"My songs. Will you sing him now?"

"If you like. Do my best. Do you trust me, though?" He grinned at the young soldier.

"Oh, yes, you mostly know what you're doing."

"Coming from you, old chap, I assume that's a compliment." He laid his violin in the case and they both walked through into the inner room where the piano stood. John closed the double doors. Gurney positioned himself in an armchair where the westering sun cast light upon his face.

John sat at the piano, shook his arms free of his sleeves, and strummed a quick arpeggio. With care, he propped up the crumpled music sheet.

"Two sharps, then, Ivor." He grinned over his shoulder and began to sing:

Only the wanderer
Knows England's graces,

Or can anew see clear
Familiar faces.

And who loves Joy as he
That dwells in shadows?
Do not forget me quite,
O Severn Meadows.

When he'd finished, tears pricked his eyes. He let his hands rest on his knees and pursed his lips.

"It's not half bad," Gurney said. "It'll do. If music ever flows again for me, I want to write a sonata for violin and piano. I'll dedicate it to you. Perhaps you'll even play it. I've thought of a title..." He gazed directly at John. "Not quite up to shaking your hand yet. I'll call it *The Smiler Sonata* because that's –"

The sound of running boots. The double doors crashed open. Sov panting in the doorway. "There you are, Smiler! You got no time, boy. I looked all over for you. Parade ten minutes or we're on a fizzer."

"Why, what's happened?"

"Moving out. Hour's notice. Heading North, up country. Travelling light. Wipers, someone said."

John's eyes met Gurney's. "Sorry, Ivor, I... Goodbye, old chap." He touched him briefly on the uninjured arm. "Fare well. May The Lord bless you and keep you safe."

But Gurney had not done with him.

The group began the march to the rail-head, John unsettled, out of step. The words of Gurney's song badgered him, he trod to their rhythm, knew they captured the true heart of the man. Such brutal sadness, seeing yourself a wanderer, an outcast who didn't belong.

Tramp, tramp, tramp.

No home, no family, looking at life and people from outside like a peeper at a window.

193

Dwelling in shadows... What shadows, what soul-pain did Gurney know?

The dark side of the spirit.

He struggled back in step, tried blocking out the thought. But...
Do, not, for-get, me, quite.

Why *quite*? Did Gurney believe he was fated to be forgotten, ignored? Did he expect it? Not with that talent, that sensitivity, surely.

John remembered Father thrusting the words of Ecclesiasticus before him one Sunday after church; he never knew why: *Let us now praise famous men, and our fathers that begat us...*

"Read those words, lad, that's the wisdom of the Almighty, that's the grandeur of God. You want to learn that by heart."

But John remembered with horror, *And some there be which have no memorial, who are perished as though they had never been.*

Unbearable – the idea of living your whole life and then being completely forgotten. The fear lingered. Life without meaning. All that striving, and caring and loving – for what, if it all counted for nothing and you were forgotten? Is this what Gurney expected? A bleak place indeed. Poor devil.

Tramp, tramp, tramp.

John raised his head, squared his shoulders and silently thanked God for his children, his wife and family. They'd remember him, wouldn't they? They at least gave life significance and meaning.

At the station, the engine blew an urgent whistle and John watched a jet of steam spurt in the air, spreading and scattering like a mist before the wind.

THIRTY-ONE

July 1917

"I can't fathom how any Corps could leave a place in this state." Sov scrubbed harder at a stain on the floor. "Who or what caused this, I don't want to think. Call this place an 'ospital? You wouldn't go bringing any wounded Tommy in here."

John looked back over his shoulder. He and Wing were whitewashing the walls of the one-time school hall; Feltham sloshed water over the windows with a screwed-up chamois leather. The glass squeaked as he polished off stubborn stains.

Only the weekend to get the place ready for receiving casualties. Some big push was coming; heavy bombardment from the British guns said so.

"What did Sarge say? How many different areas are needed?" Atherstone, also on his knees scrubbing the floor, looked up and sniffed.

Gosforth straightened his back, levered his mop and bucket forward a few feet and wiped his hands down his trousers. "Well, officially six. This'll be the reception area, I suppose." He began counting on his fingers. "They'll need a re-suss area, pre-op, a large operating room – might have to be a tent – an evacuation area and somewhere else for twenty-four-hour care."

"Is that what they call the moribunds, Gos?"

"You might say that, Sov." Gosforth dipped his mop in the bucket and began washing the floor again. A salvo of heavy gunfire shook the building; the glass in the windows buzzed.

"Hey, Smiler," Sov said, "put a cloth down, why don't you? We don't want drops o' your paint all over our clean floor. We got to get this place spotless. You watch what you're doing now."

"Don't worry," John shouted, without looking back, "we're being careful. Is it tea and fag time yet? I've had enough of arm-stretching."

★ ★ ★

Outside, the men clustered in the school yard, drinking tea and smoking. Overhead, a German spotter plane droned and puttered.

Atherstone looked up, sunlight glinting on his spectacles. "I don't like being spied on. What's he doing up there? What's he expect to see?"

"What our guns are up to," John said.

"You won't get me up in one o' them things," Sov said. "'tain't natural. What's he lookin' at, anyhow? We're miles behind the lines." He paused and looked around. "Aren't we?"

"About seven, they say," John said. "Out of range of their guns, let's hope."

"Troop build-ups, probably. That's what he's hoping to see." Gosforth drained his mess tin and slung the dregs away. "Somehow, they always know. Must be a big show coming if we're preparing this CCS as well."

"I wish he'd buzz off," Sov said. "He wants to watch out. Our lads'll be wanting a pop at him soon."

As if on cue, puffs of white smoke like soft cloud began to burst around the plane, mostly to the rear of it. The men cheered and waved at the sky.

"Over a bit, lads!" Feltham gestured as if directing the shells towards the bi-plane.

"See him off, boys!" Atherstone polished his spectacles in excitement. Tiny starbursts pinpricked the sky.

The wing of the aircraft was obscured briefly by a drift of smoke. The plane banked and flew away towards the high ground of the ridge to the north.

Nearer now to guns and action. John pushed the grim thought away.

THIRTY-TWO

Mother never told us much. I never knew she was pregnant again, for example, until the baby arrived. That was the way then. I didn't even guess that morning when she asked for help with the laundry.

I moved the stool near to the scullery sink, ready to help her bundle the wet sheets up and out of the dolly tub.

"Now, hold them away from you so you don't get soaked."

We began a slow tugging, like sailors hauling on a rope, and gradually the steaming sheets curled and flopped into the sink.

"Now, help me hotch the tub towards the gulley. Mind your feet as it goes over, and be ready to sweep any puddle back if it comes this way."

I picked up the broom, moved the stool and watched the soapy pool swirl and settle over the floor drain.

"Oof," she said, "I think we'll take a rest before we do the rinsing." She stood with her hand, red and wet, resting on her stomach. "Heavy work for a warm day. Put the kettle on, will you, and go and see if the postman's been. I'm going to sit down."

I came back with a small bundle of post. "Two letters for Aunty Daphne..."

"What have I told you? Always leave letters for Aunty Daphne on the table in the hall."

"...and two postcards for you. Are they from Daddy?" It always seemed ages since we'd heard from him. I suppose he must have written to Helen or his mother sometimes. You got used to long silences and him not being there.

Mother thrust out her hand for the post and I watched her scan the words on the first card.

"Is it from Daddy? What's he say, Mama?" She seemed to tolerate my pestering.

"He says he's very well. He sends his love and is missing us. They've all moved to another hospital now, he can't say where. Kisses to us all and an extra big hug to Rowley for his birthday. You can read it if you like." She held it out.

"He's all right, then?"

"So far, so good."

I sighed with relief. "And who's the other one from, Mama?"

"That's from Uncle Row – do you remember my brother, Uncle Row? Probably not. You were quite young when he left England."

"Where did he go? France?"

"He's in France now, but he went right over the other side of the world – New Zealand. He's just marked *I am very well* on this card. It's only a quick message soldiers can send, but he's managed to scribble one little bit himself: *Keep your pecker up!*" She smiled. "That sounds like Row. Always cheerful."

I have to admire her now. She never told us if she was worried, kept her thoughts to herself. Her way of protecting us, I suppose. She rarely showed her feelings, so I never knew whether she was anxious about anything: money, Daddy, her brother. She was tough, proud and independent, determined to manage whatever life threw at her. I wonder now how many women were like her.

THIRTY-THREE

In spite of the day's labours, John couldn't get back to sleep. Something had woken him, but he didn't know what. He hadn't reckoned on homesickness striking at three in the morning. Usually it plagued him as he washed and shaved ready for parade. He tried to imagine the routine of home, as if he could look in through the windows. Homesickness always intensified after he'd written to Em or to Helen. It seemed as strong as physical pain – this wanting of Em and the children, even little Bea whom he scarcely knew. How on earth were they managing on so little money? He missed Helen and her bright cheerfulness, too, and his parents, but also the old days – the comfort of regular school lessons – the life and work he'd left behind.

He found himself thinking about Gurney. Where was *he* now – surely discharged and back at the Front. Poor man, what on earth made him volunteer for the army after they'd rejected him initially?

Still, there were consolations. John felt closer to the men of his section since they'd found a pleasant *estaminet* in the back roads of "Plug Street". Laughter, singing and some drinks. *Carpe diem*. Life and hard labour weren't so bad when red wine was sixpence a litre. Certainly got him off to sleep. But tonight...

And then he knew what had woken him: the heavy barrage had stopped.

He was aware of the bright light first, like he'd always imagined a Biblical revelation would be – an unfolding of bright and convincing glory. Or the pillar of fire that guided the Israelites through the darkness.

Total silence. Only that light.

Then the building shuddered, vibrating and shaking as if caught in a wild shiver, and he and all the men were flung two feet in the air and cast down on the plaster floor of the attic like so many coins tossed into a busker's cap. In spite of ample straw on the floor, he'd still landed heavily on his hip. His knee hurt.

Now nothing except a persistent hissing inside, and around him. "What was that?" he shouted. But he didn't know whether any words came out.

Someone managed to light a lamp and he saw, in the light of the flickering, men everywhere rubbing their hips or elbows, shouting, swearing.

But total silence in the attic of that barn, as if The Lord had struck all of them dumb. Oh, my Lord, was this the start of Armageddon?

THIRTY-FOUR

It was always my job to bring the post up to our rooms. But one day I had a real scare and thought the worst had finally happened.

I staggered up the stairs from the front door with the long, heavy parcel. I couldn't think what it was. Perhaps a birthday present for Rowley. It had been wrapped tightly in sacking and roped at the neck. Scarlet sealing wax secured the knots and a brown tag, fixed to the rope with a lead cramp, dangled from its neck. I could make out a smudgy stamp in purple ink with the letters RAMC on it, but the writing was grown-up scrawl. I could just make out our surname – *Hemingby*.

Mother wiped her hands on her apron. A look at the parcel and her hand covered her lips. "Oh, Dorothy," she said. That alarmed me.

"What does it say, Mama?"

"Fetch me the vegetable knife from the scullery draining board." She inserted the blade under the rope at the neck of the parcel and began sawing at the fibres. "The label says *Property of Private J F Hemingby to be returned to the family*," she said.

The fastening soon gave way; the neck of the sacking opened up, and she pulled out the long case of Daddy's violin. Some of the dark leather covering was scuffed and torn and the wood casing showed through. She unclipped the fastenings. Inside, the violin and the bow lay face down, as if someone had crammed them away quickly.

"He'd never lay it in its case upside down," Mother said. "Far too fussy about it."

"What does it mean?" My voice little more than a whisper.

She said nothing, just began folding up the sacking and gathering up the cord. She looked away, sighed.

201

"Mama!"

"It means they've sent your father's violin back home. That's all. No note to say, or anything."

"Why did they do that?" My throat tightened with dread and I felt sick. "Does it mean Daddy isn't coming home?" I stared at her. "Does it?"

"I don't know what it means, child, your guess is as good as mine." Mother's impatient voice; she always covered her emotions like that. "It just means they've sent his violin home."

I turned away, my eyes filling with tears. I'd always wondered what I'd do if this happened.

Mother knelt down and pulled me close. "We have to look on the bright side. If anything has happened to him, they would have told us first, surely. They would have sent a wire or something. We just have to hope."

She did her best, but I stayed quiet all day, convinced that we'd lost him.

THIRTY-FIVE

"It's the Messines to White Sheet Ridge, I gather," Gosforth said. "Mines detonated simultaneously all along the line."

"That'll have given the Boche a rude reveillé," Feltham said. "Bad enough for us back here."

Feltham had begun to irritate – always the jaunty Cockney, always the chauvinist. Amusing as conductor on a tram back home, but not here. "Poor devils," John said, "think of the casualties. You wouldn't stand much chance with a bomb under you."

"They'd have done it to us, soon as blink," Feltham said. "Serves 'em right."

Brisk boot steps. Sov looked up. "Look out, boys, here's Sarge."

"Right, lads, early start, long day ahead. Everything's brought forward. Parade at oh-four hundred, breakfast at oh-five-thirty. After that big bang, our brave lads will have already started their push. We can expect casualties from oh-six hundred, maybe earlier."

"How many do you anticipate we'll have to deal with, Sergeant?" Gosforth said.

"Anticipate? We're bloody *required* to take two hundred first off, after that, they'll shunt 'em to another station, and another. Then it's back to us again, so we need to get a shift on. Now: Feltham, Atherstone, Poundsbury, Hemingby, stand by! Major's done his inspection and he wants three more post-op tents out on the field at the back – a chest ward, an abdo ward and, further away, the scabies tent. Corporal Russell will show you where."

"'Ere, Sarge," Sov said, "what's an abdo ward?"

"Use your bloody loaf, Poundsbury, abdomen – it's stomach wounds."

The high-geared whine of the first ambulances at about seven o'clock. John swallowed. This'd be the first time he'd seen casualties and wounds fresh from the battlefield. If Sarge was right, could be a long day. He hoped he'd remember the codes for the different wards. They wanted to avoid letting casualties know their true situation. The doctors would decide, call out the code, and the orderlies would escort or carry patients out to their destination. Straightforward enough, really: 'R' ward meant re-suss – anyone too shocked, cold or otherwise unready for an operation; 'P' ward for the very serious cases who needed to be prepared for immediate surgery; 'E' ward, that was easy – the evacuation area for anyone ready for immediate transfer out and...

"Good morning, everybody." The two doctors on duty walked into the hall as if on cue.

The orderlies stood to attention; the Red Cross nurses straightened up, their hands demurely folded.

"At ease, everyone," the major said. "I want to wish you Wessex fellows the best of luck on your first duty day here. Always remember, this is a Clearing Station. Our job is to move these men on and ship 'em out as quickly as possible. Anything you don't know, ask. It'll be a long, busy day, and a hot one, no doubt, so, as you see from my attire, regulations about uniform go by the board. Strip down, if you need to. We keep red tape to the minimum."

John craned round and saw the major was dressed in shorts. He signalled to Sov with a nod and raised an eyebrow; the captain wore lightweight flannel trousers.

"Stand by, everyone."

Echoing down the corridor leading into the hall a strange shuffling and scraping of boots. No voices.

The walking wounded first, figures in khaki, their uniforms dusty or caked with mud, stumbled in as if drunk. They had blankets over their shoulders, or greatcoats, and a swathe of bandages on their arms, or chest, across an eye or round the head. Often blood had seeped through the dressing and showed red-brown where it had dried.

Even from some feet away, John recognised the smells that accompanied them: salt sweat, strong, acrid; the oppressive reek of faeces, the sweet odour of urine.

Gosforth stood by the doorway. "Pass right up to the far end, please. Pass along now."

"Oh, fuckin' 'ell!" A tall Scotsman lurched forward and staggered on. He glared at the world out of one bloodshot eye. Others followed, shuffling.

John had to accompany the captain and check the label detailing each patient's injuries. The tags were small and often hard to decipher: official scrawls in pencil indicating the wound and the treatment so far.

John read the tally. "Private Osborne, Captain, lacerations to cheek and ear, possible buried shrapnel. Tetanus, morphia."

"P ward, Hemingby. Next."

Sov led the patient towards the captain; John escorted the wounded Osborne to a bank of VAD women. "This one's for P ward, nurse, please."

"Come on, soldier, this way," she said.

With a steady tramp of boots, the bearers carried stretcher cases in and eased them down to the floor. Gosforth, still at the entry at the far end of the hall, struggled now to direct the arrivals. "Close up the ranks, please. Use all the floor space. Keep moving."

He expected groans, cries of pain. Not a sound, no complaints. Some of the stretcher cases or the severely shocked were beyond it; others looked numb or exhausted, their fallen faces mere blanks. Many of the standing soldiers leant against the newly painted walls, a rub of mud or worse already smearing the whitewash.

He shrugged.

He began moving back to his position with the captain and struggled to pass a man leaning against the wall who had his eyes closed. "Excuse me, old chap."

No response.

He took a different route. Was it really possible to sleep standing up?

"Who's next?" the captain said.

John moved towards a red-haired man who had a muffle of bandage round his jaw but seemed otherwise uninjured.

"Excuse me, soldier," the next man in the line said, "have you got a smoke at all?"

"Sorry, not on me. I don't," John said. He turned back to the muffled man. "Right, come forward to the captain."

"What's his tag say, Hemingby?"

"Rather a scrawl, I'm afraid." John screwed his brow up. "Odo... Odontalgia. Treatment: Oil of Cloves?" He puzzled even further.

"You shouldn't be here, Private," the captain said, "taking up my time. Shouldn't have sent you here. Take yourself over to the nurses, tell 'em your trouble. They'll tell you where to go."

"Yes, sir, thank you, sir." The bandage made the soldier's speech indistinct. But his eyes smiled.

"What was his problem, Captain?"

"Toothache. Bloody scrimshanker managed to work his way out of the front line for a rest. Next?"

John beckoned to the man who'd wanted a cigarette. The man shuffled forward.

"Tag?"

John leaned forward to read the label, tied to a buttonhole on the man's greatcoat. "Complications after boil-lancing."

"What? They should have dealt with this at the aid post. Who sent you here?" The captain glared at the soldier. "Who sent him here?"

"Not signed, I'm afraid," John said.

"Typical! I shall have words to say to that MO when next I see him."

"Oh, sir, please help, I'd tear the dressing off me back meself if I could reach it. It's giving me such gyp." The soldier laid both hands on the captain's arm.

"Right, Hemingby, one for you, I think. Take this soldier to the GP tent, remove his dressing, check the problem, do what's needed and assign him to a ward – Evacuation ward, in all probability."

★ ★ ★

The soldier's back was a greasy barrel, any muscles hidden under pustular flab. His shoulders were rounded and spotty, and a ring of white stomach spilled over the top of his trousers. But he didn't smell. A freshness about him, a pleasing tang of carbolic, probably Lifebuoy Soap.

"Right, tell me what treatment you've had," John said.

"I've had me boil lanced but the doc said to have a bath and a change of clothes before he'd treat me."

"Which came first?"

"Oh, the bath, sir."

"Right, then what?"

"Well, he lanced the boil, mopped up the pus and like, and removed a large core. The sergeant took over, gave it a good swabbing with disinfectant and put a little dressing on with some strips of sticking plaster over it. He said there were a decent hole there, but I should be all right now."

"I see, let me take a look at it. Then what happened?"

"He told me to get dressed, and I put on clean shirt, pants and trousers. And socks."

"Right, brace yourself, I'm going to rip the plasters off. You know what that's like."

"I'd have done it myself in the middle of the night, if I could reach. Ouch!" The man winced.

"Now, let's have a look." The boil still had an angry red rim, the hole raw, pink and... "Oh, dear God, no wonder it's been itching." He peered closer. Nestling in the hole, pale, wriggling and fat, three lice nymphs writhed. "Chats! That's been your trouble, soldier. Three of them."

"Ooh yer bugger."

"Hold still while I dig 'em out."

John used a corner of a piece of lint, flicked the creatures out of the wound and let them fall to the floor. There they waved and struggled. He stamped and ground them with his boot.

"Should have let me use me lighter on them, sir, incineration is all they're good for."

"And it was a clean shirt, you say."

"Yeah, but you know what it's like, they lay their eggs in the seams, I think they enjoy the wash, and when you put the clean shirt on, the buggers hatch 'cos of the heat of your body. S'always happening."

"Right, I'm going to put you in the scabies ward for observation. I shan't dress the wound at present, let some air get to it, and I don't want you to put your shirt back on yet. It's not cold today. Nurse!" He signalled to a VAD nurse. "Take this man to Scabies, would you, please, and disinfect the wound." John scribbled something on the brown tag and handed it to the soldier. "Oh, and you can have that fag now, soldier."

★ ★ ★

Back in the reception hall, he sniffed and instinctively opened a couple of windows he could reach. "Let some fresh air in," he said. Already a run of sweat down his back. He stroked his chin: stubble-growth told him several hours had passed. No wonder he felt hungry.

A feeble hand gripped his ankle. He glanced down at the stretcher close to the wall. Grey tunic and trousers smeared with mud and blood, the fabric over the stomach ripped open and a crude dressing applied to a hidden gash; blood puddling. John knelt down. The man clasped his hand, rolled his eyes upwards and whispered. John put his ear to the man's lips.

The soldier flinched. "*Bitte schön*," he said. "*Wasser*."

John opened his water bottle. He lifted the young soldier's head and trickled water into his mouth. His hand on the soldier's forehead, he detected signs of a temperature. "We'll get to you soon, old chap, don't worry." No time to dredge up the complexities of German grammar. He squeezed the man's hand and left.

★ ★ ★

He found the captain kneeling beside a stocky soldier wearing New Zealand uniform.

"Nasty shrapnel wound to the femur here, Hemingby. Have to work fast. He's in shock, lost a lot of blood."

John squatted down to check the pulse. He glanced at the man's face; his stomach lurched and he felt his eyes widen. Impossible! Not out here.

The young Kiwi soldier opened bleared eyes and twitched a smile. "Watcher, mate!" His voice scarcely a rasp. "Didn't expect it'd be you." He closed his eyes and his head lolled.

"Bearers!" the captain said. Underwood and Wing appeared. "R ward for stabilising, quick as you can."

"May I go with this one, please, Captain?" John said. He stooped to pick up the handles at the rear of the stretcher. "I know him. Rowland Baxter. He's my wife's younger brother. I must make sure he's all right – for her sake."

THIRTY-SIX

"Gently now." John helped Wing ease Row Baxter off the stretcher and onto a bed. John felt the mattress and raised his eyebrows. Warm in four places.

A Red Cross nurse hurried over. "I've just removed the bottles," she said. "It's my job to look after the urn, fill bottles and keep four beds warm at all times. It does help if someone's collapsed or is in shock."

"Yes, thank you, nurse." She reminded him of Helen. Something about the soft eyes.

John leaned over and spoke close to Row's ear. "You'll be OK now, old chap. You're in good hands here." He brushed the hair back off the blanched face and felt his pulse again. Only an irregular fluttering. He tightened his lips.

Row's eyes flickered but did not open. His breathing a mere wheeze. John frowned and looked at the nurse who waited to arrange the blankets over her patient. She laboured at Row's feet, loosening his puttees and the laces on his boots.

A young doctor came up and looked at the tag. He blinked with tiredness. "Second Lieutenant Rowland Baxter, Auckland Infantry, shrapnel wound to right thigh."

"Yes, look after him, won't you, doc? He's my wife's baby brother."

"Is he? Not a Kiwi of long-standing, then. We'll do what we can. By the state of him, considerable blood loss. We'll transfuse him, see if we can't get him ready for surgery."

"Anything you can, doc." John clasped his hands together and bowed his head in a moment's prayer. He caught the doctor's eye again. "Thank you."

★ ★ ★

"Hemingby! Was it you?" Back in the reception area, the major bristled with anger. He struggled up from beside a stretcher case, his knees red from kneeling. "They said it was you."

"What, sir?"

"Opened these windows."

"I did sir, yes. I thought we needed some fresh air, cool the place down."

"What the bloody hell are you playing at? Use your brains, man! It's June. We've enough niffs in here to draw all the flies in Flanders through those windows. Think of the hygiene. Can't have them buzzing round the casualties, can we?"

"No, sir, sorry, sir. Didn't think."

"Yes, well... Shut the bloody things toot sweet and let's get on, or we'll never see this place cleared. They're leaving them in the corridors now. We just have to put up with the heat and everything." The major wiped a trickle of sweat from his cheek. "Now, go and join what's-the-fellow-" He waved his hand towards Gosforth. "And see if you can't shift some of these without waiting for one of us to examine them. Use your initiative, move 'em on." The major knelt again.

"Yes, sir, thank you, sir." John blew out his lips in silent relief. Others had overheard the exchange. Lucky not to be on a charge.

★ ★ ★

He approached the re-suss hut two hours later; he'd eaten nothing since breakfast. Ten hours ago. Maybe he could scrounge a cup of tea and something to eat from one of the nurses – unless bread was short again. But he owed it to Em to keep an eye out for her brother. He prayed Row hadn't taken a turn for the worse. He didn't want to be the first to tell her if...

His heart lurched and he took a deep breath when he saw two bearers emerge from the hut, carrying a covered body on a stretcher. They headed across the school yard away from the medical areas and disappeared. Inside the wooden building, the afternoon heat and the smells of sweat and disinfectant assailed his throat. He glanced round the room for the bed where he had left his brother-in-law.

"John, there you are, mate. Good to see you." Row lay on his side, smoking a cigarette and smiling. They had cut away his trousers, and his wounded thigh, freshly dressed, could now be clearly seen against the sheets, angry with inflammation.

"Good Lord!" John said. "This is amazing!"

"You see, God does work wonders." The padre, a small, bald man, the embers of red hair flickering at the back of his head, smiled and gestured towards the patient as if responsible for this transformation. "If anybody wants me, I'm in reception, seeing what use I can be over there." He bustled away, his jacket folded over one arm.

"Let me shake you by the hand," Row said. He eased himself up onto an elbow, put his cigarette in his mouth and gave John a firm grip. "They say you brought me in here." Strange that he spoke now with a Kiwi accent.

John took his hand. "Two of us did, yes. But this is miraculous. The wonders of blood transfusion! To put it bluntly, I thought –"

"I'd gone West. Yes, I know. Well, it takes more than a jerry bullet to put a good man down. We Baxters are tough buggers, you know. Only I wish they'd drilled me somewhere else. Twice in the same bloody leg is more than rotten luck. They tell me it's surgery this time."

"Yes?" Still not sure what you said to a wounded man. "Maybe it'll be a Blighty this time, or whatever you Anzacs call it."

"Oh, don't say that, mate," Row said. "I don't want to quit when we've just started to beat the bastards. Taken long enough."

John pursed his lips. Something brittle about Row's brightness. An unnatural glitter in the eyes.

"Yeah, blew 'em up and walked all over them. We were up the ridge and in their trenches by six. Never seen such a mess: smashed wood and earth everywhere: duckboards, shuttering, dug-out props all tumbled –"

"And dead Germans, I suppose, poor devils."

"Yeah, of course. They didn't know much about it. But prisoners, too. Lines of 'em marching away. The burying parties'll be busy tonight."

"So, how did you get hit?"

"Do you know, John, mate, I've no idea. Musta been a sniper we didn't flush out. Or a shell burst. I don't know, I was right out of it. Somebody, something got me."

A young VAD nurse came over to John carrying a plate of bread and jam and a beaker of tea. "Here you are, Private. Refreshments to keep you going."

"Oh, capital," John said. "Exactly what I needed. Thank you, nurse. Excuse my manners." He bit deep into the bread and jam, savoured a particularly large strawberry, and soon devoured the two pieces.

"Mind the tea. Don't scald yourself. It's very hot, lots of sugar," the girl said.

"Wonderful, but where did you get china to drink out of?"

"We have our secret stores, you know."

"Hey, sweetheart, what about this wounded soldier?" Row gave a big grin. "He's not the only hungry one. I haven't eaten since four this morning."

"Nothing for you, Lieutenant. Not before surgery. The orderlies will take you to pre-op as soon as our doctor has checked you over."

"Better go back to reception," John said, "move things on there. I can't get over the coincidence of seeing you. When I next write, I'll tell Em I've seen you." He shook Row's hand again.

"Do that, mate. And ask her to pass on my best to Dora and the old man. Not heard from them for ages."

John's stomach lurched. Lord, he doesn't know. His smile felt false. "I will," he said. "Next time I write." Not his place just before the operation to tell him that particular news. "Goodbye, Row, I'll be thinking and praying for you."

★ ★ ★

Back in the fetid heat, the floor seemed no clearer. The junior doctor was working down a line of stretchers. John moved to the casualty he anticipated would be next for assessment. He looked down at the man on the stretcher – a young captain, late twenties, blond hair turning silver at the temples. Didn't seem possible a man's face could be so pale. Grey, almost green. The tag said little: stray bullet in the lung. No mention of treatment, or even which lung. John knelt down to wipe away a dribble of dried blood at the left corner of the man's mouth. At the touch of the cloth, the man gagged, and a spew of dark liquid emerged through the slightly parted lips. The soldier tried to control it by swallowing, but this only caused a gargling choke and coughing. He could scarcely breathe: slight gasps and an unnerving whistle so faint John could hardly hear it.

The young doctor came forward. He did not even read the tag. He knelt down and looked briefly at the soldier's chest. He sighed. "Right, Hemingby, I want you and Feltham to take the captain calmly and with great care straight to the chest ward. See he's cleaned up, made quiet and comfortable, and kept under observation."

John stood up and took a step back. "Yes, sir." He tightened his lips, closed his eyes and bowed his head. He understood this code: no treatment possible.

Across the sprawl of bodies, he caught Feltham's eye and signalled him to come over.

"And when you've done that, report back here to me. I have some particular news for you."

John's stomach leaped. Not bad news? Not a problem at home, surely?

★ ★ ★

214

He hurried across the old playground. What did it mean that a major newly arrived had requested him personally as an orderly? Who knew he was here or where to find him?

The operating theatre had been created out of a low wooden building. A huge hut, it had fly-mesh on the windows and sliding sashes, a felt-covered roof. It looked like one of those Scout huts that had sprung up everywhere at home in the last ten years. But where to get in? A canvas corridor ran from the pre-op tent to one of the entrances. You didn't want to carry patients outside again before their op. So, not that way.

He found a porched doorway at the far end of the building. Inside, a lobby led off. His boots thumped and echoed on the wooden floor. Slow down, let your heart settle.

"Hemingby, is that you?" a voice said. A familiar tone. Where'd he heard it before?

"Yes, sir."

"Join me in here, please."

John went into the ante-room, lit by a single hurricane lamp hanging from the ceiling, and saw a figure tying the strings of a long, surgical gown. He wore a white cotton cap knotted tightly at the back. Only the tufts of grey hair protruding from underneath gave any clue as to identity.

"Good Lord!" John said.

"How are you, old man? Bearing up?" Henshaw smiled and held out his hand.

"I don't believe it. I thought you were in Kent." They shook hands.

"No, I volunteered to come over in response to the call for more surgeons. So I brushed up my skills, they made me up to a major for my pains, and here I am."

"It's excellent to see you. Very good to see a friendly face."

"My sentiments exactly. Now, I've no experience of dealing with cases fresh from the battlefield, and I don't mind admitting to you at least, I'm not feeling too confident."

"I see," John said.

"That's why, if you're willing, I'd like you in theatre as one of the orderlies. Learn the ropes with me. There'll be others, of course. But a friendly face, a reassuring grin that I'm not making a complete arse of myself... I know I can work with you, what do you say?"

"Of course. It'd be an honour – if you don't mind me being totally green in this area."

"Both in at the deep end, then, John," Henshaw said. "Let's hope I remember all the new stuff I learned on the crammer course. This first chap is very much touch-and-go. Now, if you're OK about this, get your togs on." He pointed to a separate cloakroom and began washing his hands.

John pulled on the long white gown over his shirt, tied it at the waist and fitted the surgical cap on his head. "What's the diagnosis, then, sir?" Formalities seemed appropriate now.

"According to the tag, he has a piece of shell and some fragments of helmet that have penetrated his skull. Our job's to dig 'em out. If he's lucky and we're successful in patching him up, he may only be paralysed."

"What's the operation? Tre-something."

"Trephining. Safe enough if you take your time and think what you're doing. But it'll be a long job. At least an hour. We have to make a fresh entry in the skull, look for the debris, and then patch up the damage as best we can. Right, come on. I'll introduce you to the team." Henshaw took a deep breath, then strode in, leading the way.

John looked round the hut. Four operating tables, spaced out in separate areas of the room, each with a surgeon and team at work, everyone focussed on the inert figure on the table before them. Overhead, acetylene lamps gave off white light and heat.

"Good afternoon, ladies and gentlemen, my name is Henshaw. May I introduce Private Hemingby who's here as an observer and to learn the ropes?"

John looked at the team of six clustered around the table. Heavens! Three nurses present. Obviously they don't get easily distressed. He focussed on the patient. Did the poor chap really need to go through all this only to emerge paralysed? Someone down the line decided it was worth a chance. Now, Hubert had to work the miracle.

"Still OK with blood?" Henshaw directed the comment towards John.

"All right, sir, I think. Hardened to it. I've seen enough now not to keel over."

"Good. But, look, this may be different. One or two things could make you feel squeamish. If you do become queasy, it's all right to leave the room. I'll understand. And come back if you want to. Just make sure you're sterile."

"Thank you, sir. I hope I'll stay the course." He picked up a bowl of surgical spirit that a nurse pointed out to him. The sister on the other side of the table glared.

The patient lay on his back, unconscious, his scalp partially shaved. The anaesthetist sat at his head holding a chloroform mask over his nose and mouth and monitoring his condition. The soldier, unaware, snored noisily.

Didn't expect that. I hope he's right out.

Henshaw reached into a special tool case and produced a shiny hand brace with a fine drill bit. "This is for the guide hole," he said. He laid the instrument close to hand and dipped a swab into John's bowl of spirits and carefully wiped an area at the top of the patient's brow. "About here, I think."

John swallowed, felt his fists tighten. Hubert was talking himself through the operation. No reply necessary. The room seemed very hot and John reached up with one hand to wipe his forehead with his sleeve.

"As far as we know, the brain doesn't feel pain," Henshaw said. "Anaesthetising this fellow is only a kindness – more for our benefit than his. Keeps him still." He spoke to the anaesthetist: "Better take the mask away and use the ether now. Give me more room to work."

The sweet, pungent smell wafted up from the table and caught at John's nostrils. He watched the red bead well up round the blade of the scalpel as Henshaw began cutting the skin on the brow. Fascinating, really.

A Red Cross nurse, standing close by on the other side of the table, mopped the blood ooze from time to time and placed the swabs into a bowl held by an orderly at her side.

Henshaw picked up the brace and bit and positioned it carefully. He began turning his hand and arm clockwise, the drill bit slowly penetrating the bone.

The patient snored and gave out a deep groan.

"Oh, Lord," John said.

"Don't worry, he's fine. A good sign. He's still with us. Now, let me clean the area again, nurse, will you?" Henshaw dipped a swab in the methylated spirit and began wiping with careful strokes.

Next, a bright surgical auger. John estimated the cutting edge would take out a disc in the skull about the size of a half crown. Again, the hand made steady turns as if slow-winding a clock. A grinding, a quiet rasp rose up like someone filing their nails.

The room began to sway and blur. The smell of the disinfectant and the ether made John's head swim. "Sorry, have got to..." He laid the bowl on a nearby table, gulped and stumbled towards the door.

Outside, the sun had already set and a distant blackbird fluted goodbye to the day. Another world. He bent forward and rested his hands on his knees, breathing deeply. Did he feel sick, or just hungry? In the changing room lobby, he found his water bottle, took a long drink. "Now, come on, don't let him down, pull yourself together." He washed his hands and returned inside, aware of the barrier of heat, picked up his bowl again.

The patient, still unconscious, snored and groaned as if having an earnest conversation in grunts. Immensely unnerving. John tried to make out words from the inflected noises. Just nonsense.

The removal of the disc of bone sent him queasy again. Not a time to be sick. He hurried away once more and gulped the evening air. Another drink of water, itself now warm. Cross with himself now: "Come on, Hemingby, hang on, you can do it. The lad's in good hands."

Back in the circle of white glare, he picked up the bowl once more. "Sorry."

"Don't worry," a young nurse said. "You'll get hardened to it. It's like this for all of us at first."

The sister sniffed and cleared her throat. The nurse stepped back into the shadows.

Henshaw leaned over a dark cavity in the patient's brow. He picked up pointed forceps and probed cautiously inside. A tense pause. "Got you, you blighter!" He plucked some fragment from inside. A reassuring clatter of metal hitting the enamel bowl. "That's something. Helmet, probably. Any more? Bring that lantern closer, please." He peered at the opening from a different angle. "Ah!" Another rattle into the enamel bowl. "Now, any sign of shell casing? Closer, please, bring that lamp right by my head. Don't worry. I'll make sure it doesn't burn me."

One of the other orderlies held the lamp close in and Henshaw probed the cavity once more. "No, nothing there. Ah!" Another clatter. "That should make a difference. Take the pressure off. But I think that's all we shall manage to get. So if we're all agreed, let's put him back together again."

John thought of Humpty Dumpty and felt ashamed.

Very quickly, the fragments of bone were replaced, the flaps of skin sewn back and the patient tight-turbaned in a huge bandage. Henshaw gave an injection to help the man sleep.

John sighed and smiled. But would the man wake up paralysed?

"Right, we're done." Already, bearers were carrying the man off to the recovery ward. Henshaw took off his gloves, lifted up his surgical gown and searched in his trouser pockets for his watch. "Hour and a half," he said. "Longer than I thought. Longer than I'd like. Now, who's next?"

John smiled again; Hubert still saw patients as people, not another job.

"Next is a gunner with a fractured jaw, Major," the Red Cross sister said. "Not a wound, as such."

"Now, how the devil's that happened?" Henshaw said.

"Must have been firing in quick succession, sir," an orderly said. John knew him only by sight. "The gunners is so keen to get another shell up the spout that they hurry with the next round, and forget about the recoil. We see a lot of it. The man gets his head in the way and gets his jaw well smashed for his pains."

"I see. Poor devil. Well, let's see if we can find a way of wiring and pinning him so it can heal." Henshaw stretched and arched his back. "Getting weary, John? It's all this standing, isn't it?" He put on a fresh pair of gloves and set to work again.

"I'm all right, sir. I'll see it through."

★ ★ ★

John steeled himself for the next patient: Row Baxter, drowsy from pre-op morphine. The anaesthetist began work with chloroform immediately. Henshaw began to unwind the dressing on Row's thigh. He removed the binding and the pad that straddled the shrapnel slash. He picked up the most recent bandages, already soiled with blood and yellow ooze, and thrust them towards an orderly holding an enamel bowl, who hurried away to dispose of them.

John looked now at the leg. The area around the wound glowed in an angry oval flare spreading up the thigh from just above the knee. The wound itself resembled a neat half-moon slash of swollen flesh attached to the leg, yet somehow sitting separate and above it. Like a chicken breast, he thought. He immediately hated himself. "Is he going to be all right, sir?"

"It's what's underneath that worries me. Swab, please." Henshaw held out a hand towards John. With care, he lifted the flap of flesh and clipped it back in order to work deeper inside.

John had not expected the bone to be visible or such a shocking white. The fact of it seemed immediately obvious, but he swung away, feeling himself go tense and weak behind the knees. He made himself watch Henshaw lift out a scrap of khaki cloth which dangled from a pair of forceps.

"All this gravel and filth that's been forced in," Henshaw said. "What a disgusting weapon shrapnel is! So indiscriminate. Some of this stuff's embedded. I doubt we'll ever get it all out."

"What about the bone, sir?"

"Shattered in two or three places by the look of things. Splintered, too. I must say I can't see this ever knitting properly. And I don't like the look of this artery. Even if we could sew the wound up and splint the leg correctly, I imagine it'd feel like walking with broken glass grinding inside. Poor fellow! Hmm." Henshaw lapsed into silence. "No, the kindest thing would be to remove the leg. Have done with it."

"You'd do that now, would you? Straightaway?" He hadn't prepared for this. "Where would you make the –" John could not say the word.

"About here." Henshaw touched a point high on the white flesh of Row's thigh. "We must get completely clear of the infection and the inflammation. Yes, amputation would be kindest and simplest. Now, are you able to cope with watching this, him being a relative and all? Tourniquet, please, sister." He held out his hand.

"I'll give it a go, sir. I hope I don't let you down." He closed his eyes and bit his lip. Now what am I to tell Em?

★ ★ ★

Glazed eyes. Looking, facing the table, trying not to watch. Wanting to convince himself that the body on the table was not someone he knew. The strap of the tourniquet tightened round the upper thigh until it almost cut the flesh; he heard Row's peaceful breathing, felt his own palms grow sweaty, smelt the cocktail of ether, acetylene, sweat – even, somewhere, a linger of tobacco, and the taste of bitter bile that scoured the back of his throat.

221

When that time came and Hubert picked up the saw, he closed his eyes, bowed his head and clutched his hands tightly to contain his fear and quell the tears. But he could not block out the steady grate and rasp of those metal teeth, that smell that lingered. Did not dare think about what was occurring. Bones – *stronger than concrete.* Not this one. Dear God...

Silence.

"Let's have that piece of cloth now." Hubert's voice. "Wrap it carefully. Can you manage? Do you know where it is you go?" Quiet reverential comments. Like being present at communion. Or a sacrifice.

He opened his eyes: an orderly, a drooping burden over his outstretched arms, already in the outer gloom of the hut, nearing the exit. John sighed in relief, glad to be excused that particular duty.

Hubert, relaxed again now, talked to his team: "What we have to do here... The really important part is to judge how much muscle to leave to cushion the end of the femur. This poor chap won't want the bone pressing directly on his skin. Could be agony. Now, what do you think, sister? This much?"

"That's about right, sir," she said.

"Then let's make the stump rounded and comfy for him." Henshaw began work again.

John closed his eyes again, assaulted by memories now of that childhood shop, the wooden block, the brawn-armed man, the chop and slap of knife, the thump of meat, the hammering whack of the cleaver between the bones, the busy saw, and always under foot the sawdust he stirred with his toe, or churned and piled, trying to bury under clean white heaps the brown-stained clags, drips and splashes from that butcher's table.

"Right, I think we're ready for sutures."

Safe to look again. The sister beckoned into the darkness and two stretcher-bearers readied themselves. The nurse began wrapping the stump in bandages; Hubert gave Row an injection; two orderlies stood by, ready to swab and scrub the table.

The tension eased.

The bearers lifted him away – a subdued procession to the recovery ward.

"Right, who's next?" Henshaw said.

Evening raced on into night: two more amputations – another leg, a shattered arm; the removal of a damaged eye; several extractions of bullets in the leg, the shoulder, the arms; stomach surgery – the work seemed interminable. Their table was the last to finish. John noticed how one by one the lights were extinguished over the other tables until their team worked alone. A pool of light in the surrounding darkness and silence.

Henshaw consulted his watch again as the last casualty was removed. "Four AM. Thank you very much everybody. Well done. Your support has been invaluable."

The orderlies began scrubbing again; the nurses removed the operating instruments and dropped them into a lidded tank of boiling water; John poured his bowl of spirits into an enamel bucket for disposal.

Henshaw puffed out his lips and his grey moustache fluttered. "Oh, Lord, I'm weary! How many ops have we done, John? I've lost count."

"I'm not sure, sir. Ten, at least, I'd say. Perhaps twelve." He couldn't think, didn't much care, he felt so tired. They were alone now.

"Not the fastest, then. They've told me they expect me to cover fifteen to twenty cases in a twelve-hour rush. Could do better, as you schoolmasters might say. But I have to say you've coped well."

"I'm sorry about my exits earlier."

"Think nothing of it. We all get queasy. You stayed the course; you stuck it out. That's the important thing." He pointed towards the windows. "Look at the strange light coming in now."

"Dawn, I'm afraid," John said. "Do you know I've been busy for twenty-five hours since the explosions first woke me."

"Me, too, if you count my travelling. I'm done in. And there'll be other days like it, I'm afraid, old chap, now we're so close to the

Front. Bit of a lull tomorrow, we hope. Now, off you go and get your head down." He patted John's shoulder.

"I could sleep where I drop, I think. It's reveillé in two hours."

★ ★ ★

In the green light of the recovery tent, he peered to make out faces. The sun not yet high enough to assault the tent and stifle the air with light and heat.

He counted the beds. "Twenty-five either side. But which one's Row?" He yawned, stretching his mouth. He had enjoyed his breakfast, but, in spite of the sweet tea, a headache and tired eyes told him he lacked sleep.

"Lieutenant Rowland Baxter, please, nurse. He's one of the Anzacs. Can you tell me where he is, please?"

"To be sure," she said, "we've put him in the quiet corner, where the afternoon sun leaves a little shade." Red hair, Irish lilt. "He seemed very poorly in the night. Very weak pulse. Rambling – a bit delirious."

"All right if I go and check on him? He's my brother-in-law."

"Yes, but don't tire him, will you? He needs the rest. Major Henshaw gave him a sedative earlier."

"Good heavens! He's on duty early."

"I don't think he's been to his billet. He started on his rounds about five o'clock."

"What, straight from operating? Amazing! Don't know where he gets his stamina from. I'm bushed this morning."

★ ★ ★

Row lay on his back, eyes open, staring at the sag of canvas above his head. A metal cage in the middle of the bed kept the coverings off his legs.

"How are you feeling, old chap?" John bent over the bed. Amazing blue eyes, brighter even than Em's.

The eyes crinkled, the lips moved but no words came out.

"You've had a tough time," John said, "but you're through it now. What with all this rush, I still haven't had a chance to tell the folks back in Blighty..." He balked at saying anything about the old man. "But I will as soon as I get time. Now, would you like me to inform anyone back in New Zealand? A sweetheart, perhaps?"

Row gave a faint smile and raised a finger off the sheet.

"Yes? Details amongst your papers. I'll do that. Soon as I can. Don't you worry. Just put your mind to getting..." He managed to stop himself saying, *back on your feet again*. "...fit and strong. I'll come and see you next time I'm off duty."

Row slid his hand across the sheets and grasped John's hand in silence. No grip at all. The eyes, gazing directly at him, softened and Row let them drift shut.

"Cheer-oh, old chap. Back soon," John said. He tiptoed away. Now, what about the trephining case? Is he anywhere here? He looked around and was about to ask the nurse if she had seen the soldier, when he saw a man with a bandaged head sitting on a chair at the foot of his bunk. He was reading *Punch*, smiling and holding the paper up in both hands. "Good Lord," John said to himself, and smiled. "Not paralysed at all." He hurried over to speak to the man. "How are you this morning, soldier? Good to see you up and out of bed, I was on your case last night."

"Bit of a headache, that's all," the man said. "Not surprisin' really, but the bloke, the doc, who sorted me out oughter get a medal. I'm feeling right as ninepence."

"You may see him on his rounds later: Major Henshaw. He's a good doctor. He cares. Better go. Mustn't be late for parade. Really good to see your recovery."

As he hurried off, he felt an inner glow as if association with Hubert had brought purpose into his life.

★ ★ ★

225

"Atherstone, Feltham, Hemingby, Poundsbury." The four men stepped forward. "You four are detailed off for the morning burying party. On the word, you will go to the stores and collect one pick and one shovel, and proceed with Corporal Osborne to Number Two field on the northbound road and there begin opening a new burial ground for the station's casualties. Any queries as to procedure to Corporal Osborne."

"Yes, Sarge."

★ ★ ★

Across the playground, three incinerators crackled and flared. Close by, two orderlies stoked and raked the remains of bandages, dressings, torn clothing.

"Awful smell," Sov said. "Catches the back of my throat. What's causing that, then?"

"Blood," he said, "soaked-in blood and what not else, I should imagine."

One of the orderlies plunged a swab in soiled methylated spirits and dripped it across to the fire. It immediately caught and the flames leaped and roared upwards.

"He wants to watch hisself," Sov said. "He'll have his eyebrows off doing that. Daft bugger." He pointed. "Now, is that the building where we got to go?"

"Could be. Corporal said the one on its own on the north side of the school. Well, that must be the one because it's in the shade."

The outbuilding stood squat and dilapidated. The mortar between the flaking bricks had decayed, and some of the pantiles had slipped, leaving holes where roof lathes showed through. A bird darted out.

"Well, I'll be danged!" Sov said. "There's a swallow nestin'. He ain't bothered, is he?"

"Now, we have to check that all dog tags and papers have been removed, and any other possessions that may have been missed."

226

Sov was not listening. "Typical British Army!" he said. "'Crepit ole building, but spanking new doors." He fell silent at the sight of a two-wheeled handcart, leaning against the side wall of the building. "Is that what we got to use, Smiler?"

"Seems so."

"And what are we s'posed to cover en with? I hope there's a tar-paulian, else some sacking."

"Pray their eyes are closed. It's one of my nightmares seeing a corpse like that. I've seen men go many times, but never when the spirit has definitely left, and it's just the old body." He straightened up, took a deep breath. "Anyway, let's do it. Mustn't keep the padre waiting."

The double doors scraped on the cobbles as they heaved them open. A strange waft assaulted them: disinfectant, damp stone, human waste, blood, and the sweet smell of decay.

"Oh, dear God!" John clenched his eyes and held onto Sov's shoulder. "I didn't think it'd be like this."

Lines of corpses, uniformed but unwrapped, side by side in rows, stretching into the damp darkness. One corpse, laid out below the swallow's nest, had a spat of bird mess on his forehead like a third eye.

John bobbed down and scrubbed it away with a piece of rag. The brow was ice-cold, waxy. He stood up and bowed his head.

"And have we got to deal with these and all, Smiler?" Sov pointed to a tumble of amputated legs and arms at the far end of the left-hand row. A glimpse of a severed hand clutching an amputated foot; raw flesh, white bone protruding; all of the limbs with streaks and runs of blood, a few with foot or ankle turning black.

John tightened his fists and held his breath. "Dear God, no..." He shut his eyes again, his voice a whisper. "Oh, Sov, we're just attendants in a slaughterhouse. We give animals more dignity in death than this." He rushed out of the building and vomited.

THIRTY-SEVEN

He slipped away from the camp, hoping no one saw him. The idea of talking to anyone, even Sov, appalled him. Idle chatter, passing the time, seemed obscene after all he'd witnessed. Now, if he'd remembered his violin... Its absence ached within him as if he'd left behind part of himself.

Downland now, partially cultivated. You wouldn't call these hills, not the kind Gurney yearned for, just an area where ridges tailed off towards flatlands. But a place untouched by war, too low to be of strategic value, high enough to look back over the little town, the camp, the Clearing Station. Peaceful, beautiful here, if only you could block out memories of blood and pain inside the tents and huts.

Far away, the thump and rumble of guns. Softening up the enemy before another attack. More casualties, more operations. Could he really cope with close-range medical work? Last night, he'd struggled. Perhaps he was being tested. Where was The Lord's purpose in all this? Was pain and horror human folly – or part of God's plan? Did He want to destroy mankind again, like a second flood? There must be some overall scheme beyond what the generals planned.

Against his legs, he felt the riffle and pluck of long grass, already heavy with seed. The sound of a lark. One overhead, drizzling song, too high already to be seen against the blue. Lark rise, rural peace, nature carrying on as usual. The bird's song dreamed above the world of destruction and anguish below. A second bird, further away, joined the challenge, swizzling sound over the countryside. Nearer to God than he'd ever be.

With a sigh, he sank down on the grass and lay back. Flowers crowded round, tickled and touched him: white daisies, poppies shaking their heads against the sway and tug of the breeze, even marigolds thrusting stars of colour out to the world. He pulled a stem of grass, put it between his lips, sucked the green spear. Could he cope? Was he just tired? How would he know if he was cracking up?

He'd gathered a hasty picnic: some soft cheese crammed into a baguette from one of the *estaminets*, a bottle of red wine, a borrowed tumbler. Selfish to drink alone, but even Sov's cheerful, accepting silence would intrude. He flung the grass away, poured himself a glass of wine and drank it down. He gasped aloud, rummaged in his breast pocket for Em's letter. News from home at last. He'd saved it specially.

My dear John,
I do hope you are keeping well, it has been such a long time since we heard from you. You gave us all a nasty scare when your violin appeared unannounced and unexpected. Dorothy was particularly upset and feared the worst. She slept quite badly for several nights, but settled down when I explained how no news of you could be good news. But I do think you might have sent some word of how you were and what happened.

He looked up; lark-sound still drilling the air. "Oh, for heaven's sake, Em, things have to be just so for you, don't they? Is this a slap on the wrist? I'll take your rebuke, then, but if only you knew..." His head still ached.

The children are growing up fast. Dorothy has asked if she can have piano lessons for her birthday present. I've told her we'll see. In any case, she'd have to use Daphne's piano downstairs. She has the notion of playing duets with you when you come home. She doesn't understand it will take a lot of practice.

He looked out over the flat plain below, shook his head: "Nine years old already, Dolly Daydream!" His voice a murmur. "Childhood slipping away! We'll hardly know each other. But I wish Mama was kinder. *We'll see!* What kind of answer is that to give a child?" He took a bite of the baguette. "Anyone would think she's jealous of you." He picked up the letter again.

You'll be surprised to learn that Rowley begins school in September, even though he's still only four. But he's ready for it and they have room. Everyone tells me how bright he is. He already reads quite well. I sometimes think all his growing has gone into his brains. Physically, he's still very small. Perhaps he'll grow up stocky, like his namesake.

"Now, if ever there was someone's favourite... Mama's little professor! Let's hope your stature doesn't come from our side – Perce, for example. Or his nature, come to that!" He sighed. Have to say something about Row... Write tonight, perhaps. But how to put it?

He shook his head, turned back to the letter.

Bea is walking well now and has taken to fussing over Daphne's old terrier downstairs. She cuddles and talks more to that dog than she ever does to her family. She's a very good child, placid and very biddable. No trouble.

My next child is due in mid-October –

"*Your* next child! Don't I have any part now?"

– so the doctor thinks. He says I must keep my strength up and has prescribed some dreadful-tasting tonic to ensure I stay healthy. It would be nice to have another boy. That would be ideal – two of each. Quite enough! I think the days of big families should be a thing of the past.

He looked at a daisy nodding in the breeze. He began his own nodding. Message received! No more children. Now did that mean no more... He snorted. Away from England only six months. Already she talked as if life went on without him. Oh, Lord, how can I have a marriage and see my children grow up at this distance?

I cannot imagine what life is like out there. I read the papers, but it's not the same. Perhaps you can tell us something of your work.

The sound of a saw cutting through bone. Would you want to know, Em, would you really want to know?

I hope you know you are in our thoughts. Keep well.
With my love, Emma.

"She's cross with me, that's what it is. Sitting on her feelings. Not letting me in. Oh, Em, I could have done with a little more warmth! Today of all days. I'm tired, desperately tired, I've got the hump, and you write like that."

He poured another glass of wine.

★ ★ ★

The tickling woke him and, eyes still shut, he brushed his face with his hand. But the torment continued, up his arms, around his neck. Lice, he decided, still drowsy. Now, where did I pick them up? He sat forward and began wiping his face and neck, rubbing his arms. Couldn't be lice, they preferred crevices, not the open. A ladybird, a field spider, ants or even the grass itself, perhaps. His face felt hot, his mouth stale, metallic; the sun had shifted westwards; he'd had a deep, healing sleep.

He listened for the larks. Nothing. Overhead now, sounds made by man: a spotter plane, its engine close to stall, puttered and burbled from behind the ridge. John looked up. I'm a sitting target here. Hope he's not armed.

He decided not to run. The bi-plane flew over, banking in a wide circle above the town, and came back towards the ridge. Not one of ours. He could distinctly see the German cross on the side. Two men aboard, pilot and photographer probably, their heads like two footballs protruding from the body of the plane. "Now what are you after?"

The plane turned behind him once more and with an urgent drone, followed the same curving pattern over the town, banked and returned. In a chattering roar, it flew straight above his head and over the crest behind him.

Silence settled. In the distance, a strange screeching swelled from the valley road below: clanking, squeaking like some huge ship's chain grating on a quayside. A rhythmic drumming of powerful engines, great fists of black smoke punched into the air.

He recognised what they were but had never seen one. Now, five in file proceeded at walking pace along the road, roaring, clattering, squealing, as if they needed lubrication. Alongside the machines, a few soldiers idled. They walked like off-duty guards, freed from the rigours of an inspection.

But the earth-coloured vehicles needed no protection. Metal plating tougher than a London bus or tram, he guessed, they looked like blind armoured tortoises grinding forward. He'd never seen anything so bulky or noisy on land before.

With a lurch, the leading contraption shifted direction, as a man might turn on his heel, left the road and began ramping up the slope of the ridge. It did not swerve to avoid a hawthorn bush in its path, but bent and crushed it as someone might squash a beetle, leaving it flattened in its wake. The other machines also heaved off the road.

The train of monsters would pass within fifty yards. Already he could see two cannons jutting from the side of the leading juggernaut. A mobile gun battery! Machine guns on the third and fourth monsters protruded from the flanks like spikes.

An abandoned shepherd's hut, part brick, part wood, stood in the path of the machines. The first tank reared up like a dog on its hind legs ready to pounce on its prey, overwhelmed and smashed the structure as if crushing paper. The others followed.

"Dear God," he said aloud, "who'd face one of those? They're unstoppable."

★ ★ ★

My dear Em,

Thank you very much for your letter – very welcome, I assure you. I'm sorry my silence caused such distress. Sometimes we have such a rush on that it isn't possible to keep up even basic correspondence. I miss the old fiddle very much since I find music-making good for the soul, but sadly it isn't practical here.

We have moved much nearer the Front. We're not *at* the Front as such, so don't worry, we're not in immediate danger. But we do have to cope with casualties almost straight from the battlefield.

I'm very sorry to have to tell you that Row was brought in after one battle – I cannot tell you where – so badly wounded in the leg that it needed amputation. The war is over for him, I'm afraid. He so wanted to finish the job. But he is young and fit and should recover well.

I'm glad to hear about our Rowley. Bright children need stimulation. Early schooling will do him good. If you can, will you please teach him The Lord's Prayer before he goes? I should like to think he has those words by heart. Either that or Psalm 23 – it can be such a comfort.

I shall try to write soon, but again it may be difficult. Two of us have been detailed off to go to another base – again, I can't tell you where – in order to collect new vehicles for use at the Front.

There may be no news for a while, but be sure you are all in my heart and thoughts always, as I hope I am in yours.

With much love

JFH.

He closed his eyes. "Oh Lord Jesus," he whispered, "keep us all safe, I pray, until we meet again." He tugged at his moustache. Neither the letter nor the prayer had eased the dreadful pain and doubt within.

THIRTY-EIGHT

A circle of women seated near the door, the smoke hanging blue and oppressive around the lamps. The smell of tobacco, bodies, meat cooking, hot bread and cheap perfume assaulted his senses. Loud chatter, the clink of glasses, the click of dominoes; a burst of laughter from the corner, near the piano.

"You can tell the British are in, can't you?" he said. "Now, what'll you drink, Sov?"

"Well, seeing as we're back in France, Smiler, I'll have some ving blong. You going to join me?"

"No, I'll have my usual. So, white for you, red for me." He tried catching the eye of a waiter who hurried past. Trickles of sweat had started down the man's cheeks.

"Well, make sure they don't shark you," Sov said. "You know what these bloody frog-eaters are like, more keen on food and money than they are on fightin'. Judgin' by what we heard."

"Ssh! Keep your voice down. They're still our allies. We don't want trouble."

Someone began playing the piano and singing: *In Dublin's fair city, where the girls are so pretty, I first set my eyes on sweet Molly Malone."*

"Odd, hearing one of our folksongs over here, so far from home. Nice, though," John said. "Fellow's got a good voice, I'll grant him that." He managed to catch the arm of another waiter and ordered two demi-carafes of wine.

"Alive, alive o! Alive, alive o! Crying cockles and mussels alive, alive o!" A smiling, shouting chorus – the whole platoon, it seemed.

Sov craned his neck, trying to make out who was singing. "Hey, Smiler, look here, isn't that the private you got pally with back at Base? You know, what's his name – Barney, Barnard?" His face lit up. "Gurney – that's the fellow. Tall bloke, glasses, sitting at the piano. Life and soul by the sound of it. Singing at the top of his voice."

"Gurney – here? Let me see." The two edged their way between the tables to the tangle of British soldiers. All had glasses of beer or white wine. Holding a tray above the heads, a waiter swayed through the group, came to where the two stood and began unloading wine and glasses onto a nearby shelf.

John paid him and gestured to Sov. The music stopped abruptly; the singing died.

"Well, blister my kidneys." The pianist looked in their direction. He smiled broadly. "If it isn't the Fiddler of Rouen. What brings you here?" The eyes alive behind the spectacles. A tense fire-glow about him.

"Ivor," John said, "how are you? You seem in excellent spirits. I can't believe it." They shook hands and he introduced Sov.

"Very good to meet you, my dear chap. Everything's capital, a lot going on." He tapped the side of his head. "I've got such ideas..."

"You certainly sound in good voice. What are you doing here?"

"The Glosters are on rest. Not much of that, though. They keep finding us drills and fatigues. Latest thing is practising saluting."

"Don't I know it?" John said. "But that's the army for you. We're lucky. We've been detailed to pick up a motor ambulance and cycle. So we've two days' break."

"Hey, Gurney!" A soldier interrupted the conversation. "We're going to play boules. Are you in?"

"No, count me out this time, Thorpey, I'm talking to my friend here."

Sov brightened up. "Can I join in? Make up a team?" He picked up his carafe and his glass.

"Why not, soldier? Any good at lobbing? It's good bombing practice." The men bundled out of a door at the back. The noise seeped away.

"They think I'm mad, you know," Gurney said. "Call me Prof.

Things like that. But they tolerate me. Used to be called Batty when I was a nipper."

"You're certainly much brighter than when I last saw you. What is it, a month, six weeks? Dramatic change. Quite in the swim now. How's the shoulder?"

"Oh, well enough. Twinges in wet weather. But I can ride it. Would you believe I'm our platoon's crack shot? Wouldn't think so, would you, not with these peepers?" Gurney adjusted his spectacles. "But, on form, I can get off twenty-five aimed rounds per minute. They used to time me. Still, suits me. If I have to down a Boche, I prefer it that way. I've never really reconciled myself to the thought of sticking a man."

"I don't know how you can bring yourself to any of it. If it was me..."

A sudden energetic gesture. "Now, have you brought your fiddle with you?"

"'Fraid not. The last time I played, it was with you. Abandoned it. We left Rouen in such a rush."

"Pity. We could've tried out some of my ideas."

"Tell me about your work. What's happening there?"

"Well, Sidgwicks have finally said they'll publish my poems."

"Excellent news."

"But it's my music I'm interested in. I'm working on two symphonies, you know, and there's a big choral work hammering away which won't leave me alone. It'll be magnificent, I know it." He took a sip from his cup, signalled a waiter, his foot jiggling with suppressed energy. "Something new, that gets away from all that German-influenced rubbish."

"Have you got it down? Perhaps I could look at it before we set off."

Gurney leaned forward, voice confidential: "I've developed special powers, you know."

"Oh, yes?"

"Helps with composing. I often talk to Old Ludwig."

"Sorry, how do you mean?"

"Beethoven, of course. I discuss things with him. When I'm

falling asleep. Bach's there sometimes. But I don't think he cares for me. And Schumann, he comes too, but I'm not keen on him. Queer in the head towards the end, you know."

"All Germans, then, Ivor?" John smiled but Gurney didn't see the irony.

Gurney began pacing up and down. "Do you know, they're transferring me to a Machine Gun Corps, so I can really pepper the Hun?"

John drank his wine, bit his lip and said nothing. Oh, Lord, I hope the poor fellow isn't cracking up.

★ ★ ★

They leaned planks at the back of the ambulance and managed to haul the motorcycle inside. Best not try riding it.

"Now, keep hold, kick the rear stand down, then rock him back onto it. Go on, don't be afraid." Sov watched as John wrestled with the machine. Eventually, it stood free and stable inside.

"It's heavier than you think. Not exactly a bicycle, is it? Now, shall I drive first?" John said.

Sov moved to the front of the ambulance and bent down to the crank handle. "I hope her don't kick back," he said. "Ready?" With a jerk of his arm, he laboured to wind the handle and surprise the engine into life.

After several turns, the engine faltered into an irregular rhythm. John adjusted various levers on the steering column until the engine took on the chatter of a machine gun.

"All aboard, here we go!" John grinned and sounded the horn. Its mechanical belch echoed across the parade ground. He pushed the brake lever forward and the vehicle lurched onto the road. "Thank goodness we haven't got any hills between here and Plug Street. I'm still not sure about double-declutching."

★ ★ ★

"Rum old boy, en'e?" Sov said after several miles.

"Who?"

"That Gurney. I reckon he'd had a skinful afore we showed up last night. Singin' his heart out and shoutin' like that."

John watched the road ahead. "That's the funny thing. He hadn't been drinking – nothing except coffee, as far as I could see. But I know what you mean, all that energy and excitement. Tiring to be with."

"Last time we saw en, he were down in the dumps, wouldn't talk to nobody. Now chatterin' away like a monkey as if a pendulum's swung t'other way."

"I agree," John said, "strange character, he was pleased to see me but I couldn't get through to him. Not like you and I talking. Different somehow, eccentric."

"You mean something not quite right?" Sov screwed his forefinger into the side of his forehead.

"I trust not, poor chap. He's very talented and interesting. I hope he comes through. He's got a lot to give the world of music. Poetry, too."

★ ★ ★

The young nurse in the recovery tent reminded him of someone: dark hair piled under a cap, long slender fingers. Not much more than eighteen. Something about the eyes, too.

"Excuse me," he said, "Lieutenant Rowland Baxter – where can I find him?"

"I will look, Monsieur. Ward records. A moment, please." French, then. She had all the soft charm, the pliable grace of Mademoiselle who played the piano in their duets.

That other world, three years ago.

"*Alors, parlons-nous francais,*" he said when she returned. Not Mamselle, though, she'd be in her twenties now, probably married. But something...

She seemed relieved. "Oh, thank you. I am new here since weekend. I am not speaking English very well. You know French, Monsieur?"

"I used to teach it. Before the war. So Lieutenant Baxter, where is he? His bed was over there. Have they transferred him, sent him home?"

"Ah, no, Monsieur. I regret, I believe he is dead." She gazed steadily at him. "He is not here."

"Dead? He can't be. He was only twenty-three, strong, fit. What happened?"

"It say he was weak from loss of blood –"

"In spite of the transfusion?"

"Yes. But he did not recover; he remained weak, sad as if he didn't want to get better."

He closed his eyes and shook his head. "Some kind of post-operative shock, then."

"We tried everything, even sent him back to the re-suss. He took two days to die and kept whispering 'Mother, Mother' as if waiting for her. It upset me."

"But that's impossible. He would have known she's already dead..."

"Ah, Monsieur, they say the mind of the dying is very strange, they believe things which are not real. He liked someone sitting with him, I think, that one. I did when I could but we are so busy. Sometimes I sit on the bed, sometimes on a chair. He knew a woman was there. I held his hand, stroked it – always cold." She wiped away a tear. "I am so new. It is the first time for me... I think he was Baxter."

"Poor Row," he said in English. He remembered the brittle laughter, the boasting in the re-suss ward.

Should have known...

"And I thought – I don't know why – this soldier is waiting for his maman to kiss him goodnight or goodbye. That is why I... I held his hand and kissed him. Not like I... I kiss his cheek and then his brow. 'Good night, my dear boy,' I said. He sighed and seemed to relax, to let go. After that, he slip away." She dabbed at her eyes. "I'm sorry, Monsieur. That poor soldier. I will never forget him."

He bowed his head, hardly aware of the nurse crossing herself. All that brightness lost. "Oh Lord, will this slaughter never end?" Now what am I going to tell Em?

But he hadn't been detailed for the burying party. That was something. How would he feel if he had to bury someone he knew?

THIRTY-NINE

Henshaw sent for him a few days later. John's stomach gave a lurch as if the headmaster had summoned him. What had he done wrong? More bad news? The door of the tiny room stood open, a smell of pipe tobacco seeping out. John coughed, decided to stand to attention.

On the far side of the desk, Henshaw, in full uniform, gazed out of the window. He turned round, smiled. "No, no, no. At ease, John. Nothing formal. But you might call this a serious conversation."

Still a desk between them. No chairs.

Is this an interview? he wondered. "I hope I haven't done anything wrong." Hubert had not waxed his moustache into fine points and the tufts of hair at the sides of his domed head curled and tumbled at will.

"Don't be silly. Far from it. The fact is... You must have heard by now that there's another push coming. The general wants to get the Boche on the run again while the going's good. Now, the CCS isn't shifting from here. It's a good metalled road to the Front, so the CO thinks it won't harm to stretch the communication line by using motor ambulances to get casualties back. In relays, if necessary." He paused and eyed John. "The fact is I've volunteered to be MO at the Front and set up the ADS. Some bloody unpronounceable place. Doesn't matter. I feel I'll be more use there. As you've probably realised, I'm not a very good sawbones – too damn slow for a start – just following my training and reasonably competent. But it's not a job I enjoy."

John pursed his lips, tensed himself against a shudder. As if anyone could...

"Some surgeons take immense pride in their work. Not me. I'd

242

rather not. But I'll still have to take my turn in due course."

John gripped the fingers of his left hand tightly behind his back.

"Now, I don't want you to say yes, just because I ask. But I need someone I know, and can work with. You qualify on both counts. I'd trust you with my life, too."

John looked down at the floor. So, finally, up at the Front. He swallowed. He'd wanted Hubert to choose him, but... "Thank you, sir. You can count me in. I'll come with you. I pray I'm good enough and don't make a mess of things."

"Don't be silly. I hoped you'd say yes. That's good. Now, I want you to go away and have a think. You know your fellow orderlies better than I do. I'm still new around the place. I shall follow recommendations from the mess and pick the sergeant for the Dressing Station myself, but I want you... We'll need at least thirty-two bearers – that's eight teams, plus some other odds and sods. And I'd particularly like you to choose a nursing orderly for those casualties we have to retain. So, who can you work with, who would you choose? More importantly, is there anyone you'd leave out? Up there, we'll all have to work together as a close-knit team."

He immediately thought of Sov. Have to include him. Thirty more names to go.

Henshaw opened a drawer in the desk and took out two glasses and a small bottle of whisky. "Close the door, would you? Let's drink to it. I guess you've realised I want you to lead the team. So, with that in mind, I've put things in motion to have you made up to corporal. I trust that's in order."

John lowered his eyes. Did he really want promotion and the responsibility that went with it? "Thank you, sir, it'll be an honour." He shut the door.

Henshaw held out a glass with a generous finger of whisky in it. "Good health, John, here's to you."

"Thank you, and to you, Hubert. I pray I don't let you down." He took a large swallow of the fiery liquid.

"Now, tomorrow I want you to set off in our new motor

ambulance and get up to –" He peered at his notebook. "To Poelemarck early. Certainly before the artillery's on the road, otherwise you'll never get through. And have your chum Poundsbury ride the motor bicycle up there. You never know when we shall need a runner."

The setting sun rounded the corner of the main building and cast deep red through the window. Light flashed and glinted on the bottle of Haig whisky like a lighthouse warning of danger.

★ ★ ★

From the far end of the village, the boy trundled the huge wheelbarrow towards him, its axle squealing. He staggered, head down, shoulders hunched, tongue protruding in utter concentration. A heap of items covered in black cloth which formed his load suddenly moved, a head appeared, and John made out the grey hair, the bony, hunched shoulders of an old woman clutching a bag of possessions in her lap.

"*Eh bien, mon petit*," he said to the boy, "*comment ça va?*"

The lad looked up, saw his uniform and ignored him. He puffed and strained as he passed, wove his way between two corpses and headed on towards the road where the column of field guns and limbers clanked and groaned into the village.

Perhaps he doesn't understand French, John thought. Hope he gets through. Away from here, at least. Doesn't want to stay around.

His own task was to find possible sites for the Advanced Dressing Station. Henshaw would make the final choice, but John decided it had to be near the road south so that ambulances could have access; as far away from the Front as possible, and with space and some cover so that stretchers could be laid on the ground while casualties waited for treatment. Difficult: the trenches were only six or seven hundred yards in front of the village towards the German lines. Anywhere he chose would always be within range of enemy guns. Ideally, he needed a second building for emergency operations.

If possible, somewhere safe to sleep; otherwise it would be bell tents on the fields at the rear of the village.

He grimaced at the irony: nearer our own guns.

He walked along a sunken way that ran through the middle. Corpses, mostly villagers, littered the road. He covered his mouth and nose with a handkerchief to block out the sickly smell. Difficult walking. In spite of taking cautious steps, he struggled to avoid treading on bodies. He stepped on the chest of one and gagged when the tongue flipped out under his weight like some grotesque children's toy. He removed his foot and the tongue retracted. Already birds or rats had taken the eyes. You could walk the length of the village stepping from corpse to corpse and not put a foot on the ground.

Have to organise a burying party urgently.

Only three houses had occupants. At the open door of one, an old woman stood, dressed in black with a cape over her shoulders, black ribbon in her hair and a bible in her hand. At the sound of his footsteps, a younger woman appeared. An angry stare. Soot and dust smudged her face and she wore a heavy grey garment, half-dress, half overall. A folded grey blanket over her arm.

"Good afternoon!" English seemed best to identify himself.

The women stared and made no response. Hard to decide whether their silence was hostility or terror. Perhaps both.

Amid the eerie silence, the tense peace, he met a few people in the back streets who had left their homes to make their way south with just what they could carry. All seemed terror-stricken. Not one smiled or acknowledged him. Almost as if they can't see me, he thought, or I don't exist.

★ ★ ★

"It's not ideal by any means, sir," he said. "It must have been a large house, or something like a town hall. But it gives us space and a measure of cover from blast."

Henshaw cast his eye over the huge ruin: the upper floor had collapsed; large sections of the roof had been blown away, and the windows had shed their glass. "It'll be something of a gimcrack affair," he said, "but it'll do. We don't know how long we'll be here, anyhow."

"Well, I'll get the lads started," John said. "I thought, tuck our station alongside this internal wall, sandbag it well, and have a corrugated iron roof with more bags on top. That should be strong enough to stop shell fragments. We'll have to hope we don't get a direct hit. It won't withstand that. Once it's built, we can start equipping it."

"Yes, well done, John. It'll do nicely. And if you get men to clear this rubble, we shall have a good space for the stretchers as the casualties are brought in. Now, what about somewhere to operate? Let's hope we don't have to, but chances are..."

John led him across the road towards an abandoned farmhouse. "Again, not ideal, but what persuaded me is that the kitchen's at the back and has a large table – certainly big enough to lay a man out and work around him. There's water nearby and a stove to heat it. I've got four men cleaning and scrubbing the place now. There's even another room which I thought would be ideal for your billet."

"That's if we get any sleep at all. Well, capital. You seem to have thought of everything. Now, what about my nursing orderly?"

"Do you know Atherstone, sir? He's a splendid lad, only about twenty, very unprepossessing, but he's a sticker. I'd say he has all the patience, tenderness and devotion of a woman. I've watched him dressing patients' wounds; he's gentle and has all the skill of a nurse. But, most importantly, he has a particular way with the dying. You can see the relief and gratitude in their eyes when he says he'll make sure a farewell message gets home. And then they can let go. Sort of chap who deserves a medal but will never get one."

"Quite a recommendation. So he's not going to run scared if the going gets tough?"

"Lord, no, sir. Shows outstanding courage, I'd say."

★ ★ ★

246

"So, how are things progressing, John?" Henshaw rested on a tumbled chimney, his feet stretched onto a pile of rubble. He leaned against the sandbags of the Dressing Station. Above his head, a board with a painted red cross and an arrow pointing towards the entrance.

"Well, the field at the back of the op farmhouse will be best to pitch tents for the bearers. I've got four men digging a latrine while there's still light; we've found a pump in the farmyard that works, the water tastes sweet enough; oh, and Sov Poundsbury's rather bucked. He found a couple of ducks settling to roost on a cottage roof, managed to net them and soon had them plucked and in the cooking pot. A pleasant change from bully beef."

Henshaw puffed on his pipe. "Sitting ducks, eh? Well done. Sounds as though you're well up to the mark. Sergeant Skinner's a splendid fellow, too. He's taken charge of equipping the Dressing Station and the operating room. I let him get on. Clearly knows what he's doing. Ticks items off as they're unloaded and has four orderlies running round, following his every word. Now, your bearer teams... You're obviously leading one."

"Yes, Gosforth the second, and Bourne the third. We'll all sleep in the same tent and I've put Atherstone with us, too. He knows most of us and will feel happier like that. Corporal Russell's organising the other teams."

"Yes, Atherstone. Good choice for my orderly. Keen. I already feel I can trust him to get on. Pity about that nervous sniff, I hope it doesn't start to irritate, but his heart's in the right place. Now, what about Feltham?"

John took a deep breath. "I didn't realise you knew about that problem."

"Oh, I'm well aware of that particular joker. Never stops talking, always got a clever excuse when things go wrong. Buck-passer. You think he's a good fellow and then –"

"Yes, it's all show," John said. "Most of the others are wise to him now. He irritates people like the very devil." He paused. "All that gung-ho jauntiness. I decided in the end it wasn't fair to inflict him on the other teams, so he's with me where I can keep an eye on him. I've got two other fellows I can absolutely rely on: Poundsbury, of course, and Underwood. Perhaps we can manage to water Feltham down, or at least keep him in check."

"Now, look, John." Henshaw stood up and knocked his pipe out on his heel. "I know you're absolutely bushed, but there's one last job I'd like you to do, if you would."

"Sir?"

"I'd do it myself, but I must check over this Dressing Station and the operating room, make sure I know where everything is before the rush. Otherwise, Sarnt Skinner will be after me. Now, it'd be our rotten luck for the CO to come up from Clearing tomorrow early, just to check I'm up to snuff. Now, I don't want to look an absolute arse if he asks if I know where all the Battalion Aid Posts are."

"So, you want me to go into the trenches and make sure I know where each is located. Yes, I'll do that."

"Good man. I don't suppose I'll get over there myself at all if things become hectic tomorrow, so if *you* know..."

"I'll deal with it, Major. I expect the combat troops are settling down now it's dusk, they started taking up positions about four o'clock this afternoon."

★ ★ ★

He was not prepared for this labyrinth, this zigzag of passageways. When people talked of the trenches, he expected to find a man-made ditch stretching halfway across Belgium. The notion had stayed with him since early training, never tested by logic. Expressions like 'holding the line' or the German 'Hindenburg Line' reinforced the idea of straightness. But here he walked into a maze of blind alleys, passages that dodged forward and hid from him – very few straight lines. Unwilling to ask the way, he followed an infantry platoon into a long communication trench. Going into reserve, the corporal told him.

Disturbing to find that his height exposed him to danger. Over the top of the trench, he saw a bristle of barbed wire, newly laid. Beyond that, the countryside so flat, so vast. The remains of the next village shattered, desolate, trees dismembered. No lights. But hidden over there – not that far away – Germans, as ready to fight for life as anyone here. He ducked down. Best not risk a sniper. The British front-line trenches were still yards ahead, reachable only by this warren of duckboard paths.

Have to carry stretchers along here. How on earth will we manage that?

He wandered as far forward as he could and came across groups of soldiers hunkered down in a trench about six foot wide. Two men leant against the mud wall, cleaning their rifles; further along, three squatted on their heels, hats off, laboriously writing. John noticed two army-issue postcards; one man, pencil in hand, labouring at a letter home. A surprise to find the trenches so quiet, the atmosphere sombre as if the whole countryside held its breath before a storm. One man sat alone, smoking a cigarette, his fingers shaking. He stared at the bottom of the trench.

"Are you all right, soldier?"

The man did not reply.

"Where will I find the aid post?"

No response; the soldier did not look at him but merely thrust the hand with the cigarette out along the trench, his tremor even more apparent.

John trudged on. Poor devil, he thought. But how would I be if I expected to be mown down soon. Pray, I suppose.

He came across three men, all silent, sprawled on a tumble of sandbags: one smoking a pipe, another, hands tucked behind his head, gazed at the evening drift of clouds. The third, with an enamel mug in his hand, looked up when John called out: "Where can I find the aid post?"

"Next system along, pal." He gestured back towards the village. "In the support trench. This is High Street. Not here. You wanna turn left into Primrose Way, then left again into Doctor's Lane. It's in a blind cove, timbered roof covered in sandbags. But don't disturb the doc, he'll have his head down while the going's good."

★ ★ ★

At the far end of the support trench, someone had put up a notice: *Doctor's Waiting Room – open all hours at busy times.* It hung above makeshift benches cut into the side of the trench wall, planks laid on top of the clay. An orderly sat at one end, smoking a pipe in front of a brazier. He had removed his boots and puttees and offered socked feet to the coals.

Bit early for that, John thought, even though September nights can get cold.

The man looked up. "My idea of heaven, can't beat warm feet."

John smiled. "This is the aid post, isn't it? Can you tell me what others there are nearby?"

"Dunno, mate, best have a word with the captain. He'll be genned up on where everything is. He'll have maps, I dare say."

"Right, thank you. Where will I find him?"

"Go back the way you came, pass two fire-bays, cross Primrose Way and you'll find his dugout twenty-five yards down on the right."

★ ★ ★

"Wait here, Corporal, I'll tell the captain you're here."

John looked at the wicker reinforcement of the trench walls. An ingenious system: if it rained, the clay would turn to a mud, seep into the cracks of the woven wood and create a wattle and daub wall. Damn lucky with the weather, though, could have been so wet. The trenches smelt musty and stale, unused for some time, but at least they were dry.

"The captain says he'll give you five minutes, Corporal. Mind how you go. Three steps down, quite steep." The sergeant pulled

250

aside a piece of sacking which served as a curtain and draught excluder for the dugout. The cramped stairway, the low ceiling; John hunched his shoulders, bowed his head. The dank smell of mud.

A death trap in a gas attack, he thought.

The captain sat at a desk, his back to John. A hurricane lantern on the desk hissed light. "Shan't keep you a moment, Corporal." John knew that voice. Dare he speak first?

He grinned. "*Certainement, Monsieur.*"

The captain spun round. "What the... Good Lord, it's you! How the devil do you come to waylay me in my den?" Lambert stood up, flung out his arm, shook hands. He pointed at the stripes on John's arm and smiled. "You've been promoted."

"So have you, Monsieur."

"Almost automatic out here," Lambert said. "If you survive long enough, promotion is practically inevitable." Two furrows above the bridge of his nose made him look older; the lantern light emphasised the hollows of his eyes. Below ground, his skin looked muddy, unhealthy. "Sit down a minute." He waved towards the double bunk across the cramped room. "Tell me why you're here."

The upper bunk crowded John's head. He told Lambert about his mission.

"Take this rough plan and check them out yourself. Let my sergeant have it back when you've finished. We tend to have Aid Posts in the support trenches, in a dugout if possible. Makes more sense. Also easier for you chaps to get casualties away. I'll tell you one thing: you coming in tonight will have boosted morale. The men are always glad if they see a medic around. Makes 'em feel there's somebody who'll look after them if things go wrong."

"So, it's tomorrow, for you?"

"Yes, but I'm hoping the attack will be what my sergeant calls a meat pie and cup of tea. We shall advance behind a tank."

"Is that what they call those armoured crawlers? Why tanks?"

Lambert shrugged. "A name that stuck, I gather. It started as a code word for this new weapon. And then... Anyway, I'm rather glad we shall have a huge machine lumbering in front when we go over the top. It'll give us cover and, for once, it should be a walkover. The tank will fire as it goes, it'll flatten any wire left and even bridge the Boche trenches. We have to walk behind and be ready for any German foolhardy enough to linger, who decides to take a few pot-shots. But I gather they quickly take to their heels when a tank is closing in."

"So where are they now, these tanks?"

Lambert squinted at him in mock suspicion. "Not a Hun spy, are you?"

John grinned and stroked his chin. Stubbly again. "Hardly!"

"Did you see three large barns to the south of Poelemarck?" Lambert said. "They're under cover there, where Boche planes can't spot them. Came up a few days ago, I gather. Keeping out of sight preserves the element of surprise."

"I saw a column of five the other day. Awesome things. I wonder if it's the same lot."

"Shouldn't be surprised. Not many of this new type around yet."

They shook hands again; Lambert grinned and gave a crisp salute. "*Au revoir, Monsieur Souris.* I'm glad we met again. It's lifted me, too, knowing you're nearby."

John returned the salute. "*Au revoir*, sir, and good luck." He hurried away, feeling his smile fade, sensing the tension all around. Would he ever see Lambert again, or was '*Adieu*' – the committal to God – a more appropriate goodbye?

FORTY

It began with thunder, a clout of sound that bruised the air, sped away and then slogged back at you – a demonic echo. His dream lurched into a London theatre where a tube train rumbled beneath; the ground vibrating, giving a shudder. Oh, yes, he thought, in dream-talk. Of course. But which theatre is this?

Somewhere. Back home.

He clawed his way back to consciousness. He could not see; no daylight yet. But the smells of feet and bodies, crushed grass and fetid breath told him where he lay.

It's started, then. Four hundred guns firing as fast as men could slam another shell in the breech, laying down a creeping barrage.

He had seen the shells coming along the road, the limbers loaded with them, mules staggering to haul them up to the gunnery position. Imagine what those cylinders of destruction would do if one hit a man... He clenched his eyes to change the thought.

Around him, men began unwillingly to stir, but he lay still, on his back, not yet ready to play the corporal. Hardly been asleep. Three hours, perhaps. His eyes ached. His boots, left on in frantic fatigue, pinched his feet. A crick in his neck.

He couldn't see the flashes; the shriek of the shells came first: a whee, a whistle, a hiss of their passing overhead, the sound of their firing afterwards, in turn from right to left at about a second's interval; again and again along the line, as regularly as the slow ticking of a monstrous clock.

That was the thunder. But it lacked the clap, the cutting crack of nature; no tearing tumble of sound. It thumped the air like a huge bass drum without the deep, resonant warmth, like someone dropping heavy furniture in a room above, or that empty barrel being rolled over the cobbles at Marseilles.

He longed to stretch his arms, dared not for fear of striking someone. "Morning, lads," he called upwards to the peak of the tent. "We've got this racket for the next three hours. Our day has started."

The bray of a yawn in the darkness, then a voice. "Fucking hell, already?"

"Hey, Corp!" Feltham probably. "Where's the bog?"

"Left out of the tent, head down the slope. At the bottom of the field. Don't show a bloody light, and don't trip over any guy ropes, or you'll be up to your eyes in shit." He never used to swear. Coarseness was catching. Perhaps it was the promotion.

★ ★ ★

Each man carried two rolled-up stretchers into the support trench and leant them against the mud wall. The rest were stored at the Dressing Station. John had the men wait in bearer teams, ready for action later when... He blocked the thought.

His ears hissed after the British barrage. Curious noise, like a high E flat on the fiddle. Would this bat-sound ever go away? He clapped his hand over his right ear to try to block it out. No, still there. However did Gurney cope with gunfire?

Light seeped into the sky. His stomach jittered at the thought the attack was about to start. He pictured Lambert readying himself to lead. How must he feel? John screwed up his eyes, dropped his head to squeeze out a prayer.

"'Ere they come!" Feltham said, looking back towards the village, his face lit by a gleeful grin. "Now we'll show the bastard Boche what a bit o' British engineering can do."

The clanking squeal of the caterpillar tracks; strange, drilling bursts of the motors as the drivers wrestled to prevent the engines stalling; from behind their position, the tanks clattered forward in lumbering lurches, jockeying their way across the British trenches with ease, fanning out, one to each company, to lead the coming attack. The two metal flaps on the front of the vehicles looked like drooping eyelids. Strange to humanise such monsters. The acrid rankness of exhaust smoke drifted towards them.

Bad as a gas attack, he thought. Worse still if you were inside. He stepped along the duckboards, nodding, smiling at the men under his leadership. Checking them over. His eye lighted on one. "Feltham! Where's your bloody gas mask, man?"

Feltham clapped his hands over his uniform as if searching for it. His small round head swivelled; his eyes shifted. A Cockney whine. "Some bastard's pinched it. I had it, Corp, I know I did. I swear I put it on when I come back from the shithouse."

"Go back to the tent and find it, now. And at the double! I want you back here, ready for action, not grovelling around and skulking behind the lines. We're a team now. Get a grip, man!"

Underwood looked to the sky in silent exasperation. "Trying it on, Corp, as usual. He'll learn the hard way if they do start lobbing gas shells over."

"Yes, well, we don't want that." John felt his mouth tighten. "They're sure to have a crack at us after our battery. They know the attack's coming."

"It's quiet enough now," Underwood said. "Can you hear that bird singing? Eerie."

"That's your old skylark," Sov said. "He's above us somewhere, chittering away." He looked up at the clear sky: pale blue, merging into the orange of dawn at the horizon. "See the sun in a minute."

"I tell you one thing," Gosforth called from further along the trench. "I've worked out the best way to deal with being under shellfire."

"Oh, is he off again?" Feltham back now with his gas mask. "Always some bloody theory."

"No, listen," Gosforth said. "If you accept that it's utterly unpredictable where a shell might drop, the only logical thing is to act as if there aren't any shells. To do exactly what you would have done if there was no shelling." He leant back against the trench wall and began puffing on his pipe. "If one hit you, you wouldn't know anyway."

"Sounds lunatic to me," someone said. "Like Tommies' talk. Some of them say they'll only cop it if a bullet's got their name on it."

"Gosforth's system is as good as any," John said. "I shall do my best to act on it. Stick the old tin hat on and keep going. That's what we're here for: to help others."

The big red ball that hurt your eyes edged over the rim of the plain. From a distant incline beyond the German lines, John saw a flash from a heavy gun. "OK, lads, down flat. It's started." The zipping shriek of a shell flying overhead; two seconds later, another.

"Missed," Feltham said, "the buggers ain't got our range at all."

"They're not firing at us, yet," Underwood said. "They're having a go at taking out our guns. You wait until they realise we're mounting an attack, then they'll lower their sights. Let's hope they don't start landing near the Dressing Station."

John edged his head above the support trench. He heard the sudden hammer of the tanks' engines as they began to move forward, the metallic screech of the caterpillar tracks. From yards in front of their position, the frail shrill of the officers' whistles floated back; he saw the glint of the early sun on the helmets of the men, a flash of menace from the bayonets. The soldiers scrambled out of the trench and began the slow walk behind the tank. The nearest other vehicle, about fifty yards to the right, also crawled forward.

"It's started." His fists were clenched.

More heavy shells slammed overhead, their tearing scream as noisy as any explosion. "I'm timing these and counting them," Gosforth shouted. "Pretty steady stream. Looks like thirty shells a minute."

"'Blige," Feltham said, "ain't 'e got anything better to do than count Boche shells?" He raised his voice: "Keep your 'ead down, mate, and for God's sake, shut up."

After half an hour, the bombardment stopped abruptly; a strange silence settled over their trench before more distant sounds filtered back: the sputter of a German machine gun, the crack of rifle fire, the far-off squeal and clank of the tanks, the remote sting of bullets hitting metal.

"Half an hour? I make that nine hundred shells they sent over," Gosforth called. "And not one landed anywhere near us."

"All right, lads, time to move forward," John said. "We've work to do." He gathered up his two stretchers and started moving towards the front-line trench. Oh, God, help me, I can't breathe.

★ ★ ★

The soldier must have weighed over fourteen stone, too heavy for a couple of men to carry any distance. So the four of them hoisted the stretcher onto their shoulders and began to trudge. They had not walked very far before Underwood said, "Can we stop, Corp? He weighs a bloody ton, this fellow."

"No, keep on, we're too exposed here." John's voice little more than a gasp.

"Oh, go on, Corp, we must have a breather. We ain't so big as you and Sov, we gotta have a rest." Feltham's whine.

They laid the stretcher gently down.

"Can't you see the sky's getting lighter by the minute?" Sov said. "We'll soon be easy targets. We're not invisible, you know." A star shell flared above them.

From the German trenches, the report of a rifle, and a bullet kicked up the dirt nearby.

"Oh, for fuck's sake, you two, let's get a move on or we're all done for." Sov rarely swore like that.

They heaved the stretcher on their shoulders again, their pace quickened as if they were now carrying a man of straw. Several German rifles cracked and bullets whizzed close by.

About fifty yards from the British front-line trench, an enemy machine gun opened up on the left. Aggressive, stuttering bursts.

"Oh, Christ," Feltham screamed.

"He's not firing at us. Get on," John shouted. He eased the burden of the stretcher on his shoulder. "Come on, now. Make sure you don't twist your ankle."

Another prolonged chatter from the gun. Feltham pulled the handle off his shoulder and ducked. Immediately, the stretcher tilted and the wounded man slipped off. He fell awkwardly onto a helmet lying on the ground, right onto the bleeding shrapnel gash in his side.

The man's scream of pain turned to a long exhalation and his body collapsed.

"Oh, Jesus," Sov said, quietly, after a few seconds. "We could have saved 'im. He was going to be all right if we got him to the doc. Now look."

"We can't leave him here, not now." Underwood cast glances around as if to find help. "What do we do?"

"We put him on the stretcher and take him back for burying. It's the least we can do." John turned and stared directly at Feltham. "We can't afford cowards who duck when the going gets tough."

"I didn't duck, I stumbled. It ain't easy, this ground." Feltham stayed kneeling, almost cowering.

"You bloody liar," John said. "I saw you. You ducked from underneath the stretcher, and for two pins if I'd got a gun, I'd blow your bloody lights out. You're a blasted liability."

The men fell silent, staring at him. Underwood fidgeted; Feltham looked away. "Right," John said, his voice quiet and calm, "let's carry on. Ready to lift?"

★ ★ ★

He was afraid of twisting his ankle on the rubble around the Dressing Station. Only a narrow pathway had been cleared for stretcher-bearers. Elsewhere, a scattered landscape of broken bricks and tiles, and wind-whipped swirls of lime-dust, which some men were detailed to damp down.

A brief moment for a breather now, before returning to the front line.

Three soldiers, due to go into the reserve trench, ambled past on the road which meandered through Poelemarck. Still off duty, laughing, joking. A few shells fell now, much closer to the Dressing Station than previously, a light bombardment largely ignored.

"I hope these old walls protect the station from blast, if we do get a hit," he said to Sov. He looked up at the two-storeyed skeleton of the building around them. Clouds chased across the blue of the sky. And the distinctive whine of an incoming shell, about to land close by. Both men tensed their knees, ready to duck.

The soldiers on the road heard it too, looked up into the air and broke into a trot. But a fragment of shell struck one of them, a direct hit, severing both his legs just above the knees. Bits of leg, uniform, boots, flew out across the road. The man faltered, fell onto the stumps of his thighs and continued with two or three steps before collapsing.

Then he screamed.

"Bloody hell," Sov said, "see that?"

"Doctor! Emergency!" John yelled, hoping Henshaw would appear from inside the station. "Quick, let's get his legs strapped!" He and Sov rushed into the road, fumbling in their medical bags. Within seconds, they had tourniquets on the man's thighs; John gritted his teeth as he tightened the strap; Henshaw appeared at the run. He knelt down in the road and gave the soldier a big injection of morphia and clamped dressings to the remains of the man's legs.

The soldier, eyes closed, tense, shook uncontrollably. "Take it easy, old chap," Henshaw bent close to the man's ear. "Things'll be all right."

Sov and John ran back for a stretcher, lifted the man onto it and, with tender speed, carried him round to the rear of the building where a motor ambulance and its orderlies waited. Together, they lifted the stretcher into place; a young soldier swung at the crank-handle; the engine started and the vehicle began to move; John and

Sov jumped down – the injured man now on his way south to the Clearing Station.

John puffed out an enormous breath, felt his shoulders sag.

"Well done, you two, well done," Henshaw said when they returned. "Very quick thinking. Excellent! Now, anyone else injured?" He looked around at the soldier's comrades who squatted at the side of the road – the younger one pale and shivering, the older man rocking backwards and forwards. "Oh, Jesus, hell," he said. "Jesus, hell. It could have been me."

Henshaw turned to Atherstone, standing nearby, his eyes wide, anxious. "Get these men a large rum, please." He indicated the two at the roadside.

"Sir!" Atherstone hurried away.

"Is that poor Tommy going to be all right, Major?" Sov stood awkwardly, his hands behind his back.

"He may well live, Poundsbury. Thanks to your prompt action, he lost very little blood. And the morphia I gave him will also minimise the shock. Yes, he has a good chance. Let's hope he makes it. It's these other two I'm worried about. They've got to carry on."

John hung back, eyes closed. So far he'd managed, led his men, acted calmly, got through each crisis as it came. But what if he couldn't cope? Would he know if he was cracking up? The idea still nagged.

★ ★ ★

From the shell-hole in No Man's Land, they could see the crippled tank about two hundred yards ahead. Rearing nose-high in a German trench, it resembled a ship that had started to sink. Its caterpillar tracks were damaged and slewed on the right-hand side as if someone had thrust a heavy object in to jam the wheels and stall all movement. Several large bullet holes peppered the armour plating on its side; on the other, the entry door sagged open and the body of one of its crew lolled out, the figure silhouetted against the sinking sun.

"Oh, blimey," Sov spoke in a whisper. "He's done for all right. All of 'em, probably, poor buggers. How far from our lines do you reckon they've got?"

John shook his head. "What a waste, what a sorry sight. Quarter of a mile, perhaps."

An approaching shell, that faint menacing whistle closing fast on their position. John held his breath. The end? He closed his eyes. Let it be quick and whole so we know nothing about it. He took off his helmet and thrust his face into the earth. The crump of its landing sounded as if it thudded into a mattress, but the explosion tore and flung earth skywards and outwards in a scatter of stones, helmets, earth and severed limbs. Half of a man's body, headless, cut off at the waist, whirled and cartwheeled thirty feet into the air – its arms splayed in last abandon until it landed, drooped across the left-hand tracks of the stricken tank. John gasped in relief and laughed. "See that? Like a scarecrow, poor devil."

Sov laid a restraining hand on John's shoulder and closed his eyes. "Poor bugger, that were an officer, weren't it?"

"What? How do you know?"

"Uniform. Tell by the uniform."

"Who was it, did you see?"

"I think it could have been –" Sov did not finish the sentence.

"Oh, my God, no!" John scrambled up to the edge of the shell-hole, ready to struggle over the top. He flung his medical bag forward onto the battlefield to commit himself and began using his elbows to haul himself over the rim of the crater.

"Not yet, Smiler. It's too soon. It's not safe. Come back, boy!"

John ignored him. "I've got to know. He's my pupil!" His voice a desperate scream. "I've got to know." The increasing dread rose to a choke. He began a frantic crawl, still using his elbows and dragging his dressings bag alongside. The barrage had stopped but the occasional tsing of a bullet hitting metal told him that some German aimed wildly at anything that moved in the twilight. Further away, a burst of machine gun fire – the rat, tat, tat like the knock of a jaunty postman.

A huge rat, grey against the increasing grey of night, already foraging, stopped four feet in front of him and eyed him. No fear at all.

"Geddout of it!" he hissed. He reached for something to hurl but grasped only rutted clay.

He crawled forward, glaring huge eyes at the creature. As long as it doesn't go for my face, he thought. The rat squeaked at the stand-off, sniffed the air and scurried away, fat-bloated like a sand-filled sock. The segments of its tail snaked behind.

John put his head up to gauge the distance to the tank and a rifle bullet stung the ground ahead.

"For God's sake, keep your head down, Smiler." Sov's call already strained by distance.

John stretched out to retrieve an abandoned tin hat, just within reach. He crammed it on his head, aware of another bullet kicking up the earth nearby. He lifted his head. "Red Cross!" he shouted, "Rotes Kreuz!" His voice almost a scream.

The sniper stopped.

John recognised Lambert's body by the gold signet ring on the little finger of the right hand. It caught his attention at Rouen, and, less than twenty-four hours previously, winked farewell in the last salute in the dugout. He stood up in the shelter of the tank and lifted the torso off the tank track. The arms flopped and flung out like a discarded marionette. He staggered under the weight, gently laid the body on the ground. Lambert, for sure – the officer's uniform stained with earth, smears of blood, oil. But where was his head, his legs?

A frenzy of scrabbling, searching. So much debris: weapons, helmets, human remains. Where did Lambert fall?

The head lay facing the ground, the nose resting on a rifle butt. A trickle of blood from the neck stained the earth. He drew the head to him, the dread of the moment trapped in his throat. He lay on his side cradling it close to his chest. The eyes, wide and staring, gazed up unfocussed, the blue dimming like the retreating sunset.

He wiped his fingers on his uniform and stroked the lids shut. Soft, silky. He fussed the fair hair into a parting as a mother would tend her son. He could do nothing about the mouth. It gaped at the world in one last O of surprise, perhaps a scream of encouragement to his men. Now silenced for ever.

Tears streaming, he flung his head back and howled. "Fuck you, God, fuck you! How could you allow this? Not our sons! Not our sons! Even Isaac was spared!"

He felt a touch on his shoulder, became aware of Sov beside him.

"Look, old lad, look!" The voice so gentle. Sov pointed. "It weren't the shell that done for him." A clean bullet hole in front of the ear. "That was after. Killed in action, see?"

"I must bury him. All of him. I must find all of him and bury him. I won't leave him." Kneeling, tears still flowing, he began to arrange Lambert's body like some grotesque jigsaw puzzle: the head, the torso. "His legs, his legs are missing. They must be somewhere here." He stood up.

"Get down!" Sov's voice a hiss. "You can be seen."

"I must find all of him. Get me a shroud!"

"Where?"

"Anything, something to cover him. We must wrap him in something. Please!"

Sov loped back towards the British front line, running in a half-crouch.

John began scouring the litter of the battlefield: a discarded rifle, the bayonet still fixed; helmets; boots; packs; unused bombs and, everywhere, bodies. About fifty yards away, he recognised Feltham and Underwood foraging like beachcombers for survivors to bring back.

He found the helmet first: dented, mud-covered, bloody. Inside, the initials in black ink – CDL. He'd never known Lambert's Christian name. At school, surnames only. But it was Lambert's all right. Keep it or leave it? He tossed it to one side.

The legs lay about thirty yards apart, flung out in a wide scatter by the explosion. He had to assume from the uniform they belonged to Lambert. An image returned of the orderly leaving the operating theatre carrying an amputated limb. John now carried each leg with reverence to where the rest of the body lay.

Sov returned with a large sack. "I don't know what you'll think, Smiler. I emptied the sand out. It's the best I –"

"It'll do, it'll have to do."

Together, they began emptying the pockets of the uniform: a letter from home, a tin of expensive cigarettes, a watch and chain, a few loose bullets. "Did you find his revolver?" Sov said.

John shook his head, looked away, blew his nose. Sov loosened the tie and undid the shirt to ease out the identity tag and the whistle, made the neck-line tidy.

"There's something else," John said. From a small inside pocket of the jacket, he drew out a slim volume, bound in soft pink leather: *The Rubaiyat*. Inside, as if marking a place, a head of small blue flowers, neatly pressed between fine tissue paper.

"Forget-me-not," Sov said. He turned away. From the trouser pocket of the severed left leg, he pulled out five gold coins. "Look at these!" In the last streaks of day, the sovereigns glinted in his palm. He laid them on the ground with Lambert's other possessions. "What now, Smiler?"

"He stays here, where he fell. Let the earth cherish him, since we could not."

They eased the torso and arms into the sack, then each leg either side of the body. John took a deep breath, picked up the head, gazed briefly at the gaping mouth, the closed eyes. "May you lie in the sleep of peace, my boy." He coaxed the head inside with the rest of the body, stripped off his own belt and lashed the neck of the sack closed.

"How we going to bury 'en, we ain't got a shovel?"

"Help me carry him to the bottom of that shell-hole."

They slithered down the sides of the crater, struggling against the weight of the body and the loose earth. They laid their burden at the bottom, and stood back.

"Now what?" Sov said.

They used discarded rifles with fixed bayonets as picks, loosened the bottom and sides of the hole and scuffed soil over the body with their boots. Slowly, the sacking disappeared under a covering of earth. A bright star glistened above the pit. Together, they scrambled up the side and started to pick up Lambert's possessions.

"What shall us do with these?" Sov held out the coins.

"Give them to me." He drew back his arm high and wide over the shell-hole and flung the coins into the darkness. "Blood money, Judas money. We betrayed him, we betray them all."

From the bottom of the crater came the patter of the coins landing. John stood on the edge, head bowed. Tears coursed unchecked down his cheeks.

He did not pray.

FORTY-ONE

September 1917

"Rowley! You're supposed to pick them, not eat them! You'll give yourself a stomach-ache if you're not careful."

I looked up, surprised at the sharpness of Mother's tone. She wasn't often cross with him. I thought boys were lucky, they weren't often told off, and got away with things. But then Rowley was her favourite.

"Yes, Mama." He grinned. When she'd turned back to the bramble bush, he popped another berry into his mouth.

I held up my tin. "Mama, look, I've picked all these."

She turned to see. "Yes, well, make sure you don't spill them. We need all the blackberries we can get. I want some for a pie and the rest is for jam. I need that tin full. So you'd best get on."

I asked why we needed to pick blackberries.

"Because they're good for you and we don't have to buy them. That's why."

All the best ones waved near the top of the bush where I couldn't reach them, even on tiptoe. "Mama, please may I use the walking stick now?" I liked hooking branches down and picking off the biggest and juiciest berries. They looked lovely and would quickly fill up the tin.

"You may. I shall sit and take a rest now." She walked to a bench nearby and sat down; Bea, head lolling to one side, slept in the pushchair next to her.

I hurried back to the bushes with the walking stick that had once been Grandpa Baxter's. "You'd better behave, Rowley, it's just you and me now." I wagged the stick as if it was a cane. Little brat, if only I could...

Rowley stared, put out a purple tongue and slipped another blackberry in.

"Mama, Rowley's being cheeky."

"Oh, for goodness' sake, don't fuss so, child. If you two can't be friends, we shall pack up and go home this instant, and there'll be no blackberry pie for tea."

We picked in silence. I left the lower fruits for Rowley and stretched higher to gather the fattest and darkest. Sometimes I lifted thorny branches out of the way and waded deeper into the bush, but the prickles caught my dress and scratched my arms. Filling the tin was taking for ever.

"Mama, I gotted all these. Look!" Rowley held out his tin and began to run back. She opened her eyes from a doze.

"Not yet, Rowley," I called. "There's hundreds left."

He ignored me and continued running. "Careful, now, Rowley, careful," Mother said.

Too late: he tripped on a tussock of heath grass, flung the tin forward and pitched the blackberries everywhere.

"Oh, now look," I called. "You silly boy!"

"Don't stand gazing, Dorothy," she said. "Come and start picking them up. He couldn't help it, he's only a little boy."

I stared in disbelief, crammed the lid on my tin, gathered up the walking stick and dragged over to the bench. Not so little, now you've started school, I thought. Wish I was a boy. I began picking up the scatter of berries and putting them back. "They're all dusty now, Rowley."

"Never mind, they can be washed," Mother said. "Give me your tin. I'll keep that now." She frowned. "And look at you – your fingers, they're all dirty and stained. Don't you dare touch anything until you've cleaned your hands. Here, hold them out." She took a bottle from a bag on the pushchair and began pouring a trickle of water.

I dandled my hands under the flow and rinsed them. The water swirled dark red and puddled at my feet. Looks like blood, I thought.

"Now take this rag and dry yourself off." She pulled a scrap of cloth out of her sleeve.

I wandered off, studied my arms and scrubbed at some scratches hoping they'd disappear. I worried about my dress where a bramble had pulled out some threads. Better hide that, I thought, or there'll be more scoldings before tea.

★ ★ ★

The dark liquid dripped down so slowly from the pillow case. So strange, putting all that delicious fruit inside and leaving the juice to soak through in its own time. Mother had upended a stool in the pantry and tied the pillow case onto its legs, with a bowl underneath to catch the drips. I liked this time – a quiet moment when the others had been put to bed and I had her all to myself. I took a deep breath. "Mama, when the baby comes, will it be a boy or a girl?"

"The baby? Who told you about that?" She sounded cross.

"No one told me. I guessed. I remember you wearing that smock before Bea was born and you needed to sit down a lot. I thought I must be right."

"It's not a thing for young girls to be concerned about. There's plenty of time when you're older. But if you must know, we should have a new baby sometime next month. But I don't want you tattling about it."

"No, Mama. Will it be a boy or a girl?"

"We can't choose. We have to wait and see."

I thought for a moment. "Does Daddy know?"

"Of course he does, child, don't be silly. Now, stop prattling and fetch the sugar loaf off the shelf. I shall need lots for the jelly. Bring the scales, too, we might as well get snipping and weighing now. It'll save time tomorrow."

The clock on the mantelpiece struck seven. I loved that sound. Mother called them Westminster Chimes. But it didn't really sound like Big Ben. I liked hearing it in the night when I couldn't sleep.

Very homely. It made me feel safe. I felt it was guarding the house and keeping me company. That came from Grandpa Baxter, too, and only Mother was allowed to wind it.

"Half an hour, Dorothy, then it's time."

A heavy knock at the outside door.

"Who's that at this hour?" she said.

"Shall I go?"

"No, young girls shouldn't answer the door at this time of day." She returned with a letter. "Last post is early tonight. It's from New Zealand. See, you can tell by the stamp." She tore the envelope open and stuffed it into the pocket of her apron. She stood close to the window in the fading light and read the letter. "Oh no, he's dead." She held the letter at her side and stared out of the window, chewing the little finger of her hand.

"Who's dead, Mama? Can I see?" I felt dread creeping up my throat.

"No, it's not for you. It's from a friend of Uncle Row, my brother. Killed in action, it says here. France, or somewhere. I can't believe it. Two of my family gone in the same year. Oh dear. I wonder if Dora knows." She sat down, pushed the scales and the sugar cone away and rested her head in her hands. She didn't cry. She slammed her hands flat on the table and her wedding ring banged on the wood. She shouted: "This bloody war! How is it all going to end?" She took out a rag from her sleeve and dabbed at her eyes.

"Would you like me to make a pot of tea, Mama?" I thought grown-ups always made tea if there was a problem.

"No, thank you, Dorothy, unfortunately that's not going to bring him back. You'd best get ready for bed."

I sighed. Could I never please her?

★ ★ ★

The rain pattered on the bedroom window like tiny fingers tapping.

I liked being safe and warm, and listening to the rain, but that night sleep wouldn't come. The house stood silent. Mother, the last to go to bed, had looked in, the candle flickering in her hand. She said "Night, night" and went away, the candlelight dancing and fading away along the landing, I heard her bedroom door click shut. Now I was alone, only the clock as company. I knew our kitchen was beneath my room and tried to work out where exactly the clock was. Perhaps I was lying right above it.

Outside, the rain hissed in a heavy burst and the leaves in the trees rustled. After some time, the clock started to strike. I lay tense, counting the chimes. Didn't want to miss one. Heavens to Betsy – eleven o'clock. I should have been asleep.

Such a long time since I'd seen Daddy. He was home in January for that very late Christmas and soon went again. France, Mother said. I counted up the months. Eight since I'd seen him. He'd sent a special postcard and something for my birthday – must have been my ninth – but otherwise nothing, apart from what Mother read out from his letters. His violin, closed up in its case, stood in the corner of the kitchen, neglected like a dunce. Did Daddy miss it? What was he doing that he couldn't have it with him and play it? Was he in The Trenches? That's where Elsie Dormer's daddy was.

A sudden spatter on the window.

I remember wondering if the same rain was falling in France. I knew it was Daddy's birthday soon. I hoped it wouldn't rain then. We believed it was bad luck if it rained on your birthday.

And then something reminded me of Uncle Row. He'd been in France, too. Did people remember death-days as well as birthdays?

I turned and faced the wall, even gave myself a lecture about going to sleep. But night-worries about Daddy still chased me. I sighed, turned again and clenched my eyes, trying to block them out.

* * *

Next morning, Mother was dressing Bea. Soon be time for school and another day would pass without telling anyone.

"Mama?" I waited.

She smoothed down Bea's dress and tapped her bottom. "There, miss, that's you done. Now, go and find Rowley. See what mischief he's up to." She sat back on her heels. "What is it, Dorothy?"

I waited until Bea had tottered off. "Mama, I keep having bad thoughts."

"Oh, dear, what sort of bad thoughts?" Her voice became gentler than usual.

"Bad thoughts that frighten me."

"When is this – at night? Like bad dreams?"

"No, they follow me around all day and won't leave me alone. *And* they come at night."

She went to the wicker chair and patted a space next to her. "Come here. Tell me what's troubling you." I squeezed in and leant back against her. "Now, what is it?"

"You know you said Grandpa Baxter was your daddy and Uncle Row was your brother?"

"Yes?"

"And you said you were sad because you wouldn't see them anymore."

"Yes?"

"Are they in heaven now?"

"That's what we're supposed to believe. It would be nice to think so."

I took a deep breath and rushed the worries into words. "Mama, shall I see Daddy again?"

"Of course, dear, we have to hope so – when the war's over. Now, put those thoughts out of your head and go and fetch the children. It's time for breakfast, then school."

When we were all seated, she said: "Now, you may have butter on your bread or bramble jelly, but not both."

Rowley made a disappointed "Oh, why?"

"Ssh! Because I say so." She sat down with an empty plate in front of her.

"Aren't you eating, Mama?" I said.

"Not just now. I'm not hungry. Later, perhaps."

That puzzled me. Somebody at school said that ladies who were going to have a baby had to eat for two. Now she wasn't even hungry for one. Was she sad about Uncle Row? Or was it something else?

A lot of things we didn't understand in those days.

FORTY-TWO

"I thought it the most unmitigated twaddle I'd ever heard. I ask you... The fool said to me: 'That must be the most heartfelt prayer you've ever uttered.' I didn't *pray* out there, I cursed from the bottom of my being. And meant it, too." John lowered his head. "Not that I'm proud of it." He took a sip of whisky; the chair creaked beneath him. Sunset drinks in Henshaw's office, back at the Clearing Station.

"How did he know?" Henshaw said.

"Sov must have said something. He was pretty cut up seeing me like that. He looks out for me, you know. It's mutual. Probably thought the padre could help. Instead of which, the fellow merely annoyed me."

Henshaw shook his head. "I don't have much truck with the pious brigade. Good enough for ceremonial and the like. But that's about all. They slant everything to their advantage. You notice our padre wasn't up at the Front, sharing the dangers. He was back here, waiting for the soft jobs to come in." John opened his mouth, but Henshaw went on: "I know they're not all like that. But I'll tell you another thing. I'm pretty damn sure Jesus wouldn't go along with blessing the guns and all that other clap-trap the church gets up to. We both know this isn't a holy war and no amount of churchifying can make it so. It's not Onward Christian Soldiers and Fight the Good Fight. We're a long way on from The Angel of Mons and all that. And, of course, our brother Germans invoke God's help just as much, believe in divine support, too. However, we have a secret weapon: they don't know that God's an Englishman. So that's all right." He grinned, drained his glass and leant back in his chair.

John gave a rueful smile. "I feel very raw. I volunteered for all this because of a semi-religious calling. And now it seems to have evaporated overnight. I'm rudderless. And so tired." He yawned.

"You volunteered because it's in your nature, not because of God. You're a good man, and a sensitive man, and care about others, God or not. In that sense, nothing's altered. You, the man, haven't changed." He smiled to himself. "Nearly said, 'Thank God.' But look, now we're back on rest, you must let this go. You'll drive yourself crackers if you dwell on everything. You know, there are times when a man should get drunk. We tasted hell out there and, fortunately, we've come through. Now we put all that behind us because we have to, and that's where the old whisky can help." He reached into the bottom drawer of his desk and brought out the bottle. "Have another finger of our beloved general's tipple."

John held up his hand. "No, no, not too much. Mustn't overdo it. I'm on parade in eight hours."

"That's easily solved. I'll write you a chit, excusing you, for once. Now then..." He pulled out a medical pad from another drawer. "I certify that Corporal J Hemingby is suffering from..." He looked up at the ceiling. "Suspected ubriacosis, that'll do. Should get past the sergeant-major." Henshaw grinned.

"What on earth does that mean?"

"Not a great deal. I made it up. If you remember your Italian, you'll know I've derived it from their word for *drunk*. Posh name for a hangover. You deserve a day off, especially after going that whole time out there without rest or food. I wasn't happy about that. You're too good to lose through self-neglect. And what's more, I want you sleeping in a bed tonight. There's nobody in scabies at the moment so we'll put you there where you'll have some peace." John opened his mouth to speak. "And don't worry. I've squared it with the sister. They might even bring you a cup of tea in the morning."

"OK. I shan't protest. I'm dead-beat anyway." He sighed. "I can't imagine what I shall say to Lambert's parents."

"You must leave that. I know it's on your mind, it'll stay with you for some time, but fortunately it's not your job. Lambert's superior officer will do the 'It is my painful duty' bit."

"But I must say something. I was there. I cannot let the death of one of my star pupils pass without comment. He had such a promising future. I'm devastated. God knows how his people will feel." He closed his eyes. *God* again, he thought: suddenly so far away.

★ ★ ★

"I'm sorry, Corporal, you'll have to move." The sister loomed above his bed, holding an oil lamp.

He blinked and screwed up his eyes. "What time is it?"

"Shortly after three. Sleep on the floor over there if you can, but we need this bed. It's an emergency. We've got serious gas cases coming in."

"Where from?" Stupid question; what did it matter? All cases were urgent.

The nurse busied away to the entrance to the tent. "I think someone said Saint Julien." She flung the words over her shoulder. John, bleared in thought, rolled onto his feet. He sniffed. Strange – a waft of garlic on the air.

An army of whispering ghosts began shuffling towards him, their shadows huge in the lamp-glow. A nurse or an orderly guided each one. The men clung tight and shambled forward. All bowed their heads. Coughs, wheezes. One soldier waved a hand in front of him as if wiping away cobwebs.

"Lie down there, soldier. You're safe now." The young nurse helped the man onto John's bed. "Ooh, you're lucky. This one's still warm."

Eyelids yellow-gummed and stuck together.

"I can't breathe," the man whispered, "my throat's closing up. I'm going to choke, I know I am. Help me."

But the nurse had gone.

"It's all right, soldier. Hang on!" John stood foolish in his shirt tails, without his boots.

"Who's there?" A voice of fear.

"Don't worry. I'm an orderly. Corporal Hemingby."

"A bowl! Quick!" Already the retching sound.

John snatched a white enamel basin from a tumbled stack at the side of the tent. The man struggled up onto one arm and vomited blindly over the side of the bed. A splatter of thin blood-stained muck. Some reached the bowl; droplets scattered over John's bare legs; a pink-green pool of froth bubbled on the bed. The man collapsed onto the pillow, gasping.

John beckoned a nurse and began to struggle into his trousers. No need for words. He bent down, eased into his boots and began winding on his puttees.

"Is it day or night?" the soldier said to the air.

"Middle of the night, still dark," the nurse said.

"Oh, sod it all. I'm blind, then," the man said. "I can't tell light from dark." He sank back. "I'm blind. Sod it all."

"Take it easy. It's just temporary," John said. "You've been gassed. It'll probably clear." Not sure he sounded convincing.

Near the entrance, Sergeant Skinner directed soldiers and their nurses towards vacant beds. "Lucky, dry weather has cut down the lice population, else we'd have been really up the creek where to put these buggers."

"I've seen gas cases before. Nothing like this," John said. "What is it?"

Garlic smell stronger now, or was it horseradish?

"You ain't seen the worst. The Boche have really cooked up something special. I've 'eard talk it's a mixture of mustard gas and phosgene. Burns and chokes. I reckon we'll 'ave to keep some of these ten days or so before we can evacuate them. Look, Smiler, I know you're off duty but lend a hand with the stretcher cases. We'll have to strap many of these poor bastards in their beds so they don't hurt theirselves. I'm going to detail a party to destroy all this clothing. The buggers are bringing the gas in on their uniforms. Can't you smell it? We'll all be bloody choked."

Four bearers staggered in, carrying on their shoulders a man on a stretcher. His breath a rasp of despair, he clawed at the air and wrestled to sit up. The strong leather straps checked him and he sank down again.

"Over there, lads." Skinner indicated a designated isolation area as he walked away.

The man wailed at the sudden descent. "What's happening?" He writhed and tried to sit up.

"Take it easy, you're safe now," John said. "There's a bed here."

"I'm dying, I can't see." Voice, a rough whisper.

The bearers bundled him off the stretcher. "Strap him down!" one said. "Now! Before he injures hisself." The man churned and twisted upwards as if struggling out of a smothering blanket.

"Hold him down, lads, I'll pull this belt tighter," John said. "Easy, soldier, easy."

A hoarse scream.

No time to linger. Another stretcher, another case. And another.

"Go steady with this one. He's got blisters and all sorts. Bloody hell!"

★ ★ ★

He found Henshaw in the far corner of the tent bending over a bed. Behind him, two orderlies struggled to put up netting to give the area privacy and make it insect-proof. Henshaw straightened up. "Ah, John! Good to see you. Sorry our devious little scheme didn't work out. How's the head?"

"Well, thank you, sir. Slept like a top for four hours. No sign of ubriacosis."

"Wish I could say the same. My head's very woolly. Now look, I'd like you in charge here. Pick the gentlest orderlies you know, and I'm assigning you Atherstone as well."

"What casualties are here, then?" John glanced across at two of the beds where soldiers lay with chests uncovered. "Oh, good God, what's caused that? Looks like the plague. Or burns."

"Obscene, isn't it? That's another result of the latest Boche weapon, and I don't know what the hell to do to treat it."

"You mean mustard gas causes those sores also?"

"Doesn't come out straightaway, apparently. They say it starts with a red rash which becomes a yellow blister. See that poor Tommy with a bubo under the armpit? When that bursts, you get a suppurating open sore which will be the very devil to clear. These poor chaps will be terribly scarred."

"But they'll live, though, sir?"

Henshaw tightened his lips and did not reply.

★ ★ ★

Both the man's hands showed blisters that had burst. Craters on the moon, he thought. Raw, rucked flesh tinged with yellow. He flinched at the thought of touching it.

"I'll go easy, Captain," he said, "but I have to do it. This is antiseptic ointment. It'll sting rather to start with but it should help calm it down."

The man blinked at him. "Go right ahead, I can take it." The voice a multi-toned wheeze, like blowing through tissue paper on a comb. "Never believe I was wearing gloves, would you?"

"Really?"

"Filthy stuff. They call it gas, but it gets on your clothes, stays on the ground. Terrible if you sit on anything contaminated." He coughed and swallowed. "Sorry. Almost like acid. Don't know what my wife'll say. She said she fell in love with my hands. Now look." He tensed up as John began massaging the cream in.

"Sorry, is it stinging?"

"I can take it. But I don't want to watch."

He hated using rubber gloves. So clumsy and mechanical just when the man needed reassurance of human contact. He cradled the captain's hand in his own and used his thumbs to circle the wound.

The captain sucked in breath at his touch.

"Sorry, sir, soon be done."

He straightened up and moved away. What if I return home maimed or disfigured? Chances are something'll happen; my luck can't last for ever. Dying would be simplest. Em would get a widow's pension: she'd carry on with her usual calm resolution. But what would the children make of a father seriously injured? Would Dorothy shrink from me?

★ ★ ★

"Corporal, I'm sorry, can you come quickly? I've a patient here I cannot get into bed. He keeps pacing up and down. Won't listen to a word I say. He just brushes us aside. We need a big man to persuade him." The nurse looked anxious, her hands held in front of her like a parlour maid being rebuked. John peeled off his rubber gloves and followed her.

He recognised the hooked nose and the shock of unruly hair: new was the determined striding, the hunched shoulders, the bowed head. And no spectacles. "Good Lord!" He turned to the nurse. "It's all right, I recognise him. Gurney, old fellow, what's going on?" He caught hold of the man's elbow.

"Keep away. Can't you see I'm touched by fire? It'll go, if I don't walk. I shall lose it. Leave me be. This is important." Gurney stopped to cough. He held his chest for a moment and continued pacing up and down. "*Dah*, tat, tat, tat, tat. *Dah*, tat, tat, tat, tat."

John turned to the nurse and shrugged. "He can be rather eccentric."

"I don't care if he's the King of Siam. Our orders are to get all patients into bed as quick as possible. He'll make himself worse."

"Ivor," he called, as Gurney strode past. "You ought to be in bed."

"I nearly have it. It's nothing, a cold; sore throat. A theme for my symphony. It's perfect, I know it is. Ludwig says it's been done before. But I want to capture the tattering of the machine gun.

That's new. They didn't have that: *Dah*, tat, tat, tat, tat..." Gurney tramped away.

A Scotsman in the next bed strained up off the pillow, his voice a croak: "Och, Corporal, can you no' shut the fucker up?"

"OK, Jock," John said. He turned to the nurse. "Can you get me a paper and pencil?"

"I'll try." She hurried off into the further gloom.

Gurney began pacing back. "Stop!" John said. "I think I can help. Am I right? Are you trying to do *Severn and Somme* in music, the pastoral interwoven with military rhythms?"

Gurney stopped, laughed and began coughing. "You must be reading my mind. How on earth...? I knew you were a capital fellow."

"Now, look..." John steered him by the elbow towards the bed in the corner of the tent. "Sit down there. I've sent for some paper. You hop into bed, keep the nurses happy, we'll talk about it, and I'll make some notes." His brain raced as he tried to humour Gurney.

"I can't sleep. Won't sleep. Not at a moment like this. I've got to work. If only my eyes didn't itch." He sat on the bed and scrubbed at one with the back of his hand.

"No, don't do that. You'll make it worse." John glanced round. No sign of the nurse. What next? Distract him; keep Gurney sitting down. "Now, you've got the machine gun on the side drums, presumably; the big guns – bass drum or kettle drums? Will you want the sound of the whizz bangs coming in as well?"

"You do, you understand, don't you? Marvellous." Gurney began taking off his boots and trousers.

"Now, lie back and tell me about your pastoral theme – woodwind, I suppose, flutes and clarinets?"

Gurney eased down into the bed. "It's Chosen Hill. I want to capture lying flat, gazing up at the sky. It'll come in twice: once for the sounds of the birds, distant sheep, wind in the trees – daytime stuff – and come back in the minor key to represent the scene at night. You know, like that poem of Bridges. I can just hear it."

"Yes?" John felt the nurse slide a notebook onto his lap. She said nothing. He nodded his thanks.

"Right, Ivor, what shall I put down? What key are we in?" No reply. "I'll assume it's F major like Beethoven's Pastoral, for the moment, shall I?" He glanced across at Gurney who lay flat on his back, a hand shading his eyes.

"I can't quite reach it yet," Gurney said. "It's not ready to come out."

Feared as much, John thought. "Never mind. Now look, I have to get back to my patients, but I'll leave this notebook on the table so you can jot things down when you're ready."

Gurney, eyes still shaded, nodded.

John spoke briefly to the nurse. "I think he's quietened down now. Look after him, won't you? He is a rather queer fish, but he's a very talented young man."

FORTY-THREE

Gurney chased the spoon around the tin and crammed in a second, third and fourth mouthful of plum and apple jam. In a world of his own, he stared at the tug and billow of the tent walls as the wind played with the canvas.

"Heavens, Ivor," John said, "what's going on?"

"Brain food – helps me think, especially when my guts play havoc. I need to be making music. If I can walk, I can make music. That's when I compose. But I can't walk because of this confounded thing." He tugged at the leather strap which tethered him to the bed like a wayward foal.

"It's for your own safety, old chap." And ours, too. Can't have you rampaging around half the night. "So, how did you get the jam?"

"Young nurse fetched it, specially when I said the hospital food was burning my throat."

"Likely to be the effects of gas. Take life easy, you're a casualty after all."

"No! Time is hurrying away, you fool. If you'd heard VW's Tallis Variations, you'd know what I mean. That's the way forward. Set us on fire, both Howler and me. Those marvellous echoes, that antiphonal effect."

"You're not making much sense, old chap."

"Oh, for heaven's sake – music. Isn't it obvious?"

"No, I'm sorry, I –"

"They make a special target of me, you know, the Boche."

"I guess they would. In an attack, taking out a machine gun post is always an objective. Good defence, too."

"No, not military reasons!"

"Why, then?"

"Oh, for heaven's sake! Have you no inkling? I thought at least you'd understand. You've let me down."

"No, I'm sorry, you've lost me, Ivor."

"It's obvious. Because I'm twenty years ahead of my time, idiot! And they don't like that, the Germans. They don't like the English taking over and leading. Like every dog, they've had their day. I'm to be the world-class composer now."

"But –"

"– I'm unteachable – of course I am. That's what they said at the college – Old Pince-nez Stanford. But I'll show them, I'll show you all. When I hire the Queen's Hall. Didn't you hear the applause when they brought me in here?"

John closed his eyes. Heavens, what next? He changed the subject. "Is it lonely being a machine gunner?"

"He doesn't mind it. Easier being at some remove from the men he's paid to kill. Better than all that 'fix bayonets and over the top' stuff. Don't get too close. Anyway, probably has a charmed life, Old Batty. I reckon he has. Hit twice by shrapnel, nearly taken down by a sniper. Must be a reason. But now I've had my three – like having three wishes. Significance there, see. When they're gone..."

"You've been hit twice – where?"

"The men call him a daredevil, say he doesn't look after himself. But I tell you he's saner than many." Gurney wagged a finger and looked him straight in the eye. He grinned. "They'll give him a medal one day."

"Where were you hit, Ivor?"

"Helmet dented and a scar round here somewhere." He pointed to the back of his head. "But they didn't knock his block off."

"A scar on your neck? Shall I take a look?"

Gurney shrugged and eased up onto an elbow. "Other time, it was on the belt. Sent me flying but no mark. Charmed genius, you see. I'm being looked after. But only three times, after that luck runs out."

"I see."

"And now it's raining. Will you listen to that din?" They both looked up at the sloping canvas. "Like a thousand drums." Gurney sighed. "How can I work, how can I think with that cacophony? Still, better here, I suppose, flat on my back, tied down by imbeciles, than in the trenches. I don't think I can stomach another winter in this Hell of desolation. Think of the mud waiting to suck the life out of you. That water swilling around your feet. I'm sick of living in slum conditions, sick of being away from all my friends." He yawned and relaxed as if a fever began to leave him. "I'm so worn-minded. I don't want to be out here until The Last Crump. If only I could receive a Blighty: just a little hole in the leg. That'd do it."

"Who knows, old chap, they may send you home sooner than you think." An idea began to form.

"Oh, no. That'd be evading duty. He's not a shirker. There's nothing wrong with him. Only received mild exposure. Some distance from the main trenches. The machine gun post. Sore throat, that's all – no worse than catarrh or a bad cold. Heard the gas shells landing, you know. Strange noise, not a bang at all. More a plop. Hard to capture in music. Maybe a poem."

"You've been fortunate, Ivor. You didn't get the fearful blisters some of our boys have got, but you're far from well. I doubt you could walk far. Not now. You'd need a stretcher. You're exhausted."

★ ★ ★

He stood at ease in the shadows of the mess, conscious of an itch on his thigh he daren't scratch. But Hubert insisted on his presence because of his special knowledge. He sighed, pursed his lips. Must remember to shave my moustache off. Makes me look very old-school. Don't want that. Clean-shaven is the coming man.

He tried to remember whether Gurney still had his moustache.

He'd not taken to the new colonel – almost a caricature of a senior officer. Red cheeks high-polished by gin every evening, watery blue eyes, a dangling monocle and a moustache which reminded John of the brush his mother used to sweep up crumbs from the breakfast table. Bristly of face and temper, you could see. The man brooked no opinion that didn't coincide with his own. Long service in India had fostered an imperious attitude towards anyone not his equal. How different from Hubert! He too looked the old-school officer and doctor, with his pointed moustache and neat appearance, but there was warmth and flexibility about him, even something of the rebel with his long, greying hair which fringed his bald head and wormed out from under his cap. Not a confirmed soldier. He inspired affection and loyalty: the man listened to others, his humanity not ordered by the rule book.

"Now look, Henshaw," the colonel said, "Are we agreed that we ship ninety per cent of these gas cases back to Blighty once they're fit enough? Let the wallahs over there sort them out."

"I think so, sir. We haven't the facilities to treat gas burns or the bad chest cases anyway, but if we keep 'em, we shall only clog up our own clearing. Besides, there's talk of intensifying the push towards Passchendaele which can only mean more casualties to cope with."

"My sentiments, entirely, Henshaw, so let's stick 'em on a barge and get 'em off down river. Now, what about the other ten per cent? Any chaps we can turn around and send back to their units? Those that can see again and are cough-free? They've had their rest-time here. Or shall we bung 'em all down to Base for a few weeks to recuperate?"

"I think send them on to Base, sir. Many of 'em should pick up in six weeks or so. But there is one case I'd like to bring to your attention."

"Yes, what is it?" The colonel squinted at his wristwatch.

"Well, it concerns one character, Private Gurney, who isn't badly affected by the gas as far as we can tell, but I'd prefer Corporal Hemingby here to tell you about him. He's had more close dealings than I have."

"Oh, very well."

John cleared his throat and stepped forward. Should he stand to attention? "In my view, sir, Gurney isn't a clear case by a long chalk. Quite frankly, I don't know what's wrong with him. He's not a well man, certainly. We know he's been gassed and he's making a slow recovery from that, but there is something else –"

"Not malingering is he? I won't have that. We can soon find ways to put some backbone into him."

"No, with respect, sir –"

"Yes, get on with it, man!"

"Although he's only been slightly gassed – Gurney himself plays it down – and in time could probably recover physically, there's something not quite right about him."

"Shellshocked, is he? Lacking moral fibre and playing that card?"

"Not exactly, sir, no. Gurney himself calls it neurasthenia and that might lead one to suspect shellshock. But he's not withdrawn like most cases, not now, anyway. It's either shellshock or he's not, to put it bluntly, right in the head."

"What do you make of it, Henshaw?"

"Difficult to say, sir. From what Corporal Hemingby has told me, Gurney appears to have two different moods. At the moment, he seems elated, full of energy; earlier in the year, when Hemingby came across him, he was very low. And some of his thoughts and actions are distinctly bizarre. He's not well. Talented, but not well."

The colonel blew his nose loudly and wiped its tip vigorously. "Are you talking about this schizophrenia mumbo-jumbo? Jekyll and Hyde stuff?"

John stepped forward to protest; Henshaw put a restraining hand on his arm: "Well, hardly. I'm not qualified –"

"All this split personality stuff – that's what it means, doesn't it?"

"Well…"

"Move him on. Ship him out. All right? Don't want to risk him getting doolally tap on us. If the man's showing signs of lunacy, we

286

don't want him out here. That's for certain. Ruddy liability. Let the quacks at home take a look at him."

"That's probably best, sir," Henshaw said.

"As far as I'm concerned, that goes for anyone who's malingering, scrimshanking or just not cutting the mustard. Any neurasthenic oddball is no good to us as a soldier. They're a hindrance to the war effort. Move 'em on, I say."

Maybe you're the lucky one, Ivor, John thought, back in the shadows. You'll soon be cruising down the Seine, but we'll still be here, stuck in the mud and this weather. He sighed. *Hey, ho the wind and the rain. The rain it raineth every day.* Feste's old song wouldn't leave him alone.

★ ★ ★

The two spouts dripped onto the corrugated roof with an irregular pattering. He listened to the desolate sound, the metallic rhythm. Gurney would capture that and use it in an orchestral piece. He smiled to himself. Guard duty! This futile farce of keeping watch so far behind the line. Had to be done, though: King's Regulations. An exercise even while on rest.

His life seeping away in rain: drips from his tin hat onto his cape, a trickle down his nose, the sting of water in his eyes, a run from the cape onto the back of his hands. Drenched. Far away, a crowd of men in a barn, singing music hall songs of home. Their careless, swooping voices provoked a lump in his throat. Long hours of lonely silence broken by the occasional lurch and whine of an ambulance engine; faint guns so far off that Sov snoring in the nearby guard house drowned them easily. Forty miles away, probably. No flickers in the sky. Birthday next week. John Hemingby, family man, approaching thirty-eight. He licked the rain off his lips; it tasted of nothing.

FORTY-FOUR

He propped the mirror against a shell case on the top of the trench and squatted on the fire-step. "Hope no one takes a pot shot while I'm shaving."

"You'll be all right, pal," said a Scottish soldier nearby. "Now's the quiet time – breakfast. We dinna fire at them and they dinna fire at us. They're as sick of it as we are." He held out a bucket of brown water. "Dip your mess tin in there, good soft rainwater, does wonders for the skin, lathers up a treat, too."

"Where do you get it from?" John said.

"Shell made a wee water-hole. Twenty yards away over the top, we draw all our water there." He waded away; muddy water swirled, slapped and settled in the trench.

John wetted his brush and circled it in the soap. Time for the 'tash to go. Stick with his decision. If he looked stupid or didn't like it, he could always grow it again.

Across the pocks and puddles of the glistening mud, he could make out the German line. Hundred yards away? Perhaps less. Hope Jock was right. My great head poking above the parapet.

He lathered his face and drew the razor over his cheeks. With a bold stroke, he took off a swathe of moustache and exposed the skin beneath. He dandled the blade in the water, watched the hair and foam spread and scatter.

Someone struggling against the water in the trench. He looked round.

"Good job they issued us gumboots, eh, Smiler, not like these poor buggers. Well, I've scouted round, but I can't see nowhere for a Dressing Station or an aid post. It's all bloody mud and slosh. We got to get above water level some ways."

"How do I look, then, Sov?"

"Well, I wouldn't know you, if I didn't know you. Very different, I'd say. Makes you look younger and even more smiley."

"Not too much the buck rabbit, I trust, only nicked myself twice." John dabbed below his nose. He looked round, uncertain. "Now, where do I...?"

"Cosh it over the back, boy, everybody else does, turds and all. Someone told me how to go on a shovel just now."

"I hope one gets used to this smell." John flung the water away and wiped the tin out with his handkerchief. "Fearfully strong, isn't it? That and bodies rotting somewhere."

"I brought you two medics a wee drop o' tea, set you up for the day." A square-headed Scotsman, blue eyes screwed into a mass of crinkles, handed over two mugs. "You're honoured. We usually save these for officers. You won't taste a better brew this side of the Channel."

Just room for the two of them to sit on the fire-step, back to back, knees up. They sipped their tea.

"How long shall us be out here this time?" Sov said. "This ole mud is going to be hard-going. We'll definitely be four to a stretcher."

"It's our turn, we'll just have to stick it out, hope we get through."

"I don't know how you could stand working with the doc again in the operating theatre," Sov said. "Not a second time. I'm glad he didn't want me. I couldn't have stuck it, not for a whole week."

"I hate to say it but it becomes routine after a while. I used to loathe amputations, but it's actually the kindest and quickest way of dealing with wounds out here. Better chance of checking infection or gangrene that way. And all this confounded trench foot, I hate seeing that..."

"You'll be saying you could do the job yourself next, boy."

"Not qualified, thank heavens, and I wouldn't want to do it, but after a while the procedure's fairly similar and straightforward. I know the basic steps." Silence. Sov's back tensed against his own. A slurp of tea.

"Smiler, I have to say this, I don't know how to put it. I want to tell you something... I got this feeling. I don't know what else to call it." He paused. "I don't think I'm going to make it this trick. I en't got that notion about you. But for me..."

"Sov, you mustn't talk like that. I didn't have you down as superstitious. Change the subject, will you?"

"Well, can I give you something to keep for me, and you can always give us it back if I'm wrong..?"

Sov delved inside his uniform and passed over a small Vapo-Rub jar. "Have a look if you like. It's not private."

John opened the lid and stared at the red powder inside.

"That's home," Sov said, "that's Devon soil. I put him in there to take away. I've ploughed that wet many a time till it shone in the sun, and it glows up through the grass at you when you drive the beasts out to pasture. That's home for me, that's England. You can forget the white cliffs of Dover, that's all flummery, that's for they foreigners. This 'ere's real England where I belong. I've carried him everywhere since I joined up. But Smiler, if I cop it, promise me you'll scatter en on my grave."

"Don't say such things. Be positive, you'll get through."

"But will you do that for me?"

"I'll keep it, of course I will, your little bit of England." John tightened the lid and nestled the container inside his shirt pocket, underneath his coat. "I daren't let myself think such thoughts. I have to believe... Now, come on, old lad, we'd better get on and find a different location for the ADS. Somewhere further back, higher ground if possible." He slipped his boots into the muddy water. "I hope there's a duckboard under here somewhere."

★ ★ ★

Over the wasted land towards the German lines, nothing but a morass of black mud, giving off green rankness; pockmarked with shell-holes, sumps of water. They stopped wading along the trench.

One pool, about twenty yards ahead of the front line where the Scots' platoons were positioned, rippled, stirred as if a monster had begun to rise. A mound, a uniform, eased to the surface. Difficult to say whether the body floated face up or down; so bloated it could have been the rise of the chest or the hump of the back they saw; the arms splayed in crucifixial abandon. A trail of white-bubbled scum spread out from the corpse.

"Oh, Smiler, don't say that's the shell-hole where the Jocks got water for your shave. I hope not."

"Never mind about that. Doesn't matter. But did they make our tea with the same water? I rather think so."

"Oh, Lor', I thought it tasted a bit strong. Now what? I hope we don't go down with that there pottermain poisoning. And what about the Jocks? They been drinking it, too." Sov swung round in the water. "I shall have to warn en. I can't just leave it. Us'll soon have enough with the wounded without men going sick on us and all." He waded away, his legs shooshing waves along the trench.

Somewhere behind him, John heard the slide and splatter from the trench wall collapsing. This is hopeless, he thought. Do we really expect men to stay and fight here? It's like living in a swamp. Already his heels began to feel sore and skinned. Must get thicker socks if I'm to be wearing gumboots. His thighs felt raw, too, where the trousers above the boots had chafed. How did you shift caked-on mud?

He gazed around. Very few landmarks. Over that way, the Hun; to the right and behind, more mud and supposed safety. But in the dark?

The frog looked up at him, bulge-eyes unblinking – head bobbing above the water. When John raised his telescope to search for solid ground to construct the Dressing Station, the little head vanished.

A trio of slugs inched up the side of the trench, way above the green waterline, the ground too wet to reveal their slime trail. Lucky you're out of reach. Old froggy'd soon pick you off.

A bullet thudded into the parapet at the rear of the trench two feet in front of him. A horned beetle, like a miniature rhinoceros, hesitated in its progress along the top and scurried on, unconcerned by his presence or the shot.

Sniper, eh? Good thing I stopped. I'd have walked into that. So, breakfast's over! He cursed himself for not bringing a tin hat. Head down now, you fool.

"No," he said, decision made, "we'll have to cobble something out of that ruined hut. Hardly out of harm's way, though." He heard the slip and plash of more earth washing out of the trench wall. Freed now, panels of wicker slid into the water and bobbed before him, blocking the way. He waded on, edging them aside with his thighs. Would it be safe to lob them away, or was that to invite another pot-shot? Another earth fall, right behind him; a slight tap in the middle of the back. He turned round expecting to see Sov. An arm in the muddied uniform of a French soldier lolled out of the trench wall and dangled above the water. The sharp sweet stink of death. A partially decomposed head grinned at him out of the mud and a young rat blinked out of an eye socket. It vanished.

"Oh, shit, no." He closed his eyes, made himself look again. "*Pardon, mon vieux, dormez bien.*" He bowed slightly. He'd heard the French buried bodies in the trench walls, especially under bombardment. Skeletons made good reinforcement. He could not bring himself to fold the arm back; he left it drooping.

"What a place, what a bloody, bloody place." He began making his way towards the junction with the communication trench. Soon have to report in with his recommendation for the best site. His legs ached from wading. He put his right foot down and found it snared. He struggled with dread, as if a dead man held him fast, shook his leg to free it, felt several stabs and a buckle of pain across the top of his foot. A seep of cold crept up inside his boot towards his knee.

He reached down to find what had punctured his gumboot. Ruddy barbed wire, probably.

"Corporal! Where are yous?" A Scots voice, an edge of panic to it.

"Over here! Communication trench!" He plucked the tangle of wire off his wader and freed himself. Damnation! Now his arm was wet, too. "What's the matter?"

"Will you no come quick? Emergency! Your pal said you'd know what to do."

★ ★ ★

In the front-line trench, several Scots hacked frantically with shovels at the back mud wall.

"What are you doing, what's going on?" he said.

"Three of 'em. Down there. We got to get 'em out." A young man, red-haired, freckles, eyes wide with alarm.

"It's a dugout, Smiler," Sov said, "three Jocks went down to cook bacon and have a smoke."

"Aye, we heard the earth fall, roof probably. They're only wee boys." A small man, dark hair sleeked down.

"Right, stop!" John said. "Stop! Think what you're doing."

The men ceased digging; they stood there panting. An arrow-curl of water hastened downwards through the gaps in their earth works. "This won't do at all," he said. "Can't you see? The more you dig out, the more you'll drain the water in the trench into the dugout. It's lower than we are. You'll flood it and drown 'em."

"Well, what's to do, then?"

He thought for a moment. "You might reach them through the roof. Dig 'em out that way."

"What, up there, over the back parapet? Jerry'd pick us off one by one. It'd be suicide."

"Aye, and wi' this mud, the roof would fall in anyway. It wouldna hold." John recognised the man who had brought the tea.

"Oh, Jesus no. One way they drown, the other they's suffocated.

Oh, this lousy fuckin' war." The red-haired boy flung his shovel away and leaned his forehead against the mud wall.

"I'm sorry, lads," he said. "I really don't think there's anything we can do. Even getting an air-line in would only prolong their agony. It's just a ghastly accident. You'll have to report what's happened. Where are your officers?"

The small man with the dark hair shrugged. "No here yet, we're the advance party. Always. No fooling you, pal."

"I see. I'm sorry." What more to say? He and Sov turned away.

After a few minutes of silent wading, they stopped. Sov hung his head. "Oh, Lor', Smiler, what an awful way to go, down there in the dark. They poor boys went in for breakfast and found theirselves a tomb. I'm glad we couldn't hear en."

"You know, Sov, I fear this place is cursed. It's the devil's land, not fit for honest men. It'll be the undoing of us all."

★ ★ ★

Oh, thank God. John strode towards the brazier, his hands reaching towards the warmth. "You don't know how welcome this is." He dropped his head, rubbed his hands together.

"Yes, the lads and I were fortunate," Gosforth said. "We came upon a large dump of coal, so we have as much fuel as we want. You're not the first to be drawn to get warm."

"So good to be back on solid ground," John said. "One hellish day! Do you know Sov and I were having to pull each foot in turn out of the mud? Nine inches deep in places."

"Well, of course, we're scarcely above sea-level here," Gosforth said. "Wherever you dig, you'll find water two or three feet below the surface. Previous barrages made it worse, destroyed all the drainage, turned these lowlands into a quag. Absolute madness! I sometimes wonder if the generals have any savvy at all. How can you dig trenches in that? Or even fight? Do you know –" Gosforth was off on one of his stories now. John turned round and felt the heat from the fire on his back. "They say the CO of a Guards battalion weighed the greatcoat of one of the men when they came out of the trenches – it came to eighty pounds."

"What, with the mud? That's more than five stone, isn't it? Incredible! So, how have you managed to firm up the ground here?"

"By the simple addition of sand and cement to the existing ground mud, and so far this approach road also remains in good fettle. No, keep off that area, leave it longer to set. That'll be the stretcher holding-area at busy times. We'll have to give it protection from the worst of the weather by slinging tenting over the top."

John looked at the newly-constructed Dressing Station on the concrete base of the small building. He nodded to himself: definitely the best place.

"We've built it like a Nissen hut," Gosforth said. "Curved corrugated over the brickwork and covered it with sandbags. It'll do but it won't be proof against a direct hit. Insides are hung with blankets. That was Atherstone's idea. He and Sarnt Skinner are kitting it out now, getting shelves up and so forth."

John took a look inside: probably about nine feet wide. Soon get cramped in there.

"Should do us, Corp," Atherstone sniffed. "We're into a routine now. Know where things go so we can find 'em in a hurry."

John grinned. He could still feel the warmth from the fire on his back. "Yes, I can see. Get your priorities right. Tea mugs, top shelf where you can find 'em." He cast another look inside. Not really his territory. A long bench in the entrance, a table close to the wall and a second, little more than a couple of planks on trestles, like a saw bench. He winced, quickly blocked the thought out.

Gosforth appeared. "I reckon we've done the doc proud. Come and look at his quarters."

Around the back of the building, a little hut, also well sand-bagged, with three bunks inside. It looked like the top half of an ambulance wagon. The area set aside for Henshaw was screened by a blanket hanging from the roof. It didn't quite reach the mud floor.

"He's in there now, taking a nap, best not disturb him," Gosforth whispered.

They walked away, gazing back over the mudscape that rolled down towards the trenches. Splintered trees dotted the area like the sharpened stakes of a stockade.

"We'll about get by as long as it doesn't rain," Gosforth said. "Luck's been with us so far, but there are so many streams flowing through the area..."

"You heard about the Jocks?" John said. Still on his mind.

"Yes, of course." Gosforth tightened his lips, said nothing further. He busied himself filling his pipe and cupped his hands round a lighter to get it started.

John sighed, turned back towards the brazier. He stared at the coals. So callous blocking out mention of dead men once they'd gone. As though they'd never been. That theme again. Not done to dwell, but what was acceptable to speak about? At least he could talk to Hubert after Lambert's death. "Must be difficult to keep a rifle fit to use out here," he said. "Armourers will have their work cut out with this lot, freeing up the mechanisms. Getting rid of the mud and rust."

Gosforth blew out a cloud of smoke. "Cushy job, though, back there, out of harm's way. If I was better with my hands, I'd have got in on that. Yes, funny coves the Scots. Race apart, you know. Not very practical. I mean, why pitch their cookhouse in a place that got flooded? Did you hear about it? Where's the sense in that? They should have thought. The poor bloody platoon had to live on sodden biscuits and cold stew for three days. Quartermaster so mean – no new rations until they'd finished it." Gosforth reached into his pocket and drew out a tin of cigarettes. He offered one to John, who held up a hand in refusal. "I did hear of one Jock who insisted on bringing bagpipes into the trenches. I ask you, what's he hope to do – blow bubbles?"

"But when it comes to fighting, the Scots are as brave as any, I'm sure," John said. He wished he'd still got his fiddle with him.

"Not right in the head, though, some of them. I heard of one who refused to kip in the trenches – that was *before* they got flooded. Every night when it got dark, he'd scramble up over the back parapet and sleep where any shell or bullet flying around could get him."

"Yes, I wouldn't choose to sleep amongst all the stuff that gets thrown there," John said. "But you can't sleep in these trenches unless you're standing up, because of the water. I suppose if you're tired enough, you'll sleep anywhere, you don't care: death only means sleep."

"You know where your kip is tonight, do you?" Gosforth's pipe had gone out. He laid it with care on one of the shelves. "Save that for later."

"I hope Wing and Underwood have got our bivvy up by now," John said. "Better go and find it, make sure I know how to locate it in the dark. Thanks for the warm. And well done, you've made a good job of this." He walked away, aware of the sand grinding under his gum boots.

★ ★ ★

The reek from his body convinced him he ought to bathe. His right arm was covered with green slime from the trench water and where the gumboot had leaked, his trouser leg smelled of mud and damp serge. In the dim light inside the tent, he caught sight of himself in a fragment of mirror and saw a face muddied to the eyes. "Gosforth didn't say anything," he said to himself. "You scruffy individual. Ought to be on a charge."

He peeled his uniform off and cast it in a heap on the floor. The gumboot waders he flung out through the flap onto the waiting mud. Maybe they could be patched. Now, with a clean shirt and a change of trousers, he'd be dry enough. Leave the jacket off a while, perhaps near the fire. Clean socks and everyday boots, that should do it.

The washroom was a half-tented area screened off by flaps of tarpaulin. No hot water, of course. Drums of roughly filtered yellow rainwater lined the back canvas wall. Already naked, he dipped a bucket in and poured the water over his head. He gasped, watched the water trickle and puddle over the mud. Again? He swung the bucket and sluiced himself once more, feeling his hair hanging lank against his face. With the little left in the bucket, he laboured at his chest, armpits and private parts. "That'll have to do," he said aloud. He stroked his upper lip where his moustache had been – a reflex action. Idiot! He began to shiver. Oh heavens, forgotten the towel. Just have to pad back like this over the mud. This'll scare the Boche, if they spot me. A chill touch from the mist on his back.

The rough towel smelled of vinegar. He began drying himself, hoping to warm up with vigorous scrubbing. He stopped, the towel draped over his head. Without warning, his chest began to shudder in silent panting. Tears. "Oh, God, no. Not now. Those poor boys. Not now, not here." He clamped the towel to his face, bit his bottom lip until the sobs stopped. He lowered the towel, stood there naked, features screwed in grief. "Oh, God!"

A head appeared at the tent flap. "Oh, sorry, Corp." The young private looked embarrassed. Had he heard? "Message from the major: important you report to him at his quarters. But he did say 'in your own time'." The soldier vanished.

He sniffed and wiped his eyes. "Now, why's Hubert so insistent?" He began pulling his clothes on. "Sounds like an order."

★ ★ ★

They had moved the brazier to the entrance of the medics' sleeping quarters, so that its glow was not visible. It had been capped with sand. Henshaw slumped forward on a folding stool, holding a mug of tea. At John's approach, he gave a weary smile. "Ah, Corporal, pick up a stool, will you?" Official meeting, then.

"No snifter this evening, I'm afraid," Henshaw said, "not when we're both on in a few hours. You're welcome to a beaker of this disgusting tea, but quite frankly, I shouldn't bother." He sat up and squared his shoulders. "But I did want to see you before bedlam breaks out. Are all arrangements satisfactory as far as you're concerned?"

"I should say so, sir, but I would have preferred better conditions all round."

"Couldn't agree more. I scarcely believed it when I saw this place. You hear stories about the mud and the trenches. I can believe in the Slough of Despond now, and to be quite frank – I don't mind admitting it – it's getting me down already. It's like being on the sea, but a sea of mud. I couldn't see a blade of grass or a spot of colour anywhere. Over there, where the Boche are, one presumes, is something which you might exaggerate and call a 'hill'. That must be the celebrated Passchendaele Ridge that's so important strategically." He shook his head; there was silence. "But everywhere's like a place abandoned. How can you tell what's solid and what isn't? Do you know, one of the MOs said the ground shakes like blancmange when our guns are firing?" He paused and stared into the fire. "Now, I want to say this. You must be careful out there. You don't know how deep those craters, those shell-holes are. The water could be waist-deep or maybe close over your head. I don't envy you and your teams working in the mud. It's like tottering over an abyss, a sucking hostile place just waiting for you to make a mistake. There's nowhere you can be sure of your footing."

"I agree," John said, "conditions are atrocious."

"Now listen: you must urge your bearers to keep to the duckboards the sappers have been laying. Wherever possible. They're ramshackle, I know, but at least they'll spread your weight. And another thing – you probably haven't heard. I've sent word round advising all our fellows to check their wills are up-to-date and signed, if they aren't already."

"Sov Poundsbury said something about dying earlier, and now you say this. Do you really think it'll be bad?"

"This is a life-changing place. We really don't know what's going to happen. For example: did you hear about that poor fellow earlier who wandered off the duckboards into a shell-hole? Can you imagine it? The bally thing was filled with mud like thick porridge. Stuff of nightmare." Henshaw stood up and warmed his hands at the brazier. "His mates tried to pull the poor devil out, but they couldn't. They tried to dig him out, but the mud flowed back as fast as they shovelled it away."

John winced and blocked out the image of that liquid slip near the dugout. His eyes felt sore and staring.

"In the end, someone brought up a mule. They succeeded in passing a rope under the man's shoulders and hauled him out. But they wrecked his spine. They carried him in here with such pain there was nothing much I could do. I gave him an injection, of course, and sent him on to Clearing straightaway. Couldn't even clean him up. He was caked in that clinging, stinking mud." He laid a hand on John's shoulder. "Promise me, you'll take extreme care. I really don't want accidents." John looked up and their eyes met for a second. "You look different, John – apart from your grubby face. Younger without your moustache, that's what it is. Younger, but not foolish, please."

"Is my face still dirty? I'm sorry, Henshaw." John scrubbed at his cheeks with the back of his fist.

"Think nothing of it. Only a fool martinet would worry about spit and polish out here. So, as I see it, we shall have to get casualties away at night, it's the only safe way. The ambulances will be driving without lights. Let's hope they don't come off the road. As it is, the surface will get churned up, and if the enemy find our range, it'll become pitted with shell-holes. Our fellows deserve a medal if they manage to avoid wrecking the vehicle. Now look: at least one member of each bearer team must carry a supply of morphine tablets to put under a casualty's tongue. I've already briefed Sarnt Skinner, and he'll issue them. I suspect you won't have a long carry, at least to start with – there'll be casualties pretty close by – but some poor devils will have to wait until they can be brought in. Hence the morphine."

"I'll carry some myself, sir."

"Next point: I want you to make sure you all eat and take a break from time to time. You, in particular. I don't want heroics, and I don't want you cracking up because you've pushed yourself too hard, like you did last time. Now, that's an order." He grinned, patted John on the shoulder.

"I've been thinking about Gurney. I'm glad we got him away. You were right: he was becoming increasingly disturbed out here. Not surprising. Maybe Blighty rest will level him out again. I did actually write and ask my daughter, Letty, if she'd heard anything on the grapevine about him. Apparently, he had a song cycle published some time ago which was generally well received. Juvenilia, but he made a name for himself. She remembers talk of a concert – before the war – with a particularly powerful song about yearning for sleep." Henshaw yawned. "Excuse me. I tried sleeping this afternoon but my head was so busy with things to do... Which reminds me, finally, I don't care what time of day it is, or whether I've already managed to turn in or not, I want you to report to me last thing before you get your head down. Even if you have to wake me. I guess your teams will have to do quite a bit of carrying after dark, so, for my own peace of mind, I need to know where you are and that you're safe. Is that clear? Don't look surprised. You're part of the team I rely on. I care what happens to all of you – Atherstone and Skinner, as well. You're key parts of life out here and important to me in consequence. But *we* shall be based here, and you'll be out there in danger. Besides all that, you personally are important. You should know that by now."

He shook John's hand. "Good luck, old lad. Now, go and get your head down while you can. Once our guns open up, it'll be pandemonium and you'll not get much rest."

"Thank you, sir. May I say it's a privilege to have you as a friend and senior officer." John saluted and turned away. The sort of chap I'd lay down my life for, he thought, if I had to.

★ ★ ★

301

He began padding back towards the tent, flat-footed to minimise the risk of slipping. Ahead, a flash of light out of the darkness. Certainly well behind British lines.

"Put that light out, you fool!" His shout a reflex; the damp flatness all around absorbed it and deadened it. "You'll draw enemy fire!" What idiot would do that? He hesitated, hoping it wasn't an officer on some last-minute errand.

The beam wavered into the sky, casting a shaft of light onto the low-hanging mist; it lit up the peak of one of the tents and faded, leaving a red glow like a cigarette. Someone making a late trip to the latrines. Feltham, probably, the slovenly bastard.

Why was Hubert so set on him writing a will? He'd always blocked off the idea. Death happened to other people. But now... He tried picturing his family back in that other world. Em would be big with the fourth child now. Sometime in October, she said. Mere weeks away. If he died, that child would grow up not knowing his father. What about the others? Dorothy – was she nine now? – she'd remember him; perhaps even Rowland would, but Bea, the little animal lover, she'd hardly seen him. What would she know of this stranger who came and went like a shadow in her life?

"Now stop it, you idiot!" He'd chided Sov earlier, and now... "You want to live!" His voice a hiss in the darkness. "You have to believe you'll come through." The fog caressed his cheek, cool on his face.

Blind optimism, his head said. *Fool!*

He blocked the voice out.

Em, so small in height, but determined and organised – his rock – so capable he felt ashamed of his own inadequacy.

"If I wrote a will, and I did go, my old dear, what would I leave you that you haven't got already?"

FORTY-FIVE

I've often wondered how Mother managed all those years ago. We weren't well off; she was certainly never a spendthrift. But we got by. We had Daddy's money coming in, but she must have inherited some of Grandpa Baxter's money and used that. It can only have been a few hundred pounds – a paltry figure by today's standards. But she was always *efficient* as a mother – you wouldn't call her loving. It was as if she eked out everything: emotions, money, caring. Life had to be steady, calm and ordered. She hated change.

In that autumn term when I was nine, I had a new teacher, Miss Johnstone. She was a kindly woman – young I'd say now, probably only mid-twenties, but already there was something sad about her. Quite pretty in a melancholy way; I often wondered whether she'd had a sweetheart or why she'd never married. She offered me art lessons after school and that particular evening, while she was tidying the classroom, she gave me a book to look at which had pictures of flowers beautifully drawn and painted. I never knew so many daisies existed: purples, reds, yellows and, of course, white.

"You like flowers, don't you, Dorothy?"

"Yes, Ma'am. I think they're easier to paint than people or animals."

"Why's that, would you say?"

"I like their colours, and because flowers keep still when you're drawing them. You can go right up to them without being rude and look at them closely when you want to."

I first found I liked daisies when sitting on Aunty Daphne's lawn at home. I loved the little white stars that appeared in the grass and their yellow cushion centres, but particularly those that had a touch of pink or purple on the back, or the edge of the petals. I used to wonder how that got there. Aunty Daphne taught me how to make daisy chains, and earlier in the year, one hot day, I made a necklace of daisies and put it round Bea's neck. Of course, she soon snatched it off and flung it away.

I told my teacher I wanted to try painting them, and she said she'd help me after school. So it was agreed with my mother that I could stay for an hour and have lessons. Miss Johnstone enjoyed painting watercolours herself. After that, I had to hurry home before it got dark. But being in time for tea wasn't important: it would only be something cold like bread and dripping which wouldn't spoil.

"How many daisies would you like in your picture?" Miss Johnstone said.

I decided three.

"Now, we have half an hour before you must leave. Take this piece of sugar paper and work out how you're going to present your three daisies."

I looked at the huge sheet of blue paper, turned it this way and that, and made my decision. "It's too big, Ma'am. I don't want all this. They're only little flowers."

"Clever girl! I knew you had talent. So, *you* choose what size paper you'd like and I'll cut it for you."

I decided about cabinet card size and held out my hands to the shape I wanted; after all, it was like a portrait of the flowers.

She took some scissors and trimmed the paper. "Now, how are you going to present them?"

I picked up a pencil. "I think one here, one looking straight to the front and one half sideways." I drew in three stalks, one with a bend in it.

"Very good, Dorothy. You've a natural eye for composition."

I glowed inwardly at that. She was the first person outside the family to encourage me.

"Now, how many petals do daisies have, do you know?"

Counting petals was difficult: whenever I tried in the garden, I always lost count or was unsure when I'd reached the beginning again. My mother – I still called her Mama then – suggested pulling them out one by one like the game 'He loves me, he loves me not'. But I didn't want to destroy the flower and always managed to lose count somewhere after thirty, anyway. So I still didn't know how many.

For this first attempt, I mixed green paint with more blue in it for the stalks, washed the brush and painted white strokes to suggest petals.

"Let the brush do the work. Trust it. Just give impressions of the petals this time."

When I'd finished, I swilled the brush in water and put it down.

"Very good, Dorothy. I can see you have promise and skill. We'll put it over there to dry." She took the paper away and laid it on a high shelf. "Now, when this dreadful war is finally over, talented girls like you must seize your chance. We need a whole generation of women artists to take over in the new world without men. Everyone needs to know that women can be as good as men in so many ways, and that includes quality art. If you keep practising and improving, perhaps you'll go to art college. Some already welcome women students. Times are changing. Remember that. All that's ten years away, but you can start building your portfolio now. We must keep all your best work."

I was uncertain what a portfolio was. I had to look it up in Mother's dictionary when I got home. She liked me to learn new words. But it was Miss Johnstone who first sowed the art seed in my mind.

Before I left that afternoon, she showed me one of her watercolours: a thatched cottage with the village church in the background. What struck me most was that when you looked closely, neither the sky nor the road had any colour. Just the paper, left untouched. You could say the picture wasn't finished, but it didn't feel like that. Now, that was interesting and made me start thinking what you could do with pictures.

"Later," Miss Johnstone said, "when you get skilled at

watercolours, you won't need to use pencils or ink to put in the outlines. A good watercolourist can create a picture using just paints and colours. Now, here's a question to think about on your way home. See if you can come up with an answer for next time. If you're thinking of doing a picture of white flowers on white paper, how will you manage that?

I trailed home that day, head hung low. I wasn't interested in art problems at that moment. Save that for bedtime. A leaf from a plane tree swirled down and crackled at my feet. I scuffed it away.

Something Miss Johnstone said. If the future world was to be without men, did that mean Daddy would never come back? Would the family be only Mama, the children and the new baby when it arrived, for the rest of my life? Had Daddy gone for good so I'd never see him again? That could only mean he was dead, but Mama hadn't said anything and there'd been no whispering in the house. Had there been a telegram that I'd missed?

I stopped in the street, shut my eyes and tried picturing Daddy: tall, and smiley because of his teeth. Tickly moustache. Then what? What colour were his eyes? That floored me. I wasn't sure. Was that all I could remember? I was cross now. And then, as children do, I made an excuse – that I hadn't seen him for a long time. "Not since you were a little girl."

But I remember thinking of his violin, still leaning in the corner of the kitchen, untouched. If Daddy didn't come back, who would play it? Would it ever sing again? The most disturbing thing was that I struggled, trying to hum the tune of *Salut d'Amour*.

It wouldn't come.

FORTY-SIX

Close to the tent, his right foot slipped. The ground parted and oozed up either side of his boot. The unmistakable stink of human shit. "Oh, goddammit," he said. "Who's done that – here of all places?" He cast around. "Now, how can I get rid of that? Nothing here to wipe it off."

The boots stayed outside. He stood them near the entrance to the tent, out of the way so no one should stumble over them in the blackness. He dared not take their foulness amongst his comrades. He crouched through the door-flap, felt over the ground sheet for a space to lie down. A body grumbled and shifted, disturbed by his patting hand. "Sorry, pal." His voice a hiss in the darkness. Squeeze in, somehow. Just his luck, right by the entrance. Already, the air hung heavy, warm with the smell of sweat and bully beef; on the far side of the tent, a stertorous snore, too far away to prod. He eased in, twisting himself into a sleeping position.

The silence worried him, the night unnaturally quiet as if he was the last man alive. Reveillé at three hundred hours, must be awake for it. His job to chivvy the others. The medics would hold back, give time for combat troops to take up position. Keep out of the way. He yawned. Five hours to go. He was ready for sleep.

But it would not come.

His flesh began to crawl. Was it chats hatched by the heat of the fire, or just his imagination? He knew he was asking for trouble enjoying the warmth of the brazier earlier, giving the blighters their chance. Now he was convinced creatures moved across his back and into his armpits. His crotch began to itch. They would go there. If he scratched, he'd nudge the man next to him, probably wake him again. Imagination, he told himself. Ignore it, live with it! Only lice. Go to sleep. But the itching lingered.

He didn't know when outside noises began, or if he had even slept. It seemed no time had elapsed. A horse harrumphed and jingled a harness; a voice shouting, "Come on, boys, walk on." Someone clicking his tongue. The groan of heavy axles turning on a gun carriage. Later, the unmistakable squeal and chatter of tanks on the move, their engine noise hammering forward in insistent bursts. Maybe those leviathans would get across this mud. Far off, the sputter of a motorcycle setting off. Still, his arms itched. A horse whinnied a demand onto the air, evinced a distant response, faint and distressed, perhaps from the German lines. Horse-talk knew no boundaries. Someone shovelling coal; the clank of a boiler door being flung open, the roar of the fire – a jet of steam venting. The slow rasp of men sawing timber; the scrunch of boots marching along the metalled road. He swallowed: what would this day bring?

He took a deep breath, sure he could still smell the boots.

★ ★ ★

Fine mizzle-rain out of the blackness. The boots were damp inside. "Oh, confound it all. Certainly not my day," he said. He wiped the insides out as best he could with yesterday's socks and edged the boots on. "Oh well, nothing for it." He used the socks to wipe the shit off. Better than getting muck on his puttees. "What filthy bloody swine..."

An orderly was stoking the brazier into life; John flung the socks onto the coals. They hissed and gave off a foul smell. Wasting army issue, he thought, but what the hell? Best wash his hands now, and pick up the morphine from Sergeant Skinner. No sign of Henshaw.

Orders were to muster some distance behind the flooded trenches. He found the bearer teams, shapes huddled around two stacks of stretchers, close to the track the tanks had taken. Some sat on the piled stretchers; others hunkered on their heels, smoking or drinking tea. Still dark, still unnaturally quiet. He began moving amongst the men, checking gas masks. Something to do.

"I 'ope they haven't got it like this back 'ome." Sov turned up the collar of his greatcoat. "Worse kind of rain, this, soaks right through. No good if you're wanting to finish autumn ploughin'. Mud sticks to the share, clags everything up."

"Isn't it easier now with tractors?" A voice out of the dark.

"I wouldn't know, boy. I'd stick with 'osses every time. They can plod their way up any old Devon hill, however steep. Ploughin' done. But like as not, if you're on a tractor going up a steep slope, you'll be arse over tip afore you know it. I 'eard about one fellow, he..."

John smiled and moved on. Home thoughts from abroad. Already his cheeks felt cold and his eyelashes wet as if a heavy dew had settled on them. He found Gosforth and gave him, as leader of a team, a supply of morphine tablets. "Keep 'em safe, don't let 'em get wet."

"Certainly, Corp." Gosforth began stowing them in an inside pocket. "Interesting to see if the tanks get out further this time. If they don't sink in the mud and they keep their caterpillars moving, they should fare quite well."

"Lot of bloody ifs in your theory, Gosforth." Feltham's voice. The man took a swig from his hip flask and lit a cigarette. "What they going to do if they reach the enemy trenches? They'll have to stop then."

"Well, that's where you're wrong, old fellow. They carry bridging equipment now, so I hear. We use duckboards, the tanks have fascines."

"What the fucking 'ell are they?" That grating cockney whine.

"Nothing sophisticated, only bundles of twigs or wood which they'll drop in the enemy trenches."

"Fascin-ating!" You could hear the jeer in Feltham's voice. "Proper mine of information, isn't he, Corp, old Gobspout? Don't he ever leave off? 'E should've been the teacher back in Blighty."

"Got all your kit, Feltham?" John said.

"Oh, yessir – gas mask, dressings bag." He began clapping his pockets. "Hip flask, photo of the old dutch, fags – you'd be amazed how many casualties, first thing they ask for is a smoke."

"And your helmet?"

"I got it, Corp. It's over there somewhere, on the 'andle of a stretcher."

"Go and find it. Have it with you at all times. Things could get hot today."

Feltham sniffed the air, head up like a bloodhound. "Cor blimey, it is you, isn't it, Corp, what's not nice to know today? Quite a niffty fellow, I'd say."

"You, of course, wouldn't know anything about that, would you, Feltham?"

Feltham drew on his cigarette, his round face momentarily lit up with a grin. "Absolutely nothin', Corp, Scouts' honour." He gave an exaggerated salute.

Lazy, lying bastard. John walked away. You crapped there deliberately.

★ ★ ★

The sudden spatter into the mud of a man pissing at the side of the track; a tense, religious silence, talk in awful whispers as if anything louder would provoke the enemy or betray their position; irritation at give-away sounds: a helmet clanging on a mess-tin; a man seized with coughing, quickly fist-stifled; the ring of a distant farrier's hammer on an anvil like a bell of doom, the roar of the bellows at work; from somewhere in the rear, a sudden venting of steam.

"What time's dawn?" Whispers in the dark.

"'Bout six, I think."

"What is it now?"

"Four, half-past."

John looked up, aware of a figure standing in the centre of the

310

road. He stared: Henshaw in full uniform, freshly shaved, clean shirt, tie firmly knotted. So different from last night.

Putting his brave face on.

Henshaw moving amongst the clusters of men; leaning in to encourage; smiling, patting a shoulder or an arm. Contact, a word with every man.

John felt a choke rise in his throat, a stifled sob. "Oh, God..." He bit his lip. Serious, then. The old man's never done this before.

His turn now, a strained voice in his ear: "Whatever happens today, old chap, I know you'll have done your best. Take care of your men, take care of yourself. Good luck!" Before John could speak, a pat on the shoulder and Henshaw had faded into the dark.

He bit his lip again.

A hiss amongst the group: "It's starting!"

In the distance, nearer the ground than you'd expect, the spread of blackness split with stabs of flame – a ring of red fire, each one a big gun salvo announcing the opening of the day's business.

"Can't see the point of bombardment." The last whisper of the day. It'll be shouting soon enough. "Only tells the Boche we're going to attack. Why can't we catch them off guard?"

And then... John held his breath.

The banshee wail of shells, the zip and scream of passing death, the shell-launch thunder. He swallowed. Can I bear all this day brings? Do I have that kind of blind bravery?

The ground trembled. The shiver passed through him; he couldn't tell whether he or the earth shuddered.

In a minute, he thought, in a minute, their reply.

Beyond the distant ridge, far out in the opposing sea of darkness, the yellow answering flash startled his eyes, the spit and blat of flame. He waited, heard the thump of German guns.

I know what to expect, I'm safe, still in control. He waited for the falling howl and shriek of enemy shells above his head. Not us. They won't have our range yet. It'll be our guns they go for.

Behind him, the expanding blast of a shell landing. He imagined the flying mud, the skyward fling of men, metal, debris. The echoing slog, the wallop behind, in front, everywhere. His ears sang.

Another British salvo. Death speeding away again. How long will this last? He covered his ears.

He scoured the darkness for signs of enemy guns: a distant belch of flame flared and died. Another, and another. *Crump, crump* rolled across the waiting mud towards him.

He turned and saw in silhouette against the flare of exploding shells a young private, bent forward, hands clapped across his head, clutching his helmet. He twitched at every thump and thud of nearby detonation, crouched, cried.

John struggled over, touched the boy's shoulder; wide eyes and mouth looked up. He bent to yell in the boy's ear: "It's all right, soldier, hold on. This din will stop. Soon, I promise you."

The boy sniffed sobs, sank to his knees in the mud. "I can't," he said.

"You can, you must."

But what then? his head voice said, *what shall we face then? Will you be up to that?*

He looked up. The blackness had dissolved to green-grey dark. Over to the right, through the wraith of mist, the sky split into a streak of day.

The gunfire stopped and heavenly hellish silence spread and settled.

"What do we do now, Corp?" A voice called.

"Wait," he said. "We wait."

★ ★ ★

Out of that silence, the jammer of the tank engines. A flare drooped and the machines began to slew and slide forward, exhaust drilling the air. From their tracks, mud spewed, flung out in a spray of sludge. To left and right, whistles shrilled; he saw that desperate scramble from the trenches, watched men crumble, slide and fall back in a shower of mud. But there was no opposing fire.

Once out of their hole, men waded through the eager pluck and cling of mud; slow-stepping as if shod in giants' boots, they snatched their knees out of the earth, floundered on.

Still no Boche fire.

Out there, the chatter of the tanks' machine guns raked the trenches ahead. But no crackle of rifle fire, even enemy machine gun emplacements squatted blank and silent.

Sov appeared at his side. "Is it a walkover, Smiler? Or are our boys being drawn into a trap?

★ ★ ★

"Here they come!"

Far to the right, straggles of men clambered from a sunken track lined with splintered trees. They plucked their way through the clutch of mud and slosh of water.

"Over here, boys! This way!" The bearers stood up to watch the sorry procession. Still the thunder of guns, the chatter and sting of Boche fire, all around.

John looked back, searching for the private who had cowered at the bombardment. The boy, wretched and downcast, skulked, away from the other bearers. "Now, Private, stay here. You can be most use now if you guide the walking wounded towards the Dressing Station. Support the stragglers, make sure no one falls and is left behind. Tell Sarnt Skinner or Private Atherstone I sent you. They can always do with help.'"

Red, watery eyes stared at him and blinked. The face crumpled. "Thank you, Corp." A bare whisper.

Men with white, tense faces stumbled past. None of them carried his rifle, but they staggered on, even now bowed under their packs.

"Well done, boys, nearly there." One casualty, knees and back bent, lugged a comrade, flung across his shoulder. The friend's arms hanging down behind flopped and waved at every step, a run of blood streaking his fingertips. Was he still alive?

Later, the Jocks, silent and beaten, floundered in, eyes glaring out of mud-caked faces, short bristly beards, their bare knees coated with cracking mud.

A bearer sergeant barked an order, a fellow corporal roused his men: John's cue. "Okay, lads, into teams. This is us." He watched Gosforth gather his men; all the stretcher groups spread out and readied themselves. Underwood, Feltham and Sov waiting for him to join them. He took a deep breath. "Right, let's take it steady, chaps, helmets on. Out we go."

★ ★ ★

The duckboards rocked under their weight. Mud oozed between the slats. They walked in single file.

"Take care you don't slip off," John said.

Underwood struggled with one rolled-up stretcher, Sov carried a second underneath his arm like a giant swagger stick. John led, and Feltham brought up the rear, two folded stretcher blankets draped over his shoulder.

"How far these boards go, Corp?" Sov said.

"Who knows? We'll certainly have to branch off at some point to do pick-ups."

They ducked at the scream of an incoming shell.

"I saw that bloody thing," Feltham said. "God's truth I did. Like a fucking grey streak flying by."

At times, the boards skirted a brimming shell-hole; at others, they became ramps over the uneven ground.

"Roll up, roll up, try our bloody switchback," Feltham said.

"Bearers, help! Bearers!" A faint wail somewhere to the right.

"Over there." John pointed. "See him, Sov?"

The big Devonian craned his neck. "Could be something."

"How far?"

"'Bout two hundred yards, on the edge of a crater. Blimey, it's worse out there than any rough ploughed field, and I seen en

314

waterlogged 'nough times. How're we going to reach him?"

The boy lay in the foetus position, blood puddling through his uniform onto the ground. His right boot had been dragged off, sucked into the morass somewhere; the puttee trailed like a broken tether.

"All right, lad, we're here now," John said. Sov unrolled his stretcher alongside the boy and knelt to inspect the wound.

"Oh, crike, Corp, he hasn't even fixed his own dressing."

"What is it? Shrapnel wound?" Feltham said.

"You two, get on, see if you can find other casualties. Leave us a blanket. We'll manage here." John turned again to the boy. "Right, lad, we'll have to turn you over and put a dressing on."

"Don't touch me, please don't touch me. Oh, Mam! Help me!"

"I've got to do it." Together, they laid him on his back. The boy screamed.

John began unbuttoning the tunic. Another scream: "Don't touch me, don't touch me!"

"Try the tablets, Smiler," Sov said.

John felt into an inside pocket and pulled out the small brown bottle. He lifted the boy's head. "You don't swallow this, let it rest under your tongue. It'll make you feel better in a while. Sip of water first?" He began unscrewing his water bottle.

The boy shook his head, eyes screwed in fear and pain.

John folded back the tunic and shirt so that the stomach, welling black with clots of blood, was exposed. He hated paddling his hands in it. "Can you put the dressing on, Sov? I..."

He looked at his hands and flinched, felt ashamed. Will you buck up? he told himself. Blood isn't dirt. He stood up, turned away and wiped himself dry on some lint.

"No, no, leave me alone, don't touch me. Oh, Mam, help me." The boy twisted out of the way and screamed again at the movement.

"Now, come on, boy, I gotta do this afore we can take you in. Now, bloody bite on this and shut up. You'll have every jerry sniper there is training on us." Sov wedged a small dressing in the boy's mouth.

A stifled moan of fear.

"Good lad," John said. "Take it easy, we're going to put a temporary dressing on. Grip onto this if it hurts." He held out his hand.

Sov worked at padding and bandaging the wound; the boy's nails cutting into John's palm made him grit his teeth.

At last, all done. "Right," John said, "a quick lift onto the stretcher and we'll take you in."

The boy spat out the dressing and screamed.

★ ★ ★

"Bread and jam," Gosforth said, "I've been looking forward to this since we first went out. Tickler's Plum and Apple, you'll find no equal anywhere. Take my word for it." He bit hard into the bread.

John smiled and took a drink of tea. "You sound as though you're advertising it. I couldn't stomach it at this hour. Don't you find it heavy on your digestion?"

"Not at all. All that sugar gives you energy." Gosforth took out a pocket watch and consulted it. "And, if I'm lucky, I shall have a third breakfast in two or three hours."

"I must admit I miss Em's Bramble Jam," John said. "I was fond of that. She used to make it every autumn before the war. Delicious stuff. I saw tins of Bramble Jam when we first came out. Seems to have disappeared." He paused and bit his lip. Images of the boy's black-bloodied stomach. Change the subject. "I don't know whether to put long over-boots on next time. We really struggled at one point. I was up to my knees and could feel the mud sucking, while Sov was only in slightly above his ankles. You don't know where you are. Showers of liquid mud whenever a shell came in. Needed Feltham and Underwood to pull us out."

"I think men complained about it," Gosforth said. "So it was withdrawn. There were rumours they'd been putting chips of wood in to imitate bramble pips. You know, shark the troops."

"What?" John took time to realise. Pause again. "Still straggling in, poor devils. You tend to think it's walking wounded first and then the bearers for the rest of the day. But they keep on coming. Look at that poor fellow." He pointed at a young Scot who had wandered out of the line, back onto No Man's Land. "I'd better go and bring him in."

"No, leave him. Don't put yourself in danger, Corp," Gosforth said. "He's obviously off his head. We can't help him. Not at this distance."

They watched the young man floundering around the shell-holes. "I feel powerless," John said. "I hate it." He made himself watch. The Scot's tin hat was flipped into the air like a spun coin, and down he went. "Oh, God, how long was he out there?"

"Minute, minute and a half," Gosforth said.

"I must see if he's OK."

"Nothing you can do. He's dead."

"How do you know?" Gosforth's certainty was beginning to irritate.

"You can always tell. A wounded man tries to break his fall. Instinct, you see. A dead man generally falls forward, since his balance tends in that direction. And that young Jock bent at the knees, waist, neck and ankles simultaneously. He's gone. Bury him later. Now, I think I'll..."

"What?" John said.

"Have another piece of bread and jam. When you go out again, take a cape with you. Look at that sky." Gosforth nodded towards the darker grey, building over the horizon.

Can't be matter of fact like that, John thought, I just can't.

★ ★ ★

"Eh, English! British Tommy!"

"What was that, Sov? Did you hear it? Someone calling." The

wind gusted around John's shoulders and lifted the cape. A fling of rain against his cheek. "I'm sure I heard someone calling."

"Don't like it here, Smiler. It's not safe. We're way out, more'n a mile from the ADS, I reckon. German lines can't be far. Your mind starts playing bloody tricks."

Everywhere, bodies in khaki lay merging with the mud: the dead and the dying. John shook his head. Someone called, he was convinced. "Who are you? Where are you?" A clatter of droplets on his helmet. A curtain of rain-mist drifted across the battlefield like a passing ghost.

"*Hier*, Tommy, behind you."

They both inched round, ready to raise their hands. A German soldier's head materialised out of a scrape in the ground. He wore a helmet but held no rifle.

"Oh, blimey!" Sov's eyes widened. "We're already through the flaming Boche lines."

"Stay calm," John said. "I think he's alone and unarmed. Are you hurt, Fritz?"

"*Danke, nein.*" Another volley spattered the ground. The head disappeared; Sov and John ducked into a crouch.

The voice again: "*Hier, Tommy! Englisch Kapitan hier.*" The German tried to point to a nearby shell-hole but at a rattle of machine gun fire, he vanished like a rabbit.

They found the captain with a bad gunshot wound in his right leg. Another stray bullet had punctured his lung. He tried talking: "First wave, behind the tanks, been here hours." He began spitting blood and gasping for breath.

Only a boy, could have been Lambert, John thought. Same sort of age. "You're fortunate to have fallen into a deep shell-hole, Captain. Let's see what we can do to get you out." He slid down; Sov followed. "Now, take it easy," John said, "keep this under your tongue, sir. It'll help with the pain."

"Lucky us come along, eh, Smiler? But how we goin' to carry en? We ent got no bloody stretcher. He's a big fellow."

"Second row in the scrum." The captain gave a weak smile. "So sorry."

"Where's Feltham and Underwood? They've got a stretcher," John said. "Why can you never see that bloody man when you want him?"

"They over there 'bout three hundred yards. I ent going to shout, though. Us'll have to manage."

"Right, Sov, scout around, find a couple of poles, broken trees – anything – at least eight feet long, if you can. Bring them back here. When you've done that, take your greatcoat off and keep low." John began slithering on his stomach towards the dip where the German lay. He pushed his helmet towards the back of his head. "Fritz," his voice a hiss amongst the stinging chaos of bullets, "you come with us. *Sie sind mein Gefangener.*"

The German's face reappeared and brightened into a smile. He, too, only a boy. He began to edge towards them. "*Ja wohl, mein Herr, danke.*"

"You took him prisoner?" Sov said. "Without a gun? I don' believe it."

John grinned and felt the mud crack on his face. "Let's say he surrendered. Scared out of his wits, poor lad. But now we've got a third bearer to help with the carry. Probably against the rules, but..."

The German sat cross-legged and hunched while they buttoned Sov's greatcoat up on the ground and pushed the poles down the sleeves and out of the neck.

"It'll sag rather, but it should be strong enough to take his weight, as long as the buttons don't give way," John said. "Now, somehow we must get the captain out of the hole without making matters worse."

★ ★ ★

Sov carried the two poles of the makeshift stretcher on his own at the front, one in each hand; he set a steady plod back towards

Duckboard Alley while John and the German staggered behind. John's feet dragged. Feels as though I've got ten pounds of lead in each boot, he thought. Scarcely possible to keep one lump of lead moving after the other.

"They ought to have relay posts on a long carry like this, Corp." Sov oddly formal in the presence of the stranger. "Every hundred yards or so. Make it easier. This 'ere's a heavy one. Can us rest again now?"

They lowered the drooping greatcoat gently and paused, panting. The clout and scatter of a shell-burst overhead. John looked down at the captain. The man's eyes were open but unfocussed. Drowsy from morphine, John thought. Probably bleeding inside. Very white and faint, but terribly alive. He must make it. We'll get you back, let Hubert take a look. If anyone can help…"Start again, lads?" he said.

The German watched like an eager dog waiting for instructions, and they hoisted the stretcher again.

Behind them, a machine gun chattered.

★ ★ ★

"All right, let's stop again." He knelt down and adjusted the cape – the only covering they had to keep the casualty warm. "What's this, our fifth rest? Must have been further out than I thought."

"That's Gosforth's lot up front. I reckon they've found the path," Sov said.

Four figures carrying a stretcher on their shoulders fought to be free of the mud, stamped and scraped their feet against the duckboards.

"Okay, Fritz?" The German soldier stared back towards his own lines. "You want to go back?"

"*Ach, nein, danke.*"

"We couldn't have done this carry without you," John said.

"*Bitte?*"

"Never mind. When we get back, we shall say *aufwiedersehen* and hand you over to the police. *Polizei.*"

"*Oh, ja, polizei, danke schon.*"

"Do you reckon the young shaver's any idea what's going on, what'll happen to him?" Sov said.

"I think so," John said. "Probably glad. He'll be out of it all, safe behind our lines."

The whine of a heavy shell coming in. They all ducked and shut their eyes. It passed by. You could hear the release of breath.

"That was close," Sov shouted through the blast. "Nearly got us, that one."

John took his hands from his ears. "Oh, God, it's Gosforth! It's hit them, slap on the stretcher. Stay there, both of you!" He cursed and fought the pull of the mud, struggled to where they had seen the other bearers.

Fragments of shattered duckboard peppered the remains of the bodies. He recognised Gosforth's arm from the single stripe on the sleeve; splinters of wood like thorns tangled the hair on the patient's severed head. Bandages, body parts everywhere. A photograph, badged with blood and sludge, caught under a boot, trembled with the earth; a duckboard slewed across one man's torso. "Dear God," he said, "please no. Not all four *and* the casualty?"

The young private lay on his side, serene and still, his greatcoat scorched from the blast. "Oh, Wing, thank God." He seemed uninjured. Probably knocked clear by the blast, lucky devil. He looked again. Something queer about the head, though. Not a spot of blood, but... John put his hand out. Still warm, the head felt soft under his hand, and stroking it moulded it into different shapes, the bones of the skull grating quietly beneath his palm. He picked slivers of wood off the uniform, wiped a daub of mud from the lips. He'd heard of people being killed by the concussion and now... He closed Wing's eyes.

Nothing to be done. He hated this impotence war imposed; he could do nothing for any of them – not tend them, comfort them, or even bury them. Not his job. Bow your head, close your eyes, walk away.

Above all, walk away.

They laid the captain on the concrete holding-area outside the Dressing Station.

"Let's get him a proper stretcher, and I'll redo the dressing on his leg," Sov said.

"Well done, and can you scribble a tally for him? I'm going to hand Fritz over, see if I can find Henshaw. When I come back, I'll bring two cuppers and some bread and jam. Gives you energy, I heard." He turned away, dropped his head and bit his lip.

★ ★ ★

"The bearers have taken a terrible beating." John took off his helmet, closed his eyes and let out a heavy breath. "Here you are, old chap." He passed Sov a strong tea and stood warming his hands on his own beaker. "Twenty casualties from our section: five dead, four stretcher cases, six walking wounded, five missing. The place is practically deserted. There's that young private I sent and a new relief doctor, Captain Somebody, never seen him before."

"Where's all the other casualties?" Sov said.

"Gone, all passed down the line to Clearing."

"Not snowed under, then?"

"Not now. We must get going again." He began pacing up and down. "There must be many still out there. It seems Atherstone got very cut up about so many bearers missing that he took a horse-sled and went out searching. As they'd moved on the casualties here, Skinner went out too. Probably to find Atherstone and keep an eye on him. And now Henshaw's gone as well."

The young orderly appeared carrying two hunks of bread slathered with jam. John turned to him: "Did anyone say anything before they went out? Any message?"

Big eyes stared at him. "Well, Corp, Atherstone said: 'We can't leave our own in the mud. I must see what I can do.' He mumbled something about... I thought he were close to tears," the orderly said. He handed over the two pieces of bread.

"I can't eat this," Sov said, "not straight after we seen..."

"We eat it!" John glared. "It'll keep us going, and –" His voice choked. "We eat it!"

★ ★ ★

The British tank had not flattened the German wire in its advance but dragged it along, and now the machine rested, isolated and stricken, nose down in the waterlogged Boche trench. Its door hung open, its crew either dead or escaped. Impossible to tell how long Atherstone had hung on that wire or how he had got there. The wire had snagged and torn his greatcoat, he had lost his helmet, and his spectacles, shattered into a craze of glass, were wet with the mizzle of rain. He had a single bullet wound through the back of his neck.

"Bloody 'eathens! Didn't they see the arm band?" Sov said. "Poor bugger." They untangled the stiff body from the wire and laid it gently on the ground. "He looks terrified, don' 'e, as if he was screamin', runnin' away from somethin'.'"

"We'll never know. Jimmy shouldn't have been out here," John said. "He was never cut out for all this."

"How's us goin' to get him back? I don' want 'im buried out 'ere. Not in this wet. And we ain't got no tools. Where's that horse sledge?"

John scanned the gloom of the plain. Mist rising now. Rain settling in heavily. "No sign. There's a stretcher here but no sledge. Could be anywhere. Let's take shelter for a bit, that tank over there. Get out of this weather."

★ ★ ★

They found Henshaw bending over a man underneath the tank. He looked up. "Oh, thank God, friendly faces. I shall need help. I've found Skinner."

The sergeant lay on his back, his breathing very shallow, but his eyes still flickered. Conscious, probably in pain.

"All right, old lad, I'm here," Henshaw said. "I'm glad we found you." He knelt down beside him.

"Sorry, sir, too late for our Jimmy," Skinner's voice scarcely a whisper. "Gone when I found him, and then they got me." His left leg was curved in a rough semi-circle with his boot against his ear; shrapnel had torn his belly open, and his arm rested across his stomach, covering the tangled pink entrails with his sleeve. A pool of blood welled and widened around his hand.

"It's all right, old fellow, I know you did your best," Henshaw said. "Now, we just have to work out how to get you back."

Skinner opened his eyes wide and gazed intently at Henshaw. "Please, sir, put me to sleep."

John held his breath.

"All right, Sergeant, I understand." Henshaw mopped the man's brow with a lint pad and gestured to John to pass his medical bag. "In a vein, I think." He took out a syringe from the bag, snapped his fingers for a phial of morphia. "No, next size up, please."

Sov crouched respectfully in the background, but John watched as Henshaw drew up a huge dose, flicked the syringe and squirted out a small spray. He eased the needle into the vein in Skinner's wrist. Very slowly, he pressed the plunger.

"All right now, old chap, you'll be asleep in a couple of minutes." Henshaw held Skinner's hand, his voice a reassuring murmur.

Skinner looked up, mouthed thank you; his smile faded and his eyes drooped shut.

"That was a whacking big dose," Henshaw said, "but I needed to be sure he wouldn't wake up again. Brave man, our Sam, one of the best. He knew what the score was. We shall miss him." He wiped the syringe, wrapped it in a cloth and put it back in his bag.

John lowered his head and closed his eyes. He wished he could pray.

Henshaw struggled off his knees and pushed his bag to one side. Scarcely room to stand up. They all stared down at Skinner's body. One foot lay outside, the boot already shiny with rain.

"Sorry, old chap," Henshaw said, "have to leave you and Jimmy here. Can't bury you now, too dangerous. We'll come back." He took a step away and bowed towards the body.

"Shall I..?" Sov knelt down and began to remove Skinner's identity disc and papers. "I'll rootle through Atherstone's pockets, too, sir."

"Good man," Henshaw said. "Then we must get off. This is no port in a storm."

"There's a stretcher outside," John said. "I'll get the blankets to cover them both. It's the least we can do." He ducked out from under the tank.

Behind them, the clatter and splash of an earth-slip in the German trench. The tank emitted an echoing groan and started to shift. It lurched to one side; the caterpillar tracks began to tip and sink.

"Henshaw, your bag!" John saw it all from the outside.

Henshaw moved, almost in a dive, to retrieve the medical bag, just as the tank gave a settling grumble, subsided and trapped his left wrist and the bag beneath the metal tracks. He was forced onto his back, his arm outstretched, as if thrown by a wrestler. He cried out in pain. "Confound and blast it all!" He tried wriggling the hand. "Can't shift it. It's caught fast. Now what?"

"I'm sorry," John said, "my fault. Shouldn't have called out."

"No, it's not you. You don't need to take on that guilt. I shouldn't have put the bag there. Wasn't thinking. I don't think I've anything broken."

"The bag's squashed," Sov said. He turned to John. "Shall us try digging the major out?"

They knelt, one either side of Henshaw's outstretched arm, and worked with bare hands, scooping and piling up the mud surrounding the hand. John could feel the rivets on the steel underside of the tank pressing against the top of his head. Their breath flared in the cold air. A drip of condensation. A smell of fuel.

"This isn't going to work," John said after half an hour. "The more we scoop, the more it flows back." Both men were gasping. "We must find a way of damming it or shuttering it…"

"Timber in the Boche trench." Sov began to scramble outside.

The machine emitted a metallic hollow groan and settled in the mud. It bent Henshaw's wrist and forced his hand deeper into the ground, crushing his bag still further.

"Oh, crike, what do we do now?" Sov said. "Blasted, buggering thing, beg pardon, sir."

"I'll tell you what you do…" Henshaw raised his head. Mud clung and tangled in his grey curls. "You save yourselves. That's what you do. You've spent quite enough time. Get off. Leave me here."

"We can't do that, sir," John said, "you're needed back at the station."

"You go. There are other doctors. Leave me here. I've had my life. I'm in good company. Leave me! That's an order."

"I'm not leaving you here to die!" An idea began to form. "I'm going back. I'll get help. I'll get something."

The tank groaned and shifted.

"Sov, stay with the major, see he's comfortable and keep out of the way of the caterpillar tracks."

"You're a bloody fool," Henshaw said, "and you're disobeying an order, but thank you. Now, take this. I want you to have it." He plunged his free hand into his belt and pulled out a revolver. "Use it if you have to. It's fully loaded."

"Blimey," Sov said, "where'd you get that, sir? I thought…"

Henshaw smiled. "Let's say I picked it up, Poundsbury."

"I'll be as quick as I can," John said. "We'll get you out, Hubert. Somehow."

★ ★ ★

326

The wind flung the rain at him, making him bow his head. He tucked the strap of his helmet under his chin. A brief look back. The tank still reared above the shattered trench, its stern now a haven like a cleft beneath a rock. Bloody deathtraps, he thought, but at least they'll be out of this weather. Won't draw fire, either.

On the wind, the faint jingle of a horse's harness. Somewhere, not far away. He cocked his head and began to look.

The shire horse was still yoked to the gun carriage. It stood, head bowed, placid and still, as if waiting for its driver to return. John floundered over and struggled to free it. "Would have to be white, wouldn't you?" Drops of water beaded its eyelashes and its mane draggled. A scramble onto the horse's back. They set off, the hooves making a rhythmic plash – a weary, patient sound.

"Good boy," he said. "Take me back." He clung to the tangle of mane. Would the horse find the duckboards again?

A German field gun began firing and a shell screamed overhead.

God, I'm a target. Anything that moves.

A shell whistled, landed nearby. A spray-wave of mud and water deluged him: he wiped his eyes and face and clung on.

"Good lad, keep going."

He leaned forward, head close to the creature's mane; the horse broke into a plodding trot, its head low. Rifle fire somewhere behind.

"Oh, God, though I pass through the valley of the shadow of –"

An explosion six feet away, a cascade of mud and water.

He bit his lip. "I will fear..."

Overhead, the clout of a shell; shrapnel crackled and burst; an explosion of mud and debris in front; the horse faltered and veered away.

"Though I pass through the valley of death, I will fear... I will fear –"

A fountain of mud, wood, metal, body parts spattered around him.

He screamed, "Keep going!" and ducked down.

★ ★ ★

He stumbled off the horse and tethered it to a shattered tree. His hand shook and he longed to give way to tears. Firmer ground now; he began to stagger towards the glow of the Dressing Station. His eyes ached, stinging from the rain. His heart still thumped.

And I've to go back through all that, he thought.

About two hundred yards out from the Dressing Station, he came across four bearers sprawled in the mud round the stretcher they had been carrying. The casualty, still strapped in place, gazed at the sky. Oh, God, not more. Please, not more. He lurched over. No sign of injury to any of them.

The man on the stretcher lifted his head. The wound was bandaged, a brown stain already seeping through.

"It's all right, soldier," he said to the casualty, "we'll get you in somehow." His voice a croak. He kicked the boot of the nearest bearer. No reaction.

"Leave 'em. They're worse off than me, Corp, they're done in, dead to the world."

"Stay there, don't go away. He set off, footsteps faltering. Idiot! Stupid thing to say. Incredible, four bearers too exhausted to stagger the remaining yards to dryness and warmth. He shook his head. Let sleeping dogs lie. He had work to do.

★ ★ ★

The station was deserted; only the young private sat on the bench in the entrance, biting his nails.

"Where is everybody?"

"We're pulling out." The boy was shaking. "It's not safe here no more. Too many shells. They're setting up further back."

A shell screamed in and landed close by, the blast blowing out the hurricane lantern that swung from the roof.

"There's a casualty back there..." John gestured. "See to him, will you? Get somebody to help. Don't worry about the bearers. They're deadbeat. They'll have to take their chance."

328

"What will you –"

"I'm going out again when I've found everything I want." He strode towards the shelves at the back of the hut. "And get me a lamp and a box of matches, will you? We're going to need light out there."

★ ★ ★

He lashed the two wooden cases with rope to form a loose tabard, eased them over his head so that they rested on his shoulders. Shan't lose them that way. Must wash my hands. Have a pee, too.

The horse stood, head bowed, where he'd left it. He unhitched it, gave it a drink and led it to a pile of planks where he could climb on its back.

He set off.

The horse clopped along the duckboards at a steady walk, head jerking up and down. Amazing temperament, how do they stand all these explosions? He began to plan what he'd do when he reached the tank. Would Henshaw agree? What if he said no?

The day faded into the yellow grizzle of an October late afternoon. "Glad when this is over," he said aloud. "What I'd give to get warm again!" He leaned over the horse's neck and patted the huge creature. "You deserve a medal, old lad!"

A chattering burst of machine gun fire; bullets zipped into the duckboards across the path of the horse; wooden splinters flew up. The horse reared, its great fetlocks pawing the air. It whinnied and skittered on the greasy boarding. Some instinct drove John to slip off onto the ground. He landed at the side of the duckboards, felt the mud ooze up his legs.

And then he saw the horse.

The eruption of muddy water from the shell-hole showered him. Already the horse tried to swim, its eyes rolling white with fear. It thrashed the water, pawed the air, its teeth bared in a snicker of panic. It reached the edge of the crater, tried to climb out, its hooves slipping and scouring mud from the sides. It fell back, whinnied and grumbled low in its throat. Then it stopped, began to sink. Passive now, it looked at him, eyes liquid and yielding – a plea.

Do it! The voice in his head bullied him. *Do it!*

He pushed one of the cases on his chest aside, reached underneath his greatcoat.

Do it! The voice said. *Now!*

"Oh, God, no!" His voice a scream. He dared not look, turned his head away, extended his arm, hoped.

Rapid shots sounded over the flat land. His shoulder jerked back. Then he looked through his tears.

The horse sinking into the pool. Two dark holes just above the eyes, a trickle of blood. His last impression: the white, mud-stained mop-head splayed on the surface of pink-brown water.

★ ★ ★

He heard snoring when he stumbled up to the tank. He could scarcely make out the two men. He stood outside, calming himself, summoning his reserves. The last hints of yellow light clung to the horizon. Rain stopped at last. Let's hope no one fancies a pot-shot. The battlefield grew a deathly silence, only a faint squeak nearby – the wind stirring the sagging door of the tank.

He stepped over Skinner's body and crouched underneath. He heaved off the two wooden cases he had brought and set the lamp on the mud. Both men slept. He knelt down.

"Sov! Wake up!" His voice an urgent hiss. "I'm back." He kept shaking his friend until he stirred. "Come on, we've work to do."

Sov yawned. "You brought crowbars, shovels?"

"No, that'll never work. If Henshaw agrees, you know what I must do."

"What? Oh, crike, boy, in this light? You sure you know what you're doing?"

"I've brought a lamp. It's his only chance. But I shall need help, there's a lot to do. Now open it up and light it, will you, hope the Boche doesn't see. Matches if you need them."

He moved over to Henshaw who lay, head back, his mouth gaping in silent sleep. He woke instantly when John shook him, tried to move his left arm and winced.

"Sorry. Nodded off," he said, "not much doing here." He grinned and wiped his moustache with his free hand. "So, what's the plan?"

"The decision is yours, sir, but if you agree, I'm going to amputate just below the elbow."

Bright light from the lamp burst out. Henshaw screwed up his eyes, his bushy brows knitting. He stared up. "Are you feeling confident, John?"

"Not at all. I'm absolutely terrified. But I shall go carefully and try to remember all I've seen you do."

"Good, I know I'm in safe hands, then. Go ahead, I'll stay conscious for as long as I can bear it and, if things don't work out, you can always use the morphia. There's an emergency supply in one of those cases. You'll know if it comes to that."

John took a deep breath. Time to get started. "Sov! Scrub your hands in surgical spirit, take a pair of scissors and cut away the major's jacket right up to the shoulder, then his shirt." He turned to Henshaw. "Happy for a tablet under the tongue to start with? I'll get Sov on the chloroform later."

Henshaw nodded. "OK. Make that tourniquet as tight as you can, and good luck, John."

The rasp of the scissors cutting fabric, the hollow roar of the lamp, a slight groan from the tank, the clink of surgical instruments.

The bright saw, teeth glistening, resting in its slots in the lid of the box.

John took off his coat and tunic, rolled up his sleeves and soaked his hands in disinfectant. Dip each instrument in the solution before use. He wiped Henshaw's arm.

"What do I do with this 'ere chloroform, Smiler?"

"Listen to me!" Henshaw said. "You take a big wad of lint and you stuff it firmly between my teeth, leaving a good pad exposed on the outside, then you watch my right hand. When you see me raise it, that means you're to drip chloroform onto the pad. When the hand goes down, you can stop. I wish you all the best. You're brave men, both of you. Let's hope it all goes to plan."

"Right, Sov, you work above the major's head, I'll operate from the other side. So, do up that tourniquet really tight, now." John laid out the instruments in their bowls beside the tank tracks and knelt beside Henshaw's thigh. "Ready, Hubert?"

Henshaw nodded, bit onto the lint pad and raised his right hand. After four drops of chloroform, it drooped back to the mud and he closed his eyes.

John took a deep breath, the closest he dared to a prayer and picked up a scalpel. Sweat began to prick his forehead.

He looked once or twice at Henshaw during the operation, but the eyes remained firmly shut, the teeth clenched on the lint wad. An occasional moan.

Sov, kneeling close to Henshaw's head, watched, big-eyed and reverent.

The metallic sting of a bullet hitting the tank. John paused, looked up, turned back to his work.

After about half an hour, Henshaw's left wrist flopped down onto the mud and the arm was free. "Thank God!" John said. He sank back onto his heels, rubbed his aching arm and watched the trickles of blood dying into the ground.

Henshaw spat out the wad and slowly opened his eyes. His voice was husky: "Leave the wound open. Prevent infection. Bandage it, and leave the tourniquet on."

"Oh, good God, were you conscious during that?"

"Was on call, if needed." Henshaw's eyes flickered. "But I'll have a shot now, if you will, please."

John backed off, shaking his head. Unbelievable, but the plan had worked.

★ ★ ★

Sov brought the stretcher into the gloom of the tank and together they lifted Henshaw and covered him with John's greatcoat. He slept now, heavy with morphia. Discreetly, they perched his tin hat on top of his head. A last look round: Skinner's body covered with the blanket. Atherstone's nearby; the amputation kit; Henshaw's crushed medical bag. Footprints in the flattened mud.

"I'm glad to be away from this cursed place," John said. He yawned. "We've had enough bloody trouble for one day." They put on their helmets and hoisted the stretcher onto their shoulders and began the long trudge. "I reckon it's a couple of miles. A long carry. Still traces of daylight, though." The lamp hung from his belt and banged against his hip.

"I can't believe what you did, Smiler. You got guts, I'll say that." Sov's voice floated back from the front of the stretcher.

"Couldn't think what else to do."

"The ole doc's quiet enough now, isn't he? Heavy, though."

John did not reply. He listened to the sound of their long boots battling the squelch and suck of mud. A heavy silence over the battlefield: all shooting at last at an end. Time for others to come out and bring in the bodies.

They picked their way across the mud, zigzagging; he left it to Sov to decide how best to negotiate the many pools and shell-holes. Happy to follow for once, too tired to talk. Sometimes, the sunken track was little more than a neck of mud two feet wide. The stretcher bounced with every step, the poles hard on the shoulder. Did that rhythm jar Henshaw or soothe him? I'll have a bruise there. God, I'm tired. But we did it! We got him free; we're taking him back. He sighed and tilted his head up to the brooding sky. He imagined the future: meeting Henshaw again back in Blighty. When all the hell was over.

"I can see en," Sov shouted. "We found Duckboard Alley!"

"Well done! Not so far now." John looked at the greatcoat covering Henshaw, one side drooping towards the ground. Hope that doesn't slip off. Thoughts of the horse bubbled up: quickly suppressed.

Reassuring to hear the soft stamp of their feet on the wooden boards. Tramp, tramp, tramp, the boys are marching. The old song slipped into his head.

"God, this pathway's got shot-up since we last came," Sov said. "'s not level no more, it's all upsy-downsy. You watch how you go, Smiler."

The way dipped steeply to skirt a huge flooded shell-hole and join a narrow causeway lower down. Instinct made him lower the rear of the stretcher to keep it level as Sov eased down, leaning back to take the weight.

"Steady, now, Sov."

Silence.

"Oh, bloody crike!" A scream flung into the air.

The skid of boot on plank; Sov's arms waved wildly, free of the carry; a thump; the stretcher tilted, felt light and Henshaw's body slipped, out from under the greatcoat over the stretcher head and disappeared into the liquid mud, smooth as a burial at sea. Sov, off balance, flustered, faltered, and crashed into the putrid water.

No sign now of Henshaw.

John stood above it all, still clutching the stretcher handles, unable to move.

"Smiler, for God's sake, help me." Sov, looking up, thrashed the clinging sludge, already brimming his chest. His face a mask of mud. He reached out.

John stood still, holding his breath. A warm stream coursed down his leg. He did not move.

"Smiler, help me, man, get me out!" Sov, head back, up to his neck now. The face, the fear, the arm reached towards him. All now in slow motion.

Will he drown? He watched, above it all, unable to move. *Enough*, the inside voice said. *No more.*

"Smiler! Help!" Sov shook his head, struggled to spew out the clots of mud, started to sink. His eyelashes, heavy with clay, blinked and drooped, the arm reaching still. The mud closed over the dome of his helmet and was still.

The hand reached; an air bubble blipped on the surface.

After that, nothing.

FORTY-SEVEN

The day slipped into darkness. Through a split in the cloud, the moon struggled over the horizon, flinging a blood-red, glistening path across the mud towards him. He stared unmoved, watched it swallowed by dark swirls of mist, thought nothing.

Drizzle chilled and soaked him, a wet caress on hands, face, clothes. He let it be, thought nothing.

He remained standing.

From the distant shattered trenches, a bagpipe played, floating sound across the waste of mud, mourning.

He stood, head bowed, unmoving.

A flare soared and drooped in the distance; occasional flashes stabbed the dark.

He let the hours pass, feeling the condemnation of time. He could not move, longed for the mud to dwarf and humble him into insignificance.

He remained.

A touch at his elbow. He did not look. "Come on, Corp, come in, there's nothing you can do."

He knew that Cockney voice, did not respond.

"Smiler, for God's sake, let go that bloody stretcher and come in now. You'll get soaked."

He said nothing, let himself be led.

FORTY-EIGHT

Feltham thrust a beaker towards him. "There you are, pal, get that down you. That'll sort you out."

John took a large mouthful and coughed at the liquid's fire. He stared ahead, elbows on knees, saying nothing.

"That's bloody good stuff," Feltham said. "Not watered down, nor nothing. Got it off the quarter master sergeant, he slipped it me."

John looked around. The two sat in the hut – all too familiar, like the top half of an ambulance. Three bunks, one at the back behind a blanket. Feltham lorded it from a chair.

"Doss down here tonight. No one'll come looking. I've bagged the comfy kip at the back, but you can have either of these two. The bastards have already shifted the beddin' to the new ADS. But it's a bed, innit? Off the ground. Not like those fuckin' bivvies."

A hand reaching out of a pool. Eyes staring, pleading.

John took a hefty gulp of rum and slumped forward. The drink burned; the image faded.

"I reckon we got nigh on twenty-four hours before we have to turn ourselves in," Feltham said. "Any longer, they'll think we're deserters and the questions get awkward. Me, I'm off for a Jimmy, then I'll get me 'ead down."

Feltham vanished into the night. John looked at the iron-framed bed he sat on, swung his legs off the ground, pulled a lining blanket down from the wall, bundled it over himself, and slept.

When he woke, the daylight puzzled him – fading as if it was sunset. Had he been out that long? He had no watch, tried a quick calculation. Must have slept about twenty hours. His head ached.

No sign of Feltham, but on the floor beside the bed stood a stone flagon half full of rum. He stood up, sniffed it and took a swig, drowning the faint voice that called his name.

FORTY-NINE

He stared. The wall shimmered through the swirls of steam, the glossy yellow bricks running cold with condensation. A poster there, a notice – something about *weighed*. He screwed his brow, trying to remember what it said. Already the paper curled and drooped off the wall, its gum loosened, the lettering obscure. He stared, puzzling to make sense of it. *Weighed*, that was it. He knew it now. A notice about him: THOU ART WEIGHED IN THE BALANCE AND FOUND WANTING. That was it, surely.

He still remembered his bible.

Public knowledge, then.

Other men toiled there, all, like him, stripped to the waist: one at a boiling cauldron, churning the water with a huge wooden paddle; two others, on the floor, scrubbing at bloodstains on shirts; further away, one man laboured at turning the handle of a huge mangle while the other fed clothes through the rollers, the extracted water piddling into a galvanised bucket. Were they being punished, too? He looked around, watched the hot fog spiralling through the open window as if drawn to a chimney. In the corner, two men shovelled coal, feeding the roar and heat of the boilers.

Safe, nobody watching.

He tiptoed across to the wooden cupboard where they kept soda crystals and rusting tins of soap and felt to the back of the shelf. Ah! His hand grasped a small, cool bottle, loosely corked. He glanced around. Nobody watching. Two or three furtive glugs, he gasped, hid the bottle again, felt the fire hit his stomach, longed for the fuddle to reach his brain. He walked back to his stand and relaxed as the contents of his vat changed from boiling mud and blood into dirty water tinged with pink foam.

★ ★ ★

Outside for tea break. The bottle in his jacket pocket, a coat draped over his shoulders. A chance to read her letter again.

My dear John,

I'm sure you'll be glad to know I was safely delivered of a second boy a few days ago. I've decided to call him Douglas Baxter Hemingby. I want to keep the Baxter name going now that Row has gone, especially as Arthur seems unlikely to marry and have children. His back is very bad now. I chose the name Douglas because it has no significance for either of us. If anything, it recalls our captain on the trawler who brought us back from Marseilles.

Rowley is doing well at school, especially in the three R's. The headmaster tells me he might well make grammar school one day which is very gratifying, but how they can tell such things at that age I've no idea. Dorothy grows up fast. She's a good daughter and has already become quite the little mother to the baby, as well as taking care of Bea. That helps me no end.

I do hope you're keeping well. It's such a long time since we saw you and we hear so little of you. Perhaps you're due some leave soon, I hope so.

With my love,

Em.

He groaned, put his head down on his knees. A rebuke there. Why couldn't he write? Anything, rubbish even? If only she knew. Now another mouth to feed. Four children. How would she manage? How would *they* manage, if he ever got home? What sort of father would he be now?

His hand reached into his pocket.

★ ★ ★

He rummaged at the bottom of the bag for his reserve supply and came upon the small jar. Blue glass, rusting top. He puzzled at it, and then remembered. Feeling sick, he unscrewed the lid. Inside, the dry trickle of orange-red powder, dust now, the faint smell of camphor.

He hung his head, hearing the voice, that plea he'd failed. Back to haunt him now, a promise broken.

Parade in ten minutes. Just time. He crammed the jar and his bottle into his trouser pocket and hurried round to the outbuilding, the station mortuary, where he and Sov had struggled to move the bodies for burial ages ago, in another time it seemed.

He stood amongst the nettles at the back of the building like a schoolboy up to no good and uncorked his liquor. He took several swallows, gasped and stood his bottle on the ground. He unscrewed the blue jar, upended it and watched the light wind tease the powder away so that it clung and stained the tops of the dying nettles.

"I'm sorry, Sov, I failed you."

He knew there'd never be forgiveness, but...

The words he'd coined and twisted out of the old faith rose to mock him: *Greater shame hath no man than this, that a man lay down his friends for his life.* He closed his eyes, bit his lip.

Coward! the voice in his head said. *Coward!*

He hurled the jar over the perimeter fence into a nearby field and stooped to retrieve his bottle. Now desperate with dry tears, he drained it, corked it and flung that as far as he could. Trampling the nettles and kicking at the clinging wet grass, he lurched towards the parade ground.

★ ★ ★

He stood to attention, swaying. His head throbbed and the loud

341

tumble of words from the staff sergeant made him wince.

"You're a disgrace to the Corps, man, that's what you are. How do you bloody dare to come on parade pissed as a fart and hope you can get away with it? Think we wouldn't notice? Take that stupid grin off your face. There's nothing funny about your situation, soldier. You're in deep trouble. You think being sent back from the Front, you've earned a soft number. I'll tell you now, you're wrong. None of that washes with me, old son."

Say nothing. No point.

"Stand up straight. You're slack, you're sloppy. Call yourself a corporal? Look at your feet, man. I've seen cleaner boots in a Calcutta cowshed. By God, if I have anything to do with it, you will lose your stripes. You're not fit to lead men. No one would follow you even on a free night in a Bombay brothel.

"Up before the officer tomorrow, my lad. Bet your bollocks on it. And then I'll see to it that you look the smartest you've ever been. Your own mother won't know her la-di-dah boy when we've finished with you. Now, today, you will go to the cookhouse, obtain a pint of salt water and drink it down. Clear? And when you've finished puking your 'orrible bleedin' guts out and got rid of all that Frog muck you've been swilling on the sly, you will clean out every water closet there is on-site. After that, you will set to and polish all boots in your hut twice over. I want them gleaming so brightly that I can see your stupid, grinning face in every single one. Is that clear?"

He said nothing.

"Is that clear?"

"Yes, sergeant." A mere mumble.

"Do you know something, soldier?" He put his face close to John's and whispered. "You and your type disgust me."

I know. I disgust myself.

He said nothing.

★ ★ ★

"Smiler, for God's sake, help me!" The arm stretching up towards him, just out of reach.

He woke with a start, saw the room in blackness, turned over. The bedsprings clanked. Sweat soaked his nightclothes. He clawed the pillow over his head and clamped it tight with his arm.

★ ★ ★

The major reminded him of a bloodhound – something about the long face, the drooping heavy-lidded eyes, the prim, downturned mouth. "Now, Hemingby, I've been looking at your Conduct Sheet. I see that back in October you received a Severe Reprimand and were fined half a crown." He paused. "Oh, yes, and you lost your stripes. Bit of an expensive beano, wasn't it?"

"Yes, sir!" He stood to attention and stared ahead. Something crawled and itched amongst the hairs at his waistline. He longed to scratch it. Bloody irons! Done it again, helped the blighters hatch.

The major put on his spectacles and took up the paper again. "And now here we are again: January 6th 1918 – *Breaking out of Barracks about 9.45 PM, improperly dressed and remaining absent until found in Barracks about 10.30 PM*. What was that about? Some Twelfth Night caper?" He took off his spectacles and looked straight at John.

No reply. How could he say he'd finally decided to take matters in hand with Henshaw's pistol, even went back behind the mortuary for privacy, and then thought better of it? Only a proven coward would funk shooting himself, preferring to climb out of camp and trade the gun for a flagon of cheap brandy.

Anything to block out those cries.

"Well, Private, I see we kept you for seven days CB on that occasion. Now then..." The patrician loftiness was beginning to annoy. The man had irregular protruding teeth. He leafed through a small leather-bound notebook. "You'll not have seen this. This is Major Henshaw's diary that's finally come down, and you get more than one entry here. Not exactly being mentioned in dispatches, but

343

rather complimentary. It seems he thought pretty highly of you."

God, I could do with a drink.

"I assume the esteem was mutual and you felt his loss pretty keenly."

John lowered his head. "Yes, sir." Right by his navel now, the itch.

"Very tough luck, that." He paused, but John made no reply. "Well, I'll tell you what we're going to do. I'm going to assume this is Major Henshaw's recommendation. He seems to have got the measure of you. I want you to submit to a routine medical. You'll be pronounced unfit and then we'll wangle a discharge for you."

"You're going to let me go, sir?"

"That's the general plan. You're rather long in the tooth, I gather you're a family man, and you've had a tough time out here. You're far from well. Anyone can see that. We're sending you back to civilian life, Private. Let you pick up the threads there. Sort your life out, back in Blighty. Schoolmaster, weren't you?"

"Yes, sir."

"Good!" The major stroked his hair down. "Much needed on the Home Front now, I'd guess. Now, we shall recommend you for the Silver War Badge as a matter of course, but there'll be no pension, I'm afraid, since you have a job and you leave us before the war is over. And because... Well, consider it *quid pro quo*, old chap, we overlook all this misconduct and you..." A long pause. The major snapped the book shut. "OK? Jolly good."

John hurried back to his quarters, picturing the brandy hidden in his locker. A kind of leniency, then, treating him like an officer. But really, glad to see the back of him. So, home: Em, the children and his old life.

But where was his old self?

Lost out in the mud and dragging two ghosts behind him. How would he manage this curse of survival?

He reached for the bottle, checked he was alone and took a long drink.

FIFTY

The horn groaned into the gathering darkness like a cow in distress; the sea-fog clammed around his cheeks. No land visible, no notion how long this journey would take. Could be headed anywhere. Limbo.

Safer on deck, away from others. Black smoke bundled from the funnel and drifted to mingle and darken the fog. The sweet smell of coal.

He had tucked himself into a space near the stern, his face hidden, his head bowed onto his knees. Close by, the propellers rushed and foamed in busy energy, the ship hurrying him onward. But to what? What was he good for now? And where should he go? What would Em and the children make of him?

The cold metal of the hull chilled his back, his eyes ached from tiredness. He stared at the caulked timber of the deck, and his hands, fingers spread, clamped his head as if to protect it, or tear his hair out. Anything to exclude the world.

The voice in his head would not leave him. It dredged up thoughts, words, guilt. The Bible, of course, once a support, now his tormentor. He could block out God but not The Word. That still pursued him.

Thou shalt dash them in pieces like a potter's vessel.

That was it. That was justice.

What if Dorothy ever said: 'What happened in the war, Daddy?'

What could he say? 'My friend needed help. I couldn't be a man and save him. Like a coward, I let him die.' No escaping that.

What if she sympathised?

'This is my punishment,' he'd tell her, 'let me take that like a man.'

FIFTY-ONE

I liked looking down from my attic window onto the plane trees below. A cold wind blew and the bare top-twigs rattled against each other like dry bones. I'll just wait for the streetlamp, I thought. When the gas lights, time to go down for tea. Drops of rain pattered on the window: below, a quiet street, empty apart from a soldier dragging along on the other side of the road. He wore a greatcoat and walked, head bowed, as if lost in thought. A tin hat hung from a bag round his shoulder. Dark hair, tall; one foot scuffing.

I felt a jolt in my chest and rushed away from the window down the narrow stairs to our sitting room.

"Heavens, child, slow down," Mother said. "Anyone would think the house is on fire."

"Mama, Mama, there's a soldier coming along the street and I think it's Daddy."

"Really? Coming here? Let me look." She went to the window and peered down. "I can't see anyone, are you sure? I've had no telegram. If it is him..." She lifted off her apron and began smoothing down her dress. "Quickly now, fetch me the brush from the top drawer, just time to tidy your hair. And make sure you don't disturb Douglas."

Rowley didn't look up. He sat in a chair, too absorbed in a book about warships. Bea, cross-legged near the fireguard, hammered pegs through a wooden board with a small mallet. The baby lay on a pile of towels in the bottom drawer of the dresser, sleeping after his feed.

"Does Daddy have a key?" I felt her tug the brush through my hair.

"Of course, he'll be here soon enough." She put two more lumps of coal on the range. After two minutes, she said, "You must have been mistaken, Dorothy."

"May I go outside and check?"

"If you must. But don't leave the front door open, you know how Aunty Daphne hates draughts."

I pulled the inside door shut behind me and opened the main door. Two steps down, leaning against the wall, the man sat with his back to me. Hunched forward, head down, clasping his knees. He didn't move. A bald patch on the back of his head glistened in the light from the streetlamp.

"Daddy?" I tried softly.

He made no move, his face still hidden.

"Daddy?" I said again. Still no response. "I'll go and fetch Mama." I hated closing the door on him but didn't know what else to do.

"Mama, there's a man sitting on our front steps and I think it *is* Daddy. But he doesn't answer. Will you come?"

"Heavens, child. It'd better not be some old tramp. You two little ones, stay here."

I followed her to the front door. The man remained hunched against the wall just as I'd left him.

"John, is that you? Are you all right?" She squatted down on the step beside him and put her hand on the man's shoulder. She looked at his face. He stared straight ahead as if watching something on the other side of the road. He didn't speak.

"Come on, now, John, let's go inside. You're home now." She took the man's hand and pulled him to his feet. He let himself be led.

I didn't know what the matter was. Was he blind? I held my breath and quietly closed the door.

Once inside our parlour, Mother helped him off with his coat. "Now, John, sit down. I expect you'd like a cup of tea. When do you have to go back?" Her voice unusually quiet, gentle.

He remained standing, staring down as if bewildered. Slowly, he shook his head, felt into an inside pocket and held out a folded document.

She began reading. "Discharged? That's splendid news. So you're home for good."

I went over, put my arms around his waist and pulled myself close. "Daddy, my daddy, you're home." I was tall enough now to reach his shoulders. I rested my head against his suit jacket. He laid a hand on my head, but there was no strength there, no warmth.

I pulled away and looked at him. What was wrong? The stare had gone; he clearly wasn't wounded. But no smile, no recognition.

Wasn't he happy to be home?

"Quietly now, children, come and say hallo to your father," Mother said. "Rowley, you first." She put her hand on the boy's shoulder and pushed him to his feet.

Rowland sighed, lobbed the large book to one side and wandered over to stand in front of Daddy. "Welcome home. How do you do?" He held out his hand.

No response. Daddy hardly looked at him.

Mother's smile faded as Rowley slid his hand behind his back. "Your turn now, Bea."

"No! I don't want to." She stamped her foot and hid behind the basketwork chair.

Mother sighed. "All right, we'll leave it for now, but we don't want any paddies, thank you, young lady. Learn to behave properly or you'll go straight to bed." She looked around as if uncertain what to do. "I think we'll let Daddy be. I expect he's finding it all rather strange. We'll have our tea, as usual. Dorothy, empty the teapot into the sink and make a fresh pot." She gestured towards the kettle singing on the edge of the range. "And Rowley, take Bea out with you, see she washes her hands. If necessary, do it for her."

I peered round the scullery door and watched Mother steer Daddy into a chair, in the shadows away from the hearth. "Sit there for the present, John, while we get the children's tea out of the way.

Don't mind us. Thank goodness the baby's quiet. This lot can be quite a handful. We'll talk later."

★ ★ ★

He listened to the clatter of plates and knives, the high-pitched voices, the cries of 'I want', Emma's calm, insistent control. He rested his left hand across his eyes, wished he dared reach for the bottle which nestled in his pocket. Anything to block out sounds.

"Now, Beatrice Hemingby, drink up your warm milk, it's good for you. And finish your bread and jam."

"Don't want it."

"Come along, now. Do as you're told, miss. Finish your bread and jam!"

From under the cover of his shaded eyes, John watched his right hand. The tremor had started again, the shake in his fingers obvious. He clamped his left hand over them to hide the trembling from scrutiny.

★ ★ ★

Mother took the children upstairs after tea, saying she'd read some *Alice* before bed, if they were good. They were to leave Daddy in peace; he was very tired. She scooped Douglas out of the drawer, held him up for Daddy to see and then the room went quiet. Only the crack and settle of the coals.

I squatted on the floor beside his chair. "Welcome home, Daddy. I'm so glad you're safe. You've been away for ages. I've missed you so much. I hope you'll play me your fiddle soon, will you? It's over there." I pointed to the corner of the room. "Shall I fetch it?" I looked up, but his eyes were downcast, his mouth unmoving.

"What's happened, Daddy? Why are you like this?"

He cleared his throat as if he wanted to speak but said nothing. His Adam's apple rose and sank in his throat.

I knelt up and laid my head on his chest. Beneath, his stomach spiralled sounds up to my ear. "Are you all right, Daddy? You're not wounded, are you?"

No reply. Another stomach-gurgle. And then it came to me – something I'd heard at school, sometimes men from the war were like this because... "Daddy, have you killed a man?"

I thought he hadn't heard me, but I felt him stiffen. I daren't repeat the question. Surely not, he didn't believe in killing.

Silence. The clock ticked and the coal slipped further down the grate. I put my head on his chest again and kept it there. He didn't want to talk. That was all right. We'd have all the time in the world. He was home now.

The first drop on my temple surprised me; I wasn't sure it'd happened. Then a second fell and I realised he was hunched over me. I lifted my head, saw his eyes brimming. "Daddy, don't, please. It's all right. You're home now."

He cleared his throat again, his voice husky: "Sorry, my Dolly Daydream, I'm sorry."

★ ★ ★

In the toilet outside, he sneaked several gulps of the brandy. It had seen him through transit camp and dispersal centre, eased him through the fog of the Channel. But this was the last of it. He'd need to think tomorrow about refilling the bottle. With what, though? Something strong, not too expensive. Gin might do it. He smiled sourly to himself: *father's* ruin.

But it helped.

He flushed the toilet noisily, stepped out, letting the door bang, and listened to his feet scraping up the path to the house. At least he should be able to sleep; the brandy would help dispel the voices. Just one more trial. But how to tell her?

He pushed open the bedroom door, his voice a loud whisper. "Em, forgive me, I can't... Not tonight. I cannot share your bed tonight. I'm not used..."

"Very well," she said, "I understand. Shall I make up a bed somewhere else? On the couch?"

"Here will do nicely." He pointed at the floor at his side of the bed. "I've known rougher billets."

"I see, all right, then. Do you want pillows?" She lifted two off the bed and put them on the floor. "I'll get a blanket and the old eiderdown."

"That will do, I'll not undress tonight." Did she notice him slurring his words?

"Lie down, let me cover you over."

He did as he was told and turned on his side while she fussed around, taking off his boots and covering him against draughts. Near his head now: her hand rested on his shoulder. "Good to have you back, John," she said, "after everything you must have been through. I hope you feel better in the morning." She stroked his hair and bent to kiss his cheek. She sniffed the air. "Have you been drinking?"

"Only a nightcap, Em, helps me sleep."

"I see." She straightened up and he heard her bare heels thudding round to her side. "That's all we need."

★ ★ ★

He surfaced to the sound of whispering. Grey light seeped round the heavy drapes. Peering past the chamber pot, he could make out, on Em's side of the bed, a pair of small feet on tiptoe. Must be Beatrice, he thought, what is she – nearly three?

"Mama, who's that man?"

"Now then, dear, don't say that. He's your father. We mustn't wake him."

"I don't like him. He frightens me."

"Shh, you mustn't say such things."

He closed his eyes and covered them with his hand. Could he ever belong anywhere again?

★ ★ ★

Daddy appeared at breakfast wearing his shirt and braces, no collar, and ill-fitting trousers. The others were seated already, Bea swinging her legs in her chair and clutching a spoon. Mother called out from the scullery. "I shan't be long, I'm still feeding the baby. Sit down, John, Dorothy give the porridge a stir, make sure it doesn't catch."

"Sit there, Daddy." I indicated head of the table. "I'll pour a cup of tea." For the first time, I realised why he looked different.

"You've shaved it off, Daddy – your moustache." He seemed pale and thinner than I remembered and he had big hollows round his eyes.

He looked at me and lowered his gaze. "Yes."

"When did you do that?"

No reply.

I stirred the porridge and poured his tea. I kissed the bald patch on the top of his head.

He stiffened.

I looked at my brother. "Rowley, I don't think that's a good idea." He'd taken a brown paper bag, screwed up the neck and was blowing it up like a balloon.

He stuck out his tongue at me, took a deep breath and finished puffing into the bag.

"Rowley! Stop it!"

He leaned out towards Bea's high chair and held the bag in front of him. With a devilish grin, he clapped his other hand onto it.

Bea screamed at the explosion, then laughed in surprise. Rowley cheered.

"Oh, God!" Daddy shouted. We all stared. His hands began to jitter uncontrollably on the table. The cup began to vibrate and the teaspoon jiggled in the saucer. The tea slopped over.

Mother hurried in, clutching the baby and buttoning her blouse. "What on earth's going on in here?"

I looked at Daddy. His hands still shook, but his eyes were wide with fear, his mouth half-open as if he might burst into tears.

★ ★ ★

Mother quickly restored order and the children ate in silence as instructed. "We must get you out of that dreadful suit, John, you look a tramp in that."

He nodded. He seemed very quiet.

"I've kept all your old outfits wrapped up with mothballs, I hope they still fit. I wouldn't be surprised if you've lost weight. I'll get a couple out and give them an airing."

No reply; only the sound of plates being scraped clean.

She sighed. "Will you want a bath? I rather think you might before you put on proper clean clothes. Now, will you have that here – I can easily take the tub down and put it in our room for privacy – or will you go down to the baths? If you want your back scrubbed, I'll do it for you, with pleasure."

"Council Baths." His voice a growl.

"So long as I know. Don't stint yourself, dear. Pay for a hot bath, won't you? Have a good soak, get rid of all that grime, see if you can relax," she said. "Perhaps you'll feel better."

"I'll go in the Turkish. Parcel up a suit, shirt and tie with the underclothes, please. And don't forget collar studs."

"I shan't. It'll be nice to have your old self back. And, look, take our towels. Better than paying for scratchy municipal things." She handed him two white towels which he rolled up. "Now, what about that horrible greatcoat?" She gestured to it hanging by the door. "Haven't you got to hand that back? You looked a fright when you came in."

"Twenty-eight days."

"I see." She looked grim. "Dorothy, clear these plates and cups away and put them in the sink while I make up the fire. I must bake later." She looked out of the window into the street below. "Oh, good, the coal man's here." Rowley and Bea asked if they could get down.

I glanced out of the window at the big dray horse and the long flat cart. Neat rows of black sacks leaning against each other. A heavy load. Already, the old driver was heaving the first bag onto his shoulder. Knees bent, one hand supporting the grimy sack, he began the stamp up the passage to the coal hole. The merchant's lad began to load up, too. He set off with a stagger.

At the first crash, when the coal man flung back the wooden lids to the chute, Daddy clapped his hands over his ears and sat tense, quivering. The clash and rumble of the coal came immediately afterwards, hollow like a dreadful explosion.

He stood up, half crouched, as if he saw no escape. A second thunder, a third soon after, as the load of coal roared and tumbled into the cellar.

"Oh, God, no!" His cry startled us all. He dived under the table, hands over his ears, crying, shaking, sobbing, crouching into a ball, whimpering.

Bea screamed and grew red-faced, the baby started crying, Rowland ran to hide in the scullery.

Mother whirled round from the fireplace. "Heavens above, what's got into you all? It's only the coal man. Oh, John, we really can't carry on like this."

I looked at him cowering underneath the table. I'd never seen a man afraid before. We didn't know then what had made him like this.

* * *

The smell of chlorine caught at his throat when he pushed open the doors. He spun round, stumbled down the steps and bolted along the passageway between the boundary wall and the boiler house. In a corner where moss crept over the clinker path and green slime edged up the walls, he stopped, unbuttoned his fly and paused. Behind him, the hiss and thud of the pump room. He searched around; no one could see. He let a bundle unroll and pissed urgently over one of Emma's towels. The warm trickle dripped off his fingers. Hand shaking, he buttoned himself up and held the damp cloth across his nose and mouth. He staggered back, knowing he had to go in.

"Idiot!" the voice in his head said as he barged inside the lobby. *"This is Camberwell, not Cambrai."*

★ ★ ★

Head bowed, he sat naked in the hot room. So few men anywhere now. Only an old male attendant sitting idle. Already, sweat began to prick and bead John's shoulders. He leaned forward on the bench, head in his hands, elbows on knees. When others were around, he used to pray like that. But here he sat to face himself.

"You're not mad," he said aloud. Comforting to hear his own voice whisper in the stifling steam. "You haven't lost your reason, old chap." He thought he heard Henshaw saying it. "Afterwards, you always know your reactions were foolish. So what makes you respond instinctively when a moment's thought..."

That other voice: *"Who'll give you a job when you're like this? You can't turn a form-room cupboard into a funk hole at the first bang of a desk lid. Why behave so idiotically?"* Fear welled up. Is this what the medics called neurasthenia?

And now he'd come home, not to rejoicing and relief, but to children who were afraid of him, and a wife fast losing patience.

How could you pull yourself together?

Surviving was worst: he'd carry Sov and Henshaw with him always. How to expiate cowardice? He tried imagining doing the comradely thing – visiting the widows. Sov's wife opening the cottage door to his knock. She'd know now. But would she realise his part in it? How could he tell her he'd been with her husband when he died, watched him spew and flounder, but did nothing to help? How could he pretend that cliché: that Sov died a hero's death? And could he say to Mrs Henshaw or to that favourite daughter – was it Letty? – while sitting in their house, pinch-kneed on a sofa, that he'd saved Hubert and lost him again? That stretcher – should have strapped him down. His job to think of it.

He closed his eyes, his skin prickling. *Why, this is hell nor are we out of it.* Faustus knew: you carried hell with you everywhere.

Surviving was worst.

★ ★ ★

Above the plunge pool, the shakes besieged him again. They would not let him be; they took him over, making his arms jitter and legs tremble; any step now would be a stagger or a fall. Once more as if held in a dream, he watched Sov's arm rise from the water in that desperate clawing, felt his own throat close with anguish and tears. His body shook. What would free him from this curse?

Then peace. The smell of chlorine drifted up, controllable now; the water rocked gently: still, menacing, inviting.

"*You could,*" the voice said, as he waded down into the water. The shakes began to recede. "*If you're man enough. That would free you.*"

He launched into the water, gasped at the shock of the cold clamping his body, closing his pores, heard the trickle in his ears, opened his eyes on the blue-tiled chamber he'd entered.

"*Try it. Deep breath, sit on the bottom. See how it felt for them.*"

He surfaced, gasped in air, ducked below the surface, tried squatting cross-legged. Around him, the muffling, clinging swirl. Already the held breath began to constrict his chest.

"*Stretch up, let your hand break out of the water. See that lamp overhead, reach for the light.*"

He could feel his hand in air, that other world, catching at nothing; the run of water shedding from his wrist hairs back down his arm.

"*Now, bring it back and let go. Blow the air out, release your worries, let the world drift away. One breath out down here, a deep gulp in. Don't fight it.*"

He closed his eyes, heard the soft drabble of air leaving his mouth, felt his chest clamp and tighten. He knew what to do next.

But.

With a surge and a gasp he was on his feet again, arms flailing, gulping at air, crying.

"*Coward!*" the voice said. "*When it comes to it...*"

He wallowed across to the steps. He gasped, sobbed, held onto the surround. Water trickled off his head and down his back.

Cowards were condemned to live. That was his punishment.

★ ★ ★

The house shuddered when the front door slammed. Mother looked up, gave a tut of annoyance; I wondered how things would be now Daddy was back. He was late: the kitchen clock had already struck half past one, and at one o'clock, when the meal was ready, she sighed and slid the saucepan of stew to the edge of the range.

"You're back, then," she said. "Did you go to the baths?" She wiped her hands on her apron.

Daddy stood in the doorway. He drooped into his clothes now; his own dark suit so loose it looked as though it belonged to another man. He sighed and nodded.

"Where's your greatcoat? Heavens, man, you've not come back without a top coat, surely? On a day like this? I'm not sorry to see the back of that dreadful thing. But after a hot bath, you shouldn't go wandering the streets without a coat, you'll catch a chill. Or worse. Where is it?"

"Clapham Junction."

"What, the station? Why? Did you walk?"

"You can hand greatcoats in there."

"Oh, good, and they paid you? Did you empty the pockets?"

He sighed. "Here's the demob ration book. Better take it now. And have five bob to keep you going." He thrust the book and the cash towards her and swayed, struggling to keep his balance.

"Sit down, Daddy." I pulled a chair out to face the fire. He sat, elbow on the corner of the table, his hand supporting his head.

"Is this all you can spare from what they gave you? I shall be short this week, what with the coalman and an extra mouth to feed," Mother said.

"Not been to the Post Office, have I? Can't do everything, woman. I need money, too."

I gasped. I'd never known him raise his voice to her before.

"All right, all right," she said. "Let's get dinner on the table, it's late enough as it is." She walked over to the range, her voice now a mutter. "The sooner you get your old job back, the better for all. Get some routine going again." She rapped on the window to Rowley and Bea who were out playing in the yard.

Daddy stood up. "No dinner for me, Em. I'm not hungry, don't feel like eating just now. I'll get into bed and lie down for a while."

"Oh, really!" She put her hands on her hips. "Are you ill? Shall I save some for later?"

"If you like." He stumbled out.

With a fierce sigh, Mother busied about. She bent down to the oven and banged a baked potato on each plate. She kicked the oven door to, crashed the saucepan lid onto the side of the range and began ladling the stew and carrots out.

"Don't get upset, Mama. He's tired," I said.

"I know full well the reason he doesn't want any dinner and why he has so little cash. I'd lay money on it if I had any. Now, what are we to do?" She shook her head. "What's the matter with the man? If he makes a habit of this..." She turned away and stuffed her hand over her mouth.

She didn't seem to expect a reply; her lips were tight, her eyes lowered; I could sense she struggled.

★ ★ ★

The bareness of the long avenue shocked him, the leafless trees hacked back as if a giant scythe had lopped any overhanging branches. Heavy vehicles had gouged grooves so deep in the sandy drive that it resembled a farm track.

Throughout his time abroad, he clung to the memory of the peace here, the secure seat of learning that nurtured him and its generations of boys. He tried to catch sight of the cottage where they'd lived. Would smoke still drift from its chimney?

They had created a vast clearing, the surrounding trees cut down and stacked until they could be logged. The cottage had vanished, its bricks tumbled to one side; in its place, four Nissen huts, each with a painted red cross covering walls and roof. In a row, side by side, four motor ambulances waited.

Increasing dread caught at his throat. He walked towards the main building, his footsteps crunching on the track. He stumbled in a rut created by heavy vehicles. The driveway opened onto the college lawn and the main building; he paused, mouth open, not breathing. Before him, clusters of wheelchairs in small groups; men in blue hospital uniform in the sunshine, tartan blankets over their knees; a few stood, leaning on crutches, talking, laughing; in the distance, below the headmaster's study, a small group played five-a-side crutch football, each with only one leg to kick the ball towards an open goal. Nurses criss-crossed the grass, pushing wheelchairs, carrying covered trays, tending a man's dressing, helping a soldier to drink.

"Oh, God!" The lurking memory of war rose unchecked. He turned and began to run, a peculiar limping lope, back the way he'd come. Nothing for him here but fear and misery.

Behind him a shout: "That man, halt! Stay where you are!" He ignored it. They wouldn't shoot. He scuttled on, breath already rasping.

The sputter of a motorcycle engine behind him as someone kick-started the machine. If I can just reach the road... He gasped at air. Obvious now why they called it the long avenue. Already, the urgent chatter of the vehicle seemed closer.

The motorcycle overtook and slewed across his path, a military policeman leaped off the package tray and pointed a gun. "Stay where you are!"

The tremors seized John. He stood there panting, struggling to stand upright, unable to raise his hands.

The man lowered his gun. "Who are you, what are you doing here?"

John gave his name.

"Why aren't you in uniform?"

He couldn't control the stammer: "D-d-discharged."

"Where's your Silver Badge? You should be wearing it."

"I'm sorry."

"Why are you here? What do you want?"

"Can I sit down?" He rested cross-legged on the side of the roadway. The man stood over him, the gun lowered. John clenched his hands in the hope of controlling the shaking. He managed a sentence at a rush. "My name's John Hemingby, formerly 3rd Wessex RAMC, I used to be a m-m-master here, I came to see if there's a t-t-teaching job."

The motorcycle rider laughed. "Blimey, poor sod's one of us. Bit late, though, pal. The school's been gone two years."

"What happened to all the Edwardians?"

"Gone! The old headmaster died, they say his wife was killed in a Gotha raid while he was 'ere, and it broke him. The school ran out of cash, the boys stopped comin' and those left were transferred. I reckon the guvnors was pleased when the War Office approached them. Couldn't keep going."

"Now, listen!" The military policeman motioned to John to stand up. "I'm going to believe your story. It's so stupid it has to be true. But be on your way. And if I see you hanging around again, you'll be handed over sharpish to the authorities. You mark my words. And they *will* treat you as a Boche spy."

The rider kick-started the engine and the two men mounted. "On your way, pal, and good luck. By the state of you, you should be in hospital yourself."

John began the long walk back. He'd never had a gun pointed directly at him before, but that was nothing to what he'd face when he saw Em again.

Perhaps The Station Hotel would be open.

FIFTY-TWO

The silence worried me. The house hadn't settled, the stillness different, expectant. The stairs always creaked when someone came to bed, but I hadn't heard anything. I'd climbed into bed ages before and read for an hour, but Mother hadn't looked in, as she usually did, to say good night.

And where was Daddy?

In the room below, the old clock began chiming. I held my breath in case I missed any of the strokes. Eleven o'clock. Another hour and Mother would be feeding Douglas again. Was Daddy still out? Where did he go these nights until late? Still looking for work? Hardly. Before he came back from the war, Mother had taken to going to bed about half past nine. Early to bed, she liked to say, early to rise... She often quoted it.

The front door banged and the house shuddered, I felt the tremors through the legs of my bed. Voices in the room beneath. Heavens! She must have waited up. A struggle to hear her; she always spoke quietly. Daddy was more distinct: a rumble which rose and fell with his words and his mood, like listening to a distant swarm of bees. They seemed to have a lot to talk about.

I shifted onto my side. Daddy was home; they'd soon be coming up. I began to drift off, my world safe again.

A shout from downstairs. I sat up, startled. Daddy's words were quite clear; he wailed like a dog in pain: "I hate it, I hate being like this, but I can't help myself. Don't you see? I can't stop these things. I know it's silly. Do you think I want to carry on in this way?"

I couldn't make out what she said. There were shushing noises and the voices became a hum. Mother's was patient, always steady. She explained things all the time and got her own way. Even Rowley at his naughtiest knuckled under when she reasoned with him.

"I assure you if I could help myself, I would." He was shouting again. I strained to hear her reply. Impossible.

"Of course it's not good for me," he shouted, "I know that. But it helps, I feel better. After a few, life doesn't seem so bad."

I put my feet out of bed, wondering whether to go downstairs. But they'd only stop if I appeared. *Pas devant, pas devant,* Daddy used to say in the old days. A long time before I discovered what it meant, that they wouldn't argue in front of the children.

Another outburst – Daddy again: "I'm doing my best, surely you know that? It's not easy coming back, I can't just start again. My world has changed. What use am I to anyone like this?"

I settled onto my back and stared at the ceiling. The light from the streetlamp shone up through the bare branches and made web patterns which waved and tangled overhead. What was going on? I yawned, my eyes heavy; I really must go to sleep. I had school the next day. Things would be better in the morning.

That's what Mother always said.

I tried the short prayer I'd learned when I was little – one of those Daddy taught me. That sometimes helped to send me off:

> *Now I lay me down to sleep,*
> *I pray the Lord my soul to keep,*
> *Thy angels watch me through the night,*
> *And keep me safe till morning's light.*

I repeated the last line, changing the words to include Daddy – that seemed important: *And keep us safe till morning's light.* I yawned again and told myself off. "Now, go to sleep. It's long past bedtime. Everything will be all right in the morning."

★ ★ ★

"There's no time to plait your hair," Mother said. "We're all very late. Brush it well, and I'll tie it into bunches. What colour ribbon today?"

I chose bright green because spring was coming. Always a favourite colour.

"Now, Rowley," she said, "finish your breakfast, go and do your business. Clean your teeth. You don't want to keep Dorothy waiting."

"Won't you take me, Mama?" he said. "Please..." He looked such an angel with his hair neatly brushed. You wouldn't think...

"You know very well I can't. I have to stay here with Bea and the baby. Now, be a good lad and go with your sister. She'll take you right to the classroom door. You won't get lost."

"Is Daddy all right this morning, Mama?" I said while Rowley was out of the room.

Silence.

She seemed on edge.

"Mama?"

"I should think so, child, why shouldn't he be?"

"I heard you talking last night and –"

"Did you, now?" She stared at me and unsettled me.

"I couldn't hear what you were saying. It was very late."

"You know what they say: eavesdroppers hear no good of themselves."

"Is he still in bed, Mama?"

"No, your father isn't here just now. Now, come on, child, stop dawdling, you'll be late."

"I only wanted to say goodbye."

"Yes, well, you can't, I'm afraid. Now, get along both of you." Her firm push between my shoulder blades and the way she hurried to close the door behind us, made me wonder whether she actually wanted to be rid of us.

★ ★ ★

364

The smell of hot coals and baking drifted into my nostrils as Rowley and I closed the porch door. I smiled and relaxed. Teatime: Mother must have prepared something special. I held the kitchen door open and Rowley walked in under my arm. Bea already sat up at table, a napkin folded into the neck of her dress, her little boots kicking against the foot-rest of her chair. Mother perched sideways on a dining chair, Douglas on her lap. He wore a long white dress.

"Now, Rowley, have you been a good boy today?"

"Yes, Mama, and I did sums."

I moved across and began to chuck the baby under his chin. The folds of skin felt soft, warm and moist. "How's my little Doug? Tickle, tickle."

The baby gurgled. A happy family scene we'd known many times before.

"Not now, Dorothy. Take your coat off. We need you as chef for our special tea."

"What's special about today, Mama?" I hung the coats up.

"Nothing in particular. I wanted us to have tea together and make it a treat. Today we're having crumpets, and I'd like you to toast them."

"Oh, goody! I love crumpets," Rowley said. "Please can I have the first, Mama?"

"You not only can, but you may. *May*, Rowley, that's the polite thing to say. The order will be Rowley, Bea, Dorothy, and then me. Now, wash your hands in the scullery, both of you, and we can get started."

I dragged the tumpty seat close to the fire, squatted there and speared a crumpet. I held the toasting fork in front of the glowing coals.

"Not too close, now, Dorothy. We don't want it burned. Now, when you get your crumpet, you may put butter on as a treat –"

"And jam, Mama?" Rowley bounced on his chair. "Or honey?"

"No, Rowley, butter is quite sufficient, but if you like, you *may* put on a tiny sprinkle of salt for extra flavour. There are two crumpets each, and one for me."

I loved that time of day: the light fading, the room cosy with a glow from the range, the overhead lamp not yet lit. Everything seemed to close in so that the world became just the five of us in a circle, facing the fire. I remember that moment: the scullery was in shadow and our faces glowed a soft, pinky orange in the light. Peaceful, lovely.

"Are you going to tell a fireside story, Mama?"

"Not today, Rowley, not a story, but I have got something to say."

The chairs creaked as we all swivelled to look at her. I felt it was probably all right to put elbows on the table for once. Rowley was licking butter off his fingers but Mother seemed not to notice.

"I don't know how you'll feel about this, but I wanted to tell you while it was quiet and we were all together." She paused and took a deep breath. "You know that your father has been around for a few weeks now since he came back from the war. He and I had a talk last night and it has been decided that it's probably better if he doesn't live with us anymore."

"Good!" Bea banged her hands on the table. "Didn't like that man. He frightened me."

"He was scary," Rowley said. "I didn't like it when he started shaking or hiding under things. I don't want a daddy like that."

"No, of course not," Mother said. "I expect you, Dorothy, will be most upset because you knew him the longest, but you have to understand it's for the best."

I lowered my head so that my hair tumbled like curtains across my face. "He's my daddy." My voice came out in a sad, slow whisper.

A long silence, broken only by the shift and rustle of coals.

Tears began running down my cheeks. I sniffed and felt for a hanky. "Shall we never see him again?"

"I know it hurts now, dear." Her voice was soft and kind. "But be brave and bear up. You have to understand that sad things happen to everybody some time in their lives. The pain will ease eventually. You'll get over it, I promise you."

I sniffed and said nothing. I wiped my eyes and pulled some

strands of hair out of my mouth. "Why has he gone, Mama? Why?"

"I can't tell you more now. Wait until the little ones have gone to bed."

★ ★ ★

I studied the room while Mother stayed upstairs, reading the children bedtime stories. Everywhere seemed neat, everything in its place, as she liked it.

As if Daddy had been tidied out of our lives.

And his violin had gone. That corner of the room was bare. I felt a jolt of panic. Things were serious, then. It must be true.

I sat on the tumpty, staring into the fire, trying to puzzle it out. The clock struck seven. I ought to stir myself; Mother didn't like anyone sitting idle when there were jobs to do. "Come on, now, stop moping about the place," she'd say.

I poked the coals, put a shovelful of slack on the fire and picked up the kettle for the tea things. I sniffed; my eyes ached.

"Well, Bea has quite taken to Mrs Tittlemouse," Mother said when she came into the room. "I thought it might be rather old for her, but she likes it. Animals again, you see. Oh, good girl, you've done the washing up. I can have a rest." She took off her apron and sat facing the fire.

I settled into the chair opposite. "Have you packed Daddy's fiddle away?" I tried to make the question sound casual.

"No, he took it with him, for all the good it'll do. He tried playing it the other day when you were at school but had to stop because it made him cry. Really, I don't know what to make of all this to-do. The whole thing's too upsetting."

"Did Daddy go last night or first thing this morning?"

"He left before I went to bed. He packed a suitcase with a few things while I made some sandwiches. I gave him a plate and mug to take with him, he picked up his violin and went."

"In the middle of the night? Where was he going?" My chest began to feel tight.

"Your guess is as good as mine. Perhaps he's joined some old comrades from the army. Maybe he's gone to see his family. I don't know."

"So he's gone for good?" Tears were close now. I bit my lip.

"We have to assume so, I'm afraid." She turned her head away. "We managed before..." She gulped. "...well enough without him –"

"I don't believe you. Something's wrong. He wouldn't have gone without saying goodbye, I know he wouldn't."

"You're sure of that, are you, miss? I'm telling you a lie, am I? Oh, really!" She stared at me and blew her nose.

"I know my daddy, he would have said goodbye to me, I know he would. He did when he first went to war... Unless..." The thought began to grow. "Unless you *sent* him away, told him to leave because you didn't like how he was behaving." I was shouting now. "Did you tell him he had to go?"

"I'm not going to answer that," she said in her quiet voice. "You must think what you like. What went on last night stays between your father and me. He was unsettling the little ones, he knew that. I can't have Rowley bed-wetting again, not now he's at school. You're just about old enough to understand there's something wrong, but I couldn't get your father to see a doctor."

"Oh, Mother, I hate you!" Tears now. "You did, you sent my daddy away and now we don't know where he is. I hate you!"

"Now, that's enough! Mind your manners, young lady, I know you're upset, it's not easy, but that's not the way to speak to me."

"But what has he done wrong?"

"He did nothing wrong – except we never knew what to expect. Sometimes he came home shaking and fearful, other times scarcely sober. Day after day. We're not a drinking family, and I also couldn't be doing with a husband who sat at the table and sucked his thumb. Is that the way a grown man behaves? He couldn't even hold a pen without shaking. That would have been no good in the classroom, now would it?"

"Why do you talk about him as if he's dead?"

"He might as well be for all the good he is to us now." A crack in her voice. "We need someone dependable who pays the bills – someone to keep his family, not take from his children's mouths what little food we have to go round. I know it's hard, but we must all try and forget him. Daddy doesn't live with us anymore."

★ ★ ★

Again, noises floated into my bedroom. Sounds I'd never heard before. On the ceiling above me, the shadow branches twisted and tossed. I sat up, rested my shoulders against the bars of the bed head and strained to listen: very strange – she was in her bedroom, crying; every so often I heard a choke in the sob and the weeping burst out again.

Good, I thought, at least she's a little sorry for sending him away. I'd already decided that she'd behaved like a wicked stepmother. I never called her Mama again.

FIFTY-THREE

I never knew what really happened that night. I've often thought about it. Did Mother throw him out? Or did Daddy leave for reasons of his own? Would he sacrifice himself for the sake of the family? He must have seen how life went on smoothly without him. I know what I believed at the time, and it's easy to judge Mother and say she should have been more understanding. I know I hated her with a passion, never really liked her after that.

But, from this perspective, I can see how her family was important to her and she felt she needed to protect us like a lioness driving off the male in order to keep him away from her cubs. I was nearly ten when Daddy went – always the big sister to the others – Rowley was just at school, but Bea was a toddler and Douglas a baby. I have to remember that Mother managed on her own for nearly four years after the war started. Continuity and stability were important; she hated anyone rocking the boat. Life always had to go on as if nothing had happened. She took a pride in that.

Of course, we weren't the only family to break up because of the war. Far too many men never came home and the women managed. But Daddy's absence changed all our lives, including Mother's. In spite of all her efforts, nothing was quite the same. She was only thirty-four. No age, really.

I remember her saying after Daddy had gone that 1918 wasn't a good year for her. "And I'm beginning to think July is an unlucky month." She was ironing at the time.

I asked why.

"Well, a year ago your Uncle Row died out in France; he, poor lad, would have been twenty-four this September. And now…"

"Yes, Uncle Arthur…" I could just remember Mother's other

brother – a small man stooped and hunched because of the tuberculosis.

"I'll have to go to his funeral," she said. "Somebody from the family should be there. I feel bad that none of us went to see him this year." She pursed her lips and shook her head. "Too late now, anyway. Good thing I'm not superstitious, I'll soon be the last of the Baxters. To cap it all, Dora is emigrating to South Africa."

"Whatever for, Mother?"

"Nothing to keep her, she says. She probably feels she has a better chance of finding a husband there than in England. Anyway, a woman's typing skills are always in demand." She shook her head. "I got married when I was twenty-one, much younger than Dora. Even so, far too young." She started smoothing the sheet again.

I don't think I realised how alone she must have felt. But of course, being her, she just had to tough it out.

I listened to her thumping the iron over the board. Thirteen years married, I thought – you'd still have a husband if you'd been kinder and hadn't thrown Daddy out. I daren't speak, then. She took all my blame, spoken and unspoken. What really shocked me was that she'd kept Daddy's ration card. What was he living on?

★ ★ ★

I came across a photograph recently – all four children together. Mother in her usual methodical way wrote the date on the back: September 1918. Can only have been a few months after Daddy went. But I never knew why she thought it important to have it done. Her sudden suggestion surprised me. You never know what your parents are thinking.

She didn't want to be included: just the four of us. "And you're all to wear smart clothes – and be on your best behaviour."

I remember the palaver of dressing up, keeping clean and getting to the studio. The old photographer wore a blue velvet jacket, I remember that, and his goatee beard and long grey hair like a French artist fascinated me. He fussed around getting the composition right. Douglas sat on a cushion on the table and I had to support him. And Rowley had to sit on a chair so that he looked slightly taller than Bea. "Come on, little fellow, let me help you up." The man went to lift him.

"I can manage quite well, thank you. I'm five now." His haughty independence coming out even then. He clambered onto the chair and manoeuvred into position. Mother gave his hair another smoothing down and rubbed a speck off Bea's face with a moistened handkerchief. The photographer disappeared under a black cloth which drooped over his head and the camera like a sagging umbrella.

"Smile for my Daisy," he said and waved a silly rag doll above his head.

We all watched intently but nobody smiled.

When the photographs came, Mother chose the one to keep and ordered several postcard copies. "We can send a picture of you all to members of the family. I expect Aunt Dora would like one."

I watched her addressing the envelopes and tucking the pictures inside. "Who's that one for, Mother?" Two pictures went into the envelope.

"That's for Grandma and Grandpa Hemingby, it's a long time since they've seen you."

"And who's the other picture for, then?"

"That's in case they want to give one away. Why so curious, miss?" That challenging stare.

Time to keep quiet.

Did she want to show the world how well she was managing without him? Or was I not the only one to remember that Daddy's birthday was in September.

You never knew with Mother.

★ ★ ★

The new school depressed me. The long, narrow building stood on a main road, and the sound of traffic and the clang of passing trams often distracted me in lessons. Many of the classrooms stood close to the pavement behind a mesh fence, but, because of the high windows, you could never look out. The rooms often became stuffy, and on foggy days the air smelled stale and trickles ran down the windows.

I found the tall classroom where we had most lessons specially dreary. Glossy, dark brown tiles lined the walls up to about eight feet and above them, dirty cream walls. The colour reminded me of muddy clay.

But I enjoyed new subjects: I found French easy, and words I knew years previously welled up again and gave me an advantage over the other girls who were beginners.

I loved the art room. Huge windows let in streams of northern light – the best, my teacher said, because it was constant and never spoilt by sunshine. Now I could not only paint and draw, but botany caught my interest and intrigued me. I still liked drawing and studying flowers.

The music teacher who took us for singing discovered I had some talent and encouraged me to begin learning the piano after school. And in English I came to love Shakespeare, particularly when I was given extracts to learn at home and, eventually, a part in reading *A Midsummer Night's Dream* in class.

At first, I thought nothing of the violin playing outside. Just some old busker begging. I pictured him standing on the corner near the school entrance. But the tune changed, and I held my breath and clung onto my desk as if the world had started to spin.

Can't be, I thought. Not now, not here. How has he found me?

"Dorothy, where are you?" The teacher's sharp voice interrupted my thoughts. "Come along now, girl. Pay attention. This isn't like you. It's your line – Helena's line."

"Sorry, Miss Ward." I found the place and began reading again, hesitant – uncertain:

"Wherefor was I to this keen mockery born?
When at your hands did I deserve this scorn?"

I stopped, cleared my throat, sniffed. "I'm sorry. Can someone else read, please? May I be excused today? I don't think I feel well."

Outside, the violin calling me. Playing my tune.

I glanced up at the windows which frowned down upon the class.

"Would you like to go outside for some air?"

"Perhaps a drink of water, miss. Not outside. I don't want to go outside."

"Very well. Make haste, then."

I walked towards the door, fearful, aware of the others watching.

It must be him, I thought, has to be. That tune. After all this time.

The brown-tiled corridors and stone floors echoed to the catch of my feet. Still no view to the outside, but the faint sound penetrated, even into the cloakroom.

I cupped my hands under the tap, I had a drink, splashed my face, drank some more.

Can only be him, I thought. But how has he found me, especially since we've moved?

It must be.

Like he always promised.

Outside, the violin continued playing.

The decision to go out into the road jolted me with fear. Strictly forbidden. If I was seen, there'd be a severe telling-off, possibly a letter home. But I had to know. Such a long time since I'd seen him. I needed to know if he was all right. Had anyone given him money? Or food?

The swing doors to the outside squeaked as if to betray me and I looked round to make sure no one saw. I'd no idea what I'd do if it was him.

The outside world besieged me: the clop of horses and carts, the whine of motor buses and lorries, the occasional car; the squeal and clang of trams humming along the tracks. The skip and yap of stray dogs. People hurrying past.

But no music. The busker had gone.

I hurried to the corner and looked up and down the High Road. In the distance, a policeman led the busker away by the arm. I watched them cross the road. The man wore a patched grey overcoat which didn't fit. His rounded shoulders reminded me of a crookback. His hair splayed out from the crown of his head like a grey mop and waggled when he shook his head, and his tangled beard seemed to brush his chest. He shuffled along beside the policeman.

"No, it's not Daddy," I said aloud to reassure myself, "not tall enough. Only some old tramp who can play the fiddle."

I'm still not sure if it was him. Silly, I know, but it just goes to show.

FIFTY-FOUR

Autumn 1919

The river bridge sheltered him from the bite of the frost, and enough people scurried past to make playing worthwhile. He pulled his hands from his pockets, blew on them and eased fingerless mittens on. He opened the case. His old friend nestled there, waiting to sing again. He began tuning the violin, listening to the amplified echo which the brick arch bounced back. Beside him, the brown river swirled and scoured at the bridge piers. He took a breath and began to play, leaving the violin case open at his feet.

Several people hurried by, wrapped warmly against the morning's chill, their breath flaring onto the morning air. One young woman in a cloche hat tossed a coin into the case. He looked down. Sixpence. Doing well. "Thank you," he called and continued playing.

Out of the swirl of river fog, a tall figure emerged, incongruous at such an early hour in evening dress, the silk scarf tossed over his shoulder. He stopped, put his head on one side and listened. "Ah, andante, Mendelssohn concerto. Well done. Very sweet. Played excellently, too."

John bowed his head in acknowledgment and continued playing. He tossed his hair out of his eyes.

"Down on your luck, old chap?" The man came closer and began singing the orchestral part. "Very good. Need someone like you for my sonata." He felt inside his jacket and took out his wallet. He blinked through fog-misted glasses. "Hearing you play that movement is worth a fiver of anyone's money." He lobbed the white note into the violin case. "Don't let someone snaffle it, mind it doesn't blow away."

John stopped. "Thank you very much, sir. Very generous indeed." Incredible! He bent down to retrieve the note and stow it somewhere safe.

"You're welcome to it. Money – when it's gone, it's gone, I always say."

John peered, certain he recognised the man now. "Excuse me, sir, may I ask? Is your name Gurney?"

"It is. Ivor Gurney, poet and composer. Do I know you?"

"I think you did. In France," John said. "I'm John Hemingby, one-time corporal."

"Don't believe it," Gurney said. "How are you?" He looked John over. "You were Smiler, weren't you? Of course, I recall now. Remember your fiddle-playing. Didn't recognise you, though. What's happened to bring you to this state?"

"Family break-up," John said. "This seemed best."

"My dear fellow, this is appalling. We must talk. Are you hungry?"

John lowered his eyes and nodded.

"Come on, I'll stand you breakfast. Do you mind walking?"

"No, used to it now."

"I know a tavern that's open. Sure to get food. Quite a wander, it's North of the river."

★ ★ ★

They found a table in a corner of the Smithfield Tavern, and Gurney watched him eat.

"Aren't you having anything?" John said. A struggle to remember his manners and not wolf the ham and eggs.

"No, I hate food. Makes me sluggish. Stops me working. Only eat when I have to. If my guts aren't playing up. One minute." Gurney pulled out a small notebook and scrawled a music stave. "E flat, second theme." He licked a stub of pencil and notes flew onto the page like spatters of mud. He looked up and grinned. "Can work anywhere, you know. Back at the RCM now." The table shook as Gurney's leg began agitating. "When I feel like it. Away for five years, but they had me back. Going well. VW's working with me now. Always thought he had the right idea."

"Yes?" John bit into the hunk of bread and butter and drank the hot tea.

"Trouble is, I'm five years older than the others. Some complete dolts. But I tolerate them. My music's getting performed now. Outside college. They'll do my *War's Elegy* one day."

"Is that where you were last night? At a concert?"

"Lord, no. They were fêting my poetry. Hobnobbing with Masefield and Bridges, I was. Had to read some of my stuff. They love it, you know. Afterwards, so keyed up, I had to walk and walk round this old grey waste of a city. On top of the world. Everything's going right. Couldn't be better. What about you? What have you been doing?"

"I tried selling matches first, you know, off a tray, round my neck. But people just walked past. Hopeless, and if it rained, the stuff got wet. Sometimes, in cold weather, I used to strike matches to keep warm."

"Yes? My *War's Embers* was published back in May. Must get you a copy. I'm writing more poetry again and, of course, lots of musical ideas. Two symphonies under way. Struggle to keep them separate. My father died that month. May." He looked thoughtful. "Pity that. He understood; he knew what I was about."

"You don't know how good this breakfast is, Ivor. Thank you very much. Sometimes I dream about food."

"Did you know about Margaret?"

"Margaret? Who's that?"

"That cut me up terribly. I lost her, you know. My muse: Margaret Hunt." Gurney broke off and scribbled in his notebook again. "Should be a succession of triplets. That's better. He can hear it up here, you know." He tapped the side of his head.

"They white-feathered me once or twice in the street," John

said. "Usually women, before the war ended. I didn't say anything. I took the feather, said thank you. Couldn't prove I'd served. No badge, you see. Never bothered to claim it. I reckoned I deserved their scorn anyway, because..." He lapsed into silence.

"Where are you living?" The foot was jiggling again. "Winter's coming."

John grimaced. "Where I can. Under cover, preferably, and out of sight. In the parks, sometimes."

"You can't beat barns. But ditches are good, if you avoid the nettles. Or the damp. In summer, lie under the stars in a ploughed field. Watch the turning heavens."

"By the look of you, you don't do much sleeping rough, Ivor."

"Don't you believe it. I need the outdoors. Vital. He's never happier than when he's taking long, lonely walks. Keeps his head clear. An outdoor man with an indoor mind. Would High Wycombe suit?"

John tidied his plate to one side and suppressed a belch. "That was very good, Ivor. Thank you very much. What about High Wycombe?" He took a drink of tea.

"That's where I live. A lovely taste of Buckinghamshire air. I play the organ there. But you could sleep on the sofa. Unless it's too far out."

"You come in from Bucks to the Royal College? By train?"

"Walk it, if I can. Not those contraptions. Every Sunday night after Evensong, I set off."

"And then what?"

"Kip down where I can in London. Someone always gives me a bed or a floor. Or rent something if I'm flush. Occasionally college."

John's beard started itching in the warmth. Ivor was right: winter was coming. Best get under cover. But where? High Wycombe? Long way out. An idea began to form. Worth a try anyway.

"Bring any books away with you? I'd buy them off you," Gurney said.

"Afraid not, Ivor. Travelling light these days."

"Pity, can't find my Housman. Left it somewhere, probably. Or did I lend it?" Gurney raised his hand to catch the barman's eye. "Landlord, give this man a pint of your finest. Look, old chap, terribly sorry, I'm going to have to shoot. Composition tutorial with VW. Late already. But stay here and have a drink on me. Get warm. Very sorry to see you in such sore straits. Hope you manage to grin and bear it." He tossed three florins on the table. "That should cover it. Well, goodbye..." He reached out to shake hands, seemed to think better of it and patted John on the shoulder of his overcoat.

John half got to his feet but Gurney had gone as if blown forward by a following wind.

The landlord appeared at the table and slid a tankard of bitter in front of John. "'ere's your beer. Now, drink up quick, then 'op it. This isn't a day hostel. I don't know why he brought you in. Fellows like you get us a bad name. We'll have the bobbies in afore we know it." He scooped Gurney's three coins into his huge fleshy palm and turned away.

Strange being the outsider, but you got used to it. Part of the punishment. Well done, Gurney, though. Making a decent fist of his talents. Never seen him so confident and determined. Still strange, though. Brittle, tiring to be with. You couldn't keep up.

★ ★ ★

He'd crossed the Rubicon, then. Gurney had brought him over the Thames to the North side. Nearer now to his parents and childhood home than his wife and children. If he was in luck, he knew where he might find quiet winter quarters. A long haul to walk up Goswell Road to Islington. Could take the tram. He laughed. Could afford it, thanks to Gurney. But imagine offering a fiver to the conductor! They'd throw him off or call the police. He picked up the violin case and began to trudge North.

★ ★ ★

The housekeeper looked him up and down. "No, sorry, we've nothing here for you." She shrank back and began to close the door.

"Mrs Banks, wait! Will you get Mrs May for me? I need to see her."

"How do you know my name?"

"Just get her, please. I don't want to make a fuss."

He could tell from the blank look on Helen's face that she didn't recognise him. "How can we help you? What do you want?" she said.

"Sis, please, it's me – Fordie."

She peered at him. "What? Oh, dear God, John, look at the state of you. What's happened to you?"

"Are you alone?"

"Apart from Mrs Banks, yes, the boys are at school and Howard –"

"Can I come in? I need to talk."

He wiped his boots carefully and took them off. The grime of his toes showed through the holes in his socks. "I'm so sorry to arrive like this, but winter's coming and I need help. You were the only one I could turn to. It's hard going being on the road for fifteen months, sleeping outside or going to Salvation Army hostels. But I've survived. The army taught me a lot about roughing it."

She hurried him through to the parlour at the back of the house, overlooking the garden. A small fire crackled. "We can talk here. This is where I check household bills and write my letters. We won't be disturbed." She motioned him to sit on a rocking chair, close to the hearth.

"Must be careful," he said, "too much warmth will start my chilblains off."

"My dear boy, why didn't you come sooner? What are family for? I feared the worst when your letters from the Front stopped – must be two years ago now. But we never heard anything. Em stopped writing, cut us off, I suppose. Ages ago. So we thought..." Tears began to brim her eyes. "And now you're alive..."

"Just about, Sis, just about. I didn't want to impose. Besides, I felt ashamed."

"Oh, you fool, you silly fool! As if we'd turn you away."

His sister hadn't moved with the times, thank God. No sign of her skirts shortening. Her simple elegance reassured him that not everything had changed with the war; she was still his ideal of womanhood: her dark hair long, full and gathered up, with a centre parting, calf-length skirt, pretty white blouse with a string of pearls. He looked at her large, brown eyes, caught her concerned gaze and struggled not to weep.

"I only knew you by the Hemingby eyes," she said, "and the teeth, of course. Long hair and a beard are pretty good disguise. But how can we help? I'd love to put you up, but, you know…"

"If you agree, I don't want Howard or the boys to know about me. I'll try not to be an embarrassment, but the war has left me… Do you know about shellshock?"

She nodded. "I've heard of it."

"I think that's what it must be. I can't cope with sudden loud noises. Explosions, say. A car backfiring, even a coal delivery. They overwhelm me and I begin to shake. I can't help my sudden fear. It's uncontrollable. As if I'm back in the war. Things are better when I'm outside on my own; I don't feel trapped. Quiet and isolation help, and I can manage then. But in order to keep the shakes at bay, I drink. I hate to say it but it dulls the senses. I feel well again. And it keeps out the cold. I know the world's against alcohol at the moment – Ma and Pa wouldn't understand at all, but I think of it as my medicine. It's the only way I can live with myself. The worst thing has been the nightmares. I get terrible dreams about something I did."

Helen looked indignant. "Out there? In the war? I don't care what it is. Whatever happened, you'll have had your reasons. I wish you wouldn't punish yourself. You always did. There's very little on earth that can't be forgiven. Christianity has taught us that."

He put his head in his hands, said nothing. How could he tell her, in all her simple goodness, that his faith had vanished?

"What do you want me to do, darling?"

"Can it be our secret? I don't want Ma or Pa to know – or Perce, for that matter. I need a refuge for the winter. And the idea came to me this morning. In short, may I be your lodger?" He saw her eyes widen. "No, not indoors. May I sleep winter nights in your garden shed? I'll be no trouble, shan't even be there during the day, but with the cold nights I do need to be under cover. Think of me as your wounded soldier, if you will. Though I'm more like a wounded animal that goes away to be alone and to lick his wounds."

"Oh, Fordie, I can't bear to think of you condemning yourself to this life. Of course you must have somewhere out of harm's way. We never go in there once the warm days have gone. No one need know and I'll keep the boys away. You can slip in by the back gate whenever you want to, the shed's well away from the house and close to the fence. You can do your hibernating there for sure. But there's one condition, something I want you to do for me first..."

"If I can. What is it?

"I want you to go and see Em one more time. You've been away over a year now. She might have changed. Things could be different. Better your proper home than cooped up here."

"But she made it quite clear. When we talked about it that night, she said, 'If you go now, you go for good.'"

"Women say these things at the time, they don't necessarily mean them for ever."

"You don't know my rock."

"I know she's a good woman, who's seen her children through difficult times while you were away. She's been very strong. And proud, too. She never asked for help from any of us. Please – you must give it one last try for your children – and for my sake."

He lowered his eyes and sighed. "Very well, but I'm not optimistic. I'll go soon."

"No, go tomorrow. It's Saturday, you'll see the children as well. That's settled." She frowned in mock sternness. "Now, more importantly, we must get you cleaned up. I'll have Mrs Banks run you a bath, you can have a shave and become more your old self and, if you'll allow it, I'll trim your hair for you. I'm no barber, but I'll do my best to make you look presentable."

"Sis, you're lovely, thank you. But what about clothes? I can hardly wear these."

"I shall have them burnt and you can start again. You're in luck. Ma gave me some of Pop's old clothes only the other day to give to the poor. If you don't mind turning into a tweedy old gentleman, I'm sure they'll be a reasonable fit."

Upstairs, he lay in the bath, feeling the forgotten, blissful touch of hot water. He thought of the VAD nurses he'd encountered in France; many of them angels comforting the wounded and giving them hope, or peace of mind. And here was another, in his own family, to whom tenderness came naturally. Perhaps Helen's optimism was justified. Was it really time to return from exile?

FIFTY-FIVE

I found the breaststroke easiest. The front crawl quickly became tiring and I hated having to put my face in the water. The breaststroke was slower but seemed more genteel. I watched older ladies doing it, their bathing caps bobbing up and down the pool like buoys on a choppy sea.

Saturday morning was Pool Day when the whole family went to Camberwell Baths. Mother stayed out of the water and had never been able to swim. "I'm too old to learn now," she'd say when anyone asked, "but I think it's important you children pick it up while you're young." She sat in the public seats, Douglas on her lap, while we all had half an hour in the pool. Any longer and your fingers became pinched. In any case, staying in longer cost more.

I was expected to keep an eye on the others but Rowley could swim well for his age. He battled against the water with a busy dog-paddle he'd learned, but he often called out to Mother to make sure she was watching.

Definitely Mummy's boy.

Bea showed no fear and had already developed a kind of side stroke, though she looked more like a little corkscrew churning through the water.

The younger ones had twenty minutes before Mother called them out to get dressed. This gave me ten minutes to see how many widths I could do. I challenged myself to swim further each week.

We all looked forward to the after-swim treat. I have to admire Mother for that. She made a ritual of it: each child, whatever their age, was given two pieces of chocolate and a biscuit – the special weekend extravagance – always worth waiting for. But I've gone over and over what happened one Saturday, trying to work out what was going on. Was Mother protecting us? Or herself?

★ ★ ★

Rowley saw him first – standing at the front gate when we reached home. He slipped his hand into Mother's. "Who's that man?" he said. "Is he waiting for us?"

"I've a very good idea who it is. I wonder what he wants after all this time." Mother tightened her lips.

I recognised him, of course. You could tell from his build it was Daddy, but I held back from rushing to greet him. How would he be after all this time? And why was he dressed in old-fashioned clothes that didn't suit him?

"Why are you here?" Mother said, her voice steady, almost cold.

"You took some finding," he said. "I didn't know you'd moved. Fortunately, Daphne..."

Bea looked up and whispered, "Who is it, Mama?"

"Well, we won't stand here gossiping for all the neighbours to see. You'd better come in." She led the way to the front door, we followed and Daddy came last.

"When did you move?" Daddy said. He put his hat on the table and stood with his hands folded awkwardly before him like a shy boy in front of the class.

"Dora sold up and went to South Africa. This is my share of the family home."

"When did that happen?" His hand had started to shake.

"It suits us very well, and the children like their schools in this neighbourhood. Why have you come, John? I don't want the children upset."

He clasped his hands behind his back, but his right arm still shook. Was he nervous? "Is there any chance of a cup of tea since I've come all this way?" He looked around. "So, you're managing all right?"

"I can't afford to give out cups of tea just like that."

I gasped. I knew we had to watch the pennies as Mother put it, but...

Daddy put his hand in his pocket and threw two coins on the table. "Here's tuppence. Can I *buy* a cup of tea, for old times' sake?"

Mother sighed and moved the kettle onto the gas stove. "Very well, but please don't stay long. I've the children's dinner to think about. Besides..."

"Is it all right if I sit down?" He pulled a chair out and sat at the table, his hands in his lap. He looked around the room. "So, how old are you now, Rowley?"

My brother looked towards Mother and said nothing.

"I see, cat's got your tongue. Are you doing well at school?"

"Very well, thank you. He's a bright boy," Mother said.

"And what about you, little girl? What's your name?"

"Beatrice Hemingby, I'm four." She twisted her hands together and swayed from side to side on her heels.

At last he looked towards me, his eyes big and brown exactly as I remembered. "And how are you, Dolly Daydream? I hope you haven't forgotten me. Are you still painting?"

I gulped. So long since he'd called me that. "I'm very well, thank you, Daddy. I'm..."

I couldn't stop the tears. I pulled a hanky out of my sleeve and withdrew into the corner to mop my eyes and blow my nose.

Mother put a cup of tea on the table. "I can't remember if you take sugar or not."

"I take it as it comes these days, Em. Beggars can't be –" He stopped, cleared his throat and took a sip of tea.

"I don't think coming here was a good idea, John. You can see it's upsetting the children. You'd better drink up and go. I'm sorry. There's nothing here for you now."

He stood up. "Perhaps you're right. I shouldn't have come. I'm sorry, too. I didn't realise how upsetting it would be – for everybody. But at least I know." He picked up his hat and walked towards the

door, his shoes creaking. "Goodbye, everybody. I'll see myself out."
He cleared his throat, swallowed and left.

Complete silence in the room. I waited for the bang of the front
door. I daren't go to the window and watch where he went.

"Now, then," Mother said, "let's get on and hang your wet
swimming costumes on the clothes-horse."

The two children began to move. "He smelled of mothballs."
Rowley wrinkled his face.

I blew my nose and dabbed my eyes. What really hurt was he
didn't say goodbye to me. I vowed I'd never love anyone, ever again.
It hurt too much and always ended in tears.

Anyway, I broke that resolution soon enough.

But the image of those two pennies lying untouched where
Daddy had thrown them stays with me, even now.

FIFTY-SIX

July/August 1922

"Who is he? Do you know?" The man at the bar lowered his voice. He cocked his head towards the corner where John sat.

The landlord worked the pump handle to pull the new beer through. "Not really, no one does, but he comes in every night, months now, maybe over a year. Has three pints and a chaser, then leaves. Always before closing time." He looked up at the pub clock. "Half past eight. He'll be off soon."

"Scruffy bugger, ain't 'e?"

"He's seen better days, but he's no trouble. Looks like a tramp, but between you and me..." The landlord softened his voice so that John struggled to hear. "I reckon he's a gen'leman down on his luck. He's there outside every night when we open up, orders a pint and goes and sits in that corner. Never speaks to no one. Keeps his head down."

"What they call him?"

The landlord shrugged and began pulling beer for another customer. "Someone nicknamed him Fiddler John," he said over his shoulder. "'Cause of the music case. Gets all over. He's been seen in the Aldwych, outside King's Cross, even downa Tube. Busking for beer money, I suppose. Funny sort of life."

"Old soldier, most like." The man lifted his cap and scratched his head. "Though he don't look like 'e's seen action."

"Nah, too old. Look at it 'im. Just some old soak."

"Ah well, sod him, then."

Sod you, too, John thought. What do you know? He'd reached the stage he sought every night where his eyes felt heavy and his head began to nod. Time to kip down somewhere before the dream caught him up.

★ ★ ★

My headmistress became more like a lanky witch in her gown and hood. She stood on the dais and looked down on the assembly of girls and parents. A shaft of sunlight burst through the topmost windows onto where I'd have to walk. Heavens, I hope it doesn't get any hotter. I could see motes of dust dancing.

"And, finally, we come to the Junior Art Prize which is awarded to one of our second year girls. Congratulations to Dorothy Hemingby for her painting "Chrysanthemums.""

Deep breath. Wait for the applause. Hope you don't trip on the steps.

I stood up, feeling my neck grow hot, and made my way towards the dais.

Take the book in your left hand, leave the other for the handshake. Don't forget to curtsey.

The Duke of Connaught looked old. His huge spreading moustache reminded me of the bottom branches of a fir tree draped with snow. He was very bald. His face looked fierce and formal, but his blue eyes had crinkles so he seemed kindly. "It's an honour," Mother had whispered as I stood up, "he's the King's uncle."

"Well done, um, Dorothy." The Duke glanced at the book I'd chosen. "Watercolours of London, eh? Splendid. Hope to attend art college, do we?"

"I'd like to, sir," I said in a small voice. "But I also want to join the Junior League of Nations when I'm older, to prevent future wars." Stupid remark, really, since he'd been a high-up military man, I think.

"Do you now? Splendid, well done!" The Duke handed me the book and shook hands. His palm felt very dry and hard.

The headmistress gave a thin smile and led the applause. "Well done, girl."

I took a step back, bobbed a curtsey and sighed in relief.

★ ★ ★

The first thunder of the day overhead. John shot awake, tense with fear, then relaxed. No, not the early bombardment, not now; only the milk train drumming over the bridge. Sleepers often sheltered here, the last few creeping in, he guessed, long after drink and sleep had claimed him. He sat up, eased out of the cardboard box and wandered to the far wall where he pissed the night's drink away. Most sleepers lay huddled in the centre, away from the drips and seepage down the walls.

Bundles of humanity starting to stir. He coughed – a dry, lingering hack – until his throat felt sore.

At the far end of the arch, a man sat up, clapped his hands over his ears and began to scream as if in torment.

"Oh, for fuck's sake, pal, shut up!" A beggar nearby gathered his scraps of wool and cloth, stuffed them into a sack. He tied his overcoat around his waist with some horsehair string and shambled away, ignoring the screams.

One by one, other rough-sleepers staggered to their feet and prepared to depart. One man paused to light a pipe, inhaled the sweet smoke and grunted with pleasure; another hawked and spat thick phlegm into a shallow puddle and dragged off into the grey light outside. Other sounds of coughing.

Soon, John and the screamer were alone, only the smell of tobacco lingering on the air. The man squatted now, head bowed, hands still covering his ears. He wore a baggy dark suit, and rocked back and forth. Can't leave him like that. John folded up his cardboard box and leant it against the wall. It'll do for someone if I'm not back tonight. He gathered up the violin case and his battered luggage and approached the man.

"Are you all right, friend? Are you in pain?"

The man screamed again and curled into a ball. "I'm not a spy,

391

I'm not a spy. Turn it off, I beg you." He cried out again. "Do you have a gun? Give me it, for pity's sake, and I'll finish it."

"Turn what off, old chap?"

"The electricity, the wireless. Stop tormenting me. I'm not a spy."

"There's no electricity, no wireless here, I promise. Only the trains." John looked up at another drumming clatter overhead.

A stillness came over the man and he uncovered his face and peered up. "Who are you?" He stared. "I know your voice. It's you, Hemingby, thank God."

"Heavens, what are *you* doing here?" Hard to recognise Gurney now he'd grown so thin. He wore no glasses, and heavy eyes stared as if he was haunted. "Come on, let's go and find some breakfast. We could both do with a cupper tea and a bite. There's a stall nearby."

Gurney struggled to his feet. Apart from his overcoat to cover him, he had lain all night on bare hummocked ground. He bundled his arms into the coat sleeves. "If only I could go back to France. Life was steady then."

"Don't wish yourself back in that hell, Ivor."

"I could write there, music *and* poems. It held together." He made a loose fist-grasp with clawed fingers. "Inspiration flowed. I'm lagging, they're moving on without me."

"Who are, old chap?"

"The others: old Howler, Bliss, Holst. He's as much Gloucestershire as I am."

Walking calmed Gurney. His face relaxed; he put his glasses back on, whistled tunelessly under his breath – more the Gurney John remembered. Only the furrowed brow, the anxious stare remained. He took furtive glances over his shoulder, as if expecting to be followed.

"What's all this about being a spy, Ivor? This way." He pointed out the canopied stall on the Embankment. He put his luggage down and rummaged for coins to buy a beaker of tea and bread and dripping for the two of them.

"They arrested me one night, said I was a spy," Gurney said. "But I love my country. I wouldn't do that. I was only walking the docks. They said I was a spy because I had no identity. Pockets stuffed with letters from Masefield, Bridges, Stanford and what not, but I couldn't prove it. I B Gurney, I told them. But they didn't know who I was, just mocked me. 'Be you,' they said, like the old days at school."

John laughed.

"You see, even you find it funny."

"Sorry, old chap."

"In the end, I managed to root out my discharge papers. But they torture me now. Bombard me with electricity to control me. Stop me working."

They sat down on a bench facing the river.

"So what's happened to your music, your poems?"

Gurney tapped his fingers to the side of his head. "All up here, waiting for the surge to release them. I love it when it comes; the racing fire possesses me. When ideas teem, I'm invincible, I can sweep the world before me with my music and my words. But it's topsy-turvy. I don't understand why. When I'm on my heights and brimming with inspiration, when I feel elated, that's when people find me difficult. I know that now. They like my work, but they don't like me. At the time, I think to blazes with them. The me that I need to be is not what they like. People prefer me down where they can reach me, hold me back and tame me. They want to keep me in a four-four, common time world." He hid his head in his hands. "And that's what I fear."

"And do you think this electricity blocks your energy, your inspiration?"

"If only I could find somewhere away from it all where I could work." He began to pant and looked round wildly. "Oh, God, it's back. Where's it coming from?" He put his hands over his head and gave an anguished scream. People on the Embankment turned to look.

John's mind raced. "Ivor, why don't we drink up and set out for Regent's Park? If there's electricity in the air, the trees will diffuse it or block it. And the animals in the zoo will trumpet their distress if electric waves and currents are troubling them. What do you say? Shall we go and see?"

"Promise me it'll be safe, you'll stay with me?" Gurney's eyes widened.

"Of course."

They turned their backs on the river and walked north through the streets. Gurney stared at the pavement, head down as if lost in thought. Poor devil, John thought, how did he get in this state? Am I wise to go along with these delusions? It may give him short-term reassurance and win his trust, but does it merely reinforce his view of the world? Should I explain reality to him?

★ ★ ★

"I'll row." Gurney bolted into the wooden boat which rocked and jostled under his weight. Ruckles of water sped out over the lake.

"I'm sorry, Ivor, I haven't any..."

"Get in! Don't worry about that." He tossed a florin towards the attendant, took off his coat and began to wriggle onto the sliding seat of the skiff. "At least an hour, maybe two, please."

The man began to push them out from under the willows with a long boat hook. John settled in the seat at the stern of the boat and let the rudder-ropes drape over his shoulders. He laid his luggage behind him in the boat. For a few minutes, Gurney pulled hard on the oars as if striving for exhaustion. He didn't speak. John felt his head jerked by the power of the strokes, his spine rammed against the ornate metal back of the seat. Strange to see someone rowing in a suit, jacket and all. Going to be hot, too.

"At last. Away from it," Gurney said. "It can't reach us here. The electricity won't cross water. Are you a sailor?"

"Not in small boats, I have to say."

"A poor substitute this; I wish I could be in my boat, but this'll have to do. This brings some peace."

"You have your own boat?"

"Only a small one but I love sailing her when I can. I miss *The Dorothy*."

John looked at the planking at his feet. He closed his eyes, unable to block out the thoughts. Must be fourteen now, quite the young woman. Even Douglas must be nearing four. He sighed.

Another world. Don't dwell there.

Silence. Gurney continued rowing.

John looked up and tugged on the rudder lines. "Pull, you lubber, unless you want to swing from the yard-arm!" His sudden shout caused a flurry of rapid heaving, and for the first time that day Gurney laughed.

★ ★ ★

"Calmer now, Ivor?"

"I'm safe here and my head's clear. You've helped. Now we're going at nature's speed. Look at that." He stopped and let the oars patter over the water. About ten feet away, a swan butted through the water. It eyed them in hope of food and paddled on. Gurney began rowing again. "I love the eddies the oars make. See, clear puddles where we've been." He continued to row gently and looked straight at John.

> *The songs I had are withered*
> *Or vanished clean,*
> *Yet there are bright tracks*
> *Where I have been,*
>
> *And there grow flowers*
> *For others' delight.*
> *Think well, O singer,*
> *Soon comes night.*

John sat, eyes closed. Beneath the boat, the gentle dribble of water.

"Ivor, that's exquisite. So simple and direct. That is *you*, presumably. When did you write it?"

"Recently, some time ago, I forget now. I can be brilliant when the fire takes hold, I know I can. It's what comes after I hate. I work, and create – music, poems – until I collapse. Sometimes it takes me over, brings me back to earth. I hate it. You always fear it coming. You watch out for it. 'Am I going again, you think, shall I plunge down?'"

"How do you mean, Ivor?"

"It's like standing on a hilltop, Ivinghoe Beacon, if you like, watching some purpling cloud massing on the horizon at sunset. And you wonder if it's going to sweep up and overwhelm you. Or a gas cloud. Darkness coming. That's what I dread. I've had troubles, something's wrong with me, I know it. The medics have slapped this label on, or that: neurasthenia, shellshock – deferred, if you please – or a nervous breakdown. But it doesn't help, it doesn't rescue me. Times I've begged for help but nothing's forthcoming. It's that going down, the abyss I fear. When nothing feels worthwhile."

"But, Ivor, doesn't experience teach you –"

"People tell me it goes in cycles and I'll bounce back up again. But when I'm down, it doesn't feel like that. That's when I know I'm a failure and life is meaningless. It's like being buried in a smothering fog. You cannot see any way forward."

"Oh, don't say that, old chap."

"That's when I pray for death. When things feel bad. I tried to finish it all, you know. Thought of drowning myself or jumping under a train. I wrote letters to all my friends to thank them and say goodbye. But my courage failed." Gurney shook his head.

I know, John thought, I've been in that place.

The boat rocked gently, the water trickle-slapping its sides. Across the lake, echoing, the squark of a moorhen, its wings clapping the water. A squabble of gulls, fighting for bread that bobbed in the shallows.

Gurney looked up. "Think of the bliss. Finally grasping the elusive peace. Some of our lads out there were lucky. No known

396

grave. They sleep well." He shook his head. "Most profoundly to be wished, I think now..." He gave a rueful smile. "Back in Gloucester once, I went into the police station and demanded a gun so I could end it all. I asked for police protection from my voices. So, what did they do? They sent for my sister to take me home. I don't need to be humoured. I don't want my sister, however much I love her. I long to be rescued from this torture while I'm still sane. I have my troubles, heaven help me, but I'm not crazy or mad. I'm saner and more innocent than many. I see the truth and beauty of life; I *know*. But if I go home, our Ron will do for me one day, I'm sure he will."

"Who's Ron, Ivor?"

"My brother. Since father died, he's turned against me. That time I lived with them, he said I was violent, threatening and dangerous, called me childish because I don't eat or sleep properly like he and Ethel do. I don't need food! I can do without sleep." Gurney shook his head. "Didn't work staying there. No sympathy. He kept saying, 'Trouble is we don't know whether you're mad or bad.' He don't understand what I'm about. Says all my stuff should be destroyed. Me as well, I shouldn't wonder."

John spotted a heron motionless on the island of the lake, watching them. He thought of Percy. He'd do for me too, if I ever cross him. "Brothers!" He gave a rueful smile.

"I have to go back, though," Gurney said, "it's home. Where I belong. I hate the houses, the drainpipe streets life in London. Nothing for me here. I've decided. I'll set off when we land. Have to get away."

"What, tonight? What about the college?"

"No place now. Failed my stupid exams, so I withdrew. Said goodbye to VW. But he keeps in touch, wants to help. The college isn't for me, or I for them, it seems. They said I was irresponsible and immature. Some fools found me annoying. To them, I'm merely unfulfilled promise."

"But you still have somewhere to live? High Wycombe, didn't you say? What about that? I thought you were happy there."

"Finished there, too. No more pious organ playing. Now and then I've played piano for the cinema to earn cash. I could get by. Plumstead way, that was. I slept on the Embankment on a bench or under a bridge, occasionally in cheap lodgings if the weather turned around. Nearly robbed one night, sleeping out of doors. But what the devil! Money's not the issue..."

"How will you get back? Have you enough for the train? I'd give it to you gladly, if I had it."

Gurney leaned forward and put a hand on John's arm. "I can't stand those machines. Don't you worry. I'll walk it like I've done before. Walking helps. Soothes the brain."

"I don't believe it. How far is it? Must be miles."

"A hundred or so. Depends which way I go. Greatest reality I know, feet on the ground, travelling at the speed of a man. No confounded machine, no horse. Keeps my head clear for the things that matter. Push myself physically. Dig for six hours, I feel well. Rowing today, I've settled. *Corpore sano,* all that, I s'pose. When I get... I love walking the Ridgway, away from man, in touch with the old people. Avoid Oxford whatever I do. I'll go tonight. Past Buckingham by moonset."

"You'll walk all night?"

"It isn't nature's dark I fear."

The skiff glided to land and jolted against the wooden decking. Gurney shipped the oars and leaped onto the bank holding the painter – all in one movement. The boatman hurried to take over; John tottered to keep his balance in the rocking boat. He gathered his things together and stepped ashore.

"May I walk a little way with you, Ivor?"

"I should welcome it. Feel the miles go sliding by."

They set off, but the prospect of their separation loomed and John had nothing to say. They trudged in silence northwards.

They chose Camden Town for the parting of their ways. Awkwardness between them now: intimate strangers again. John wanted to head towards family territory, either Islington or Stoke

Newington; Gurney intended to tackle the long hill to Hampstead and the heath.

"You take the high road and I'll take the low road." John gave a foolish grin to cover the farewell.

"Here, have this." Gurney thrust out a half sovereign, several sixpences, a shilling and an assortment of copper coins clenched in his hand.

John recoiled. "I can't take this. Won't you need money for your journey?"

"I shall neither eat nor sleep while I'm travelling. If I need anything, I shall work for it. That is the way of the wanderer." Gurney gazed around the busy junction. "I'm glad to be away from here, Hemingby. Look at that abomination!" He pointed towards the maroon tiles of the tube station. "What grace is there in that? Who needs to travel beneath the ground when we have air?"

"It's progress, my dear chap. What we all fought for."

"When I fought for my country, I fought to save the hills and rivers, the fields and farms from any Hun invader, not to advance the infernal machine."

"And for the freedom to write your music and your poems, Ivor. Don't forget them."

"I hope they live on, for I fear I may not." He looked wild-eyed, close to tears. "I'll tell you this: everything I've done – music or poetry – stems from my sorrow. It had to be thus." He shrugged, trying to rally himself. "Fare well, Hemingby. You're a good sort. I pray life lifts for you. Thank you for giving me time and a little joy today. I fear we'll not meet again." Gurney looked him briefly in the eye, shook his hand and swung away, head lowered. He pulled the collar of his coat up and set off, his hands clamped back over his ears, a determined stride up the hill. John watched him go and shook his head. Walking wounded, certainly, but was Gurney a casualty of war or had his burden been always deep within his soul? "Farewell, fellow wanderer." He felt the need to whisper – almost a blessing. "There *are* bright tracks where you have been. Please God, you somehow find peace."

FIFTY-SEVEN

Excellent, he thought, as he dragged along Seven Sisters Road, I know where the next drink's coming from. The image of a quart bottle of beer, perhaps even a whisky chaser, drew him onwards. He rested his luggage, rummaged in his trouser pocket, enjoyed the trickle of coins through his fingers. Thank you, Ivor, you're a pal. He coughed and held his chest.

On the air, a strong smell of fish frying. Hunger taunted him, his mouth watered. Cooking steam billowed out from the brightly lit shop on the other side of the road. Perhaps today he'd allow himself some chips. Anything to ease the hunger pain. He searched for a way through the late afternoon traffic. He began crossing the road, avoided a pile of horse manure, hesitated, and the klaxon of a lorry belched a warning. He mouthed an apology.

"Tuppenny bag of chips, please." He held out the coins and kept his eyes lowered; he rarely looked shopkeepers or barmen in the eye now. The shop was warm, the rich smell of cooking overwhelming.

"Old soldier, are you?" The cockney accent was strong.

"Passchendaele." The less said the better. No point in talking about his war.

"Silver badge?" The old man's eyes narrowed. He stopped shovelling the chips into the paper.

"Pawned it." Easier to lie than give the truth.

"That bad, eh? Down on your luck, then. I understand." His manner changed. "Look, chum, tell you what I'll do. I got some tail ends here, give us five minutes, I'll dip them, fry them off and I'll throw them in as well. If you don't mind skin, there's still some goodness there."

"God bless you, guvnor." The persona was beginning to fit. He hated it. He'd been himself with Gurney; for a few brief hours, he could forget the beggar on the street whom the world shunned or didn't see.

A heavy drizzle had set in; nothing for it but to cram the newspaper bundle into his suitcase and look for shelter. Still be food, hot or cold. He remembered something Gurney had said about cemeteries. "You'll always rest in peace there, my friend, no one disturbs you, and the residents never complain." Give it a try, then.

He reached the gates of Abney Park about closing time. Stoke Newington and home territory now; his parents and Percy lived nearby. Wouldn't visit, though, they wouldn't want to see him. Not like this. Five o'clock on a wet evening, the leaves on the trees turning now. He slipped through the gates and scurried out of sight before any attendant saw him. There'd be ways in or out after hours anyway; there always were. Tall trees closed the last of daylight in – cedars of Lebanon by the look of them. And the undergrowth: ivy and brambles creeping round the older graves. They'd take over the world if man ever turned his back. Peaceful within the walls, though.

Best avoid the chapel. A cosy kip there, no doubt, especially if you pushed two benches together. "But don't risk being caught by an early funeral, old boy." He talked to himself often now. Company of a sort.

He bundled his luggage in the undergrowth behind a gravestone. "Excuse me, Ebenezer. May I leave my belongings here a while? Would you mind?" The dead didn't bother him.

Except in dreams.

He set off to scout around. If he could find some Victorian tomb: something under cover and out of the way. An old vault, perhaps. Already, the trees were trickling leaves. Soon be time for winter quarters – at the bottom of Helen's garden again. She was the only one he could turn to. His right heel began chafing. A blister coming, if he didn't rest. He paused at a prominent grave – William Booth, the Salvation Army chief. Never had much time for them before the war. All oompahs and marching. Now, more than once, a refuge at difficult times. Anti-drink though, which didn't help, you were forced to pretend, and you had to swallow claptrap scriptures if you wanted support. Too militaristic. Enough of armies and fighting the good fight. No fight was good.

They had built the war memorial over the top of the catacombs. He limped down the old steps; a rusting metal gate blocked his way. "Oh, bugger it," he said. His voice boomed a flat echo in the darkness inside. "No room at the inn." He shook the bars, put his shoulder to the gate and barged it, felt the lock grate and give. The gate squeaked open. He smiled. "Good old Abney Park, takes all sorts, even unbelievers and the living."

He stepped into the gloom, just able to make out a low flat monument, about knee-high. "Perfect. No climbing into bed. Best move in before the light goes." Up the stairs, a quick look round, and back on the path to pick up his stuff.

★ ★ ★

He sat on the floor of the vault, his back to the tomb that would be his bed. The flame on the nub end of a candle he'd found swayed in the draught from outside. He'd made strict rules: food in the morning – essential; food in the evening – desirable. Anything else, a bonus. And no drinking until seven in the evening, but tonight he'd broken his rule. He had a whisky starter while the barman at the tap room hunted out a large brown bottle and filled it with beer.

"Don't drop it, mate." The man handed the bottle over. "There's money back on that."

It amused him to ape the niceties of his old life. He poured his beer into the enamel mug Em gave him when he left. Two mugfuls, then food. You had to live by rules to make it tolerable. The cold fish and chips waited on the tin plate. Beer, food, beer. When the candle starts to gutter, bed.

He gobbled the fish and chips but soon became bloated. He teased out a rogue bone from his front teeth. "A feast, a veritable feast." His voice resounded dully. He left a fish skin and a few chips and laid his plate to one side. He took another swallow of beer and belched into the darkness. "Beg pardon, gentlemen," he said to the listening coffins. No doubt about it: an evening drink made it bearable. His eyes began to feel heavy; his head nodded. He looked at the candle. "Come on, Hemingby, time to turn in. Will you excuse me, gentlemen?" He lurched up the stairs to burrow into the wet shrubbery. Another rule: never crap on your own doorstep. He'd decided: as long as no one knew, this vault would become base for a while.

★ ★ ★

A distant clock struck three. Something woke him, he didn't know what. Complete darkness in the vault. From outside, a steady hiss: the rain heavier now. Drips and patters on the stone steps; the rustle and chatter of droplets on dead evergreen leaves. From further away, a dashing sound like the rushing sea. Wind in the tall trees, he supposed. Good thing to be under cover tonight.

But what had woken him? He lay on his back to ease the pain in his hip caused by the stone. He coughed twice and listened, pulled Em's blanket up to his neck. Sounds inside the vault, too: scutters, rustling, the occasional gibber and squeak. Then, the giveaway: the tang and scratch of something on his plate. "Help yourself, brother." He yawned. "We all have to." When he woke in the slow light of morning, the fish skin and the chips had gone.

★ ★ ★

Bent double, his collar turned up against the rain, he hobbled along the perimeter path of the cemetery. A church clock chimed nine. He'd long ago pawned his watch. Must find somewhere for a hot drink and something to eat – the station buffet, perhaps.

The name on the gravestone beside the path jolted his attention.

He stopped. In a broad sweeping curve over the top, the words FAMILY GRAVE OF J F HEMINGBY. A sudden catch in his throat as if he wanted to be sick. His own name on a gravestone. "Oh, God," he said aloud. "What's going on?" A trickle of rainwater ran down his face from his hair. His first thought was that he'd died and was viewing his own grave from a different world. He quickly dismissed the idea. The dead didn't feel hunger like this. Besides, ivy already twined and clung to the stone, obscuring other details. His second thought kicked him in the stomach: something had happened to Em and the children. But why bury them here? They all lived south of the river.

He started to rip the ivy off the stone, breaking its cling by firm tugs at the stems. Several tendrils snaked across, the green leaves shaped like spades in a pack of cards. The ivy roots left strange tracks on the stone as if some ghostly millipede had walked across its face. But names were beginning to appear. He brushed away lichen which turned the stone sandy in places. He studied his hand, now yellow with grime. He knelt in the mud, hoping his knees were not on the grave itself.

"Good Lord," he said aloud. "They've both gone, have they?" He sighed in relief. Not Em, then. Ma scarcely spoke of her two half-sisters – he only knew them as Aunt Louisa and Aunt Mary, one had spent her days in an asylum. He never knew why.

These things happened.

At the bottom of the stone, more recent carving. To take it in, he read the inscription twice. "1920 – two years ago. Why wasn't I told?" His father, John Frederick Hemingby, was dead and John knew nothing of it. Guilt flooded in that he'd missed the funeral. A stab of grief. Then anger. There were ways. Percy, with all his council connections, could surely have tracked him down and told him.

He struggled to his feet – a twinge of rheumatics in his knees. Not surprising, really. He limped along towards the exit, still hunched against the wind and the rain. Ahead, an angel on a pedestal, serene and impassive, gave the world and the dead a stone blessing. He stopped to look, fascinated by the branch of an elm sapling, wind-tossed, which lashed in fury across the angel's face. He shook his head, gave a rueful grin at the irony.

He thought again of his brother.

Over tea and a bacon-fat sandwich, his fury grew. Percy, self-appointed head of the family now, would have arranged that funeral. Once, it would have fallen to himself. The more he considered it, the more he became convinced his brother had deliberately kept the information from him. Well, then. Sunday – the perfect day to go and beard Percy at home and ask his reasons for this total exclusion from a family occasion. He drained his mug of tea, used the station toilet and set off, battling against the rain.

'He'll do for me one day, I know he will.' Gurney's words lingered in his head. John gritted his teeth.

FIFTY-EIGHT

He lurched up the front steps and clutched the brass knocker. Another squall of rain clattered the door-glass and stung his cheeks. His knocking echoed through the hall; the place held its breath. Was it the silence of an empty house? He waited, rain dripping off his beard and hair onto the quarry tiles at his feet. He peered through the bobbles of glass into the dark hall.

Come on, Perce, let me in.

Silence. But it still seemed the house was listening.

He slid down the door jamb and squatted on the top step. Hardly out of the rain, though. He reached up for the brass ring and thundered a knock again. "Oh, sod it. I'm not staying out here." He dragged himself upright, lifted one leg up and tugged off his boot. With a quick backhanded swing, he smashed the glass of the lower window to the left of the door and saw the shards tumble inside. A glance up and down the road. Safe. All sensible people indoors. Not a burglar, anyway. I'm family.

Taking care not to snag his wrist on the glass, he eased up the lower sash, scrambled up onto the stone sill and managed to put one leg inside the room just beyond the fragments of glass. He sat back on the window sill and lowered his other leg onto the floor. Glass crackled beneath his boot. He levered himself upright, stepped into the room and stood panting. He pulled off his remaining boot, flung his sodden overcoat across an upright chair and clawed a blanket off the headrest of a wing-backed leather chair. Where the hell was Perce? Not at work on a Sunday, surely.

The sofa beckoned. It faced the unlit fire and had two or three cushions. The chill of the room struck at his face. At least it was dry. His head ached and the damp clamped his neck and shoulders. Kip down until Perce comes home. Apologise later for breaking in. He curled his feet up and settled onto the sofa, the rug giving him rough comfort. He tucked it around his neck, squashed a cushion into shape and began to give way to sleep.

The door of the room banged open. "Who are you? What the devil do you think you're doing?"

He reached for the back of the sofa and clawed himself upright. Percy stood in the doorway, a stout walking stick raised in his hand.

"I, er... Perce, it's me." John looked at his brother.

Percy stared. His shirt hung open and his long johns looked twisted as if pulled on in haste. Behind him, a muscular youth, about nineteen, his bare chest oiled and smooth. A strong smell of pomade.

The young man stepped into the room, fists clenched. "Want me to do the bleeder over, guvnor?"

"No, no, I know him, he's my... leave him. And you, get out!" Percy's voice sounded shrill.

"What about my –?"

"Not now! Go on, get out! Get out!" Percy tried to bundle the half-naked boy out. The youth turned in the doorway, narrowed his eyes and pointed at John. "You'll pay for this, mate, next time I see yer, I got your number now," he said.

"For God's sake, get out!" Percy's voice rose to a scream. He swung round to John. "And you! Get off my sofa, you're filthy, what on earth makes you think you can break into my house?"

Sounds of the young man running up the stairs, crashes and thumps in the room overhead, footsteps cascading down the staircase, the crash of the front door shutting.

John slowly stood up, his back to the cold fireplace, and faced his brother. He held up his hands in surrender. "I'm sorry, Perce, I didn't know what else to do. It's cold and wet out there. I had to get under cover. Besides, we need to talk."

"Well, I don't want to talk to you! How dare you barge in on my privacy? And who's going to pay for that window? I shan't forget this. Panes of glass aren't two a penny, you know, and you're not in any position to contribute. Look at you. No better than a tramp."

John shook his head. "I'm sorry about the window, sorry for appearing unannounced, but it seemed you were out. I wanted to talk about Father. I didn't know he was dead. No one told me."

"I'm going to put some clothes on. I'm not getting into any argy bargy with you until I'm dressed." His bare feet pattered towards the door.

"Can't I make myself a hot drink – tea or something?"

"If you must, but don't think for one minute you're staying tonight." Percy sniffed and disappeared.

John put his boots on and wandered through to the back kitchen. His left foot squelched. Boot leaking, obviously. Must find some cardboard. He filled the kettle from the tap, set it on the gas. Now, what chance of finding rum or whisky to keep the cold out? He began searching the pantry shelves. If he's got any.

Padlocked away, probably.

"You know, if you had a modicum of self-control and greater powers of self-denial..." John turned round. As always, Percy appeared without warning. He stood in the doorway, a neat waistcoat fastened over his shirt, his trousers sharply pressed. "I know what you're looking for and you won't find any. Drink is a waste of money, you should know that, and I'd have thought you have precious little cash to feed your indulgence."

"Percy, why didn't you let me know Father had died? It was a shock, upset me seeing the grave."

"No one knew where you were, simple as that."

"You, if anyone, could have found me. You have contacts, you're always round the streets. I've never been far away."

"I had to take on head of the family. A lot to arrange. People turn to me now. Besides, who wants a drunk at a funeral? You disgrace the Hemingby name. No job, you don't support your family, you look a fright. I certainly wasn't going to have Ma distressed still further."

"You won't understand. Some things... Drinking helps. Hate myself for it. It's like a wound. I've done things... It's a punishment I feel I have to bear."

"Oh, fiddlesticks, what do you mean wounds? You haven't a mark on you. You're no hero returning from the war. Try squaring up to life. Slinking around, making excuses like this, you only reveal your own weakness. Who'd want to admit to you as a brother, as you are now? Maybe you should talk to a vicar, somebody who can talk sense into you, give you some backbone, make you face your responsibilities."

John closed his eyes and took a deep breath. "All right, I'll go. I'm obviously an embarrassment here." He paused. "In more ways than one."

Percy lowered his gaze, wouldn't look him in the eye. You could hear his fast breathing. Abruptly, he glared at John, his eyes glittering. "Just get out of our lives, will you? And don't bother the family again. Unless you want to force me to find a way of dealing with you."

I know, John thought, as he stumbled down the steps into the darkness and rain, hide behind your whited sepulchre, if you will. I shan't say anything.

★ ★ ★

Too early to go to a pub. He dragged round to the churchyard and nestled on the bench in a corner of the porch. Out of the wind and rain, at least. You could even spend the night if it wasn't for the metal gates they locked across the entrance. He'd learned now: wood was warm; stone was always cold.

They were holding Evensong: a soft glow seeped through the coloured windows into the darkness; a parsonical voice fluted and droned; a ragged refrain responded with a fervent Amen. He knew the service so well. The closing hymn next. Would it be one he knew?

The day thou gavest, Lord, is ended. A choke caught at his throat.

One of his favourites – in the old days. Right from boyhood. When he belonged. That was the curse of it: though his mind rebelled, God still held his heart. He listened to the congregation swooping the tune, revelling in the Victorian sentiment, the confidence of faith. Mostly female voices, some elderly, quavering. This hymn often sung at funerals. He bit his lip and swallowed.

Probably held Father's funeral here, perhaps they sang this for him. I should've been told; should've been here. We didn't see eye to eye, the old man and me, but I should have been allowed to say a goodbye of sorts.

The image caught him unawares: the hand stretching from the mud-rucked pool. Those words chasing him: *Smiler, for God's sake, help me!*

No goodbye there, either.

No easier to bear, even in exile.

A fit of coughing racked him. He stuffed his fist into his mouth and tried to stifle it, stood up to catch his breath. Someone thrust the heavy door of the church open and light flooded out. He had only a brief impression of the man: dark overcoat, hair plastered down and parted in the middle, wire-framed spectacles.

"Will you be quiet? We have a service in progress." The churchwarden looked him up and down. "And be off with you! We don't want your sort idling around here. This is the House of God. Move on."

John hung his head and shuffled out of the porch. Still raining. High above him, the church clock struck seven. Head for the pub, then. They'd be open. Comfort and a welcome of sorts there. Words drifted into his head: *My God, my God, why hast thou forsaken me?* Quickly stifled: self-pitying blasphemy.

This life was what he deserved.

★ ★ ★

In the entrance of The King's Arms, where they did the off-sales, he pulled out the brown quart bottle from his bag and passed it through the hatch to the barman. "A fill-up, please. London bitter." He began to count out coins from his pocket. "And can you spare a crust or two, please, mate?"

He breathed relief as he saw the beer pouring from the metal jug into the neck of his bottle. Not long now. "Not too tight with the stopper, please, fingers are cold tonight."

The two crusts were stale and biscuit-like; on the edges of one, a speck of blue-green mould had begun to blossom. He plucked it out and flicked it on the ground outside – for the sparrows. The bread would be tolerable after dunking in beer. Couldn't afford to be choosy, after all.

He stood in the yard wondering where to take his supper. Somewhere dry – the vault perhaps. Bright light flung out of the pub entrance as a young man swaggered out. He wore a light brown bowler hat at a jaunty angle, his dark jacket revealed a white shirt, rolled at the neck, a bright neckerchief, tight trousers.

John tried to turn away.

"'ere, you!" The young man strode over and seized him by the overcoat. He wagged a finger in John's face. "Still around, are yer, poking your nose in where it ain't wanted? I'll teach you to butt in on other people's tricks. Perhaps this'll take the smile off your stupid face."

John felt a stinging blow to his right cheek and another full in the mouth. The bottle of beer spiralled out of his hand. Something in his mouth cracked. He felt a stinging pain, the force of the blow spun him round, and his face and mouth hit the cobbles. A hefty kick at the side of his stomach. He doubled up, gave a loud groan and lay still. Around him, broken glass and a spreading pool of foam.

★ ★ ★

The raddled face peered down at him, her blue eyes crinkled with concern. "Are you all right, darlin'?" she said. "He didn' arf crack you one." The woman squatted beside him, her bright red lips pouting. "He wants to pick on someone his own age. I know 'im, little basket, always tarting himself around. Nasty piece of work. Blackmail his own grandmother, he would." Her long straggly hair, already an over-ripe blonde, she had bundled up and adorned with strips of ribbon. He studied her through bleared vision. Weird, what is she – a witch or a clown?

The woman wore several layers of clothes over her dress, a waistcoat, a fur stole, a cloak, even an apron. She picked up her cloth bag which bulged with mysterious objects. "Come on, darlin', you're coming with me. I'll look after you."

John sat upright on the cobbles, aware of blood coming from his mouth and running down his chin. He patted his jaw with care.

"He's done for your teeth, love, them two front ones. Big gap there now. I'll take a look when we get back." She helped him to his feet. "Takes it out of you, gettin' knocked down like that, I know."

He tried a step. "My ankle, I think I've sprained it." He could hear himself lisping now. Everywhere ached.

"'ere, I'll 'elp you." She hooked his arm round her neck. "You lean on Sarah, go on, I can take it. Let's get you home. Get them clothes off you. You stink of beer."

He did not argue.

★ ★ ★

Sarah had two rooms she called home. Amazing how warm they were. She sat him at the table. He slumped, groaned and began to relax. She patted the wall at his side. "Feel that!" She picked up his hand and placed it against the wall. "Thass where their boilers is. It's all right backin' onto a laundry. Means it's always warm in 'ere. Now, I reckon I've got some clothes as'll fit you. Soldier, were you? My Jack was an' all. He was a big fella, 'bout your size. I reckon some of 'is clobber will fit. Come on, darlin', strip off and let's get you cleaned up." He hesitated. "Don't be shy, I seen it all before. More times than I care to remember." Her lips seemed large, almost

412

inflated, and the lipstick had wandered to exaggerate the outline. Fascinating, he thought, has she seen herself? How can she bear to look like that?

She lugged in a large hip bath and began pouring jugs of hot water into it. "I have as much 'ot water as I like. On tap, straight to the sink. Not many places can say that. They ran a pipe and tap through on the sly, like, from next door. And they brought the electric through for me, an' all. They wanted paying, of course, so I had to give them a bit of what for, but I don't mind. I'm used to that and it don't mean anything. If it makes a bloke feel better, why not? They're either old blokes – they're always grateful, if they can get it – or they're young boys who need guiding all the way."

He stood there in his shirt and long underpants. "My teeth," he said, aware of the lisp. "Can I wash my mouth out?"

"Oh, love, I'm sorry. Come on, come over 'ere." She led him at a gentle hobble through to the kitchen-scullery and prepared a mug of warm salt water. In a scrap of mirror above the sink, he examined the bloodstained gape. Clots of blood clung to his beard. Where his teeth had been, a jagged black gap. He lowered his eyes and screwed his mouth into a painful grimace.

Goodbye, Smiler.

"Come on, darlin', 'ave a rinse-out. It's a good disinfectant. It'll clean your mouth, help your gums to heal. But don't swallow it, though, will yer? Otherwise..."

He shook his head and tried a rueful smile. He still remembered the sergeant's punishment. Hadn't stopped him drinking, though. He swilled his mouth out with care and watched the pink water puddle into the sink. His mouth throbbed.

"Come on, soldier, bath-time!" She began guiding him back. "What *is* your name, love? I can't keep calling you nothin'."

"John." His voice sounded muffled and strange through the swelling.

"Johnny," she said. "I'll call you Johnny. This poor Johnny didn't come marchin' 'ome, did you, love?" She began unbuttoning his

413

shirt. "Neither did a lot of them, did they? My Jack for one. Out there somewhere. No one knows where he's buried. One of the many with no known grave, isn't that what they say? Covers a multitude, that does."

He began to shake, unable to control the giant shiver. Too close to Sov and Henshaw now. He stood on the edge of the drowning pit. His head lashed from side to side in involuntary jerks.

"All right, darlin', all right. You're safe now. Come on, let's slip your linin's off." She unbuttoned his long johns and jockeyed them down his legs. "What did your missus think when she saw you in this state?" She burst into a snatch of song: *"Johnny, I hardly knew yer.* Well, that's not your fault, darlin', I know."

She helped him into the bath and began sponging hot water over his head and shoulders. She rummaged in her cloth bag. "I got a bit of nice soap I half-inched – bit of Pear's. Now, relax, be a good boy and let Sarah baby yer. I'll give yer a bottle, too. Help yer sleep."

The tremors began to subside and he let his head rest against her body while she sponged and soothed his arms and chest. He winced as she dabbed his beard to remove the clotted blood. "Sorry, darlin', I'm bein' as gentle as I can." He leaned against the swell of her breast as she sponged and soaped his arms and legs. The warm smell of female sweat. "Right, darlin', sit up and I'll rinse you down." He did as he was told and she poured warm water out of an enamel pitcher over his head. It cascaded over his shoulders and down his back. He could feel the tension and pain flowing away. He sighed with relief. "Thanks, Sarah." His voice barely a whisper.

She dried him down and slipped a flannel nightshirt over his head. "Now, Johnny, bedtime." Behind a heavy curtain, a feather bed in the corner, close to her kitchen-scullery. She lit a candle and put it on a small cupboard at the bedside. "Don't s'pose you want to eat, but there's a bottle, there, and a glass, top shelf. Take what you want, it'll help yer sleep. I'm just goin' to get in your water while it's still hot." She switched off the overhead light, tugged her clothing off and tumbled it onto a chair.

The gin stung his mouth. May have started the bleeding again, he thought, but he took several swallows and felt reassured by its fire. He watched her bathing, fascinated: the first time he'd seen a naked woman. Her rounded white flesh swelled and curved like a mother goddess. Not a young girl by any means, but still attractive.

She slipped on a nightdress and joined him in bed. "Have you had all you want, darlin'? Shall I take the glass?" He nodded. She put it to one side and blew out the candle. The room was swallowed by hot darkness.

He felt her turn towards him and rest on one elbow. She stroked the hairs on his chest with her fingers. Her voice a soft whisper now: "You can have me, you know, if you want to. I shan't mind. We're not hurtin' anyone. Come on, darlin', rest your head here. See how you feel."

She put her arm around his shoulder and pulled him to her breast. He inhaled deeply, felt a catch in his breath, and then tears came in uncontrollable shudders. "Oh, God! Oh God!"

"It's all right, Johnny, I've got you, you're safe. I've got you."

FIFTY-NINE

Mother was never one for photographs. She didn't mind having them taken but she never had any on display. "I know well enough what people look like," she said once. "Why do I need to remind myself and clutter up the mantelpiece or the dresser?" So there were never any family pictures, not of her father, Aunt Dora or even Uncle Row. The portrait she'd had taken of us children was tucked away in an old wooden box with a hinged lid. But it was strange. She took care to date and label pictures as if that was important, as if one day somebody might be interested. But then, she was always methodical.

Certainly no picture of Daddy, of course. I remember coming across an envelope in the wastepaper basket and inside was a torn-up photograph. Out of curiosity, I did my best to reassemble it, like a jigsaw puzzle. It was a picture of their wedding and it looked as though someone had cut across it first of all, deliberately separating the two of them and had then torn both halves up. Symbolic, really. I don't know if she ever divorced him.

After Daddy had finally gone, the one picture of him in full uniform at the beginning of the war disappeared from her bedside table and was never seen again. Thrown away, too, I should imagine.

She never mentioned him and behaved to the world as if she was a widow. She wouldn't have married again, anyway. Never a hint of anybody else. I can understand now: she'd had enough of marriage.

I came across one of my old school exercise books recently. I must have had it as a rough book or perhaps I never finished it. At the back, I found a letter I'd started writing – what was I? Twelve? Thirteen? After Daddy had gone, anyway. The pain of his absence still lingered. It's so hard when you know someone isn't dead. But you had to think of him that way, knowing he'd gone for good, like someone who'd died. For me, he really was the 'dear departed' as the saying used to be.

Dear Daddy,

It's your birthday today and it's pouring with rain. I hope it's not bringing you bad luck. I still miss you and often think about you. I wish you would write to me. I wonder what has happened to you and if you still play your violin. Wherever you are, I do hope you are keeping well. I hope you have found a new home and somebody to love and look after you, as you deserve.

And there I broke off. I wouldn't have sent the letter. No forwarding address, anyway. All too painful for an emotional teenage girl. I remember wondering if Daddy started another family with someone else. I couldn't bear that thought, hated the idea he might have another Dorothy in his life.

We never heard of him again. If Mother did, she wouldn't have told us. She protected and controlled all our lives.

But we were all losers as a result of that break-up. Certainly Bea and I were. We both had to change our ambitions. The money just wasn't there. I feel most sorry for Doug. He grew up not even knowing what his father looked like. If he'd passed Daddy in the street, he wouldn't have recognised him. Doug was always a handful and Mother struggled to control him. In the end, when he was sixteen, she herself signed him on in the navy and let them discipline him.

She eventually had to admit defeat and give up the independence she'd guarded so jealously and that changed everything for all of us. You could say Rowley was the one survivor. It's as if Mother put all her hopes, all her eggs in one basket. He did do well in his career and Mother was no doubt very proud of him. But she couldn't have foreseen that there'd be another war.

Even now, I wonder if it was Daddy playing the violin outside my school. I can't forget it. Silly, isn't it?

But I would have liked to see him just one more time.

SIXTY

Close by the cemetery's perimeter wall, two men, shoulder deep in a wide pit, heaved great clods above their heads, banged their spades on the ground to dislodge the clay. "Oh, Lord," he murmured, "thought I'd seen the last of these." Mass burials still haunted him, but he made himself face horrors now when he could. His way of controlling the shakes.

He stopped to watch. No one would challenge him: he was in disguise. Over the days he'd stayed with Sarah, she'd given him two changes of clothes, another bath and a haircut. He could easily pass for an office worker, slightly old-fashioned in dress, but smart. The dark suit and waistcoat fitted tolerably well, but he had to wear a white scarf over an open neck. Couldn't fasten the collar stud. "Don't worry about it, Johnny. Who cares these days? You can always say you've got a rash."

The two men clambered out of the grave, panting. One leaned on his shovel and tipped the peak of his cap in greeting.

"Easy digging, would you say, after all the rain?" John's hand hovered in front of his mouth. Still embarrassing his lack of front teeth.

The second man lit his pipe and drew on it. "All the same to us, sir, rain or sun. We do this twice a week."

"A mass grave?"

"Yes, sir, every Tuesday and Friday we get a workhouse hearse in with the week's burials. St Pancras today. There's five coming, two of 'em children."

The first man spat on his hands and picked up the shovel again. "We're about ready now."

"A communal grave?"

"Yes, sir. These are the unmarked – the paupers and the unclaimed." He took off his cap and looked away down the path.

The clop and trundle of a horse and cart in the distance; a glimpse of a chaplain, leading the way, his vestments ballooning in the chill breeze.

"Beg pardon, sir, I wouldn't linger unless you've really a mind to." The man tapped his pipe out on his heel. "They sometimes take the coffins back, you see, for next time. The bodies is wrapped, but that's all. They's just as nature left them. No one's worked on 'em, if you take my meaning. If you're not used to it, can catch at the throat."

"I see, thank you gentlemen. I'll take your advice and bid you good day." He raised his hat and headed towards the vault, aware still of a slight pain from his sprained ankle. He closed his eyes.

A pauper's funeral.

He took a deep breath, shook his head and walked on.

★ ★ ★

The garden shed seemed like home now. He'd agreed with Helen to take up residence after Michaelmas, when the old gardener had given the lawn its last mow and all the tools had been cleaned and oiled. John could live there undisturbed until late February. He loved the woody smell of the place, the lingering odour of grass and the tang of linseed oil. He placed the suitcase on the workbench and propped his violin case in the corner amongst the canes and pea sticks. Have to go busking soon. In spite of his frugality, Gurney's money was almost gone.

"Oh, marvellous," he said. Helen had left an array of provisions: a caddy of tea, a saucepan, a billy-can of water, a jar of sugar cubes, several tins, a can-opener, cutlery. On the floor underneath the bench, he found a trug with windfalls from the garden, a few carrots and late runner beans, potatoes – and a primus stove.

Pinned to the inside of the door, a note:

Dearest Fordie, make yourself as comfortable as you can, use the deck chairs and please feed yourself. On the top shelf, you'll find emergency supplies, if you really need them. I shall be down in the morning to see you and bring other items. With my special love, Helen.

He glanced up to the shelf and could make out two flagons of beer and a half bottle of whisky. "Oh, you darling," he said, "what would I do without you?" With her support, exile became bearable. And she didn't judge. She accepted how things were and made no adverse comment about his appearance, the life he led.

Or his drinking.

He set up a deckchair and relaxed with a mug of beer from the bottle he'd brought with him. Beef Broth tonight, he decided. These winter quarters were luxury in comparison with the vault. It had served him well but it always smelled musty – the biscuit taste of death, he called it. But his things had stayed dry. Nevertheless, he couldn't come and go as he pleased, always had to be cautious, went in fear of being discovered. It wouldn't be long before someone else found the vault and took up residence, or the authorities came across his break-in and padlocked the gate.

Shortly after nine o'clock, he lay down on the floor and prepared for sleep. Yes, luxury here. Could even use the outside toilet, now down-graded to the gardener's toilet after Howard had modernised the plumbing in the house. Best used after dark, though. No one would hear him: family life took place at the front of the property. In the shed, he found a dusty cushion for a pillow and settled under the heavy overcoat Sarah had given him.

Sarah: a ragged angel, there when he needed her. Without her help... Couldn't stay, though, not fair. He couldn't work, couldn't keep her. Time to go. His presence would only cramp her style.

He listened to the sounds of the night: the distant rattle of a train, the hesitant, questing hoot of an owl, the distinctive whine of a car driving off in the street at the back. Ah, lying on wood again! He stroked the floor: a slight grittiness beneath his fingers, like sand.

Be careful of splinters. A tickle of something running across the back of his fingers. Ant? Beetle? Spider, probably. Harmless, anyway. He grinned in the darkness. The one thing Em was afraid of. Not much else frightened her, but a spider...

Stop it, stop it! No point in upsetting yourself.

He turned over and let himself drift. Thank heavens for safety and beer. This life was tolerable, after all.

★ ★ ★

A knock at the door. He tensed up. Nowhere to hide. Helen came in carrying candles and a bottle of milk in an earthenware cooler. He relaxed.

"Fordie! You're here," she said. "I hoped you'd come back to hibernate. Are you warm enough? I could let you have –"

"Very cosy, thank you." He moved to greet her. "Hallo, Sis." Self-conscious, he held his hand in front of his mouth, uncertain whether to kiss her.

"How are you?" She looked him up and down. "You look well: haircut, change of clothes." She noticed his missing teeth. "Oh, my darling, what's happened? Have you been in the wars?"

He tightened his lips in a grimace.

"Sorry," she said. "Tactless of me. What happened?"

He told her the bare essentials, omitting all mention of Percy.

"So, you've lost the famous Ford teeth. What a shame. How horrible. Does it still hurt? I suppose you didn't think to summon a bobby."

"No point. To them, I'm only a vagrant who got into a fight. Not exactly a breach of the peace. They see it all the time. But you look radiant. Are you expecting again?" She smiled and nodded. "When are you due?" He admired the swell of her belly. Pregnant women were always beautiful. "Do you want to sit in the deckchair?" He moved to set it up.

"No, thank you!" She raised her hands in demurral and perched on the edge of the workbench. "If I got down there, I'd never get up again. Baby's expected in about six weeks – early November. Howard's hoping for a girl this time." She smiled. "He's threatening to call it Guy if it's another boy."

John shook his head, puzzled.

"You know, Bonfire Night, Gunpowder Plot."

"Oh, yes," he said. "I can't stand fireworks. Last year I got really drunk, trying to block it all out."

"My poor dear. How are things generally? I daren't ask about your family."

"Nothing to tell. Getting on well without me, I'd imagine. I've heard nothing." He paused. "I wish I'd known about Pa."

Helen lowered her gaze. "Yes, that was bad. I felt they ought at least to look for you and tell you, but Percy vetoed it, and Howard agreed it was better you weren't included."

"I came across the grave."

"Oh, that's insufferable. What a horrible way to find out. I'm so sorry."

He shrugged. "That's Perce for you."

"I know, dear. But the trouble is he's so efficient. Everyone turns to him. Ever since he earned promotion, he's become so bossy. I wish he'd find some nice girl who could tame him."

John looked at the floor and shook his head. He said nothing.

"And what about you?" she said. "Do you feel ready for some sort of job now? I hate the thought of you sleeping rough. I lie awake some nights, wondering..."

"Don't lose sleep over me, please. I'm not worth it."

"You mustn't say that! You're my brother! I will worry!"

"I get by. This life suits me. I don't have responsibilities, no demands to cope with. I can please myself. Sounds selfish, but it keeps those dreadful shakes away. I think if I had to work, the pressures and tensions would return, and I wouldn't manage." He gave a dry cough and held his chest.

"It's not good for your health, though, is it, all this? Listen to you."

"Nothing to worry about. Probably a trace of gas poisoning. Scores of former Tommies live with it."

"You must look after yourself, anyway. Make sure you eat, and keep warm. I shan't be able to come and see you very often. I mustn't. I'll try and visit once a week. I'm not very happy about keeping all this from Howard. But you are family, after all. It has to be our secret. I'll come when I can. If you need anything, put something – this milk-cooler, if you like – in the window here." She gestured towards the cobwebbed pane. "I'll see it from my little office."

★ ★ ★

Bonfire Night began before his first beer. In the darkness of a garden two houses away, the first rocket soared and burst like a flare above the battlefield. He saw the brightness scatter, heard the wallop of a banger, as if the enemy had thrown a hand grenade. A childish scream, he flinched, heard distant running footsteps; soon another cannon slogged the air. Through his window he saw a drift of smoke, smelt gunpowder, tasted war again. His head knew all the tricks of jumping jacks, but now he could hear only the rapid crack of a sniper's rifle, the futtering menace of the machine gun, the cries of men. The bonfire cast a blaze high into the sky, lit up and shadowed weirdly the tools in his shed. The outline of a scythe cut across the door. He looked in awe at the lit sky, fountaining light across the gardens, clenched his eyes and saw only a tank ablaze with Boche fury, its crew scattering and stumbling like fiery scarecrows.

"Oh, God!" His voice little more than a gulp. He snatched the bottle of beer on the top shelf, unfastened the stopper and hurried to tip the liquid into his mouth. It poured down from the corners of his lips, trickle-soaked his jacket. He gasped, belched, drank again. Reason deserted him, lurched aside; fears and memories began to rampage. Fingers trembling, he thrust the bottle on the workbench for fear of dropping it. Shaking seized him, sidestepped all reason, flung him cowering, shivering, drivelling to the floor. He heard the scream of shell and passing mortar; saw the spit and flare of gunfire, the frenzy of battle.

"It's not safe here, it's not safe, it's all wood. No sandbags."

He burst open the shed door and fled at a scuttling crouch, hands cradling his head, towards the brick safety of the toilet. He bundled into the building, grazed his knee on the concrete floor, took pleasure in the reality of the pain, crouched in the corner at the side of the pan, hands over his head, gibbering: "Oh, Jesus, Jesus, make it stop."

★ ★ ★

He emerged only at the soft return of silence on the air, the sweet smell of bonfired apple wood, a pall of smoke, the reek of gunpowder, mist drooping over the gardens. He recalled the strange quiet of after-battle when he and Sov went hunting for the wounded, fearing what they might find. He remembered the plodding trudge of carry-back, the jolts of the stretcher and the groans, curses, coughs and retching gargles of wounded men.

Safe now, though. All that horror behind him. Life couldn't hurt him anymore.

He knew he was beaten.

He tiptoed back to the shed, turned to look towards the house where a rear bedroom window cast light across the garden. Had anyone spotted his fearful flight?

Exhaustion, flatness, relief squatted on him, welcome after all that fear-wringing panic. Beer now; afterwards, bully beef and mashed potato. He'd no idea what time it was. Past bedtime, surely.

But he needed that drink.

★ ★ ★

The first scream came as the moon, shrouded in mist, edged above the ridge of the house roof. He woke, tense and listening, uncertain where the sound came from. A woman's scream, not a child's. Fear or pain? Bleary, his head fuddled by alcohol, he propped himself up, tried to think. He scrambled up off the floor, edged towards the window and peered out. A cobweb clung to his hair; he snatched it away. Outside, the silvered garden lay peaceful and silent as if all was well with the world.

Had he dreamed it? Not impossible. Screams often shattered his sleep.

The cry came again, seeming to shock the neighbourhood into listening silence. He winced, tense with fear. Now he knew: Helen. Clearly in agony, she must be in that one lit room at the back, where they'd drawn the curtains against the world. Time for her confinement, obviously. He understood so little about childbirth – always a whispered secret in the ways of women. He knew they experienced pain – but like this? Helen was suffering and he dared not emerge from hiding. If only he could hold her hand, suffer with her, reassure her... Easy enough on the battlefield. But here... Not a brother's place, anyway. Where was Howard? Would he be comforting his wife or downstairs, pacing?

Another scream. He winced with fear.

"Bloody fireworks! They've done this, they've brought the birth on."

Hungover, he rubbed his aching temples. "Pray God her two boys can't hear this." Would they still be at home? He tried to remember when Rowley was born. Did Em send Dorothy away? And where was he? Classroom, probably. They kept men away from this mystery of life, told them later.

After everything, he still knew as little about birth as a child.

Another scream, prolonged and chilling. "For God's sake," he whispered ferociously, "have you no ether? Who's with her – a doctor, a nurse? Give her something." Why didn't they take her to hospital? Now, if Henshaw... His mind leaped to block the thought.

He dropped to his knees and squeezed out a prayer: "Lord, help her, save her, protect her through this ordeal."

The screams intensified. He clapped his hands over his head, tears pricking his eyes. What if she were close to death? "Lord, save her, I beg. Watch over her now, I pray. And I... And I will return to Thee."

Toady, the voice in his head said, *why bargain and grovel now?*

One last desperate scream. A silence. A chilling, stunning, awful silence. "Lord, hear my prayer. I beg you."

He opened the door of his refuge, his ears straining. A robin in the next garden trilled. A hint of dawn.

But there, high-pitched and distant, a thin wail, a child's cry upon the air.

He let his breath go. "Thank God! She is delivered."

★ ★ ★

He lit the primus stove to boil water for tea. Forget sleep, this will soothe you, old chap. Now, will anyone spot me if I use the closet? He stifled a cough and stepped into the chill air, rubbed a stab of tight pain in his chest.

He tiptoed across the garden, his shoes leaving grey footprints on the dew-sodden grass. "Bright tracks where I have been." He remembered that Gurney line he loved. "Literally." Could betray him, though. He gazed up at the window, its blank face staring, the light a faint glow through the curtains.

"Calm after the storm," he murmured. "Thank God. I hope she's all right now." He looked round at the neighbouring gardens, the sky brightening to slate-grey now. High on the roof of the house next door, the chatter and squabble of sparrows drowned the morning calm.

Instinct told him all was not well. He could see nothing of the road at the front, but sifted sounds reached him – worrying sounds. He tried to deduce what was happening: the slam of a car door, hurrying footsteps, the ring of the doorbell. He shrank behind the brick extension. "Something's not right," he said to himself: no human sounds from the house, no baby's cry. "What's going on?"

A familiar noise: the high-revving whine of an ambulance engine, the grinding as the driver wrestled with the gears, the cough of the engine as it stopped.

Silence.

Footsteps, faint, urgent voices. A chill at heart made him hold his breath. Door slams, the din of motor vehicles, then silence drifting back.

And now, closer to him, a new sound, coming from the house: the rattle of curtain rings on a metal pole. He inched round the corner of the building and saw the drapes in Helen's office tightly shut.

One by one, at each window, someone was closing the curtains.

That could only mean one thing.

★ ★ ★

He waited as long as he dared, drank the tea, half-heartedly brushed the sleeves of his suit to smarten his appearance, thumbed through a seed catalogue and tried to feign interest in new cultivars, stood up, put his scarf on, tidied the cushion away, attempted to comb his hair using his fingers; he crouched to see his reflection in the cobwebbed window – anything to pass the time. He stroked his beard, shook his head: no chance of a shave.

Outside in a high tree, a pigeon soft-hooted a greeting to the day. "When the sun catches that upstairs window," he murmured, "time to knock on the kitchen door." Sick dread clamped his throat. "I hate being helpless. I cannot skulk in hiding and do nothing. I have to know."

★ ★ ★

He was faced with a suspicious stare. Mrs Banks, the housekeeper, stood barring the entrance. She wore a long black dress buttoned

428

up to the neck, a strand of hair straggled at the side of her face. She tried to tuck it away.

"Good morning, Mrs Banks, I'm sorry to appear like this. I'm John Hemingby, Mrs May's brother." His hand covered his mouth.

"I know who you are, sir, and where you've been." Her tone was cold, almost hostile. She stared at his ill-fitting suit, his straggly beard.

"May I come in? Not too early, I hope." He tried to look past her in the hope of seeing a kitchen clock.

"You may step into the kitchen, sir, but no further. Please do not disturb our peace today. This is a house of mourning."

She knows. Be straight with her. "I realise that. I'm so sorry. I am family, you know."

"Yes, sir, I suppose so."

"Did the poor baby not survive? How is Mrs May this morning? Feeling better, I hope." Might as well reveal what he knew of the night's anguish.

"Oh, sir, don't you realise? You have it wrong. It's Mrs May. She passed away early this morning."

"Oh, no! Not that. Not Helen. Because of the birth?" He lowered his head, covered his face with his hands. A struggle to know what to say. "I'm so sorry. I cannot tell you how sorry I am." Another pause. "What about the baby, did that survive?"

"Touch-and-go, sir. Mr May is at the hospital now. The poor mite's very weak. Thank heaven her boys don't yet know."

John bowed his head again, bit his lip. "I'm so sorry." He shook his head. "Not Helen. I can't believe it. She was always so strong, full of life. I thought the world of her."

"Quite so, sir."

"Oh, please, can I see her? I'd like to pay my respects. I may not be able... the funeral..." The sentence died. "I need to say goodbye."

"She wouldn't want that, sir. Not as she is, not now. Not even Mr May... I volunteered to lay out the body, make sure she's at least presentable for the undertaker."

He kept a long silence, eyes closed, lips tight.

"Did she suffer?" His voice a whisper.

"Not at the end, sir. That, at least, was peaceful."

★ ★ ★

He hurried back to the shed, his left hand crammed into his mouth. He bit hard on his forefinger to stop himself crying out. Silent tears flowed unchecked. Under cover again, he sank to his knees, sat back on his heels, head bowed. "Oh, Sis, Sis, I wasn't ready to say goodbye, not to you. Not like this." Almost a prayer. "What'll I do without you? It's unbearable." He raised his head, listened intently as if she might say something out of the wooden silence to comfort him. He blew his nose, swallowed his grief. He'd not done with tears. "But I know one thing for sure: God has no mercy." His voice a vehement hiss. "He could have spared you." He looked up at the wooden roof. "Why take *her*, you bastard?"

Silence, of course.

A blackbird outside chattered and flew away over the fence. John scrambled to his feet. He snatched off his neckerchief and stretched up to the top shelf. This was an emergency.

Helen would understand.

SIXTY-ONE

When his mother did not answer his knock, he barged round to the back door and crashed inside. His head ached. Dizzy, might be sick. He slung his luggage and violin case in the scullery and lurched towards the back sitting room. "Ma, you there? 's me!"

No reply. The house wasn't locked; where was she? He clung onto the doorframe, trying to think.

In the room which his mother loved for its cosiness, the curtains were drawn, the room unlit, her chair empty. He felt the seat cushion. Still warm. Not far away, then. A fire drizzled smoke in the grate.

He grasped the mantelpiece to steady himself, put his head back and shouted. "Wh'are you? 's John!"

A slight rustle of fabric. His mother stood behind the door, eyes wide. A poker in her hand.

"Wha' you doin'? 's me."

"You could have been a burglar, crashing in here like that." He'd forgotten how strong the Suffolk burr could be. "What do you want? We need peace today."

He stumbled towards her, holding his arms out, desperate for comfort. "She's gone, Ma. Whad'll we do now without her? I can't bear it."

She stiffened, held the poker awkwardly out to one side. "Oh, son, must you drink like this? You never used to. I don't know what Father would have said, seeing you in this state. Coming in like the wild man of Borneo. What's happened to your teeth? Have you looked in a mirror lately?" She was dressed in black. Her head now had a permanent tremor and the hair was white. "Sit there, in Father's chair." She turned him towards the other wing-back chair and stirred the fire up with the poker.

John sat, head in hands. "Helen's gone, and I can't stand it. 's so unfair."

"Life is unfair, boy, we have to be strong and bear it. We can't all give way to our feelings or drink ourselves into a stupor at every trial The Lord sends. I've enough to live with, too. First, Father goin', that was hard enough, now Helen, and you in this state. I heard the stories. I don't know what's the matter with this family. But I can't afford weepin' and wailin'. We carry on. That's what we have to do. I going to put a kettle on, make a cup o' tea."

He hung his head. Should have known she'd be like this. Never really warm. Only Helen gave him what he needed. And she... He bit hard on his fist.

★ ★ ★

His mother set a cup of tea and a plate of biscuits on a table beside his chair. "Help yourself, son." He buried his head in his hands. How could she be so composed? Tea and biscuits! He wanted to shout: for God's sake, Mother, your daughter has died a most horrible death, and you sit there, taking it all so calmly.

He crammed two biscuits into his mouth.

"Haven't you had breakfast?" she said.

The tremor was unnerving. It looked as though she was in a state of permanent disapproval. Her hands lay limp in her lap: a picture of still dignity. "I don't like funerals," she said. "But they have to be gone through. People expect it. I'll do what I can to comfort those poor boys, I don't suppose Howard'll bring them to the funeral. Too upsettin'. And you won't be there, will you? Not as you are, anyway. It'll only be Perce and me from our side. I expect the dress I wore for Father will do."

He took another two biscuits. What could he say?

She looked straight at him, head shaking. "You're not my John anymore. I don't know why. I don't understand what's going on, why you can't live in peace with your wife and children."

"Do you know about shellshock, Ma?"

432

"I know the war finished four years ago and it's time we forgot our troubles and moved on."

He closed his eyes, half shook his head. "There's no going back, Ma. Em made that clear. 'If you go, you go for good,' she said. This is my life now."

"She doesn't want the children upset any more than they have been, and who can blame her?"

He took a deep breath, wondered how to respond and felt a sharp pain stab at his chest. He held his hand over the upper ribs. Easier to take shallow breaths. His mother seemed not to notice. She hated fuss. He'd forgotten her strange habit of ignoring you when you were in pain or distress.

Silence.

"Talkin' of Em, I kept something for you," she said. "You might as well have it. She sent me two copies. Out of the blue, we hadn't heard for ages. I forget when the letter came; before Pa died, because I remember him sayin' what a good-looking girl Dorothy was turning into." She stood up and reached behind a jug on the mantelpiece and passed a postcard photograph to him. John nodded his thanks and stared at it.

A family portrait. All four children. He turned the picture over. Em in her usual way had dated it: September 1918 – four years ago. Soon after he'd left. Heart not totally iron-clad, then. He stuffed the picture inside his jacket and began to cough – tight spasms that hurt. He choked, held his chest, felt a trickle into his beard and saw a spray of foaming blood had spattered the lace cover of the chair-arm.

"I don't feel well, Ma." His voice a painful wheeze.

She stood up. "Oh, dear, today of all days. You stay there. I going to ring Perce. He should be in his office now. He'll know what to do."

His head ached, his chest stabbed, breathing was painful. He closed his eyes, leaned back in his chair, listened to her shuffle into the hall and pick up the telephone.

Perce, he thought, that's all I need.

★ ★ ★

He woke at the click of the light-switch to see a dark figure in the doorway: crisp-cut, smart suit, immaculate black tie, polished shoes and a black silk arm band. A sweet smell upon the air. Percy running to his mother's rescue.

"Has he been bothering you, Mother?" Percy said.

"Well, I wasn't expectin'..."

"We can't have you upset, not today of all days. You've enough to worry about with poor Helen." Percy pulled the chain of keys out and freed himself from his case. He placed it carefully out of sight behind his mother's chair and peered down at John. "What were you thinking of, coming here when we're in mourning? It really isn't done. Not in a state of intoxication. You might at least have the decency to arrive sober."

"I wouldn't expect you to understand, Perce." He paused. "But don't forget she's my mother, too." John remained in the chair, holding his chest; his voice a hoarse whisper. He dared not cough again.

"What do you think we ought to do, Perce?" She stood beside her chair wringing her hands. "I mean, look at that chair cover."

"He needs medical care, Mother, no doubt about it. There's something seriously wrong if he's coughing blood." Percy wrinkled his nose, his thin lips twisted with distaste. "Fortunately, I thought to make some telephone calls before I came, and I've managed at short notice to find a place that will give him the treatment he should have."

"Oh, that's wonderful." She turned to John and spoke in a louder voice as if he'd gone deaf. "You goin' to be all right now, son. Our Perce's fixed somethin' for you."

I'll bet he has. John nodded and closed his eyes, too tired to speak or resist.

"In fact, Mother, as I guessed, it would be better if they took him in an ambulance to a hospital. See the doctor there. I've a vehicle and a couple of men waiting outside for just such an emergency."

"You arranged that, Perce? You are a good boy. You think of everythin'. Shall I put the kettle on? I'm sure the men would like a cup of tea."

"No, don't worry, Mother, they're busy people, and it's best to get him away as quickly as possible. I'll go and call them." Percy's shoes emitted an officious squeak as he bustled out of the room.

John opened his eyes and saw his mother bending over him. "They're going to take you away in a minute, son. It'll all be for the best." Her head shook as if contradicting her own words.

"I'm sorry I upset you, Ma." His voice a croak. "But I needed to see you when I knew about Helen. I shouldn't have come. But I was so upset."

"I understand. It's a terrible blow to us all. You'll be all right now."

"The room at the back, gentlemen. Go ahead." Percy's precise voice, deliberately louder, from the passageway, and the tread of heavy feet in the kitchen.

"Good afternoon, ma'am." The attendant came into the room and stood aside to let Percy pass. A second man, also dressed in a crumpled, dark serge suit, began to open out a stretcher on the carpet.

"Oh, Lord in heaven, it's that bad, is it?" She'd started to wring her hands again.

"It's best, ma'am, saves him walking, eases the pain."

"Oh, I see."

"Give him some of this," Percy said. John was aware of his brother reaching into his pocket and producing a small bottle. He heard the squeezed pop as the cork was withdrawn. Percy gave it to the attendant.

"What's that you're givin' him?"

"Don't worry, Mother, it's a little medicine to help his cough. Do you have a teaspoon?"

"I'll get one." She hurried out of the room.

"How much should I give, sir?" The first man whispered his question.

"Two teaspoons, maybe more," Percy said. John could hear the straps being loosened on the stretcher.

The attendant came over, balancing a teaspoon of liquid. He cradled John's head. "Steady, now, soldier. This'll ease things for you."

John felt the spoon pushed through his lips. I know that taste, he thought. But what's Perce doing with laudanum ready to hand? He swallowed the liquid. That's me done for.

Sleep crept over him and he offered no struggle when the men lifted him onto the stretcher. They began fastening straps across his legs and chest. His mother stood in the background, watching.

Only the wanderer knows England's graces, he murmured. Gurney's poem, somehow comforting.

"What about his luggage?" his mother said.

"It's all right, ma'am, we'll take it. Check it in at the same time as the gentleman. Ready, Harry?" John felt himself lifted up. He opened his eyes to the smell of cologne and saw Percy bending over.

"Soon have you somewhere safe, old fellow." Percy gave John's hand a pudgy squeeze. "Don't you worry."

All for show, as always. John's head already felt cloudy from the drug. Ma will be impressed, but you don't care tuppence what happens to me. Gurney's words again. *And can anew see clear familiar faces.* Already his speech sounded slurred. He smiled wryly and shook his head. A white pustule sat on the tip of Percy's nose.

Percy Pimple. He wouldn't like that.

The men began to manoeuvre the stretcher out into the corridor. "I think straight out of the front door," Percy said. "I'll fetch his things."

John raised his head and looked towards his mother. She stood behind her chair, hands clasped before her breast as if in prayer, head shaking.

"*Do not forget me quite*," he said. The straps strained on his chest and he lay back, his eyes closed.

SIXTY-TWO

A cool breeze blew through the window to the left of John's bed. The sash was opened wide and the curtains shook and clacked against the sill. He lifted his head. A large room, more than thirty beds. Most of them empty. His head ached. No idea how long he'd slept. He gauged the time now at mid-afternoon.

Next to him, a patient with a spray of white hair tumbling over his skeletal face. The old man coughed frequently, his tongue protruding from his lips whenever a fit overtook him. Frequent hawking and spitting into a bowl at the side of his bed. "Awake, are you?" The man's voice a wheeze. "Been asleep long enough."

"How long was I out?"

"Oh, I dunno. Lose track. Ages."

"Where's everybody else?"

"Day room, probably. Teatime soon."

"So where am I? What is this place?"

"Don't you know?" Another fit of coughing; the man gulped a drink of water. A long silence. "Can't believe you don't know. This is 199 Dartmouth Park Hill, mate."

"I don't understand," John said. "Is that significant? Is this a hospital?"

"Sort of. This part's the infirmary. You're in the workhouse now."

SIXTY-THREE

1926 was a turning point for us all, eight years after Daddy had gone. The family split up, we left the Streatham house, most of our furniture, and went our separate ways.

I don't know how long Mother had been planning it. She told me shortly before my eighteenth birthday. I had just two or three months after I'd finished school to find some flat for Bea and me to live in. I suppose the cash legacy from Grandpa Baxter had finally run out and Mother decided she'd have to start earning, so she'd taken a job as a live-in housekeeper with a gentleman in Hove. Doug would go with her; he was barely eight. Her decision was probably helped by the fact that Rowley had won a scholarship to a posh school and would board there, so would be off her hands. His career was probably mapped out early. Plans to go into the navy were often mentioned. Mother never considered the army. Perhaps she thought it'd jinxed the family after what happened to Uncle Row and Daddy.

I'll never forget that terrible day. Douglas was always a little devil. That morning, he was dancing about on the table and peering out of the window to watch the family trunk being loaded onto a lorry.

I told him to get down. He just thumbed his nose. Big sister or not, he took no notice of anybody except Mother.

"Mother's coming," Bea said. "I heard her on the stairs."

"No, she's not!" He put his tongue out at her. Then he realised and leaped off the table as Mother staggered in under a pile of sheets, towels and blankets.

That did it. The next thing we knew, he gave a piercing yell and lay on his back, drumming his heels on the floor. His fists clenched, he stared wide-eyed at the ceiling. Blood welled up from his mouth and ran down his chin onto his neck. The tip of his tongue draped like a pink worm over his lips.

"Let me look!" Mother knelt down. "Bea, pass me a pillowcase, any one, an old one." She held up a hand and flicked her fingers. I was told to run to the telephone box and contact the doctor, and say Douglas had bitten some of his tongue off. Mother turned back to him. "Now stay where you are, don't talk, put your head back. Lie still and keep swallowing the blood." She shook her head. "You are a naughty boy, always into some scrape or other. Today of all days."

That was a major upset. The doctor came and Douglas needed stitches. I remember Mother and I had to hold him down on the table; Bea went out of the room. The doctor gave him an anaesthetic and told him to keep as still as possible. I remember Doug's eyes filling with tears when the doctor began sewing the tongue tip back on. We held him down, but Mother looked up at the ceiling, couldn't bear to watch. She was always softer towards her boys.

That accident meant that Mother and Doug couldn't leave after all and had to stay on for a few days. But with us, she was adamant: "Now, you two, on your way! I'd like to think of you settled in before dark."

I took a deep breath. "Come on, then, Bea, let's go."

Mother offered her cheek to be kissed and gave me a pat on the back as we embraced. "Goodbye, dear, I know you'll look after Bea. Make sure you write."

"I don't want to go..." Bea choked back tears. "Why can't I stay with you and come to Hove? I won't be any trouble, I promise."

"I know you wouldn't. You're the quietest and best behaved of the lot, so I know you'll get on well with Dorothy. Now buck up, be a brave girl, you're eleven now. Give me a kiss and be on your way. Think of it all as an adventure."

★ ★ ★

We struggled up the stairs to the second floor of that house in Gray's

439

Inn Road. Two dark-painted doors faced us on that narrow landing. We put our cases down and I took out a key and unlocked the right-hand door. It swung open slowly with a faint squeal of hinges.

Two metal bedsteads dominated the room, and between them a wobbly wicker-seated chair. A narrow sash window with curtains made from old army blankets looked over a slate roof, a walled yard and the backs of other houses.

Bea was very resentful about the move. She sat on the bed nearest the window and sniffed the air. "It smells dusty in here, this mattress feels lumpy. Where do we hang our clothes? And there's no carpet, not even a rug. This place can't have been scrubbed for ages."

I told her we'd have to hang our clothes on a few hooks behind some curtains in the corner.

"And do we have to cook on this?" She pointed at a gas burner on the hearth. "It'll only take a small saucepan." She turned the tap on at the wall. Silence. "No gas, either."

I said we'd have to start saving pennies and sixpences for the meter.

"And what do we do – light a fire in that poky little grate if it gets cold, or sit around the stupid gas ring? Honestly!"

I sighed. "This was all I could find. We'll have to make the best of it until I earn some money. Then perhaps we can move."

"There aren't any lamps," she said. "Somebody's taken them off the wall. There's just the bit where they used to be. Oh crumbs, that means candles."

"Or my bicycle lamp. I did pack that, just in case."

"Something else missing." Bea stood up. "Where do we wash?"

I looked down. "Sorry, the sink's on the landing."

She hurried to the door. "There isn't even a doorknob on the inside. We'll have to lock the door just to keep it shut."

I remember at the end of the landing beneath a frosted-glass window, a small square sink jutted out at knee-height.

"Are we supposed to wash in that?" Bea said. "You'd have to

kneel down. It's all chipped and dirty." The white glaze had disappeared from the edge of the sink, a large graze revealing the dirty yellow biscuit of the pottery.

"I'm sorry," I said, "I didn't notice when I first looked round. It's only cold water." I turned the brass tap on. It emitted a sucking sound, then a frantic hammering before water gushed out.

"Oh, golly," she said. "I'm glad I've got short hair. How will you manage?"

"We'll get by, we'll have to," I said. "We must find out where the nearest baths are. Perhaps I'll have my hair short, too."

"Dot," a voice of dread, "where's the lavatory?"

I pushed open a narrow door to the right of the sink to reveal the back stairs. They went down to what was once the scullery. "The WC is downstairs and outside in the yard."

"That's two flights down. Did you pack a potty?"

I shook my head. "We'll get one tomorrow."

A long silence. She looked at me and bit her lip. "I want to go home."

"We can't, I'm afraid. This is home now."

SIXTY-FOUR

My dear Dorothy and Bea

I do hope you've settled into your digs and are now feeling comfortable there. I'm glad to say Douglas's tongue is getting better quite quickly and he seems none the worse for his adventure. We shall leave here for good by and by, probably Thursday. I've sent a letter to Mr Ashworth telling him of our plans so our arrival is not unexpected.

I was surprised and pleased that the doctor, rather than sending a bill, asked if he could have some of my preserves in lieu of payment. He must have glimpsed them on the shelves in the pantry when he was in the scullery. That suits me nicely. I thought I'd have to leave them for the next tenants. I can't take them with us. I much prefer they go to a good home where they'll be appreciated. I've packed some nice jars of jam, chutney and pickled onions in a basket and will take them round to the surgery before we leave.

That's all my news for now. It's probably better if you write to Hove in a day or two.

With my love
Mother

★ ★ ★

"Who's that?" Bea held out a small sepia photograph, already curled at the edges.

I took it from her. A man in military uniform sat tall and proud on a huge horse. "Good heavens! Where did you get that? Where was it?"

"I found it on the floor. It may have fallen out of this book." She held up a copy of *The Secret Garden*. "I wanted to read this and the snap must have been tucked inside. Who is he, anyway?"

"That must be my old copy. I probably tucked the picture in there ages ago to keep it safe. I often wondered what happened to it. Fancy that turning up after all this time."

"Who is he?"

"Don't you know? You must do. It's Daddy. Before he went to France. While he was still training. I took that picture. I was very little. You were only just born."

"Let me see." Bea held out her hand and studied the picture. She snorted. "Could be anybody. Just a soldier. So, it's Daddy. Well, who wants to keep that?" She tore the picture in half, and then again, and threw the pieces into the wastebasket.

"What are you doing?" I rushed across the room, dropped to my knees and began rummaging amongst the waste. "It's not yours to destroy. What are you thinking of?" I picked up the pieces and reassembled them on the palm of my hand. "How could you do that, Bea?"

She puffed out her breath. "What's the point of keeping a picture of *him*? He didn't want us, he didn't want his family. That's why he left."

"He didn't leave!" I felt myself grow hot.

"He did! It's his fault we're stuck in this poky little place and Mother's miles away having to keep house for somebody else. What sort of man leaves his wife and young family to fend for themselves?"

"You don't understand. You were only little. You don't even remember him. He wasn't well, certainly wasn't suited to being a soldier. Something happened during the war to make him crack up. Mother threw him out when all he needed was time and understanding. Just a little love and patience."

"Mother didn't throw him out. He spent the money on drink, upset the family and then he left us. Who wants a father like that?"

I sat back on my heels. "Oh, Bea. You didn't know him. He was a lovely man before the war – kind, gentle, understanding. I adored him."

"Well, he's no use to us now, is he? He's gone, and good riddance."

"Poor Daddy. I wonder where he is now." I started to count on my fingers. "He'd be forty-seven. I hope somebody was kind to him in his new life, anyway."

"He's probably dead. From what I've heard, if he was a drunk on the streets, he wouldn't have lived long." She sat on the bed; a spring clanked beneath her. "Oh, I hate this place!"

"We'll find somewhere else, I promise. When I'm earning steady money."

Silence. Bea got up and opened the window at the top. "I'm sorry I tore your picture. Perhaps we can glue it together on some backing paper."

"No, you're probably right. He's gone, nobody knows where. Best not think about him. The good times were long ago. Poor Daddy."

And then I crossed the room and threw the pieces of photograph back into the basket.

SIXTY-FIVE

The annual medical inspection. "Yes, that pleurisy and pneumonia certainly weakened your heart." The doctor lifted the cold stethoscope off John's chest. "The beat's irregular, touch of flutter there."

"Yes?" John said.

"And the kidneys are probably rather dicky now after your time on the road, all the alcohol and so on. Are you drinking water now?"

"Oh yes, doctor. And tea." No chance of a drink in here, anyway.

"Now, anything troubling you? Any pain anywhere?"

"Only toothache from time to time."

"Really? Let me take a look. Open your mouth, please."

John still felt self-conscious about the gap at the front. Now a wooden spatula held his tongue down and the doctor peered inside his mouth.

"Not too sure I like the look of those gums. Gingivitis, I suspect. I'll put you on the list for the dentist, let him take a peek when he comes in next month. Maybe one or two teeth need whipping out. I suggest rinsing out with salt water twice a day. That should help a bit."

"I'll speak to one of the nurses, doctor."

"Good man." The doctor dropped his stethoscope into his bag and gathered up a cardboard folder. "Put your shirt on. You'll live, Hemingby." He strutted away, his feet turned outwards, the scuff of his shoes echoing down the stone corridor.

SIXTY-SIX

And then Peter. I'm amazed at how bold I was. I asked him if he'd go to the pictures with us. It was daring because the man was always supposed to make the first move. Bea was horrified: "I don't understand why you've palled up with him." She went very red. "He's not your young man, is he? I don't want to play gooseberry."

"No, of course not, silly. He lives next door, and he seemed lonely."

"But he's German, isn't he? Why pick *him* as a friend?"

"You mustn't think like that. The war's been over eight years. It makes sense now to befriend people from other countries, even Germans. It's the only way we can hope for peace between nations in the future. I don't ever want to see another war."

"But what's he doing here? How do you know he's not a spy?"

"You're just being silly now."

But if I'm honest, I did feel daring. Idealism coming out, I suppose. Peter had piercing blue eyes and blond hair and a strong nose like a Roman emperor. Stunningly handsome, I thought, and when he looked at me, I held my breath and my heart beat faster. Nothing came of it, of course. Romance can hardly blossom if you take your young sister everywhere with you. We went to the cinema once or twice, and I took us to a Lyons Corner House for tea and toast.

I remember he drank very weak tea without milk and floated a slice of lemon on top. That was the first time I'd seen tea drunk the continental way. He asked me what I did.

"I'm starting as an uncertificated teacher with young children in September."

"You will be good. You are patient and sympathetic, Miss

Hemingby." He made me blush. "I have proposal to make." He paused, and I held my breath. "Would you like to teach English this summer to Russians? I have some Russian friends. I meet them at The Institute. You visit them to their house in London and give them lessons in English. They will pay well."

"Russians?"

"Ah, naturally you are worried. But these are not Red Bolshevik, they are good White Russians who live in England now. They want to learn English if you will teach them."

Bea must have been really bored. She may even have been jealous.

I nodded. "Well, it's all good experience. Why not? The money would come in handy."

"That is good. Then I will tell them and arrangements will be made."

Fancy that, I thought, as we all walked back, I've really joined a league of nations, if I do this. But how much should I charge for lessons?

I don't think Peter ever talked about himself, or said why he was in England, and certainly never did invite me out. He was a typical German of the time: always formal, clicked his heels when we met and bowed. I was impressed, but really I knew very little about boys, apart from my brothers: one was being groomed to go to a snooty school and become posh, the other was a little brat. In the end, we drifted apart. I remember thinking he wasn't a lot of fun. He never made me laugh, didn't have a sense of humour and seemed rather cold. With those looks, he would have fitted well into Hitler's Germany. Perhaps that's what became of him. I was really naive in those days.

★ ★ ★

I enjoyed the chance to spread my wings, but I don't think Bea liked independence at all. None of us ever found Mother particularly loving, but I think Bea missed the security of home. She often

447

seemed resentful of being thrust away from the family and being dependent on me.

"I'm just an orphan," she used to say. "My father left us, my mother doesn't want me and you're always too busy doing other things."

She became a typical adolescent very early. You couldn't reason with her when she was in that frame of mind. But Mother and I had agreed that, if possible, she shouldn't change schools. And so, every day Bea took a bus across the river back to her school in Streatham. Long, tiring days. But she never really settled in the flat. I think she always thought she'd missed out. Perhaps eleven was too young to be out in the world.

She also thought I was selfish starting evening classes. For years it'd been my ambition to go to art college and I found somewhere I could go twice a week after I'd finished teaching. But Bea wasn't happy and made that clear more than once.

I'd never managed to get a portfolio together – certainly couldn't have taken it with me to the flat – so I entered a competition for a place on that art course. By a twist of fate, it was Bea who spotted it and encouraged me to enter. As it turned out, I got into a terrible pickle because of those classes. I *was* naive in those days.

* * *

"I've painted the place I'd like to live," I said, "my dream cottage in the country. Don't suppose I ever shall. People don't these days."

Bea looked at my competition entry and smiled. "You like your flowers, don't you? All those pinks and reds, and yellows. It's clever how you've managed it. Are they hollyhocks? You've done those well. Lot of hard work keeping a cottage garden tidy, though. I wouldn't want to live there. Did you copy it from somewhere?"

"No, I didn't! I made it up. All my own work," I said. "Honestly, Bea!"

"I tell you what I do like: that path leading through the gateway into the woods. There's real mystery there. Leading you into the unknown. I hope the judges like it."

★ ★ ★

Maud Esslin's breath caressed the top of my head as she leaned over my shoulder. "The picture's very pretty, Dorothy, as far as it goes: the composition, the balance of colours. Just right. But, dear, it's so predictable. I don't want to be harsh after all your hard work, but you're never going to become a great female artist if you mimic Victorian sentimentality. It's time we abandoned the corsets of convention, moved on and showed what women can really do."

Her scarlet tie dangled over my right shoulder. Her closeness was comforting but also embarrassing.

"You know, dear," her voice so quiet and persuasive, "you'd be magnificent, if you could only break free of tradition and let yourself go. I could help you, if you'd let me."

★ ★ ★

I listened to Bea breathing in the other bed. Fast asleep, thank goodness. I'd no idea what the time was. Well past midnight, certainly. What an evening! No wonder sleep didn't come, but it wouldn't have been right to stay. Bea would have worried if I hadn't come home.

I could still feel the taut tingle where Maud had caressed me. Is this what grown women enjoyed with their friends? It felt so soothing sitting at her feet, an elbow on one of her knees, even laying my head back so that it rested on her stomach. We talked about life, art, even read poetry to each other. Drank sherry. I told her about Daddy. All so natural and comfortable. I'd never known such closeness. Mother rarely held or cuddled me; only quick kisses or pecks on the cheek were encouraged. Nothing more. Even Bea and I never hugged, though we shared so much.

449

But when Maud stroked my hair – "It looks so much better, Dot, now you've cut it", when she cradled my head, ran her fingers down my neck and traced the lines and hollows of my throat and shoulders, when her hand strayed inside my shirt and found a breast, when she leaned over, kissed the top of my head tenderly and cupped the breast and teased my nipple into excited firmness, it all felt so natural and comfortable. My body purred with the affection like a stroked cat.

"Is that good?" Maud said. "Is that what you like, Dot?"

"It's wonderful." My head was drunk with sherry and delight. It was like nothing I'd known before. Even my tongue buzzed.

"True sisters at heart can bring such softness and gentleness, comfort and love that passes any rough embrace a man can give. You'll see, we'll discover new heights together, you and I." It was the first time I'd felt special since I was very little.

And yet... Doubts crowded in.

★ ★ ★

"I do think it'd be nice if *you* wrote to Mother this time. She likes to hear from us both, you know." I bent over that wretched gas ring and gave our porridge a final stir and poured it into two bowls.

"And what should I tell her – that I hate living in this poky place?" Bea said. "That we're always getting colds? She's not interested or she wouldn't have left us to fend for ourselves like this."

"You know why she's had to take up work."

"Yes, but it's always the boys, isn't it? To keep Douglas out of mischief, or so Rowland can have his chance with the navy. What's wrong with me having a career?"

I handed her the bowl. "Careful, it's hot. Why not talk about how you're getting on at school? About your friend Winnie? You can say I've started this course in the evenings, tell her I'm managing large classes at school quite well, you'd better not mention the little devils who won't do as they're told. Write what you like: how you've learned to make omelettes, talk about your weekend job helping out at the kennels. Anything newsy, so long as she knows we're managing and she doesn't have to worry. See if you can make her laugh."

"That's an impossibility for a start," she said. "Sometimes I hate her. I'll tell her we're doing all right, considering we've been abandoned by both parents, that we have to eat our meals in a canteen because of your wretched evening classes, and that I'm browned off with having to sit on my own in that library every night, doing my homework. I can't wait to leave school and get a job." She thumped the bowl down on the floor. "I can't eat this. It's all lumpy and it's burnt my tongue."

"Oh, Bea, when you're in this mood, there's no reasoning with you! Why not ask Mother to write to Aunt Dora, she's got plenty of money now. Perhaps she'll sub you in a year or two so you can go to full-time college on a vet's course. That's what you want to do, isn't it?"

She sighed. "What's the point? Girls are never going to be equal to boys."

"Maybe not, but we can have a jolly good try to prove the world wrong."

★ ★ ★

"I don't want to go," Bea said. "She doesn't really want me there."

"You have to. Mother's arranged it specially with Mr Whatsisname for you to stay during this half-term. Besides, you'll enjoy it when you get there. Nice breath of sea air for a change."

"As long as Rowley isn't there, lording it over everybody and talking posh. I couldn't stand that. I don't know what you're going to get up to, but I think you want to be rid of me for a few days."

"Don't be so silly!" I lowered my eyes. But it might give me a chance to... I blocked the thought out. "Come on, we're late. Get your mackintosh on, we'll have to take the bus tonight."

I never told Bea, but I was looking forward to seeing Maud that night. She'd arranged for us to see some film in Hampstead and have supper afterwards. The prospect of going out in public with my tutor made me feel really special and grown up.

"Just us, no need to worry," Maud said. "And afterwards, we'll go back to my flat and unwind with a nightcap. That's splendid, now we know you haven't to rush back."

"Yes, lovely," I said. My stomach squirmed, but was it fear or excitement?

I didn't realise what her intentions were. You don't know at that age what frenzy you can provoke in others. I certainly didn't.

We sat on her settee drinking red wine. Maud's hand drooped along the back behind my head. A man's gold signet ring winked from her little finger like a serpent's eye. I sat with my hands in my lap, uncertain.

"Why not stay the night, dear? Come on, snuggle up." She blew a stream of smoke into the air and stubbed out her cigarette. Her arm slipped round my shoulder and drew me close.

"Put your head there, dear. Relax. Make yourself comfortable." My head rested on her bosom in a heady aura of cigarette and musky perfume. "No rush. We've all the time in the world. Comfy?"

I nodded.

Her hand wound into the front of my blouse, down and under and round. "You like that, don't you?" The slow rolling of my nipple began again.

"Yes." My voice was hoarse as if I'd a frog in my throat.

"Let me just loosen up, then perhaps you'd do it for me too." She freed her tie with one hand and unfastened her shirt buttons. "Come here now." She lifted my hand and put it inside the shirt. "Have you ever done this before?"

I gave a slight shake of my head. The breast was naked inside the shirt and I began to wonder then if she'd planned all this.

She put her head back and gasped. "Oh, my dear, kiss me. Keep on with that and kiss me." I became frightened. She pulled me into an embrace and her kiss became firm and passionate, demanding more than I knew how to give. I strained away, struggling for breath. I'd never kissed anyone like that.

And then she asked me to do something which really worried me. Then I knew she had seduction in mind.

"I can't," I said. "Please stop. It wouldn't be right."

"All right, my dear, all right. Too quick, I'm sorry." Her voice was soothing. She took a deep breath and began buttoning me up, then turned to her own shirt. "I'm so sorry, you're not ready yet. But do you think you could, in time, love me just a little?"

★ ★ ★

I cried in bed that night. The room was cold, seemed damp. Maud had been good and kind, walked me down to the taxi rank to see me off. She seemed so understanding and didn't blame me. She even paid the fare. But that just increased my guilt at not being able to respond in the way she wanted, at wanting to go back to that lonely room when I could have stayed the night in comfort, and no one would have known.

My whole body ached with the evening's pleasure, but what worried me most was the fearful realisation that I could so easily have come to enjoy what we did. I'd never felt so excited and loved and wanted – and special. And that was what hurt: it was wrong. I didn't believe in sin and all that, but a nag somewhere told me it wasn't natural – women shouldn't be like that with each other. Physical love was between men and women, surely. And where would it all end?

I burst out crying again when I considered losing all that tenderness, that cherishing of me alone. It felt as if I was young and foolish, and had betrayed Maud after all she offered, but to be true to myself, I knew I'd have to let that strange intimacy go.

That night, at least, I couldn't bear the thought.

SIXTY-SEVEN

Being in the workhouse wasn't bad. Nothing to be ashamed of. Not now. The stigma of being inside had gone. There was talk of closing them gradually; but he'd still stay on if the place did become a hospital for the long-term sick. Nowhere else to go. They'd assessed him Ufi – whatever that meant, but he wasn't expected to work. Unfit for industry, perhaps.

Not too harsh, really: fed, clothed, a bed for the night. Out of harm's way – out of the family's way. Never any visitors. He thought his mother might come, but Perce probably controlled that, too. John wrote a couple of letters, but she never replied. One was returned with *Gone Away* scribbled on the envelope. He didn't know whether to believe it or not.

No, life wasn't bad. Inmates didn't have to wear uniform now. Bath and shave once a week, sometimes more often. You could wear what passed as your own clothes, they gave you pocket money, you could go out for walks, they let you sign out as long as you came back, they even took you to the pictures sometimes. And always a newspaper to read. That passed the time. Sitting on a bench in the sun with your back to the wall – an old man before time.

It was a life.

SIXTY-EIGHT

1928

I never told Bea the reason why I changed my course. I couldn't. She challenged me, of course: "I thought you were mad keen, you always said you wanted to go to art school. And you seemed pretty thick with your tutor." She finished buffing her school shoes and laced them up.

"Yes, well, I've decided it's not me." I didn't look at her. "Best to keep painting as a hobby. I don't like working in oils and I'm not really in tune with current thinking in art. Besides, botany's a science – much more useful in the modern age, and the tutor's a man, which I prefer."

"You've changed! You used to hate maths, and all sciences." She crammed her straw hat on and stood by the door. "I hope I pass today's geometry test."

"Anyway, I still get to do artwork, drawing plants and so on. Ah! You've reminded me. I must give my little darlings a spelling bee today. So, meet you at the college canteen about half past five."

"Don't you ever get fed up with studying?"

"No, it's hard work, I'm sometimes pretty whacked, but at least I'm working towards a degree. Got your geometry set? All your pencils sharp?"

"Oh, Dot, don't fuss. You sound like Mother. I'll see you at Birkbeck after netball." She picked up her satchel, straightened her hat and clattered off down the stairs.

Why does life have to be such a compromise? I thought. I've had to let go two things that I cared about.

★ ★ ★

"Don't look round!" I banged my cup down and wiped my mouth.

Bea peeped over her shoulder.

"I said, don't look round." My voice a hiss now. "He's here again."

"Who?"

I took a casual sip of tea and stared over her shoulder. "Leslie Sutterton I think his name is. He's about three tables behind. Don't look round!"

She sighed. "I think you only come here so you can eye up the young men."

"I wonder if he's on an honours course, too."

"If I'm not allowed to turn round, describe him. What's he look like? Is he handsome?"

I felt myself blush. "*I* think so. He's tall, medium build and he always wears the most fashionable plus-fours. He's got on a sandy-coloured suit tonight and beautiful fawn socks. Really show his legs off. He must have money, that's the second lot of plus-fours he's worn this week. He looks really stylish. Perhaps his father's a tailor."

"Could you really love a man who plays golf?" she said.

"Oh, Bea, he doesn't have to be sporty. He's just following fashion. I really would like to marry someone who cares about his clothes."

"Marriage? Are you thinking about getting married? Have you spoken to him?"

"Oh, no, I daren't. I'm only dreaming. You're supposed to wait until they approach you. In any case, he must be terribly posh, he speaks frightfully, frightfully, you know."

"Doesn't sound your type at all. I can't stand snobs."

"The only thing I don't like is his wavy blond hair. It looks as though he's had it permed. I can't tell whether that's natural or not. Still, can't have everything."

★ ★ ★

"What do you think, then?" Bea passed the letter over. "It's only a rough version."

I bunched the pillow up behind me, leant against the bedhead and began reading.

Dear Aunt Dora,

Mother has encouraged me to write to you. I do hope you are well and enjoying life in South Africa. I believe you know that Dorothy and I are sharing a flat in London. She's doing quite well as an elementary schoolteacher and is also studying for a degree at evening classes. She hopes to be a qualified teacher soon.

"Yes, leave that bit out about us sharing. And the degree course. I'm sure she already knows."

Bea turned back from staring out of the window at the damp roofs. "The trouble is padding it out. I can't just come straight out with what I want. It'd be rude. It all seems rather short."

I picked up the letter again:

I start on my two-year school certificate course in September which means I shan't be leaving school just yet. I've always liked animals ever since I was little and spend many of my weekends working at kennels out at Finchley and occasionally help at stables nearby. All this has made me realise that I'd like to train to be a vet when I'm older. It will mean working to get the basic higher qualifications, particularly in biology, but I'm determined to do well. I wonder, though, particularly as you have no children of your own, whether I could ask you to help support me financially from sixteen, after my school cert, until I've qualified as a vet. It would mean a great deal to me, and I would be very grateful if you are willing to help me in this way.

"Oh, dear." I shook my head. "I should leave that bit out about her not having any children, it rather rubs it in."

"What can I say?"

"Well, she doesn't know you very well, you were only little when she emigrated. Tell her something about yourself. Why not mention what your teachers say in school reports. That would help to fill the letter out and give her some reasons to support you."

"And how do I end it – *Yours sincerely*?"

"Oh, you have to put *Love*, surely."

"I hate having to write a begging letter like this. It's so... so..."

"I know it's degrading, but we *are* the poor relations."

★ ★ ★

I hated lying to Bea, pretending I wasn't looking for a young man. But something had to be done. The sensations Maud had roused had frightened and confused me. Must have been sexual. That feeling I was out of control – something I loved and hated, but with a woman – that was surely wrong.

Then I remembered going to a friend's wedding and listening intently to the words of the service. I'd no time for all the ceremony and mumbo-jumbo, the veiled bride being given away by her father, the blessing. Putting the fear of God into the young couple. Marriage in church hadn't worked for my parents. But those words the parson said about marriage – so that *natural instincts and affections* "should be directed aright" – that made sense. In spite of all the clap-trap, there was wisdom there, a clear guide as to what I now had to do to protect myself. What I'd felt with Maud was a *natural instinct*. That was a relief. But I had to make sure it was *directed aright*. That was my logic: I had to find a man.

I pretended not to notice the first piece of bread. It landed on the desk in front of me and bounced forward into the next row. I couldn't even be sure whether it was deliberately thrown or not. I turned to my friend Eileen. "Did you see that? It's raining bread."

"Silly idiots. They're trying to attract attention. Ignore them."

But the General Studies lecturer was boring. You had to strain to hear him, and the Franco-Prussian war was hardly modern history and politics. Not after The Great War.

Eileen leaned towards me to whisper. "I'm not bothering with notes. You can always read it up if you're interested."

But I felt sorry for the lecturer. His voice was high-pitched – I'd even heard some people imitating him, a hoarse squeak which echoed down corridors in the college. General Studies was compulsory and the little grey-haired man seemed to wrestle with his subject and the indiscipline of his students. Nobody wanted to be there. Midweek purgatory – every Wednesday night throughout the term.

He turned towards the blackboard to chalk up in slow copperplate handwriting *Otto von Bismarck*.

The next piece of bread hit my ear and bounced into Eileen's lap.

"Ow! That was hard. Must be stale."

"Don't turn round," she said, "it'll only encourage them."

I caught sight of Leslie out of the corner of my eye – further along and one row behind. Wasn't him. Beautiful cufflinks glinted at me from his desk. His notebook lay open, he appeared to be listening intently, but he was doodling. Next to him, a very attractive blonde girl, quite made-up, her short hair rippling elegantly in beautiful waves. They seemed absorbed in each other, sitting very close. No chance with him, then. You couldn't cut in on that.

I glanced up at the clock. Coming up to eight – nearly time.

Another piece of bread landed, then a second.

"Oh, really!" I brushed the crumbs onto the floor. "I hope the caretaker doesn't think I've done this."

"Thank you very much, ladies and gentlemen, next week we shall look at –"

The lecturer's words were drowned by a buzz of voices, the flipping of seats, the closing of books. I sneaked a look up the tiers behind. Two young men about five rows back remained sitting. Early twenties, probably. One, tall and dark with heavy-rimmed spectacles, looked serious. The other, hair swept back, high forehead, beautiful long fingers, I noticed – he smiled broadly, cocked his head, and winked.

SIXTY-NINE

I hurried along the street, enjoying the sunshine and a day off. Teaching the Russians suited me; they were keen to learn English and paid well. Certainly easier teaching adults, they didn't play me up. Next time, I thought, I must try the different ways of spelling the sound *ay*.

Two new ten shilling notes crackled in my coat pocket. A lucky night! Bea and I could go to the pictures and have a meal out.

At the corner near the Mount Pleasant sorting office, I bumped into someone running in the opposite direction. The huge parcel he was carrying spun out of his hands, hit a lamppost and split.

"Oh, 'eck, now look," he said. He bent down and began gathering items of clothing strewn across the pavement and in the gutter.

I immediately apologised and offered to help repack everything.

"No, I'll do it. You don't want to go picking up my mucky smalls." He looked up, touched the peak of his cloth cap and grinned. "It's you," he said and stood up.

The young man from the back of the lecture theatre, the one who'd winked at me.

"Oh, heavens," I said, "what are you doing here?" I must have blushed.

"I could say the same. I were rushing to catch the post. Get this lot of washin' off to me mam for Monday morning. But I can't send it like this, can I? Now what'll I do?"

"Stay there," I said, "I've an idea." I left him picking up the rest of his clothes while I hurried round the corner, where I knew there was a Smith's.

What an extraordinary experience, and what a piece of luck! I brought back some large sheets of strong brown paper, a ball of string and some sealing wax. Together, we rested the scattered garments on a public seat and began bundling his washing into a new parcel. I spooled off a length of string.

"Hang on, I'll do it," he said. He took out a penknife and cut the string.

I tied the parcel up really securely. "Put your finger on that, hold it tight and I'll tie the knot."

. He grinned. "Thanks ever so, lass," he said, "you've saved my bacon, though I reckon I've missed the post now. I owe you for paper and string."

He began sorting coins out.

"I'll tell you what you can do." I felt myself blushing. "Instead of that, there's a Joe Lyons not far away, you can buy me a cup of tea and a slice of *fresh* bread and butter. As long as you promise not to throw it at me." I looked straight at him.

He grinned again and lowered his eyes.

I'd done it again – made the first move!

★ ★ ★

"Where are you from?" I said. "You're not a Londoner, I know."

"Well, can you guess?" He looked better without a hat. He'd folded his cap onto the table at his side.

"Judging by your accent, I'd say up North somewhere. Yorkshire?"

"Close enough. Lincolnshire, near the Humber river."

"You're far from home," I said. "And you send washing to your mother every week? You don't use a laundry?"

"That's right. Saves money, and if me mam gets the washin', she knows I'm all right – stops her worrying. I don't always get time to write with all my marking. And the college work."

"Marking? Are you a teacher?"

"I am. Me first job. Lucky to get it. Risinghill Juniors, up Islington way."

"That makes two of us. I teach infants in the St Pancras area."

"I'm doing the general degree at college with a maths specialism. That's quite enough for me. How about you?"

"Oh, I'm on the honours course – Botany and English."

"And what about you?" he said. "You're a Londoner – by the sound of you."

"I suppose I am." I told him briefly about myself and how the family had split up.

"So, you're an orphan in the big city, too."

"That's right." Some instinct told me not to mention Bea yet. "My father was a schoolmaster, too. He went through the war, but for all I know he may be dead now."

"Don't you know?"

"I haven't seen him for years." I worried then I'd said too much. He'd probably think what a funny family we were.

"Me dad's an engine driver. I'm one of nine, the eldest is twenty-eight, the youngest are still at home."

"Heavens, I thought we were a large family. We're only four – and Mother."

He looked directly at me. "I like your fringe, your bob, is that what they call it? – very modern, and you've got nice eyes."

"Well – thank you. I've been admiring your lovely smile."

"Aye, and my teeth too. They're like stars – come out every night." I laughed. Idiot!

"I'd like us to meet up again," he said. "Can we? It gets lonely round 'ere at the weekends."

"Well, that might be possible, but there's one big problem."

"Oh, no, don't say that. What is it?"

"I'm Dorothy, but I don't know who you are. I can't possibly meet someone without a name."

He smiled. "I'm Chester Drawers, but you can call me Fred."

I laughed again. "I see. Then my real name is Ida Down, you know." I warmed to his humour and high spirits, but was he joking, or was he really called Fred?

463

SEVENTY

1929

John was proud of some things he could do. Old Sam, admitted to the workhouse before the war; he'd taught him to read and write after a fashion. The old man had been in the Boer wars, had stories to tell. No other schoolteachers inside, though. You weren't expected to sink like this. But they let him play his fiddle from time to time: at Christmas, little concerts for the inmates, that sort of thing. The superintendent had found some music: some Irish jigs for him to play, even some gypsy music. New stuff to learn. But the hands had stiffened up now and the finger pads were soft.

It hurt to play – in more ways than one.

Bedtime was the worst. Thirty-two beds in one dormitory, with snorers and groaners and screamers and snufflers. And the smells. Like sleeping in a zoo after dark. Sleep was slow in coming unless you were lucky and got the nurse who'd give you a spoonful of Collis Browne's for your sudden cough. That helped. Otherwise you knew Sov lurked in the shadows behind the bed head, and you remembered how you might have done things differently, if only...

Fair punishment, then. Penance, really. Certainly no bitterness. Leave all resentment about life to Perce, who'd always nursed enough for them both.

SEVENTY-ONE

"What do you make of this, then?" Flushed, breathless, Bea flung the letter onto the bed.

I recognised the writing. "She's taken long enough to reply." I tidied my college papers into a folder and picked up the letter.

Dear Beatrice,

I was interested to receive your letter full of news. It is very pleasing to hear how one's nephews and nieces are doing so well. I'm sure your mother will be proud of you all, especially Rowley, as you grow up. And it's good to hear that you are making a success of your studies also.

It is true that Herbert left me well provided for when he died and I am quite comfortably off, but, to be blunt about it, I am sorry to say that I really do not think becoming a vet is a suitable career for a young woman.

I am willing to help financially where I can but not with this particular idea. Come up with a more suitable alternative, let me know, and we can look at the matter again. There will always be a need for stenographers. Why not consider taking that up until such time as you want to get married? It is a good job for a hard-working girl such as yourself, and typing and shorthand are always useful skills. I'm sorry to disappoint you.

With my love to you and Dorothy,
Aunt Dora

"Oh, Bea, I'm so sorry. What a blow."
"Rowley again! I wish I hadn't grovelled now. Let her keep her

bloody money. She's stuck in the last century. Well, that's that. No point in staying on now. I might as well get a typing job like she says. That's all I'm good for." She tore the letter into small pieces and threw them on the bed.

"Don't say that! At least take your school cert, get some basic qualifications. They'll always stand you in good stead."

"You talk just like a teacher now."

"Well..." Was this a good time to break the news? I'd promised I'd say something at the weekend. But now...

I took a deep breath. "I've something I want to tell you. I hope you'll be happy about it."

Her mouth tightened and she stared at me.

"Freddie and I got engaged last night, after the class." I couldn't hide the smile.

"You're just twenty-one, same age as Mother when she got married. I thought you swore you'd never –"

"We shan't marry for a year or two, we must save up for somewhere decent to live, for a start. We're just *engaged*. Freddie wants me to meet his people either next weekend or sometime soon."

"You're not expecting, are you?"

"Bea!"

"Do you love him?"

"Well, we get on well, he makes me laugh, we go to the same classes, we're both teachers. What is love, anyway?"

"I remember you telling me you'd met someone called Fred, not Freddie. I thought nothing would come of it. You said you couldn't bear to walk out with someone called Fred who wore boots around town."

"That was easily solved. I changed him to *Freddie*. Sounds more modern and fashionable. He doesn't mind. 'A rose by any other name would smell,' he said. He knows I like Shakespeare. He's always mucking about." I smiled. "So, he's Freddie. Aren't you pleased for me?"

"It's rather sudden. Are you sure it's what you want? You'll have to give up teaching, won't you? Isn't that the rule? No married women teachers?"

"That'll be no great loss. I'll find something else. I'm not really cut out for –"

"I can see it now! A couple of children by the time you're twenty-five. Just become any old married woman."

"Not necessarily. You can plan families these days. You only have to read Marie Stopes –"

"So where will you live? And what about me, what'll happen to me?"

"It's not happening next week, there's plenty of time yet."

"Well, say you wait two years, and then get married. You'll be twenty-three and I'll be sixteen."

"Oh, Bea, let's not argue. A lot can happen in that time. You'll have finished your exams, you'll probably have found a job by then. There are plenty of nice boarding houses where young people –"

"That's it, farm me out, shove me off. First Mother, and now you, when it suits you. Well, don't worry about me..." She began bundling clothes into a bag. "I'm off to somewhere I *am* wanted –"

"Where are you going?"

"I'll see you on Monday evening at your beloved college. I'm off to Winnie's for the weekend, at least her mother makes me feel welcome." She zipped up the bag.

"Oh, Bea, don't go!"

"That'll leave the coast clear for you to canoodle with Freddie, bring him back here, why don't you, and be really modern. Let him see how we have to live in this dreadful dump." The door crashed against the bed frame as Bea flung it open. Her footsteps rattled away down the stairs.

That argument upset me. I can't bear family rows. But I didn't really know what I'd said to spark it off. Bad timing, I suppose. Aunt Dora's letter didn't help.

I began gathering up the torn bits of paper. This wedding wasn't going to be easy.

SEVENTY-TWO

I threw the pieces of bread into the pond and watched the ducks scoot across towards us, my head bursting with wedding plans. "I tell you what, Freddie, let's be modern on our wedding day. Let's both wear white."

"How do you mean, lass?" He stood watching me, his head bowed, hands behind his back.

"We're not having a church wedding, and I certainly shan't be wearing some old-fashioned lacy creation and hiding behind a veil. Let's see if we can both find light-coloured suits to wear."

"Is that what you want?"

"Yes, something bright, modern. Break with tradition. You don't need a dark suit, you wear one every day in the classroom. It's a happy occasion. Let's have you in something light and fashionable."

"You'll have me in plus-fours next."

"No, I won't. Don't be silly. But can we please get you out of those awful country-boy boots?"

"Don't you like them? I need them. They support my ankles when I'm standing all day."

"Well, we're getting married, we're not going to be on our feet the whole time, are we?" I put the bread bag down, slipped my arms round him and pulled him to me. "Let's have you in a pair of smart brogues. Will you, for me?"

He laughed and put his arm round me. "We'll see about that. Folks'll think I'm your fancy man."

"No they won't. They'll think you look very smart and handsome."

He steered me towards a bench overlooking the pond and we sat down, the sun off the water dazzling us. "I'm bothered about one thing, though, lass. Are you sure about not getting wed in church? I think some of my folk will think it queer if we didn't. And I reckon me mam would like to come down, see me get married."

A gust of cold wind blew across the pond, ruffling the surface into wrinkles. It caught the ducks' backs, lifted the feathers and blew the birds across the water like miniature galleons.

"Oh, darling, I thought we'd agreed," I said. "We're grown up now, we're both over twenty-one. We certainly don't need mothers or fathers giving us away, making speeches, shedding tears. I definitely don't want *my* mother there, if I can help it, she'd cast a blight over the whole proceedings, wouldn't even smile for the camera. You'll discover her disapproval soon enough. And in any case –"

"Yes, I'm sorry, love, I forgot. You haven't got a father. All right, then, we'll leave things be. Unless you want to ask your brother, of course."

"That little snob? No, thank you! I'd rather... Who shall we invite? Who's going to be your best man?"

"Oh, that's easy, Artie, of course. I shall need another Northerner to give me support." I remembered the serious-looking man with the heavy glasses at college.

"So, Arthur and Alie, that's two. And Bea, and perhaps her friend, Winnie, to keep her company. I'll ask Bea to be bridesmaid, that'll keep her happy. And I'd like Eileen from college and her new husband. It's not far to come from Wimbledon. Is there anybody else you want to invite?"

"No, I don't think so. Don't know that many folk down here." He recited the names again, counting them on his fingers. "Two, four, six and the two of us, eight. Just a nice number for a booze-up afterwards."

"Freddie! I thought we might go somewhere nice to eat. Leave that to me. I'll think of somewhere and book it."

"So, when?

"Well, we agreed the school holidays, when we've both broken up, so how about August – not the first weekend, that's the bank holiday, but the next, the Saturday?"

He was looking through a diary. "That's the eighth."

I put my arm through his and smiled at him. "Let's arrange to be man and wife on the eighth of August, then. Now, it'll have to be the registry office where one of us lives. Let's see if we can find somewhere round here. I don't want some dreary place in the city centre. Let's get married out here, in the fresh air of the heath."

"Rightho, now what about snaps? Who'll do that?"

"Eileen's husband is a photographer, I think he's got flash. Shall we ask him?"

"Whatever you want, love, is OK by me."

"Oh, Freddie, you're lovely, you make things so easy."

"Well, shall we book it all, then?"

"Yes, let's enquire, see what papers they need." I took a deep breath. "You know when we're married, I'd love to live round here with that view over Parliament Hill Fields. I wonder if we can afford one of those flats."

"I don't know, lass," he shook his head, "your champagne tastes..."

"Only a little flat, Freddie, I want us to get off to a good start."

I suppose we all have high hopes at the beginning. After years of penny-pinching, I so wanted life to be perfect...

SEVENTY-THREE

John paused on the footpath round the pond and watched the sodden bread bobbing in the water. Grey and bloated now, and covered with green algae, it rocked in the scum near the edge. People liked feeding the birds, even in times of hardship. He closed his eyes. Not so long ago I'd have fished that out. He shook his head. Terrible stomach upset. Never again. Being on the road was not the place to have diarrhoea.

He lifted his head, looked out across the water and marvelled at the swallows swooping over the pond. They skimmed and twittered, plucking things he couldn't see from the still surface. The world was a better place when the sun shone and swallows returned to dart over the water.

A few yards away, a small boy, perhaps three, stiff-armed and important, held a piece of bread and flung it with all his might towards the ducks. It landed in the water at the child's feet amongst older soggy contributions.

He smiled. Dorothy used to like feeding the gulls.

He moved on, anxious to buy the *News Chronicle* before they all went. The tobacconist opposite the register office saved him a copy only if he arrived before eleven. Life was simple now. Breakfast, a short walk, buy the paper and read it on a bench by the pond, then lunch. An afternoon snooze. No responsibilities, no demands.

Unfit for industry.

He glanced at the paper before tucking it under his arm. Still long columns about Al Capone. American gangsters! Surely they could convict him on *one* charge. And France, saying they couldn't afford to send a team to the Olympics next year. Hard times indeed, then.

He crossed the road by the studded crossing. Walk back on the other side. Sunnier there. The same route most mornings.

The name Hemingby leaped out of the noticeboard. Funny how you could always see your own name in a mass of irrelevant information. Drawn to it, he paused to read. Somebody called Hemingby getting married. Frederick George Burgess marrying Dorothy Mabel Hemingby.

Good lord! It had to be. He closed his eyes and tried to calculate. The age was right, and the middle name Mabel, just like Em. Dorothy was getting married here on August 8th. Was she living nearby?

Well now, old lad, how about that? His stomach jittered for the first time for years. He smiled.

It'd be marvellous if... How could he manage to be part of her big day? He shook his head. No! After all this time his appearance would be an embarrassment. Wouldn't want that. One possibility, though. It might just work.

SEVENTY-FOUR

"Come on, Hemingby, we haven't got all day. Others want their turn. Get a move on and get out."

You couldn't linger in the bath. No time for privacy or reflection. If you were first in, the water was scalding and you came out pink and sore. You weren't allowed to run cold water in either. That'd make it too chilly for the last chap. Expensive to heat – water. Mustn't waste it. Best go was number three: temperature about right and the water not too dirty. Wednesday was bath day for his ward – bath and shave day just once a week. Pity that, he'd look a scruff by Saturday.

He lay down full length in the bath – not used for treatments now. Big enough and long enough to drown in, if you felt inclined. That was why they had an attendant at each end of the bath-house to keep an eye on you. Not that they'd care if you did, but it saved awkward questions. The men just read the paper and shouted from time to time. Like the army, but without the uniform.

A long time since he'd shaved himself. Same reason, in case you harmed yourself. The once-a-week scrape, he called it. If you were lucky, they stropped the razor before your turn. Otherwise you had little nicks and runs of blood. Old Pinchnose was best, he lathered you properly and moved your face how he wanted it by holding your nose. You didn't feel safe with the other one, Chinny Chin Up. Vulnerable, letting someone near your throat.

He'd had three weeks to think how best to go about it. He stopped buying the newspaper and saved all his allowance, stuffed in a sock in his locker. Took it with him when he went for his walk. He listened in to the news on the wireless in the day room instead. Some music, too, but not much he liked.

Could just about afford the shirt and tie, he decided, with all his savings, especially if he touched Old Tom for a loan. He'd help out.

Have to ask to go out on Saturday. You had to have permission to do anything. But a good enough excuse, surely – as long as they believed him.

★ ★ ★

His new collar chafed in the heat. He tried easing it with his finger. From the inside pocket of his jacket, he drew out the photograph, held it out in the sunlight and peered at it, narrowing his eyes. Should have spectacles now: eyesight, teeth, both gone. They looked after him well enough, fed and clothed him, but no one actually *cared* for him. No spectacles. And in his haste, he'd left the magnifying glass behind.

He knew the picture well, anyway, stared at it often in private moments, his only link with the children. The sepia portrait, tattered and curling at the edges. How would they look thirteen years on? Douglas's age, now. Dorothy he'd know surely, centre of attention as the bride. Perhaps Rowley, too, nudging manhood at eighteen. Would he have filled out and grown tall or still take after his mother, small and slight?

And Em – mother of the bride – would she be there? Best keep at a distance, if so. He drew back into the shade of the shop's awning. She might recognise him – even now. Couldn't face that staunch implacability – not again. Best hide. And yet, maybe time had softened her. Something lingered if she sent that photograph. Just a curious glimpse then, see if her hair had also greyed and she'd turned matronly in middle age.

A knot of young people laughed and jostled out of the registry office and onto the pavement opposite.

Husband and wife, now. So where was Dorothy?

He slipped behind a pillar box near the kerb and craned to look across the road. A bright green Austin Seven busied past, its hood folded back for the sunshine. An omnibus stopped on the opposite side and blocked his view. He cursed, willing it to move off.

And then he saw her. He gasped, his mouth hung open, tears blurring his eyes. He knew that shy smile immediately. Her figure, full and womanly now in a white linen suit, reminded him of his mother, but that fringe of hair over her brow made her seem thoroughly modern. Should have thought of that. She wouldn't keep long hair for ever.

"And that must be Frederick," he murmured. The tall young man, with hair swept back off his forehead and pleasant smile, seemed at ease. "Handsome fellow, aren't you, in your new summer suit? No wonder she fell in love with you." He watched Dorothy gaze up at her husband. She slipped her hand into his, smiled, and Frederick took out a handkerchief and mopped his brow. John looked away and bit his lip. So hard to bear.

"Come on, you two, say cheese for the camera," someone shouted.

A blare of light, an exploding puff of smoke.

John's eyes widened; he flinched, ducked, then relaxed. Not now, you idiot, it's safe now. He grinned at his foolishness. His hand shook only slightly.

"Give it a minute, let it cool down, I've enough powder for one more." The young man laboured with his camera. "I'll just move the tripod."

John scanned the group: no sign of Em, nor anyone who could be Rowley. Friends not family, then.

"Over here, Dot, this way." A slender girl of about sixteen stepped forward, put her hand into a bag and flung a fistful of something high into the air. A hail of rice fell on the couple.

"Oh, Bea, you promised you wouldn't," Dorothy's laughter floated across the road.

Now, is that really...? John shook his head and smiled. Another young lady with bobbed hair. Wearing trousers, too. Could this rebel really be little Beatrice? Impossible!

And now, best get ready. Mustn't miss his moment. He drew back under the tobacconist's awning and began preparing.

★ ★ ★

"Come on, Dorothy, let me straighten that for you."

I flinched when Alie moved to adjust the single red rose Freddie had given me. He'd pinned it himself to my lapel, got up especially early and bought the flower fresh from the market.

But nothing too flash, we agreed.

I wasn't sure whether I liked Arthur's wife. Alie thought she was it, laughed a lot and spoke confidently, rather dazzled Freddie. Most men, actually. And why on earth wear that fox fur on a hot day? Absolutely ridiculous! Just showing off. That and the cloche hat.

"There, that's better. It's straight now!" Alie patted my lapel.

I looked at the spray of lily-of-the-valley she wore on her breast, the tiny bunch set in a silver container-brooch. Beside it, fox's eyes dangled and glinted. So competitive, always flaunting her money.

"Did you hear from your mother?" she said.

"Only a letter and a pound note. She wishes us well, says she'll meet Freddie one day. She hasn't come, anyway."

"What will you do now you've had to finish teaching?" Alie said.

"Oh, I shan't miss it, I was never much good in the classroom. Freddie's the disciplinarian, he's set to make teaching his career."

"Like Arthur, then."

"I'll probably wait a while and then take up coaching foreigners again," I said. "When we've settled into marriage."

"What about your degree course?"

I paused. "I don't think we'll miss it. I said Freddie should keep going and finish it, but he said he'd rather sit at home with me after a hard day's work. We've both had enough of swotting; we've done two years. Besides, it'll save money with only one salary coming in."

"Listen, I'll let you into a secret," Alie said. "I've persuaded Father to let us have the Rover. Arthur wanted to give Freddie a treat

476

today, so we'll take everybody on to the restaurant. Just about squeeze in. The car's parked round the corner."

"Can he drive, then? I didn't know that." I looked at the pavement and bit my lip. Alie taking over again. Why couldn't we just keep things simple? All I wanted was a quiet wedding. No fuss. And now... "I think I'd better go and find Freddie," I said and walked off to where the men had gathered to smoke. Why didn't people realise whose day it was? I didn't want that sort of extravagance...

Across the road, an old busker began playing a violin. I stopped, broke away from the group and listened intently to the frail sound drifting towards me, mingling with the noise of traffic.

"What's up, lass?" Freddie said. "You look as if you've seen a ghost." He ground his cigarette out on the pavement.

"I'm all right," I said. "Listen, darling! I know that tune, I haven't heard it in years. I used to love it. *Salut d'Amour* – my father used to play it for me when I was little. It was my favourite. Oh, that takes me right back. How special to hear it now. I remember Daddy promised when he went off to war..."

I stood there, tears pricking my eyes.

Freddie squeezed my hand. "I'll see if I can get him to play it again. Now, don't run off with anyone, will you?"

That made me smile. Dear Freddie, always the joker then.

★ ★ ★

The young man stood before him, straightening his tie. "Now then, old man, how are you?" His strong Northern accent a surprise.

"Well enough, thank you, sir. Congratulations..." Embarrassed, John covered his mouth with his hand. His chin stubbly, too.

"That piece you just played... My wife..." The young man gave a foolish grin. "I shall have to get used to calling her that... Do you think you could play it again for us?"

"Of course I will, sir, with pleasure."

"I'm Fred, by the way, but she likes to call me Freddie. I don't know why. Here..." The young man reached into his jacket and pulled out a ten shilling note. "Take this for making our day special." A pause. "Go on, take it."

"I wouldn't dream of it, Fred. You keep it, please. For your honeymoon. For your life together. Tell her to think of my playing as a small greeting of love on your wedding day. Congratulations to you both. You've got yourself a good girl there, I'm sure."

"Oh, aye, I have."

"Look after her, won't you?" John lowered his eyes. Because I could not, the voice inside said.

"I will that. I'd best be off. Thank you very much, then." His boots squeaked as he hurried away.

John picked up his violin and prepared to play. Already, his arm ached and his fingers hurt through lack of practice. But this was special. It had to be.

"Sing for me now, won't you, old thing," he whispered.

Into his playing he poured all the pain, all the love. The last thing, the only thing he could do for her now. Hello and farewell across the years; after this, he could let everything go.

He floated the old melody over the distance between them. Music from a lost world. He swayed with the tune, his tears falling unchecked. I was a lousy father, but I loved you. I loved you all.

He played on. The horsehairs on his bow began to break and fray, flaring in the wind.

Blood on his fingers now.

He played on.

When he had finished, he let his fiddle hang at his side and watched them both from afar. "Goodbye, Dolly Daydream." His voice a whisper on the warm breeze, he watched the couple walk away arm in arm. "May your world be safer and happier than mine. I hope life blesses you."

He bent down, laid his violin and bow gently in their case, lowered the lid and snapped it shut.

★ ★ ★

Everywhere still and dark. He stirred and raised his head at the familiar cry. "Smiler, for God's sake, man, help me." Sov, looking up, thrashing the sludge which brimmed at his chest. The face a mask of mud.

Sov's arm reaching out...

But it's so easy, after all, John said. I just have to... He sighed in relief.

Standing at the side of the morass in the clear light, he stretched out, felt Sov's fingers slither and slip, then grasp his own. The grip tightened, his arm hurt at the strain, then a strong pull, down, down, towards the welcoming dark.

He smiled.

AUTHOR'S NOTE

In 1922, shortly after he disappears from this story, Ivor Gurney was committed by his family to an asylum in his hometown of Gloucester and then shortly afterwards confined permanently in the City of London Mental Hospital, Dartford, where he was diagnosed as suffering from "delusional insanity (systematised)". Even before he went to war, Gurney had had a breakdown as a student, and it is likely that his mental health was always fragile. In 1917, when he was sent home, he was considered to be suffering from shellshock – a common enough diagnosis in those days. Over subsequent years, it was thought that he was suffering from schizophrenia, and only recently has it been more widely accepted that he was a victim of bipolar disorder (manic-depression), for which, at the time, there was no known cure or treatment. It is the behaviour symptoms of that disorder that I have tried to portray here, working within the limits of what is known about Gurney's life and thought. He remained incarcerated in the asylum for fifteen years, composing less music but still writing poetry of sorts. He died in 1937 from tuberculosis.